OXFORD WORLD'S CLASSICS

# COUSIN PHILLIS
### AND OTHER STORIES

ELIZABETH GASKELL was born in 1810, the daughter of Elizabeth Holland and William Stevenson, who trained as a Unitarian minister and was subsequently a farmer, journalist, and civil servant. After her mother's death, she was brought up by her aunt in Knutsford, Cheshire. In 1832 she married William Gaskell, Junior Minister at Cross Street Unitarian Chapel in Manchester; the couple had seven children, of whom four survived to adulthood. Gaskell's first novel, *Mary Barton*, published in 1848, was very successful and brought her to the notice of Charles Dickens who subsequently asked her to write for his new periodical, *Household Words*. Her second novel, *Cranford* (1853), began as a series of papers in this journal. Her other novels are *Ruth* (1853), *North and South* (1855), *Sylvia's Lovers* (1863), *Cousin Phillis* (1864), and *Wives and Daughters*, published posthumously in 1866. She also wrote many stories and non-fictional pieces, and the first biography of Charlotte Brontë (1857). She died in Hampshire in 1865.

HEATHER GLEN is Professor of English at the University of Cambridge. She is the author of *Charlotte Brontë: The Imagination in History* (2002), and editor of *The Cambridge Companion to the Brontës* (2002) as well as editions of Emily Brontë's *Wuthering Heights* (1988) and Charlotte Brontë's *The Professor* (1989; new edition 2003) and *Tales of Angria* (2006).

## OXFORD WORLD'S CLASSICS

*For over 100 years Oxford World's Classics have brought readers closer to the world's great literature. Now with over 700 titles—from the 4,000-year-old myths of Mesopotamia to the twentieth century's greatest novels—the series makes available lesser-known as well as celebrated writing.*

*The pocket-sized hardbacks of the early years contained introductions by Virginia Woolf, T. S. Eliot, Graham Greene, and other literary figures which enriched the experience of reading. Today the series is recognized for its fine scholarship and reliability in texts that span world literature, drama and poetry, religion, philosophy, and politics. Each edition includes perceptive commentary and essential background information to meet the changing needs of readers.*

OXFORD WORLD'S CLASSICS

ELIZABETH GASKELL

# Cousin Phillis
## and Other Stories

*Edited with an Introduction and Notes by*
HEATHER GLEN

OXFORD
UNIVERSITY PRESS

# OXFORD

UNIVERSITY PRESS

Great Clarendon Street, Oxford OX2 6DP

Oxford University Press is a department of the University of Oxford.
It furthers the University's objective of excellence in research, scholarship,
and education by publishing worldwide in

Oxford New York

Auckland Cape Town Dar es Salaam Hong Kong Karachi
Kuala Lumpur Madrid Melbourne Mexico City Nairobi
New Delhi Shanghai Taipei Toronto

With offices in

Argentina Austria Brazil Chile Czech Republic France Greece
Guatemala Hungary Italy Japan Poland Portugal Singapore
South Korea Switzerland Thailand Turkey Ukraine Vietnam

Oxford is a registered trade mark of Oxford University Press
in the UK and in certain other countries

Published in the United States
by Oxford University Press Inc., New York

British Library Cataloguing in Publication Data

Data available

Library of Congress Cataloging-in-Publication Data

Data available

Typeset by Glyph International Ltd., Bangalore, India
Printed in Great Britain
on acid-free paper by
Clays Ltd, Elcograf S.p.A.

ISBN 978–0–19–923949–8

11

# CONTENTS

# INTRODUCTION

*Readers who do not wish to learn details of the stories' plots will prefer to treat the introduction as an Afterword.*

ELIZABETH GASKELL has long been one of the most popular of Victorian novelists. Her novels were much esteemed and widely reviewed in her lifetime. There is today a growing recognition of her artistry both as a novelist and as a biographer; but the shorter fictions that made up a large proportion of her literary output are rather less well known. These shorter fictions—more than thirty in all—range from ghost stories and melodramas to historical vignettes and sketches in domestic realism, and from 'tales' of a few pages to several 'novelettes' of 40,000 words or more.[1] They were popular in Gaskell's lifetime, and were much reprinted and pirated; but few are available in cheap scholarly editions today. Like other nineteenth-century short stories, they were rarely noticed by contemporary reviewers; and, with the exception of *Cousin Phillis*, they have received comparatively little critical attention since. The consensus appears to be that they are in some way subsidiary to Gaskell's main achievement as a novelist. Yet as readers of this volume will discover, they do not deserve this neglect.

## Short Fiction in the First Half of the Nineteenth Century

By the middle of the nineteenth century the novel was becoming established as the dominant literary genre. Valued for its moral teaching, and for what it had to say about society, seen increasingly as a vehicle for serious intellectual debate, it was beginning to be a 'formidable' presence in British cultural life.[2] In comparison, what we have now come to call 'the short story' had little prestige. The origins

[1] 'Tales' and 'novelettes' seem to have been the accepted terms for short fiction in the 1850s and 1860s: 'story' could refer to a fiction of any length. 'Novelette' was used of a longer work that was shorter than a novel, and perhaps because of its connection with women's romantic fiction, the term was frequently used depreciatively. 'Novella' has now become the preferred term for a longer short fiction; but in the mid-nineteenth century it seems to have been used only in connection with Italian works.

[2] Thus David Masson, in the first extended theorization of the genre, *English Novelists and their Styles* (Cambridge: Macmillan, 1859), 211.

of the genre in oral storytelling, and in chapbooks and nursery tales, meant that it was associated with women and children; with the pleasures of 'gossip', the thrill of romance or adventure, rather than with the formal shaping of high literature. Short 'tales' were enduringly popular: indeed, by the middle of the nineteenth century the expansion of the reading public had led to a proliferation of short fictions of various kinds. Huge quantities of melodramatic and sentimental 'penny fiction' (both serialized novels and shorter stories) were appearing in periodicals aimed at the working classes; there was an answering outpouring of 'improving' tales designed for the same public in religious periodicals and tracts.[3] Short fictions were thus associated with the lower orders: with the immediate gratifications of popular entertainment or with simple didacticism, rather than with the more enduring pleasures, the more sophisticated demands, of higher literary forms.

The status of short fictions was further lowered by the economics of book distribution. 'Short tales' were not welcomed by the circulating libraries through which the middle classes largely encountered new fiction. Since the income of such libraries depended on charging by the volume, it was far more lucrative for them to stock novels that were published in three volumes. 'The librarian wont encourage short stories,' declared an article in *Fraser's* explaining what it called 'the English prejudice against short stories' in 1856. 'Three volumes are indispensable to him. They are the "means whereby he lives".'[4] Shorter fictions for the privileged classes did appear in more prestigious periodicals, such as *Blackwood's* and *Fraser's* itself, and were sometimes collected in volumes, though these were likewise unpopular with circulating libraries.[5] They might also be found in the fashionable illustrated 'keepsakes' and 'Christmas books'. But the promotion of these as gift-books, their appeal to the seasonal market, even their fine illustrations (usually finer than their literary contents), reinforced the sense that the 'tales' they contained were slight, ephemeral commodities, rather than works of art.

Yet serious writers were producing shorter fictions, and such fictions seem to have been of considerable importance to them. It is

[3] See Louis James, *Fiction for the Working Man 1830–1850* (London: Oxford University Press, 1963).

[4] 'The Art of Story-Telling', *Fraser's Magazine*, 53 (June 1856), 725.

[5] Ibid. 726.

true that the 'short story' was in this period hardly theorized as a separate genre. But, as twenty-first-century scholars are beginning to discover, there had been a good deal of experiment with its possibilities since the early years of the nineteenth century.[6] Writers in this period do not seem to have seen short fictions simply as condensed novels, but as works of a different kind. Most were early and deeply familiar with that favourite of the late eighteenth- and early nineteenth-century nursery, *The Arabian Nights' Entertainments*, perhaps the world's most famous collection of short tales. Allusions to this are everywhere in the writing of the first sixty years of the century—not least in Gaskell's own fiction, and in the periodical in which five of the stories that follow were published, Dickens's *Household Words*. *The Arabian Nights* was not, however, just a fertile source of images. It offered also a potent example of how the short tale might be different from more ambitious narrative—more various, more provisional, more responsive to the inconsequential and the arbitrary. The fact that each story contained suggestions of further stories was a constant prompt to serious or ironic metafictional reflexiveness. The frame narrative of Scheherezade telling stories to King Shahryar, always holding out the promise of another tale, provided a suggestive image of endless deferral of closure, of storytelling as riposte to absolute authority.

The associations of the 'tale' with magic and with fairy story seem to have chimed in the early nineteenth century with a growing interest in popular customs and beliefs. This led to a number of collections of folk tales, such as Edward Taylor and George Cruikshank's *German Popular Stories* (1823), a translation and adaptation of Grimm's fairy stories, and T. Crofton Croker's *Fairy Legends and Traditions of the South of Ireland* (1825). Both these were much reprinted, and influential in prompting further collections.[7] But perhaps most important for the literary development of short fictions were James Hogg's *Winter Evening Tales* (1820) and *The Shepherd's Calendar* (1829), and Walter Scott's *Chronicles of the Canongate*.[8] These collections, which placed ostensibly oral narrative within a

---

[6] Tim Killick, *British Short Fiction in the Nineteenth Century* (London: Ashgate, 2008) is the first comprehensive account of short fictions published between 1800 and 1830.

[7] See Jennifer Schacker, *National Dreams: The Remaking of Fairy Tales in Nineteenth-Century England* (Philadelphia: University of Pennsylvania Press, 2003).

[8] These are the dates of their publication in volume form.

more sophisticated frame, brought the local, the regional, the primitive, into suggestive relation with a more cosmopolitan modernity. In their experiments with the relation between frame narrator and tale they drew attention to the ironies of transmission; they offered the self-reflexiveness of conscious 'storytelling' rather than the novel's illusion of immersion in events.[9] Their interest in the supernatural was taken up in the tales of terror for which *Blackwood's*, especially, was famous in the 1820s and 1830s,[10] and forged an association, that was to be important to Elizabeth Gaskell, between Gothic stories of curses and hauntings and the regional tale.

The other main kind of serious short fiction in this period was that of the literary 'sketch'. The Anglophile American Washington Irving, whose immensely successful *Sketch-Book of Geoffrey Crayon* had appeared in 1820, was the most famous contemporary writer of short fictions of this kind. His success inspired English writers, of whom perhaps the most popular in the 1820s and 1830s was Mary Russell Mitford, author of *Our Village: Sketches of Rural Life, Character and Scenery* (1824–32). If tales such as Hogg's had their roots in rural oral storytelling, the 'sketch', with its connotations of polite accomplishment, was rather more urbane. It dwelt on the quotidian, evanescent moment. It did not tell a 'story' but represented scenes and characters in a more inconsequential way. Like its prototype in the visual arts, it did not pretend to overview or conclusiveness. It aimed rather at an effect like that which Nathaniel Hawthorne was to describe in distinguishing a collection of pictorial sketches from a 'finished picture': 'the charm lay partly in their very imperfection; for this is suggestive, and sets the imagination at work'.[11]

The dual traditions of the 'tale' and the 'sketch' were to prove of seminal importance for the next generation of writers. In the 1840s Poe and Hawthorne in America were experimenting with short fictions: indeed, critical reflection on the short story has sometimes been seen as beginning with the former's famous review of Hawthorne's *Twice-Told Tales* in 1844. It was as authors of sketches and papers that Dickens and Thackeray, who were to be the most

---

[9] On this subject see esp. Ian Duncan, 'Introduction' to *Winter Evening Tales*, *The Stirling/South Carolina Research Edition of The Collected Works of James Hogg*, vol. xi (Edinburgh: Edinburgh University Press, 2002).

[10] See Robert Morrison and Chris Baldick (eds.), *Tales of Terror from Blackwood's Magazine* (Oxford: World's Classics, 1995).

[11] Nathaniel Hawthorne, *The Marble Faun*, ch. 15.

famous English novelists of the mid-century, began their literary careers. Yet both were to move away from these early beginnings. If *Pickwick Papers* commenced as a series of disconnected comic 'sketches', it was to be followed quickly by *Oliver Twist* and *Nicholas Nickleby*. If *Vanity Fair* bore the subtitle *Pen and Pencil Sketches of English Society* it was as *A Novel without a Hero* that it appeared in three-volume form. Although both Dickens and Thackeray continued to produce some short stories, both were to develop their writing careers primarily as novelists.

Gaskell's trajectory seems to have been rather different. She first became known as 'the authoress of *Mary Barton*': it was thus that Dickens addressed her when he asked her for a 'short tale' for the first issue of *Household Words*.[12] In a famous review of that novel in *Fraser's* Charles Kingsley had declared that 'had we wit and wisdom enough, we would placard its sheets on every wall, and have them read aloud from every pulpit, till a nation, calling itself Christian, began to act upon the awful facts contained in it'.[13] Yet unlike Thackeray, the 'puppet-master' of *Vanity Fair*, or Dickens, the 'conductor' of *Household Words*, Gaskell seems to have been uneasy with narrative authority. She was to follow *Mary Barton* with *Ruth*, another novel with a purpose, but as she completed the first volume in November 1851 she was pulled in a different direction, which seems to have been more in accord with her fictional bent. By then she had contributed several 'tales' to *Household Words*: she now followed these up with a little sketch of village life—'*one* paper', she recalled later, 'I never meant to write more.'[14] She did, however, write more: an irregularly appearing series that gradually evolved into something closer to a novel without ever quite becoming one. *Cranford*, which in the end appeared before *Ruth*, retained some characteristics of the 'sketches' with which early nineteenth-century readers were familiar. It dwelt on apparently inconsequential detail, rather than developing a coherent pattern of

[12] Charles Dickens to Elizabeth Gaskell, 31 January 1850, *The Letters of Charles Dickens*, ed. Graham Storey, Kathleen Tillotson, and Nina Burgis, vol. vi. *1850–1852* (The Pilgrim Edition; Oxford: Clarendon, 1988), 22.

[13] Charles Kingsley, from an unsigned review, *Fraser's Magazine*, 39 (Apr. 1849); quoted in Angus Easson (ed.), *Elizabeth Gaskell: The Critical Heritage* (London and New York: Routledge, 1991), 152–3.

[14] Elizabeth Gaskell to John Ruskin, Feb. 1865, in *The Letters of Mrs Gaskell*, ed. J. V. A. Chapple and Arthur Pollard (Manchester: Manchester University Press, 1966), 748.

imagery; it replaced the suspense, the rapid pace of melodrama, with a loosely connected series of atmospheric vignettes. Yet the pleasures it offered were also those of narrative. It was not merely that as the series continued it gradually developed a gently unfolding plot. The world it portrayed was one of stories and embedded stories: the tales told by and to the characters, the snobbish or consoling fictions they construct about their lives. Its interweaving of different voices and perspectives, its sense that any single story was merely one among many, stood in suggestive counterpoint to the more purposive dominant mode of *Household Words*.

This kind of fiction appears to have been peculiarly congenial to Gaskell. Throughout her life, within domestic circles, she was famous as a storyteller: Dickens addressed her as 'Scheherezade'. She had a keen feeling for the primitive pleasures of storytelling—the delights of 'sketching' as well as of developing character, of suspense resolved in a shorter space. She also had a keen interest in popular forms of story. She was mindful not merely of the slowly building perception of pattern and significance that the Victorian novel enabled, but of the older, simpler shapes of parable and fairy tale. She could draw on a well-established tradition of the short story, not as a vehicle for artless realism but as a peculiarly self-conscious genre, both alert to fictional convention and closely connected to popular forms: a genre that might at once be accessible to readers without the time or the inclination to read a three-volume novel, yet allow a sophisticated play with aesthetic effect. Precisely because they did not attract so much critical attention as her novels, her shorter fictions gave her more freedom to experiment with different voices and subjects. Precisely because they were more 'occasional', they enabled her to respond to immediate contemporary concerns without requiring her to take a stance as a public moralist. Above all, perhaps, she found creative possibilities in their relative brevity.

There is tantalizingly little in Gaskell's marvellous, gossipy letters about the processes of her writing, but the few remarks that there are suggest that she was acutely aware of the aesthetic implications of narrative's extension in time. In May 1854, whilst *North and South* is appearing in parts, she laments to a correspondent that she has 'never had time to prune it. I have got the people well on,—but I think in too lengthy a way'.[15] She battled with Dickens over the serializing

---

[15] Elizabeth Gaskell to John Forster, 17 May 1854 (ibid. 290).

of its ending, complaining that she felt 'compelled to desperate compression' but she came to feel that the shorter version she tailored to his requirements, with its tighter structure and economy of detail, might be the better one.[16] She was drawn to the leisurely expansiveness of the high Victorian novel, that 'loose baggy monster', with its descriptive elaboration, its slow building up of character, and its gradually unfolding plot. *Wives and Daughters*, especially, demonstrates her assurance with the form. But she was also interested in brevity: in the effects that might be achieved through the single telling detail, the telescoping of time. She seems to have been sharply aware that reading a short story was an experience rather different from becoming immersed in the absorbing world of the novel: that the reader of a shorter fiction is more likely to see it, consciously, as a fiction, if only for the simple reason that s/he comes more quickly to the end.

This selection aims to give some sense of Gaskell's variety and originality as a writer of short fictions and to enable a thoughtful reading of some of her finest achievements in the genre. It begins with a tale published near the beginning of her career as a professional writer, and ends with a novelette written almost at its end. The first five stories were written for Dickens's *Household Words* in the 1850s. Their subjects range from the plight of the fallen woman to episodes in seventeenth- and eighteenth-century English history, a Wordsworthian story of Westmorland, and a tale of city life. The last, *Cousin Phillis*, written in 1864 for the more highbrow literary periodical *The Cornhill*, is a longer rural 'idyll' shaped partly by allusions to the classics and to literary pastoral. To read these tales in sequence is to see a trajectory akin to that which we see in Gaskell's novels, from her early attempts at 'fiction with a purpose' to a more disinterested art. Yet it is not a straightforward progression. For even the first and apparently simplest of these stories is considerably more artful than might at first appear.

## Lizzie Leigh

The first chapter of *Lizzie Leigh* appeared anonymously in March 1850, in Dickens's 'new cheap weekly journal of general literature',

[16] Gaskell to Anna Jameson, Jan. 1855 (ibid. 328); Jenny Uglow, *Elizabeth Gaskell: A Habit of Stories* (London and Boston: Faber and Faber, 1993), 368.

*Household Words*.[17] It was particularly prominent as the first item in the first number, appearing immediately after the editor's 'Preliminary Word'. *Household Words* was very different from *Blackwood's* and *Fraser's*—those monthly reviews for the privileged classes in which Scott's and Hogg's (and also Thackeray's) tales and sketches had appeared. A weekly miscellany, priced at twopence, at a time when the cheapest ticket to a working-man's theatre in London cost three-pence, it aimed to appeal to readers used not to three-volume novels but to the formulaic—melodramatic, sentimental, didactic—fictions of the popular penny periodicals. But it also appeared in forms more likely to attract the middle-class and even upper middle-class reader, in paper-covered monthly parts, and semi-annually as a bound volume; and it prided itself especially on the quality of its fictions. As Lorna Huett puts it: '*Household Words* was an oddity: a cheap publication welcomed into the drawing rooms of the middle classes, and into the reading rooms of such reputable institutions as the first public library in the country, the Manchester Free Library. Its fiction was composed by some of the most respected and celebrated authors of the day.'[18]

Gaskell had for years been interested in writing for 'the people'. Her first stories had been published in the short-lived *Howitt's Journal of Literature and Popular Progress*, which aimed to provide the working classes with improving reading matter. But she knew that what they wanted was not simple didacticism. She was to refer one Evangelical editor who asked her to write a moral tale to the review of *Mary Barton* in *Fraser's* in which Charles Kingsley defended the appetite for the romance and excitement of penny fictions amongst those who pass their lives in 'the stifling shop, the crowded and pestilential work-room, the noisy and dust-grimed manufactory' as 'really Nature's own craving for her proper medicine'.[19] To her, the extremes of melodrama were reflective of what she had called in

[17] Thus Dickens described it in a letter to Gaskell, 31 January 1850, writing to request her to contribute 'a *short* tale, or any number of tales' (*Letters of Charles Dickens*, vi. 21–2).

[18] Lorna Huett, 'Among the Unknown Public: *Household Words, All the Year Round* and the Mass-Market Weekly Periodical in the Mid-Nineteenth Century', *Victorian Periodicals Review*, 38 (2005), 70.

[19] Elizabeth Gaskell to Fanny Mayne, *c.*1853, *Further Letters of Mrs Gaskell*, ed. John Chapple and Alan Shelston (Manchester: Manchester University Press, 2003), 106; Charles Kingsley, 'Recent Novels', *Fraser's Magazine*, 39 (Apr. 1849), 423.

the Preface to *Mary Barton* the 'lottery-like nature' of the people's lives. In that novel, she had begun to explore how the tropes of sentimental fiction might be invoked and reconfigured to point toward the transforming possibilities of 'sympathy'. *Household Words*, with its lively interest in 'the amusements of the people'[20] and its repeated appeals to 'fancy' and to fairy tale, gave her a space within which she could publish serious fiction ('dont think that it is necessary to write *down* to any part of our audience,' wrote Dickens to one contributor[21]) that was also genuinely popular.

'Lizzie Leigh' appears to have been perfectly pitched for its audience. The liberal middle classes who had been stirred by *Mary Barton* approved its concern with the plight of the fallen woman, its portrayal of urban poverty. It appealed to less practised readers by the way in which it drew on and developed familiar tropes of the penny fictions—the girl from the country who is 'ruined' in the city, the father disowning his daughter, the redemption of the prodigal. The tale became immediately popular. Less than two weeks after the final episode was published, 'a Drama of intense interest entitled "Lizzie Leigh"' was announced at the Royal Surrey Theatre; 'Lizzie Leigh, by Charles Dickens' appeared as the lead story in Washington Irving's *The Irving Offering: A Token of Affection for 1851*.[22] Yet if Gaskell's story could easily be adapted as a melodrama, appropriated as a sentimental gift-book tale, it is rather different from the usual run of writing in either genre. And if it was pirated as 'by Dickens', it is also suggestively different from the fiction that he was writing in the 1840s and 1850s for readers used to the conventions of melodrama and of sentiment.[23]

What one hears in 'Lizzie Leigh' is the voice of a quieter realism. Instead of Dickens's strong rhetorical patternings, there are the accents of a regional speech—*whatten*, *childer*, *shippon*; instead of his emphatic play with key words and phrases, a restrained, economical prose. Whereas Dickens achieves his striking effects through the stark oppositions and exaggerated gestures familiar to his readers

[20] The first part of a two-part article on this subject was published in the first issue of *Household Words*.

[21] Dickens to W. H. Wills, 12 Oct. 1852, *Letters of Charles Dickens*, vi. 776.

[22] Advertisement in *The Era*, 28 Apr. 1850. In July it was playing in Manchester (*Manchester Times*, Wednesday, 16 July 1851).

[23] See Sally Ledger, *Dickens and the Popular Radical Imagination* (Cambridge: Cambridge University Press, 2007).

from melodrama, this tale's distinctive artistry lies in its observation of particulars, its rendering of psychological nuance, its depiction of a domestic moment not as a striking tableau, but as a multifaceted reality:

When tea was ended,—it was merely the form of tea that had been gone through,—Will moved the things away to the dresser. His mother leant back languidly in her chair.

'Mother, shall Tom read you a chapter? He's a better scholar than I.'

'Aye, lad!' said she, almost eagerly. 'That's it. Read me the Prodigal Son. Aye, aye, lad. Thank thee.'

Tom found the chapter, and read it in the high-pitched voice which is customary in village-schools. His mother bent forward, her lips parted, her eyes dilated; her whole body instinct with eager attention. Will sat with his head depressed, and hung down.

He knew why that chapter had been chosen; and to him it recalled the family's disgrace. When the reading was ended, he still hung down his head in gloomy silence. But her face was brighter than it had been before for the day. Her eyes looked dreamy, as if she saw a vision; and by and by she pulled the bible towards her, and putting her finger underneath each word, began to read them aloud in a low voice to herself . . . (pp. 4–5).

This anticipates D. H. Lawrence in its delicate portrayal of the dynamics of family life, its concern with how the protagonists affect and yet are unnoticing of one another, its rendering of feelings of which they are only half aware. There is no single controlling perspective but an intimate evenhandedness, a flexible imaginative sympathy.

The familiar shapings of melodrama are evident in 'Lizzie Leigh': its extremes of feeling; its emphasis on chance and coincidence; its appeal to sentiment. Yet there is also, throughout, a precision of observation, an intelligent unexpectedness, that points to a different way of reading the social world. The parable of the prodigal gives a clear moral shape to the story that its readers might expect and recognize. But Gaskell is also attentive to the different ways in which it is read—by the boy with his 'high-pitched' village school training, and the mother who has to put 'a finger underneath each word'. Where Dickens abstracts, and stylizes, and emphasizes, Gaskell differently registers both the unconscious poetry and the awkward ongoing prose of ordinary life. Thus, at the story's outset, Mrs Leigh, newly widowed, sits 'rocking herself to and fro by the side of the bed, while the footsteps below went in and out' (p. 4): the parallelism of the sentence marking both the distance between and the simultaneity of the instinctive rituals of grief and the business that must be done. The difficult journey across the moors that follows is described in a sentence that recalls the rhythms of a funeral march:

Two and two the mourners followed, making a black procession, in their winding march over the unbeaten snow, to Milne-Row Church—now lost in some hollow of the bleak moors, now slowly climbing the heaving ascents. (p. 5)

Where Dickens's coincidences attest to the triumph of overview, there is a quieter matter-of-factness in the patient attention to the humble reality of things that leads to Mrs Leigh's discovery of her daughter's child:

The writing was no clue at all; the name 'Anne,' common though it was, seemed something to build upon. But Mrs Leigh recognised one of the frocks instantly, as being made out of a gown that she and her daughter had bought together in Rochdale. (p. 18)

As Catherine Waters has shown, descriptions of second-hand clothes, by George Augustus Sala, were to be prominent in *Household Words*. In these articles clothes become potent images of the bewildering variety, the proliferating objects, of the new world of mass production and consumption, indicative of the depersonalizing logic of a whole society.[24] But this opening story in the journal offers a suggestive image of Gaskell's less assertive art. A woman noticing the 'large patterns' that suggest that a child's clothes might be made from its mother's, another recognizing a particular familiar fabric, a private memory of a time 'together in Rochdale': one by one these unstressed details trace a world of human connection, fragile, resourceful, tenacious, a woman's world of making do.

## Morton Hall

Gaskell's implicit dialogue with Dickens was to continue in the stories she went on writing for *Household Words*. But 'Morton Hall', the next story in this volume, is very different from 'Lizzie Leigh'. It is not a simple 'tale', but three interconnected stories, with a distinctive

[24] Catherine Waters, '"Fashion in undress": Clothing and Commodity Culture in *Household Words*', *Journal of Victorian Culture*, 12 (2007), 26–41.

frame narrator—the bigoted elderly spinster Bridget Sidebotham. By the time of its publication in *Household Words* Gaskell's readers knew her not merely as a writer of 'social problem' fiction, but as the author of the popular series of Cranford 'papers' that had appeared intermittently in that journal during the preceding two years. They would have recognized Bridget Sidebotham and her sister as Cranfordian creations: 'Ethelinda always maintained that the long chapters in the Bible which were all names, were geography; and though I knew well enough they were not, yet I had forgotten what the right word was' (p. 58); 'I said that old families, like the Mortons, generally thought it showed good blood to have their complaints as high in the body as they could—brain-fevers and headaches had a better sound, and did perhaps belong more to the aristocracy' (p. 63). Here, as in *Cranford*, they would have found neither melodrama nor fiction with a purpose, but a subtler balance between irony and sentiment. Yet 'Morton Hall' tells a darker story than *Cranford*, one that reaches backward over nearly two hundred years of English history.

   Those who began 'Morton Hall' in *Household Words* on 19 November 1853 had for months been reading a 'History' of a rather different kind. The journal's serialization of *A Child's History of England* was drawing to a close. Dickens's trenchant, dogmatic anti-monarchical history, originally written for his children, set out with polemical gusto to instruct the people of England, still largely unenfranchised, in what he saw as the meaning of their nation's history. Its sardonic account of 'the merry things that were done' in the 'merry England' of the Restoration, when 'everybody found out all in a moment that the country *must* be prosperous and happy, having another Stuart to condescend to reign over it', had appeared in *Household Words* for 29 October 1853. 'Think, after you have read this reign,' Dickens urged his readers, 'what England was under Oliver Cromwell . . . and what it was under this merry monarch who sold it, like a merry Judas, again and again.' His is not a nuanced history, as its title indicates. But its emphatic simplifications allow a powerful rhythmic stylization of the complexities of the past into a narrative with an unambiguous import, one that might indeed enable those who had been powerless within it to gain some purchase on it.

   Gaskell was to untease some of the strands of that same history in the tale whose first part appeared in the following month. The more alert of her readers might well have been struck by the difference between Dickens's scathing picture of 'the merry days' of the Restoration and 'Morton Hall' 's portrayal of the returning cavaliers, 'laughing, and talking, and making merry, and speaking gaily and pleasantly to the village people', whilst the Puritan Alice Carr sits weeping in 'the chill house shadow . . . [a]ll through that summer's day' (pp. 35–6). Unobtrusively but distinctly Gaskell takes the key word of Dickens's polemic, and makes it part of a more subtly chequered history: the 'village bells' heard that day 'through the upper windows—which were open because of the heat . . . ringing merrily through the trees' (p. 36); the young squire of the following century, riding through the village 'in his bright scarlet coat, his long fair curling hair falling over his lace collar, and his broad black hat and feather shading his merry blue eyes' (p. 43); Phillis Morton, 'merry and comical', 'making cheeses' whilst dressing for a ball (p. 44–5); she and her brother, 'sometimes sad enough, sometimes merry as ever' as their inheritance disappears (p. 46). With her keen interest in etymology, Gaskell may well have been aware of the root of 'merry' in an old High German word meaning 'short', picked up in its associations with 'pastime', the pleasant whiling away of time. For the short space within which her story narrates the passing of several lifetimes, no less than its striking contrasts, conveys a darker intuition of the transience of 'merriment'. The suggestion is not laboured, but the narrating housekeeper pauses to dwell on the strangeness of a long-remembered moment on that day of the cavaliers' return:

Between the last cottage in the village and the gates to the old Hall, there was a shady part of the road, where the branches nearly met overhead, and made a green gloom. If you'll notice, when many people are talking merrily out of doors in sunlight, they will stop talking for an instant, when they come into the cool green shade, and either be silent for some little time, or else speak graver, and slower, and softer. And so old people say those gay gentlemen did . . . They used to tell how the cavaliers had to bow their plumed hats in passing under the unlopped and drooping boughs. (p. 35)

'Morton Hall' is sharply different from Dickens's 'ungentlemanly' history (as G. K. Chesterton called it); and this is not merely because of its narrator's reverence for rank. For the gently ironized Bridget Sidebotham is less a mouthpiece for Gaskell's own political sympathies than an image of her wry awareness of the difference of her art from his. Here, instead of an authoritative master-narrative, there are stories handed down by women—the Sidebotham sisters, Alice Carr's 'old nurse', the two housekeepers at the Hall. The world this tale configures is one of neighbourhood gossip, of rumour and oral tradition, in which events are variously reported, discounted, or mythologized, gradually forgotten or never spoken of. 'By and by there was a talk'; 'we did not hear so much'; 'the children of the village got up a tale'; 'he . . . tried to form words, but no sound came out of his lips': the phrases like these that punctuate the telling point to Gaskell's deliberate refusal of the straightforward power of polemic, her quiet articulation of a different view of 'history'. If throughout there are stories, there are also counter-stories. With its references to the Corn Law debates and the Catholic question, the opening paragraph points toward competing narratives of Englishness; indeed, the opening sentence registers a division between the narrator's loyalty to a vanishing past and the opposing story of progress that is transforming the countryside. The marriage of the conclusion might seem to hold out the promise of a romantic resolution to the long history of conflict between Cavalier and Puritan, but this sense too is countered by Bridget Sidebotham's tart interjection: 'I longed to tell her to pluck up a spirit, and be above a cotton-spinner' (p. 66).

'Morton Hall' replies to Dickens with a subtler fictional reflection on how the events of 'history' are experienced and remembered, what kinds of meanings can be discerned in or retrieved from them. In this, it perhaps owes something to Thackeray's *History of Henry Esmond*, which had appeared the preceding year. In that novel, Thackeray likewise contemplates the England of the Restoration through the troubled story of an aristocratic house. Gaskell's Phillis Morton is a little like Beatrix Esmond—spirited, beautiful, 'like a little princess for the imperious sway she exercised'; her closeness to her nephew—'you would have thought them brother and sister rather than nephew and aunt'—recalls *Henry Esmond*'s more shocking transgression of kin and generational boundaries. Most centrally, perhaps, Gaskell's story follows Thackeray's novel in its scepticism regarding grand historical narratives and in its concern with questions of legitimacy and usurpation: who is the rightful head of the nation? of the family? But this far shorter story, appearing on the cheap paper of a twopenny periodical, and told by one who is after all of the servant class, is also suggestively different from Thackeray's three-volume novel, with its patrician narrator and its eighteenth-century typeface and wide margins, priced at a guinea and a half.

What sense can be made of the troubled, divided past? Gaskell poses the question not, as Thackeray does, by an elaborate meditation on 'the Muse of History', but by evoking the kind of story that would have been familiar to all readers of *Household Words*.[25] 'Morton Hall' is punctuated by a series of suggestions of fairy tale: the feast with the meat on the spit, shut up in a room for years; the brambles that slowly grow up around the abandoned hall; 'Miss Phillis' looking at the food on the table 'as if she feared to shut her eyes lest it should all vanish away'. The story's pivotal moment is the curse of Alice Carr:

She doomed them to die out of the land, and their house to be razed to the ground, while pedlars and huxters, such as her own people, her father, had been, should dwell where the knightly Mortons had once lived. (p. 42)

It is a curse that seems fulfilled with the pulling down of 'the old stone dining-parlour where the great dinner for the preachers mouldered away—flesh from flesh, crumb from crumb!' (p. 67). Gaskell's readers would have known of the long-standing folk-tale tradition which held that the curses of the injured and the powerless had a peculiar efficacy.[26] 'Alas!' says Bridget Sidebotham, 'we have seen' (p. 43). Yet the events she narrates might also be seen as disclosing a more optimistic story, of progress and reconciliation of division, in which 'streets' are built and the people become prosperous, and the first disastrous marriage between the Mortons and the Carrs is succeeded by a second happier, more fruitful one.

Is Bridget Sidebotham's a story of the reconciliation of division, or of a retributive logic working itself out? Gaskell leaves both possibilities enigmatically suspended. Instead of a strongly moralized narrative, she offers a series of seemingly random details: the 'mighty cold rounds of spiced beef, quarters of lamb, chicken pies' that Alice Carr sets out for the preachers; the 'scent of the *maréchale* powder

[25] *Henry Esmond*, Preface to Book I. The connection between *Household Words* and fairy tale was intimate and well established. On this subject, see Elaine Ostry, *Social Dreaming* (London: Routledge, 2002), ch. 5. 'In an utilitarian age, of all other times, it is a matter of grave importance that Fairy tales should be respected,' Dickens had urged, in his 'Frauds on the Fairies', which appeared in the journal on 1 Oct. 1853, a few weeks before the first part of 'Morton Hall'.

[26] See Keith Thomas, *Religion and the Decline of Magic* (Harmondsworth: Penguin, 1973), 602–11.

with which Miss Phillis's hair was just sprinkled'; the 'eggs all shattered and splashed, making an ugly yellow pool in the road just in
front of the cottage'; little Cordelia Mannisty reciting a geography
lesson, of which Bridget Sidebotham remembers only 'that Pomfret
was famous for Pomfret cakes' (p. 57). But 'Morton Hall' is not simply
a succession of unconnected vignettes. For Gaskell confronts her
readers also with a shocking central image: the remembered starvation
of the Mortons, 'like . . . a sad, terrible dream' (p. 64). This is the fact
that makes a charged silence at the centre of her story's world of gossip.
Bridget Sidebotham and her sister never discuss it; the child Cordelia
is enjoined 'not to speak about all this to any one' and 'never has
named it again' (p. 64). Their silence registers that history is not
merely story, but traumatic reality.

How might readers of *A Child's History of England* have responded
to this tale of aristocratic downfall? Those whom Dickens was
addressing as the coming agents of history appear only at the edges of
Bridget Sidebotham's narrative as 'the clumping sound of the clogs of
the village people' on the day of the cavaliers' return to Morton, or,
later, as 'people working in mills' (p. 65). Yet Gaskell, whose view of
the Corn Laws was rather different from her narrator's, knew that the
people had their story, too. 'It was the spring of 1800,' she was to
write eight years later in *Sylvia's Lovers*. 'Old people can yet tell of
the hard famine of that year':

The harvest of the autumn before had failed; the war and the corn laws
had brought the price of corn up to a famine rate . . . Rich families denied
themselves pastry and all unnecessary and luxurious uses of wheat in any
shape; the duty on hair-powder was increased; and all these palliatives
were but as drops in the ocean of the great want of the people. (ch. 44)

She who had written three years earlier of the people 'clemming' in
Manchester knew that for many in mid-Victorian England hunger was
not merely a story held within living memory, but a more immediate
threat. She would have expected her story's central image of death by
starvation to reverberate with readers of *Household Words*. Hunger was
a frequent subject in that journal.[27] In the early 1850s *The Times* was

---

[27] In 1850, for example, it reported that 'two little children whose heads scarcely
reached the top of the dock' had been charged 'with stealing a loaf out of a baker's shop.
They said, in defence, that they were starving, and their appearance showed that they
spoke the truth. They were sentenced to be whipped in the House of Correction'
(W. H. Wills, 'The Great Penal Experiments', *Household Words*, 8 June 1850, 252);

still publishing accounts of actual starvation amongst the labouring classes, several in November 1853, as 'Morton Hall' appeared.[28] The gulf between the lives of the privileged classes and those of the lower orders was as great as in the 1790s, those years of war and famine in which, partly in order to conserve flour for foodstuff, a tax of a guinea a year had been imposed on the hair-powder that the fashionable wore. Hair-powder had been one of the most potent and many-faceted symbols of that time of ideological warfare. But perhaps its simplest and longest remembered meaning was as an image of the luxuries enjoyed by the upper classes whilst the people starved.[29] Gaskell might have expected readers to whom the 1790s were closer than the Second World War is today to make their own connection between two of her narrator's apparently inconsequential memories: the recent repeal of the Corn Laws and 'the scent of the *maréchale* powder' sprinkled years before on the youthful Phillis Carr's hair. She does not drive the point home: these remain simply details, for the reader to notice or not. But at least some of those who pondered Bridget Sidebotham's lament for the Mortons of Morton Hall might have found another and perhaps more subversive story in its contrasting images of a laughing girl wearing hair-powder and of the same woman, years later, dead of starvation, 'grey ragged locks about her face' (p. 51).

## My French Master

'My French Master' appeared in two parts in *Household Words* in December 1853, the month after 'Morton Hall'. This tale, too, replaces authoritative 'history' with a story told from the viewpoint of one on the edge of events. The narrator, less strongly marked as a character than Bridget Sidebotham, is an elderly woman, looking back to her girlhood in the New Forest at the time of the French

in 1854–5 it was to serialize Gaskell's *North and South*, with its accounts of starvation amongst the Manchester poor.

[28] e.g. *The Times*, 5 Nov. 1853, p. 5; 22 Nov., p. 8; 30 Nov., p. 10.

[29] 'Since the famine in seventeen hundred and ninety-nine and eighteen hundred there had been a tax on hair-powder,' notes Gaskell, not quite accurately, in *My Lady Ludlow*, published *in Household Words* in 1859. She seems to be following the account in George Lillie Craik's *The Pictorial History of England: being a History of the People as well as a History of the Kingdom* (1849), iii. 665. For a more complex recent account of the hair-powder tax debate, see John Barrell, *The Spirit of Despotism: Invasions of Privacy in the 1790s* (Oxford: Oxford University Press, 2006), 145–209.

Revolution and recalling how news of the Terror impacted upon a peaceful English rural community. Her own story of the death of parents and spinsterhood and exile emerges obliquely, round the edges of her memories of her beloved 'French master', the émigré M. Chalabre, with his 'dainty, courteous politeness' and his grief for his king and queen. Here, once again, the tale unfolds through a series of vignettes: the shaded glades and sunny spaces of the New Forest; the courtesies of friendship; the news that filters through from France; at the end, the present-day Paris of salons and matchmaking. Here, once again, there is a central image of a horror that will not bear speaking of: 'the news was too terrible to be put into plain English, and too terrible also to be made known to us children, nor could we at once find the clue to the cypher in which it was spoken about' (p. 73). The executions of the French king and queen are seen from the perspective of two gently bred English girls for whom they meant 'a fortnight's entire cessation of French lessons'. The narrator portrays herself and her sister 'sitting up in bed . . . arms round each other's necks', weeping for '[t]hat beautiful queen, whose portrait once had been shown to us, with her blue eyes, and her fair resolute look, her profusion of lightly-powdered hair, her white neck adorned with strings of pearls'. 'We . . . vow[ed],' she recalls, 'in our weak, passionate, childish way, that if we lived long enough, that lady's death avenged should be' (p. 74).

It is a moment that reverberates with more than private sentiment. Gaskell is here evoking one of the best known and most ideologically charged passages in English political writing: the moment in Burke's *Reflections* when a description of the French queen in the bloom of her youth and beauty is presented at once as an elegy for a vanished past and a clarion call to war. 'I thought ten thousand swords must have leaped from their scabbards to avenge even a look that threatened her with insult. But the age of chivalry is gone.'[30] The passage, famously lampooned by Paine as a meaningless lament for 'a Quixotic age of chivalric nonsense',[31] was being recalled in a different way in mid-nineteenth-century England: '"The age of chivalry is gone," said Edmund Burke; and young England with a sigh repeats the

[30] Edmund Burke, *Reflections on the Revolution in France*, ed. J. C. D. Clark (Stanford, Calif.: Stanford University Press, 2002), 238.

[31] Thomas Paine, *The Rights of Man*, pt I, in *Rights of Man, Common Sense, and Other Political Writings*, ed. Mark Philp (Oxford: Oxford World's Classics, 2008), 100.

ejaculation,' declared one writer satirically in 1844.[32] He is referring specifically to the romantic conservatism of the Tory 'Young England' group, but the remark points toward what became in the middle years of the century a much more widespread nostalgia amongst those of widely differing political persuasions for what was seen as a golden age of feudalism—of 'dignified obedience' and civil- ized grace and 'courtesy', when the strong were protective to the weak and the rich looked after the poor. The power of this configur- ation of feeling in the England of the early 1850s is attested by the huge success of Charlotte Yonge's *The Heir of Redclyffe*, the best- selling novel of 1853.[33] This novel, whose hero, Guy Morville, is a quintessential figure of 'chivalrous courtesy', with 'highstrung notions of love, friendship and honour', was adopted by the young Pre-Raphaelites as a pattern for actual life, and became favourite reading for officers during the Crimean War.[34]

Gaskell's story, published ten months later, is rather more equivo- cal in its portrayal of 'chivalry'. There is a brief but telling acknowl- edgement of a radical counter-perspective, as the narrator, looking back, quietly contrasts 'the shudder of horror that thrilled through the country at hearing of this last execution' with 'the silent horrors endured for centuries by the people', the emotive reaction of 'a moment' with a history endured 'at length' (p. 74). But this kind of challenge to 'chivalry' is not the story's main concern. Its centre of interest lies rather in Gaskell's more subtle pondering of that 'chival- rous code' embodied in the figure of the girls' French master, which they themselves echo in their 'weak, passionate, childish way'. 'My French Master' portrays the romance of chivalry not as an oppressive delusion, but with a gentler irony. It is countered not by insistence on the people's sufferings but by the contrast between M. Chalabre's dreams of noble service to his 'sovereign' and the snub he receives when he goes to pay homage to a 'mass of corpulence' in a London hotel (p. 78). And it is also countered more unexpectedly, by his happy marriage to a 'good, respectable woman' without imagination who regards the French 'as frog-eating Mounseers' (p. 82).

[32] *The Student: a Magazine of Theology, Literature and Science*, vol. i (London, 1844), 209.

[33] Gaskell describes the novel and its 'immense success' in a letter to a French correspondent in March 1855 (*Further Letters*, 131).

[34] J. W. Mackail, *The Life of William Morris*, 2 vols. (London, 1899), i. 43.

The brevity of the tale is an essential part of its art. What has happened to the 'forest circle' in the years of war between 1793 and 1814, the growth of the narrator and her sister 'from children into girls—from girls into women', is summarized in a single paragraph (p. 75). The narrator's sudden sense that 'youth had passed away—gone without a warning—leaving no trace behind' (p. 80) is mirrored by the speed with which her story traces the replacing of the old France by the new mercantile one of the mid-nineteenth century, in which M. Chalabre's ancestral home is occupied by one engaged in the dyeing and selling of Turkey-red wools. The tale's central story is of fidelity to the past: of the beloved French master who leaves a garland of 'immortelles' on the grave of a dead friend, who remains faithful to his sovereign and his youthful vows, who 'lived to be eighty-one, but . . . had the black crape band on when he died' (p. 75). But its narrative momentum speaks of ongoing time and change. Within its story of enduring affection Gaskell quietly includes one of her apparently inconsequential details, the narrator's father's loss of memory:

Then came the return from Elba—the hurrying events of that spring—the battle of Waterloo; and to my poor father, in his second childhood, the choice of a daily pudding was far more important than all. (p. 80)

Where 'Morton Hall' suggested that the meanings of history reverberate beyond the individual lifespan, there is an ironic, elegiac sense of fleetingness in this shorter story's narrative of constancy.

### Half a Life-Time Ago

'Half a Life-Time Ago', published in three parts in *Household Words* in October 1855, is a story of rather different kind. At its opening, the 'life-time' of its central character is over: the introductory paragraphs present it as an epitaph not merely for an individual but for 'a class now passing away from the face of the land'. The story's focus on a 'Stateswoman' of Westmorland would for readers in the 1850s have immediately evoked Wordsworth, a long obituary for whom had appeared in *Household Words* on 25 May 1850. Gaskell, who had admired the poet since girlhood, was almost certainly familiar with the recently published letter in which he had written to Charles James Fox of his attempt in 'Michael' and 'The Brothers' to 'draw a picture of the domestic affections, as I know they exist among a class of men who are now almost confined to the north of England. . . . small independent *proprietors* of land, here called statesmen, who daily labour on their little properties'.[35] Much in 'Half a Life-Time Ago' recalls the Wordsworth of *Lyrical Ballads*: its basis in local story, its powerful tale of the strength of 'domestic affections' and of rootedness in place, even the 'idiot-brother' with his senseless repeated cry. 'A prose Lyrical Ballad', Angus Easson has called it.[36] Yet it is not exactly Wordsworthian.

A large part of the difference lies in the simple fact that the blank verse of 'Michael' and 'The Excursion', elevating its subjects into tragic inevitability, is here replaced by the unpredictability of prose. But it lies also in the unWordsworthian sharpness of Gaskell's attention to particulars. Thus, she describes Susan and her brother huddling together in the orchard 'where the fruit-trees were bare of leaves, but ghastly in their tattered covering of grey moss: and the soughing November wind came with long sweeps over the fells' (p. 96); she registers with unidealizing distinctness the drunkenness that is a part of the statesmen's culture, Susan's ageing body, the hardness of caring for the idiot. 'Half a Life-Time Ago' is unWordsworthian, too, in its depiction of love not merely as fidelity and endurance but also as longing, expectant desire:

She hurried over her household work, in order to sit quietly at her sewing, and hear the first distant sound of his well-known step or whistle. But even the sound of her flying needle seemed too loud—perhaps she was losing an exquisite instant of anticipation; so she stopped sewing, and looked longingly out through the geranium leaves, in order that her eye might catch the first stir of the branches in the wood-path by which he generally came. Now and then a bird might spring out of the covert; otherwise the leaves were heavily still in the sultry weather of early autumn (p. 111).

The connection made in this passage between intensity of feeling and almost hallucinatory perception of minute detail was one that Ruskin had noted in Pre-Raphaelite painting in a famous letter to *The Times*

---

[35] William Wordsworth to Charles James Fox, 14 Jan. 1801, in Christopher Wordsworth, *Memoirs of William Wordsworth* (London, 1851), i. 169. Gaskell would almost certainly have read this, the authorized biography of the poet, by 1853.

[36] Easson, *Elizabeth Gaskell* (London: Routledge, 1979), 22.

written in May 1854.[37] The precise, detailed observation that is evident throughout this tale bespeaks the impact upon Gaskell both of the first two volumes of Ruskin's *Modern Painters* and of the Pre-Raphaelite paintings with which she was becoming familiar both in London and in Manchester.[38]

Unlike a painting, however, a narrative tells not merely of the moment, but of the passing of time. Gaskell is not imitating another medium but exploiting the distinctive potentialities of her chosen form. Even the just-quoted moment of waiting intensity is not static: Susan hurries over her housework, stops sewing; there is a suggestion of passing time in its final word. As its title suggests, time is central to this story. But it tells two stories of time. One is of time as relentless, in face of which Susan is helpless, a sense that is registered in the tale's recurring images of the harshness of the Westmoreland weather, its repeated references to the passing of 'the long monotonous years that had turned her into an old woman before her time' (p. 126). Near the story's ending, the reader sees her amidst her dead lover's family, 'pierced to the very marrow', but standing 'as still and tearless as the great round face upon the clock' (p. 128). It is an image of blank imperviousness and rounded finality: of the ultimate authority of time. As Susan herself puts it, in a moment of self-reflection that is also a moment of narrative self-reflexiveness: 'Life was short, looking back upon it' (p. 126). Her story, known in the district, has the brevity of an epitaph. Yet like an epitaph it speaks not simply of a life's ending, but also of a life. The story of time as inexorable process is countered in the telling by another, in which the finality of closure is complicated by the prose of life going on. Susan devotes herself to her idiot brother, goes out in a winter storm in response to a human cry, takes her dead lover's family to live with her. Within her narrative of loss Gaskell quietly places the counterpointing suggestion that life is possibility and not mere meaningless process, that time can be redeemed. It is a suggestion that is imaged with unsentimental precision in another moment of heightened attention, when the childless, motherless woman notices

[37] *The Times*, 25 May 1854. Ruskin is describing *The Awakening Conscience*, a painting by Holman Hunt belonging to Sir Thomas Fairbairn, with whose family the Gaskells were friendly in Manchester.

[38] Gaskell and Charlotte Brontë talked of their admiration for *Modern Painters* at their first meeting, in the summer of 1850, at Ambleside, close to the place in which this story is set. (Elizabeth Gaskell to Catherine Winkworth, 25 Aug. 1850, *Letters*, 123).

the clock ticking with the peculiar beat [she] had known from her childhood, and which then and ever since she had oddly associated with the
idea of a mother and child talking together, one loud tick, and quick—a
feeble, sharp one following. (p. 123)

What she hears is not the mechanically marked measure of mere
duration, but that shortest of stories, tick tock.[39] It is a story that for
her bears testimony to unforgotten tenderness.

## The Manchester Marriage

If 'Half a Life-Time Ago' portrays a small community where the
stories of all are known, the next story in this volume speaks of a far
less rooted modernity. 'The Manchester Marriage' was Gaskell's
contribution to an extra Christmas number of *Household Words* in
December 1858: one of four stories, by Dickens, Wilkie Collins,
Adelaide Procter, and herself, set within a frame narrative entitled
'A House to Let'. The theme of the number is a familiar 'Dickensy'
one:[40] the alienating anonymity of city life, symbolized in the mystery
of 'the house across the way', and countered in a manner appropriate
to Christmas by the telling of a series of stories of those who have
lived in it. The denouement sees it become a children's hospital.
Gaskell's story has a less rosy ending, and it bears little relation to the
number's 'mystery' narrative. But like the others it is set in an urban
world of estrangement and displacement, in which—as both its title
and that of its frame suggest—things are temporary. The story it tells
is not of the sufferings of the dispossessed but of the social mobility of
the commercial middle class. Alice Openshaw and her servant Norah
are natives of Liverpool, who move to Manchester and then London:
'the Manchester marriage' is contracted on the way. The London
setting, required by the frame story, is unusual in Gaskell's fiction.
But Mr Openshaw, who has risen in the world by 'fighting his way
through the hard striving Manchester life with strong, pushing
energy of character' (p. 134), is a self-made man from Manchester.
 Here, once again, there is a suggestion of a dialogue with Dickens,
whose *Hard Times*, with its scathing portrait of Bounderby the

---

[39] On *'tick-tock'* as fiction, see Frank Kermode, *The Sense of an Ending* (Oxford:
Oxford University Press, 1967), 44–5.
[40] The word is Gaskell's, in a letter written during the period of her growing annoyance with him (*Letters*, 534).

self-made man, had recently appeared in *Household Words*. Gaskell's description conveys, by contrast, a part admiring, part respectful acknowledgement of the hardness of the struggle to get on in the world, the 'energy' and 'character' required for it. Her Manchester man is not a caricature, but a complex creation, who changes in the course of the story, finding unexpected reserves of tenderness within him as he grows to love the crippled Ailsie, and, by the end, an unexpected brotherhood with the man whose place he has usurped. Gaskell was to return to the tale of one believed lost at sea who comes back to find that his betrothed is married to another in her later *Sylvia's Lovers*. But in this shorter story of brittle modernity one hears perhaps more clearly the echo of an older, more haunting one, that she would have known from traditional ballads such as 'The Demon Lover': the story not of a living lover's return, but of one who comes back from the grave as a revenant. For here the returning husband appears as a liminal figure whose sense that he can no longer have a place in ongoing life is expressed by his suicide.

Within Gaskell's story there are, however, suggestions of other stories, troubling and complicating that archetypal tale. It is not the wife, but the second husband, with his 'strong pushing energy', who is to be haunted forever by this excluded other—a figure for all the losers in life's competitive struggle, those who have no place in the narrative of getting on. And it is not the wife but the servant, who had been 'the only bridesmaid' at Alice's first wedding, who recognizes the strange man, with his 'eager, beautiful eyes'.

Norah plays a pivotal part in the Openshaws' story. Its happy outcome is brought about largely by her fidelity to her mistress, by her quick-wittedness in face of the unexpected intruder and her self-effacing silence when accused. But Gaskell also sketches in Norah's story and Norah's perspective. To Norah, the stranger's eyes are beautiful and familiar because she has seen them daily in the face of a child she loves. Her feelings for the family she lives with include not merely love and loyalty and a fierce protectiveness, but also resentment—'It almost put her out of patience to see Mrs Openshaw come in, calmly smiling, handsomely dressed, happy, easy, to inquire after her children' (p. 144)—and a prosaic acknowledgement of a hard reality: 'I have cared for her and her child, as nobody ever cared for me' (p. 149). The story registers her position as a servant, moved from place to place to suit her employers' convenience; as an unmarried woman, who has no child of her own. Required to be loyal and devoted to her charges, she is at once expected and not expected to have emotions: there is a bitter irony in the fact that she is suspected of having a follower. With economical precision Gaskell delineates the contradictions of her situation. The moment of the apparently dead husband's return is thus charged with complicated feeling: 'Norah and he looked at each other; gradual recognition coming into their eyes' (p. 141).

The recognition is not merely Norah's, of the stranger's identity, but a mutual one. The husband's dawning awareness of the disaster of his return is also a recognition of shared exclusion from the stories of those who (as Charlotte Brontë put it at the ending of *Villette*) have 'a happy succeeding life'. The haunting suggestion is of a strange affinity between the man who seems to come from the world of the dead and who is shortly to return to it, and the woman who occupies the lower world of the servant class. If 'The Manchester Marriage' tells an optimistic story of the humanizing of the self-made man, it contains also the under-story of those who have no place in nineteenth-century England's official narratives of happiness and success. It is a story subtly at odds with the cheering message of Dickens's Christmas Book.

## Cousin Phillis

The last and longest tale in this volume was published in a periodical very different from *Household Words*. Appearing monthly, priced at one shilling, the *Cornhill Magazine* was a more prestigious journal addressed to a more sophisticated audience, carrying much more ambitious fictions: when the first part of *Cousin Phillis* appeared in November 1863, the journal had recently finished serializing George Eliot's *Romola*. With its fine illustrations by artists and wood engravers, the *Cornhill* also much more explicitly invited its readers to see those fictions as works of art. Gaskell's 'Curious, if True' appeared in the first issue: a curious little story that reflects ironically upon the fictionality of fairy tale.

*Cousin Phillis* is neither a short story, nor a novel like *Romola*. It is designedly a shorter fiction that plays upon the dual origins of the genre in the traditions of the 'tale' and the 'sketch'. For central to the telling is a tension between the onward movement of linear narrative and the lyric suspension of time. It opens like an example of that well-known nineteenth-century genre, the *Bildungsroman*, as its retrospective narrator, Paul Manning, tells of setting out to begin the world. There is a gentle irony in his account of his 'new independence', which is in fact a rigid routine: 'I was at my desk by eight o'clock, home to dinner at one, back at the office by two' (p. 157). But within this familiar story there soon appears a second story, that which is adumbrated in the title: 'It is about cousin Phillis that I am going to write.' 'Phillis' is a name with pastoral and amorous resonances, familiar both in Greek poetry and English Renaissance verse. Like such verse *Cousin Phillis* places the girl who is at its centre in a pastoral setting: but it is a richly detailed, sharply seen mid-Victorian one, in which plants are named with Pre-Raphaelite precision: 'fraxinella', 'stone-crop', 'fumitory'. The aestheticism of the *Cornhill*, with its fine illustrations, is echoed by this narrator, in whose memory 'scenes rise like pictures', and who first sees Phillis lit up, standing in a doorway, framed:

I knocked with my hand upon the 'curate' door; a tall girl, about my own age, as I thought, came and opened it, and stood there silent, waiting to know my errand. I see her now—cousin Phillis. The westering sun shone full upon her, and made a slanting stream of light into the room within. She was dressed in dark blue cotton of some kind; up to her throat, down to her wrists, with a little frill of the same wherever it touched her white skin. (p. 162)

Phillis appears within Paul's narrative as an aesthetic object, seen with a Pre-Raphaelite clarity. Yet she is also, we see as the story unfolds, a person with her own story, her own aspirations and frustrations, her own inner narrative of change. She is not a generalized figure of lost pastoral innocence, but a particular 'tall' girl brought up in the old Independent faith, eager to learn and think for herself, straightforwardly accepting of her own dawning sexuality. Like the Pre-Raphaelite paintings that Gaskell saw and admired in Manchester and in London, *Cousin Phillis* portrays a particular historical moment of cultural and technological change. Time and place are becoming different. The story registers the speed of the new technology: steamships arrive quickly, the railway comes. The quotations from Virgil that seem to invoke an eternal classical truth are in fact taken from a series of 'sketches' about farming in New England published in the same year as this story in an American periodical.[41] Life at Hope Farm is not a timeless pastoral idyll, but open to new technological developments in agriculture: the local is becoming part of a wider world.

Yet *Cousin Phillis* is not simply the story of Phillis but also the story of Paul: of his leaving home and becoming 'independent', and above all of his encounter with a world that questions his. Gaskell portrays the rather differently 'Independent' way of life at Hope Farm with a seriousness that recalls Ruskin, whose *Unto this Last*, with its Gospel-inspired challenge to the values of political economy, had appeared in *Cornhill* two years before. For her tale is subtly inflected by the teller's sense that he is describing a culture in comparison with which his own is shallow and unexamined, a way of life more beautiful, a discipline far deeper than his. It is a sense that is summed up in his description of the minister leading a psalm in the fields:

He lifted his spade in his hand, and began to beat time with it; the two labourers seemed to know both words and music, though I did not; and so did Phillis: her rich voice followed her father's as he set the tune; and the men came in with more uncertainty, but still harmoniously. Phillis looked at me once or twice with a little surprise at my silence; but I did not know the words. There we five stood, bareheaded, excepting Phillis, in the tawny stubble-field, from which all the shocks of corn had not yet been carried—a dark wood on one side, where the woodpigeons were cooing; blue distance seen through the ash-trees on the other. (pp. 167–8)

Paul feels the beauty of the moment but cannot join in. It is not just that he does not 'know the words' of the psalm: the life that he sees at Hope Farm is tuned to a higher pitch than the one he is beginning to lead. The world of these others is not exactly simpler than that of his new 'independence'. In many ways it is more complex: characterized by fineness of perception, intellectual strenuousness, spiritual awareness, an austerity that is also richness ('home made bread and newly churned butter'; a courtyard 'full of flowers'); by a seriousness of purpose that gives it the beauty of a work of art. Hope Farm is not idealized: Paul registers, for example, the minister's struggles with irritation and failures of charity; his blindness to his daughter's growth to womanhood. But what he sees there causes him to feel,

[41] See p. 265, second note to p. 225.

obscurely, the limitations of his own ambitions, of his pride and satisfaction in his new life.

*Cousin Phillis* does not, however, simply ironize its narrator. For it
is Paul's faithful recollection that renders this other life in all its
sharpness of detail, that registers its beauty and places it in the past.
Throughout, the telling is inflected both by his imaginative feeling
for what he sees, and also, more poignantly, by his sense that it is
gone. Looking back, he recalls not merely 'the bright colour of
Phillis's hair, as the afternoon sun fell on her bending head', but also
'the silence of the house, which enabled me to hear the double tick of
the old clock which stood half-way up the stairs'. His narrative is
shaped by a constant tension between the loving attention that seeks
to hold time suspended and an awareness of ongoing time. 'The
tranquil monotony' of a summer afternoon spent reading to Phillis
and her mother 'made me feel as if I had lived for ever, and should
live for ever', he recalls. But he also recalls 'the clock on the house-
stairs perpetually clicking out the passage of the moments' (p. 177):
his repeated 'I see her now' is countered by the past tense of the
unfolding story he tells. Through his narrative emerges a subtle
metafictional reflexiveness. Thus, he describes watching Phillis read
the letter which tells that her lover will not return:

How peaceful it all seemed in the farmyard! Peace and plenty. How still
and deep was the silence of the house! Tick-tick went the unseen clock on
the wide staircase. I had heard the rustle once, when she turned over the
page of thin paper. She must have read to the end. Yet she did not move,
or say a word, or even sigh. I kept on looking out of the window, my hands
in my pockets. I wonder how long that time really was? It seemed to me
interminable—unbearable. (pp. 223–4)

The scene is tense with the opposition between the silent, motionless
girl and the turning page, the unseen clock. It remains for Paul
arrested in memory. Yet what he recalls hearing at this moment of
disaster is not the 'tick-tock' of meaningful story but the relentless-
ness of 'tick-tick'. This is at once an 'interminable' moment and part
of an unstoppable movement toward 'the end'. His description encap-
sulates the tension that shapes this quietly sophisticated narrative.

Gaskell's short fictions, of which the six given here are only a
sampling, are easy to enjoy. But they are also complex, thought-
provoking, resonant. Most were not designed to be read 'at a sitting'

(one of Poe's criteria for the short story, in his famous early attempt to define the genre); all those collected in this volume, except 'The Manchester Marriage', were published in parts. Their first readers would thus have had to take time to read them, to mull them over and ponder them. The present-day reader will find much to reward such pondering.

Each of these stories differently testifies to Gaskell's sharp aware-ness of those issues of class and gender that have preoccupied con-temporary historians of early Victorian England. But a reading that moves too fast to abstract these familiar themes will overlook the delicacy with which she registers particularity, her alertness to the complexity of the actual, the obliquity of her approach to charged subjects, her sharply intelligent engagement with other, perhaps less familiar issues of her time. These are not simple stories, but stories animated by other stories, under-stories and counter-stories. Each delineates an actuality that resists any single narrative—whether of polemical history or of social purpose, of disillusionment or of romance. They are moving, compelling, entrancing. But they are also stories that reflect upon stories in a quietly subversive way.

# NOTE ON THE TEXTS

THE texts given are those of the first British publication in volume form, which differs very little from that of the original periodical publication. Divisions between parts in the original periodical publication are marked thus in this edition: *   *   *.

'Lizzie Leigh' was first published in three parts in *Household Words* 1, on 30 March and 6 and 13 April 1850. It first appeared in volume form in *Lizzie Leigh and Other Tales* (London: Chapman and Hall, 1855).

'Morton Hall' was first published in two parts in *Household Words* 8, on 19 and 26 November 1853. It first appeared in volume form in *Lizzie Leigh and Other Tales* (London: Chapman and Hall, 1855).

'My French Master' was first published in two parts in *Household Words* 8, on 17 and 24 December 1853. It first appeared in volume form in *Lizzie Leigh and Other Tales* (London: Chapman and Hall, 1855).

'Half a Life-Time Ago' was first published in three parts in *Household Words* 12, on 6, 13, and 20 October 1855. It first appeared in volume form in *Round the Sofa*, 2 vols. (London: Sampson Low, 1859).

'The Manchester Marriage' was first published in the extra Christmas number of *Household Words* on 7 December 1858. It first appeared in volume form in *Right at Last and Other Tales* (London: Sampson Low, 1860). In this case, Gaskell removed a few references to the original frame narrative.

*Cousin Phillis* was published originally as a four-part serial in the *Cornhill Magazine*, appearing monthly from November 1863 to February 1864. It was published in volume form in what seems to have been a pirated edition by the American firm Harper & Brothers in 1864. It was first published in Britain in volume form in *Cousin Phillis and Other Tales* (London: Smith, Elder & Co.) in 1865.

# SELECT BIBLIOGRAPHY

## Gaskell's Short Fictions

During Gaskell's lifetime she published five volumes of shorter fictions:

*Lizzie Leigh and Other Tales* (London: Chapman and Hall, 1855).
*Round the Sofa*, 2 vols. (London: Sampson Low, 1859).
*Right at Last and Other Tales* (London: Sampson Low, 1860).
*The Grey Woman and Other Tales* (London: Smith, Elder, 1865).
*Cousin Phillis and Other Tales* (London: Smith, Elder, 1865).

Collected editions of Gaskell's shorter fictions include:

*Novels and Tales by Mrs Gaskell*, 7 vols. (London: Smith, Elder, 1872–3).
*The Works of Mrs Gaskell: The Knutsford Edition*, ed. A. W. Ward, 8 vols. (London: Smith, Elder, 1906).
*The Novels and Tales of Mrs Gaskell*, ed. C. K. Shorter, 11 vols. (Oxford: Oxford University Press, 1906–19).

All the shorter works that Gaskell is known to have written are to be found in *The Works of Elizabeth Gaskell*, gen. ed. Joanne Shattock, 10 vols. (London: Pickering & Chatto, 2005–6).

## Biography and Letters

Foster, Shirley, *Elizabeth, Gaskell: A Literary Life* (Basingstoke: Palgrave, 2002).
Gaskell, Elizabeth, *The Letters of Mrs Gaskell*, ed. J. V. A. Chapple and Arthur Pollard (Manchester: Manchester University Press, 1966).
—— *Further Letters of Mrs Gaskell*, ed. John Chapple and Alan Shelston (Manchester: Manchester University Press, 2003).
Gérin, Winifred, *Elizabeth Gaskell: A Biography* (Oxford: Oxford University Press, 1976).
Uglow, Jenny, *Elizabeth Gaskell: A Habit of Stories* (London and Boston: Faber and Faber, 1993).

## Selected Criticism of Gaskell

Billington, Josie, *Faithful Realism: Elizabeth Gaskell and Leo Tolstoy. A Comparative Study* (Lewisburg, Pa.: Bucknell University Press, 2002).
d'Albertis, Deirdre, *Dissembling Fictions: Elizabeth Gaskell and the Victorian Social Text* (New York: St Martin's Press, 1997).
Easson, Angus, *Elizabeth Gaskell* (London: Routledge, 1979).
—— (ed.), *Elizabeth Gaskell: The Critical Heritage* (London and New York: Routledge, 1991).

Matus, Jill (ed.), *The Cambridge Companion to Elizabeth Gaskell* (Cambridge: Cambridge University Press, 2007).

Schor, Hilary, *Scheherezade in the Martketplace: Elizabeth Gaskell and the Victorian Novel* (New York and Oxford: Oxford University Press, 1992).

Stoneman, Patsy, *Elizabeth Gaskell* (Brighton: Harvester, 1987).

### Criticism of Gaskell's Short Fictions

Foster, Shirley, 'Violence and Disorder in Elizabeth Gaskell's Short Stories', *Gaskell Society Journal*, 19 (2005), 14–24.

Hardy, Barbara, '*Cousin Phillis*: The Art of the Novella', *Gaskell Society Journal*, 19 (2005), 25–33.

Murfin, Audrey, 'Victorian Nights' Entertainments: Elizabeth Gaskell and Wilkie Collins Develop the British Story Sequence', *Romanticism and Victorianism on the Net*, 48 (Nov. 2007).

Pettitt, Clare, '"Cousin Holman's Dresser": Science, Social Change and the Pathologized Female in Gaskell's *Cousin Phillis*', *Nineteenth-Century Literature*, 52/4 (Mar. 1998), 471–89.

Rogers, Philip, 'The Education of Cousin Phillis', *Nineteenth-Century Literature*, 50/1 (June 1991), 27–50.

Turner, Mark, 'Time, Periodicals, and Literary Study', *Victorian Periodicals Review*, 39/4 (2006), 309–16.

Watson, J. R., '*Round the Sofa*: Elizabeth Gaskell Tells Stories', *Yearbook of English Studies*, 26 (1996), 89–99.

### Further Reading in Oxford World's Classics

Gaskell, Elizabeth, *Cranford*, ed. Elizabeth Porges Watson and Charlotte Mitchell.

—— *Mary Barton*, ed. Shirley Foster.

—— *North and South*, ed. Angus Easson and Sally Shuttleworth.

—— *Ruth*, ed. Alan Shelston.

—— *Sylvia's Lovers*, ed. Andrew Sanders.

—— *Wives and Daughters*, ed. Angus Easson.

# A CHRONOLOGY OF
# ELIZABETH GASKELL

| *Life* | *Historical and Cultural Background* |
|---|---|
| 1810 (29 Sept.) Elizabeth Cleghorn Gaskell born to William Stevenson and Elizabeth Holland in Chelsea. One surviving sibling, brother John, born 1798. | |
| 1811 (29 Oct.) Mother dies. (Nov.) Baby Elizabeth taken to Knutsford to be brought up by Hannah Lumb, Mrs Stevenson's eldest sister. | |
| 1812 | Charles Dickens born. Robert Browning born. Byron, *Childe Harold's Pilgrimage* (to 1818) Crabbe, *Tales in Verse* |
| 1813 | Jane Austen, *Pride and Prejudice* |
| 1814 William Stevenson remarries: new wife Catherine Thomson. | Abdication of Napoleon. Jane Austen, *Mansfield Park* Scott, *Waverley* |
| 1815 | Battle of Waterloo. Napoleon banished to St Helena. |
| 1816 | Charlotte Brontë born. Jane Austen, *Emma* Coleridge, 'Christabel' and 'Kubla Khan' |
| 1817 | Jane Austen dies. Keats, *Poems* Robert Owen, *Report to the Committee on the Poor Laws* |
| 1818 | Emily Brontë born. Jane Austen, *Northanger Abbey* and *Persuasion* (posthumous) Mary Shelley, *Frankenstein* |
| 1819 | Peterloo Massacre in Manchester. Queen Victoria born. Mary Ann Evans (George Eliot) born. John Ruskin born. Crabbe, *Tales of the Hall* Scott, *Ivanhoe* Byron, *Don Juan* (to 1824) |

| *Life* | *Historical and Cultural Background* |
|---|---|
| 1820 | Accession of George IV. Anne Brontë born. Lamb, *Essays of Elia* (to 1823) Malthus, *Principles of Political Economy* |
| 1821 Goes to boarding school at Barford, Warwickshire, run by Byerly sisters, relations of her stepmother. School moves to Stratford-upon-Avon in 1824. | Napoleon dies. Keats dies. *Manchester Guardian* started. John Stuart Mill, *Elements of Political Economy* |
| 1822 | Shelley dies. |
| 1824 | Byron dies. |
| 1826 (June) Leaves school. | James Fenimore Cooper, *The Last of the Mohicans* |
| 1827 | Treaty between Britain, France, and Russia to determine independence of Greece (confirmed 1830). |
| 1828 Disappearance of John Stevenson on way to India. Elizabeth goes to live in Chelsea with father and stepmother. | |
| 1829 (22 Mar.) Father dies. Elizabeth goes to stay with uncle, Revd William Turner, in Newcastle-upon-Tyne. | Carlyle, *Signs of the Times* |
| 1830 | Revolutions in Germany, Poland, Belgium, and France. Accession of William IV. Christina Rossetti born. Tennyson, *Poems, Chiefly Lyrical* |
| 1830–1 Newcastle. Visits Edinburgh with cousin, Ann Turner. | |
| 1831 Visits Knutsford and Liverpool. Goes to stay with Revd John Robberds, senior minister at Cross Street Unitarian Chapel, Manchester, and his wife. Meets here Revd William Gaskell, Robberds's junior minister. | First Reform Bill introduced. |
| 1832 (30 Aug.) Marries William Gaskell at St John's parish church, Knutsford. Gaskells set up house at 14 Dover Street, Manchester. | First Reform Bill passed. Walter Scott dies. Harriet Martineau, *Illustrations of Political Economy* (to 1834) |

| *Life* | *Historical and Cultural Background* |
|---|---|
| 1833 (10 July) Birth of stillborn daughter. | Charles Lyell, *Principles of Geology* Carlyle, *Sartus Resartus* *Tracts for the Times* (to 1841) |
| 1834 (12 Sept.) Birth of Marianne Gaskell. | Coleridge dies. Charles Lamb dies. |
| 1835 | Dickens, *Sketches by Boz* |
| 1836 | Dickens, *Pickwick Papers* |
| 1837 (Jan.) 'Sketches Among the Poor' (written with William), *Blackwood's Edinburgh Magazine*. (7 Feb.) Birth of Margaret Emily (Meta) Gaskell. (1 May) Death of Hannah Lumb. | Accession of Queen Victoria. Dickens, *Oliver Twist* |
| 1838 | Anti-Corn Law League founded in Manchester. Dickens, *Nicholas Nickleby* Lyell, *Elements of Geology* |
| 1838–41 Birth and death of unnamed son. | |
| 1839 | Chartist Petition presented to Parliament. Carlyle, *Chartism* |
| 1840 'Clopton House' in William Howitt's *Visits to Remarkable Places*. | Marriage of Victoria and Prince Albert. Robert Browning, *Sordello* Charles Darwin, *The Voyage of HMS Beagle* Dickens, *The Old Curiosity Shop* |
| 1841 (July) Visits Heidelberg with William. | Ralph Waldo Emerson, *Essays* (i) Dickens, *Barnaby Rudge* |
| 1842 (7 Oct.) Birth of Florence Elizabeth ('Flossy') Gaskell. Moves to 121 Upper Rumford Road, Manchester. | Tennyson, *Poems* |
| 1843 | Carlyle, *Past and Present* Ruskin, *Modern Painters* (to 1860) |
| 1844 (23 Oct.) Birth of William ('Willie') Gaskell. | Robert Chambers, *Vestiges of the Natural History of Creation* Elizabeth Barrett Browning, *Poems* Dickens, *Martin Chuzzlewit* Disraeli, *Coningsby* Emerson, *Essays* (ii) |

| *Life* | *Historical and Cultural Background* |
|---|---|
| 1845 (10 Aug.) Willie dies on family holiday in North Wales. | Potato famine begins in Ireland. Disraeli, *Sybil* Margaret Fuller, *Woman in the Nineteenth Century* Edgar Allan Poe, *Tales of Mystery and Imagination* |
| 1846 (3 Sept.) Birth of Julia Bradford Gaskell. | Repeal of Corn Laws in Britain. *Poems by Currer, Ellis and Acton Bell* (Brontë sisters) Dickens, *Dombey and Son* Edward Lear, *A Book of Nonsense* |
| 1847 'Libbie Marsh's Three Eras' (June) and 'The Sexton's Hero' (Sept.), *Hewitt's Journal*. | Anne Brontë, *Agnes Grey* Charlotte Brontë, *Jane Eyre* Emily Brontë, *Wuthering Heights* Tennyson, *The Princess* |
| 1848 (Jan.) 'Christmas Storms and Sunshine', *Howitt's Journal*. (Oct.) *Mary Barton*. | Revolutions in France, Sicily, and Austria. Emily Brontë dies. Formation of Pre-Raphaelite Brotherhood. J. S. Mill, *Principles of Political Economy* Thackeray, *Vanity Fair* |
| 1849 (Apr.–May) Visits London and meets Dickens, Forster, and Carlyle. (June–Aug.) Visits Lake District and meets Wordsworth. (July) 'The Last Generation in England', *Sartain's Union Magazine*; 'Hand and Heart', *Sunday School Penny Magazine*. | Garibaldi enters Rome. Charlotte Brontë, *Shirley* Ruskin, *Seven Lamps of Architecture* |
| 1850 (Jan.) Approached by Dickens to write for his new periodical, *Household Words*. (Feb.) 'Martha Preston', *Sartain's Union Magazine*. (Mar.–Apr.) 'Lizzie Leigh', *Household Words*. (June) Moves to 42 (later 84) Plymouth Grove, Manchester. (Aug.) Meets Charlotte Brontë at the Kay-Shuttleworths' house, Briery Close, near Ambleside. (Nov.) 'The Well of Pen-Morfa', *Household Words*. (Dec.) *The Moorland Cottage*; 'The Heart of John Middleton', *Household Words*. | Wordsworth dies. Tennyson becomes Poet Laureate. Dickens, *David Copperfield* Nathaniel Hawthorne, *The Scarlet Letter* Charles Kingsley, *Alton Locke* Tennyson, *In Memoriam* *Household Words* started by Dickens |

| *Life* | *Historical and Cultural Background* |
|---|---|
| 1851 (Feb.–Apr.) 'Mr Harrison's Confessions', *Ladies' Companion and Monthly Magazine.* (June) 'Disappearances', *Household Wards.* (July) Visits London and Great Exhibition. (Oct.) Visits Knutsford. (Dec.–May 1853) *Cranford* serialized in *Household Words.* | First Women's Suffrage Petition presented to Parliament. Great Exhibition in London. Melville, *Moby Dick* Ruskin, *Stones of Venice* (to 1853) |
| 1852 (Jan.–Apr.) 'Bessy's Troubles at Home', *Sunday School Penny Magazine.* (June) 'The Shah's English Gardener', *Household Words.* (Dec.) 'The Old Nurse's Story', *Household Words.* | Harriet Beecher Stowe, *Uncle Tom's Cabin* |
| 1853 (Jan.) *Ruth*; 'Cumberland Sheep-Shearers', *Household Words.* (Apr.) Charlotte Brontë visits Plymouth Grove. (May) Visits Paris. (June) *Cranford* (book form). (July) Visits Normandy. (19–23 Sept.) Stays with Charlotte Brontë at Haworth. (Oct.) 'Bran' (?with William), *Household Words.* (Nov.) 'Morton Hall', *Household Words.* (Dec.) 'Traits and Stories of the Huguenots', 'My French Master', 'The Squire's Story', 'The Scholar's Story' (?with William), *Household Words.* | Turkey declares war on Russia. Charlotte Brontë, *Villette* Dickens, *Bleak House* |
| 1854 (Jan.–Feb.) Visits Paris. (Feb.) 'Modern Greek Songs', *Household Words.* (May) 'Company Manners', *Household Words.* (Sept.–Jan. 1855) *North and South* serialized in *Household Words.* | Crimean War begins. Dickens, *Hard Times* Henry Thoreau, *Walden* |
| 1855 (Feb.) Visits Paris. (Mar.) *North and South* (book form; Feb. in USA). (31 Mar.) Charlotte Brontë dies. (June) Patrick Brontë asks her to write his daughter's biography. (Aug.) 'An Accursed Race', *Household Words.* (Sept.) *Lizzie Leigh and Other Tales.* (Oct.) 'Half a Life-Time Ago' (revision of 'Martha Preston'), *Household Words.* | Charlotte Brontë dies. Robert Browning, *Men and Women* Tennyson, *Maud* Walt Whitman, *Leaves of Grass* |

| *Life* | *Historical and Cultural Background* |
|---|---|
| 1856 | Visits Brussels to research for Charlotte Brontë biography. (Dec.) 'The Poor Clare', *Household Words*. | Crimean War ends with the Paris Peace Congress. |
| 1857 | (Feb.–May) Visits Rome and meets Charles Eliot Norton. (Mar.) *Life of Charlotte Brontë*. (May) Faces libel action for misrepresentation brought by various people mentioned in the *Life*. Meta engaged to Captain Charles Hill, widowed officer in Indian army. | Indian Mutiny. Elizabeth Barrett Browning, *Aurora Leigh* Dickens, *Little Dorrit* Anthony Trollope, *Barchester Towers* |
| 1858 | (Jan.) 'The Doom of the Griffiths', *Harper's Monthly Magazine*. (June) 'An Incident at Niagara Falls', *Harper's Monthly Magazine*. (June–Sept.) 'My Lady Ludlow', *Household Words*. (Aug.) Meta's engagement broken off. (Sept.–Dec.) Visits Heidelberg. (Nov.) 'The Sin of a Father' (in later collection as 'Right at Last'), *Household Words*. (Dec.) 'The Manchester Marriage', *Household Words*. | George Eliot, *Scenes of Clerical Life* |
| 1859 | (Mar.) *Round the Sofa*. (June) Visits Scotland. (Oct.) 'Lois the Witch', *All the Year Round*. (Nov.) Visits Whitby and gains material for *Sylvia's Lovers*. (Dec.) 'The Ghost in the Garden Room' (in later collection as 'The Crooked Branch'), *All the Year Round*. | War of Italian Liberation; Garibaldi in Sicily. Dickens starts *All the Year Round*. Darwin, *On the Origin of Species* Dickens, *A Tale of Two Cities* George Eliot, *Adam Bede* J. S. Mill, *On Liberty* Tennyson, *Idylls of the King* |
| 1860 | (Feb.) 'Curious if True', *Cornhill Magazine*. (May) *Right at Last and Other Tales*. (July–Aug.) Visits Heidelberg. | Lincoln elected president of the USA. George Eliot, *The Mill on the Floss* Hawthorne, *The Marble Faun* |
| 1861 | (Jan.) 'The Grey Woman', *All the Year Round*. | Outbreak of American Civil War. Unification of Italy; Victor Emanuel becomes king. Prince Albert dies. Elizabeth Browning dies. Dickens, *Great Expectations* George Eliot, *Silas Marner* Trollope, *Framley Parsonage* |

| *Life* | *Historical and Cultural Background* |
|---|---|
| 1862 (May) 'Six Weeks at Heppenheim', *Cornhill Magazine*. Visits Brittany and Normandy to gather material for 'French Life' (1864) and to plan memoir of Madame de Sevigné (never written). (Summer) Marianne secretly engaged to her second cousin, Thurstan Holland. | Christina Rossetti, *Goblin Market and Other Poems* Ruskin, *Unto This Last* |
| 1863 (Jan.–Mar.) 'A Dark Night's Work', *All the Year Round*. (Feb.) *Sylvia's Lovers*; 'Shams', *Fraser's Magazine*. (Mar.) 'An Italian Institution', *All the Year Round*. (Mar.–June) Visits France and Italy. (Apr.) *A Dark Night's Work* (book form). (8 Sept.) Florence Gaskell marries Charles Crompton. (Nov.) 'The Cage at Cranford', *All the Year Round*. (Nov.–Feb. 1864) 'Cousin Phillis', *Cornhill Magazine*. (Dec.) 'How the First Floor Went to Crowley Castle', *All the Year Round*; 'Robert Gould Shaw', *Macmillan's Magazine*. | Lincoln's Gettysburg address. Thackeray dies. J. S. Mill, *Utilitarianism* |
| 1864 (Apr.–June) 'French Life', *Fraser's Magazine*. (Aug.–Jan. 1866) *Wives and Daughters, Cornhill Magazine*. (Aug.) Visits Switzerland. | Browning, *Dramatis Personae* |
| 1865 (Mar.–Apr.) Visits Paris. (Mar.) 'Columns of Gossip from Paris', *Pall Mall Gazette* (Apr.) 'A Letter of Gossip from Paris', *Pall Mall Gazette*. (June) Buys 'The Lawn', Holybourne, Hampshire, as a surprise for William. (Aug.–Sept.) 'A Parson's Holiday', *Pall Mall Gazette*. (Sept.) Visits Dieppe. *The Grey Woman and Other Tales*. (12 Nov.) Dies at Holybourne. (Dec.) *Cousin Phillis and Other Tales*. | Assassination of Lincoln; end of American Civil War. W. B. Yeats born. Rudyard Kipling born. Lewis Carroll, *Alice in Wonderland* Dickens, *Our Mutual Friend* Ruskin, *Sesame and Lilies* |
| 1866 (Feb.) *Wives and Daughters: An Every-Day Story* published in book form, posthumously and unfinished. | |

# COUSIN PHILLIS
## AND OTHER STORIES

# LIZZIE LEIGH

## CHAPTER I

WHEN Death is present in a household on a Christmas Day, the very contrast between the time as it now is, and the day as it has often been, gives a poignancy to sorrow,—a more utter blankness to the desolation. James Leigh died just as the far away bells of Rochdale Church were ringing for morning service on Christmas Day, 1836. A few minutes before his death, he opened his already glazing eyes, and made a sign to his wife, by the faint motion of his lips, that he had yet something to say. She stooped close down, and caught the broken whisper, 'I forgive her, Anne! May God forgive me!'

'Oh my love, my dear! only get well, and I will never cease showing my thanks for those words. May God in heaven bless thee for saying them. Thou'rt not so restless, my lad! may be—Oh God!'

For even while she spoke, he died.

They had been two-and-twenty years man and wife; for nineteen of those years their life had been as calm and happy, as the most perfect uprightness on the one side, and the most complete confidence and loving submission on the other, could make it. Milton's famous line might have been framed and hung up as the rule of their married life, for he was truly the interpreter, who stood between God and her;* she would have considered herself wicked if she had ever dared even to think him austere, though as certainly as he was an upright man, so surely was he hard, stern, and inflexible. But for three years the moan and the murmur had never been out of her heart; she had rebelled against her husband as against a tyrant, with a hidden, sullen rebellion, which tore up the old land-marks of wifely duty and affection, and poisoned the fountains whence gentlest love and reverence had once been for ever springing.

But those last blessed words replaced him on his throne in her heart, and called out penitent anguish for all the bitter estrangement of later years. It was this which made her refuse all the entreaties of her sons, that she would see the kind-hearted neighbours, who called on their way from church to sympathise and condole. No! she would stay with the dead husband that had spoken tenderly at last, if for three years he had kept silence; who knew but what, if she had only been more gentle and less angrily reserved, he might have relented earlier—and in time!

She sat rocking herself to and fro by the side of the bed, while the footsteps below went in and out; she had been in sorrow too long to have any violent burst of deep grief now; the furrows were well worn in her cheeks, and the tears flowed quietly, if incessantly, all the day long. But when the winter's night drew on, and the neighbours had gone away to their homes, she stole to the window, and gazed out, long and wistfully, over the dark grey moors. She did not hear her son's voice, as he spoke to her from the door, nor his footstep as he drew nearer. She started when he touched her.

'Mother! come down to us. There's no one but Will and me. Dearest mother, we do so want you.' The poor lad's voice trembled, and he began to cry. It appeared to require an effort on Mrs Leigh's part to tear herself away from the window but with a sigh she complied with his request.

The two boys (for though Will was nearly twenty-one, she still thought of him as a lad) had done everything in their power to make the house-place* comfortable for her. She herself, in the old days before her sorrow, had never made a brighter fire or a cleaner hearth, ready for her husband's return home, than now awaited her. The tea-things were all put out, and the kettle was boiling; and the boys had calmed their grief down into a kind of sober cheerfulness. They paid her every attention they could think of, but received little notice on her part; she did not resist—she rather submitted to all their arrangements; but they did not seem to touch her heart.

When tea was ended,—it was merely the form of tea that had been gone through,—Will moved the things away to the dresser. His mother leant back languidly in her chair.

'Mother, shall Tom read you a chapter? He's a better scholar than I.'

'Aye, lad!' said she, almost eagerly. 'That's it. Read me the Prodigal Son.* Aye, aye, lad. Thank thee.'

Tom found the chapter, and read it in the high-pitched voice which is customary in village-schools. His mother bent forward, her lips parted, her eyes dilated; her whole body instinct with eager attention. Will sat with his head depressed, and hung down.

He knew why that chapter had been chosen; and to him it recalled the family's disgrace. When the reading was ended, he still hung down his head in gloomy silence. But her face was brighter than it had been before for the day. Her eyes looked dreamy, as if she saw a vision; and by and by she pulled the bible towards her, and putting her finger underneath each word, began to read them aloud in a low voice to herself; she read again the words of bitter sorrow and deep humiliation; but most of all she paused and brightened over the father's tender reception of the repentant prodigal.

So passed the Christmas evening in the Upclose Farm.

The snow had fallen heavily over the dark, waving moorland, before the day of the funeral. The black storm-laden dome of heaven lay very still and close upon the white earth, as they carried the body forth out of the house which had known his presence so long as its ruling power. Two and two the mourners followed, making a black procession, in their winding march over the unbeaten snow, to Milne-Row Church—now lost in some hollow of the bleak moors, now slowly climbing the heaving ascents. There was no long tarrying after the funeral, for many of the neighbours who accompanied the body to the grave had far to go, and the great white flakes which came slowly down, were the boding forerunners of a heavy storm. One old friend alone accompanied the widow and her sons to their home.

The Upclose Farm had belonged for generations to the Leighs; and yet its possession hardly raised them above the rank of labourers. There was the house and outbuildings, all of an old-fashioned kind, and about seven acres of barren unproductive land, which they had never possessed capital enough to improve; indeed they could hardly rely upon it for subsistence; and it had been customary to bring up the sons to some trade—such as a wheelwright's, or blacksmith's.

James Leigh had left a will, in the possession of the old man who accompanied them home. He read it aloud. James had bequeathed the farm to his faithful wife, Anne Leigh, for her lifetime; and afterwards, to his son William. The hundred and odd pounds in the savings'-bank was to accumulate for Thomas.

After the reading was ended, Anne Leigh sate silent for a time; and then she asked to speak to Samuel Orme alone. The sons went into the back-kitchen, and thence strolled out into the fields regardless of the driving snow. The brothers were dearly fond of each other, although they were very different in character. Will, the elder, was like his father, stern, reserved, and scrupulously upright. Tom (who was ten years younger) was gentle and delicate as a girl, both in appearance and character. He had always clung to his mother, and dreaded his father. They did not speak as they walked, for they were only in the habit of talking about facts, and hardly knew the more sophisticated language applied to the description of feelings.

Meanwhile their mother had taken hold of Samuel Orme's arm with her trembling hand.

'Samuel, I must let the farm—I must.'

'Let the farm! What's come o'er the woman?'

'Oh, Samuel!' said she, her eyes swimming in tears, 'I'm just fain to* go and live in Manchester. I must let the farm.'

Samuel looked, and pondered, but did not speak for some time. At last he said,—

'If thou hast made up thy mind, there's no speaking again it; and thou must e'en go. Thou'lt be sadly pottered* wi' Manchester ways; but that's not my look out. Why, thou'lt have to buy potatoes, a thing thou hast never done afore in all thy born life. Well! it's not my look out. It's rather for me than again me. Our Jenny is going to be married to Tom Higginbotham, and he was speaking of wanting a bit of land to begin upon. His father will be dying sometime, I reckon, and then step into the Croft Farm. But meanwhile—'

'Then, thou'lt let the farm,' said she, still as eagerly as ever.

'Aye, aye, he'll take it fast enough, I've a notion. But I'll not drive a bargain with thee just now; it would not be right; we'll wait a bit.'

'No; I cannot wait, settle it out at once.'

'Well, well; I'll speak to Will about it. I see him out yonder. I'll step to him and talk it over.'

Accordingly he went and joined the two lads, and without more ado, began the subject to them.

'Will, thy mother is fain to go live in Manchester, and covets to let the farm. Now, I'm willing to take it for Tom Higginbotham; but I like to drive a keen bargain, and there would be no fun chaffering* with thy mother just now. Let thee and me buckle to, my lad! and try and cheat each other; it will warm us this cold day.'

'Let the farm!' said both the lads at once, with infinite surprise. 'Go live in Manchester!'

When Samuel Orme found that the plan had never before been named to either Will or Tom, he would have nothing to do with it, he said, until they had spoken to their mother; likely she was 'dazed' by her husband's death; he would wait a day or two, and not name it to any one; not to Tom Higginbotham himself, or may be he would set his heart upon it. The lads had better go in and talk it over with their mother. He bade them good day, and left them.

Will looked very gloomy, but he did not speak till they got near the house. Then he said,—

'Tom, go to th' shippon, and supper the cows.* I want to speak to mother alone.'

When he entered the house-place, she was sitting before the fire, looking into its embers. She did not hear him come in: for some time she had lost her quick perception of outward things.

'Mother! what's this about going to Manchester?' asked he.

'Oh, lad!' said she, turning round, and speaking in a beseeching tone, 'I must go and seek our Lizzie. I cannot rest here for thinking on her. Many's the time I've left thy father sleeping in bed, and stole to th' window, and looked and looked my heart out towards Manchester, till I thought I must just set out and tramp over moor and moss straight away till I got there, and then lift up every down-cast face till I came to our Lizzie. And often, when the south wind was blowing soft among the hollows, I've fancied (it could but be fancy, thou knowest) I heard her crying upon me; and I've thought the voice came closer and closer, till at last it was sobbing out "Mother" close to the door; and I've stolen down, and undone the latch before now, and looked out into the still black night, thinking to see her,—and turned sick and sorrowful when I heard no living sound but the sough* of the wind dying away. Oh! speak not to me of stopping here, when she may be perishing for hunger, like the poor lad in the parable.' And now she lifted up her voice, and wept aloud.

Will was deeply grieved. He had been old enough to be told the family shame when, more than two years before, his father had had his letter to his daughter returned by her mistress in Manchester, telling him that Lizzie had left her service some time—and why. He had sympathised with his father's stern anger; though he had thought him something hard, it is true, when he had forbidden his weeping, heart-broken wife to go and try to find her poor, sinning child, and declared that henceforth they would have no daughter; that she should be as one dead, and her name never more be named at market or at meal time, in blessing or in prayer. He had held his peace, with compressed lips and contracted brow, when the neighbours had noticed to him* how poor Lizzie's death had aged both his father and his mother; and how they thought the bereaved couple would never hold up their heads again. He himself had felt as if that one event had made him old before his time; and had envied Tom the tears he had shed over poor, pretty, innocent, dead Lizzie. He thought about her sometimes, till he ground his teeth together, and could have struck her down in her shame. His mother had never named her to him until now.

'Mother!' said he at last. 'She may be dead. Most likely she is.'

'No, Will; she is not dead,' said Mrs Leigh. 'God will not let her die till I've seen her once again. Thou dost not know how I've prayed and prayed just once again to see her sweet face, and tell her I've forgiven her, though she's broken my heart—she has, Will.' She could not go on for a minute or two for the choking sobs. 'Thou dost not know that, or thou wouldst not say she could be dead,—for God is very merciful, Will; He is,—He is much more pitiful than man,—I could never ha' spoken to thy father as I did to Him,—and yet thy father forgave her at last. The last words he said were that he forgave her. Thou'lt not be harder than thy father, Will? Do not try and hinder me going to seek her, for it's no use.'

Will sat very still for a long time before he spoke. At last he said, 'I'll not hinder you. I think she's dead, but that's no matter.'

'She is not dead,' said her mother, with low earnestness. Will took no notice of the interruption.

'We will all go to Manchester for a twelvemonth, and let the farm to Tom Higginbotham. I'll get blacksmith's work; and Tom can have good schooling for awhile, which he's always craving for. At the end of the year you'll come back, mother, and give over fretting for Lizzie, and think with me that she is dead,—and, to my mind, that would be more comfort than to think of her living;' he dropped his voice as he spoke these last words. She shook her head, but made no answer. He asked again,—

'Will you, mother, agree to this?'

'I'll agree to it a-this-ns,'* said she. 'If I hear and see nought of her for a twelvemonth, me being in Manchester looking out, I'll just ha' broken my heart fairly before the year's ended, and then I shall know neither love nor sorrow for her any more, when I'm at rest in the grave—I'll agree to that, Will.'

'Well, I suppose it must be so. I shall not tell Tom, mother, why we're flitting to Manchester. Best spare him.'

'As thou wilt,' said she, sadly, 'so that we go, that's all.'

Before the wild daffodils were in flower in the sheltered copses round Upclose Farm, the Leighs were settled in their Manchester home; if they could ever grow to consider that place as a home, where there was no garden, or outbuilding, no fresh breezy outlet, no far-stretching view, over moor and hollow,—no dumb animals to be tended, and, what more than all they missed, no old haunting memories, even though those remembrances told of sorrow, and the dead and gone.

Mrs Leigh heeded the loss of all these things less than her sons. She had more spirit in her countenance than she had had for months, because now she had hope; of a sad enough kind, to be sure, but still it was hope. She performed all her household duties, strange and complicated as they were, and bewildered as she was with all the town necessities of her new manner of life; but when her house was 'sided,'* and the boys come home from their work, in the evening, she would put on her things and steal out, unnoticed, as she thought, but not without many a heavy sign from Will, after she had closed the house-door and departed. It was often past midnight before she came back, pale and weary, with almost a guilty look upon her face; but that face so full of disappointment and hope deferred,* that Will had never the heart to say what he thought of the folly and hopelessness of the search. Night after night it was renewed, till days grew to weeks, and weeks to months. All this time Will did his duty towards her as well as he could, without having sympathy with her. He stayed at home in the evenings for Tom's sake, and often wished he had Tom's pleasure in reading, for the time hung heavily on his hands as he sat up for his mother.

I need not tell you how the mother spent the weary hours. And yet I will tell you something. She used to wander out, at first as if without a purpose, till she rallied her thoughts, and brought all her energies to bear on the one point; then she went with earnest patience along the least-known ways to some new part of the town, looking wistfully with dumb entreaty into people's faces; sometimes catching a glimpse of a figure which had a kind of momentary likeness to her child's, and following that figure with never-wearying perseverance, till some light from shop or lamp showed the cold strange face which was not her daughter's. Once or twice a kind-hearted passer-by, struck by her look of yearning woe, turned back and offered help, or asked her what she wanted. When so spoken to, she answered only, 'You don't know a poor girl they call Lizzie Leigh, do you?' and when they denied all knowledge, she shook her head, and went on again. I think they believed her to be crazy. But she never spoke first to any one. She sometimes took a few minutes' rest on the door-steps, and sometimes (very seldom) covered her face and cried; but she could not afford to lose time and chances in this way; while her eyes were blinded with tears, the lost one might pass by unseen.

One evening, in the rich time of shortening autumn-days, Will saw an old man, who, without being absolutely drunk, could not guide himself rightly along the foot-path, and was mocked for his unsteadiness of gait by the idle boys of the neighbourhood. For his father's sake Will regarded old age with tenderness, even when most degraded and removed from the stern virtues which dignified that father; so he took the old man home, and seemed to believe his often-repeated assertions, that he drank nothing but water. The stranger tried to stiffen himself up into steadiness as he drew nearer home, as if there were some one there for whose respect he cared even in his half-intoxicated state, or whose feelings he feared to grieve. His home was exquisitely clean and neat, even in outside appearance; threshold, window, and window-sill, were outward signs of some spirit of purity within. Will was rewarded for his attention by a bright glance of thanks, succeeded by a blush of shame, from a young woman of twenty, or thereabouts. She did not speak or second her father's hospitable invitations to him to be seated. She seemed unwilling that a stranger should witness her father's attempts at stately sobriety, and Will could not bear to stay and see her distress. But when the old man, with many a flabby shake of the hand, kept asking him to come again some other evening and see them, Will sought her down-cast eyes, and, though he could not read their veiled meaning, he answered timidly, 'If it's agreeable to everybody, I'll come, and thank ye.' But there was no answer from the girl, to whom this speech was in reality addressed; and Will left the house, liking her all the better for never speaking.

He thought about her a great deal for the next day or two; he scolded himself for being so foolish as to think of her, and then fell to with fresh vigour, and thought of her more than ever. He tried to depreciate her: he told himself she was not pretty, and then made indignant answer that he liked her looks much better than any beauty of them all. He wished he was not so country-looking, so red-faced, so broad-shouldered; while she was like a lady, with her smooth, colourless complexion, her bright dark hair and her spotless dress. Pretty, or not pretty, she drew his footsteps towards her; he could not resist the impulse that made him wish to see her once more, and find out some fault which should unloose his heart from her unconscious keeping. But there she was, pure and maidenly as before. He sat and looked, answering her father at cross-purposes, while she drew more and more into the shadow of the chimney-corner out of sight. Then the spirit that possessed him (it was not he himself, sure, that did so impudent a thing!) made him get up and carry the candle to a different place, under the pretence of giving her more light at her sewing, but, in reality, to be able to see her better; she could not stand this much longer, but jumped up, and said she must put her little niece to bed; and surely, there never was, before or since, so troublesome a child of two years old; for though Will stayed an hour and a half longer, she never came down again. He won the father's heart, though, by his capacity as a listener, for some people are not at all particular, and, so that they themselves may talk on undisturbed, are not so unreasonable as to expect attention to what they say.

Will did gather this much, however, from the old man's talk. He had once been quite in a genteel line of business, but had failed for more money than any greengrocer he had heard of; at least, any who did not mix up fish and game with greengrocery proper. This grand failure seemed to have been the event of his life, and one on which he dwelt with a strange kind of pride. It appeared as if at present he rested from his past exertions (in the bankrupt line), and depended on his daughter, who kept a small school for very young children. But all these particulars Will only remembered and understood when he had left the house; at the time he heard them, he was thinking of Susan. After he had made good his footing at Mr Palmer's, he was not long, you may be sure, without finding some reason for returning again and again. He listened to her father, he talked to the little niece, but he looked at Susan, both while he listened and while he talked. Her father kept on insisting upon his former gentility, the details of which would have appeared very questionable to Will's mind, if the sweet, delicate, modest Susan had not thrown an inexplicable air of refinement over all she came near. She never spoke much; she was generally diligently at work; but when she moved, it was so noise-lessly, and when she did speak, it was in so low and soft a voice, that silence, speech, motion, and stillness, alike seemed to remove her high above Will's reach into some saintly and inaccessible air of glory—high above his reach, even as she knew him! And, if she were made acquainted with the dark secret behind, of his sister's shame, which was kept ever present to his mind by his mother's nightly search among the outcast and forsaken, would not Susan shrink away from him with loathing, as if he were tainted by the involuntary relationship? This was his dread; and thereupon followed a resolution that he would withdraw from her sweet com-pany before it was too late. So he resisted internal temptation, and stayed at home, and suffered and sighed. He became angry with his mother for her untiring patience in seeking for one who, he could not help hoping, was dead rather than alive. He spoke sharply to her, and received only such sad deprecatory answers as made him reproach himself, and still more lose sight of peace of mind. This struggle could not last long without affecting his health; and Tom, his sole companion through the long evenings, noticed his increasing lan-guor, his restless irritability, with perplexed anxiety, and at last resolved to call his mother's attention to his brother's haggard, care-worn looks. She listened with a startled recollection of Will's claims upon her love. She noticed his decreasing appetite, and half-checked sighs.

'Will, lad! what's come o'er thee?' said she to him, as he sat listlessly gazing into the fire.

'There's nought the matter with me,' said he, as if annoyed at her remark.

'Nay, lad, but there is.' He did not speak again to contradict her; indeed she did not know if he had heard her, so unmoved did he look.

'Would'st like to go back to Upclose Farm?' asked she, sorrowfully.

'It's just blackberrying time,' said Tom.

Will shook his head. She looked at him awhile, as if trying to read that expression of despondency and trace it back to its source.

'You and Tom could go,' said she; 'I must stay here till I've found her, thou know'st,' continued she, dropping her voice.

He turned quickly round, and with the authority he at all times exercised over Tom, bade him begone to bed.

When Tom had left the room, he prepared to speak.

\* \* \*

## CHAPTER II

'MOTHER,' then said Will, 'why will you keep on thinking she's alive? If she were but dead, we need never name her name again. We've never heard nought on her, since father wrote her that letter; we never knew whether she got it or not. She'd left her place before then. Many a one dies in—'

'Oh my lad! dunnot speak so to me, or my heart will break outright,' said his mother, with a sort of cry. Then she calmed herself, for she yearned to persuade him to her own belief. 'Thou never asked, and thou'rt too like thy father for me to tell without asking—but it were all to be near Lizzie's old place that I settled down on this side o' Manchester; and the very day at after\* we came, I went to her old missus, and asked to speak a word wi' her. I had a strong mind to cast it up\* to her, that she should ha' sent my poor lass away, without telling on it to us first; but she were in black and looked so sad I could na find in my heart to threep it up.\* But I did ask her a bit about our Lizzie. The master would have her turned away at a day's warning (he's gone to t'other place; I hope he'll meet wi' more mercy there than he showed our Lizzie,—I do,—), and when the missus asked her should she write to us, she says Lizzie shook her head; and when she speered at\* her again, the poor lass went down on her knees, and begged her not, for she said it would break my heart (as it has done, Will—God knows it has),' said the poor mother, choking with her struggle to keep down her hard, overmastering grief, 'and her father would curse her—Oh, God, teach me to be patient.' She could not speak for a few minutes,—'and the lass threatened, and said she'd go drown herself in the canal, if the missus wrote home,—and so—

'Well! I'd got a trace of my child,—the missus thought she'd gone to th' workhouse to be nursed; and there I went,—and there, sure enough, she had been,—and they'd turned her out as soon as she were strong, and told her she were young enough to work,—but whatten kind o' work would be open to her, lad, and her baby to keep?'

Will listened to his mother's tale with deep sympathy, not unmixed with the old bitter shame. But the opening of her heart had unlocked his, and after a while he spoke.

'Mother! I think I'd e'en better go home. Tom can stay wi' thee. I know I should stay too, but I cannot stay in peace so near—her,— without craving to see her,—Susan Palmer, I mean.'

'Has the old Mr Palmer thou telled me on* a daughter?' asked Mrs Leigh.

'Aye, he has. And I love her above a bit. And it's because I love her I want to leave Manchester. That's all.'

Mrs Leigh tried to understand this speech for some time, but found it difficult of interpretation.

'Why shouldst thou not tell her thou lov'st her? Thou'rt a likely lad, and sure o' work. Thou'lt have Upclose at my death; and as for that I could let thee have it now, and keep mysel by doing a bit of charring. It seems to me a very backwards sort o' way of winning her to think of leaving Manchester.'

'Oh mother, she's so gentle and so good,—she's downright holy. She's never known a touch of sin; and can I ask her to marry me, knowing what we do about Lizzie, and fearing worse? I doubt if one like her could ever care for me; but if she knew about my sister, it would put a gulf between us, and she'd shudder up at the thought of crossing it. You don't know how good she is, mother!'

'Will, Will! if she's so good as thou say'st, she'll have pity on such as my Lizzie. If she has no pity for such, she's a cruel Pharisee,* and thou'rt best without her.'

But he only shook his head, and sighed; and for the time the conversation dropped.

But a new idea sprang up in Mrs Leigh's head. She thought that she would go and see Susan Palmer, and speak up for Will, and tell her the truth about Lizzie; and according to her pity for the poor sinner, would she be worthy or unworthy of him. She resolved to go the very next afternoon, but without telling any one of her plan. Accordingly she looked out the Sunday clothes she had never before had the heart to unpack since she came to Manchester, but which she now desired to appear in, in order to do credit to Will. She put on her old-fashioned black mode* bonnet, trimmed with real lace; her scarlet cloth cloak, which she had had ever since she was married; and always spotlessly clean, she set forth on her unauthorised embassy. She knew the Palmers lived in Crown Street, though where she had heard it she could not tell; and modestly asking her way, she arrived in the street about a quarter to four o'clock. She stopped to inquire the exact number, and the woman whom she addressed told her that Susan Palmer's school would not be loosed* till four, and asked her to step in and wait until then at her house.

'For,' said she, smiling, 'them that wants Susan Palmer wants a kind friend of ours; so we, in a manner, call cousins.* Sit down, missus, sit down. I'll wipe the chair, so that it shanna dirty your cloak. My mother used to wear them bright cloaks, and they're right gradely* things again a green field.'

'Han ye known Susan Palmer long?' asked Mrs Leigh, pleased with the admiration of her cloak.

'Ever since they comed to live in our street. Our Sally goes to her school.'

'Whatten* sort of a lass is she, for I ha' never seen her?'

'Well,—as for looks, I cannot say. It's so long since I first knowed her, that I've clean forgotten what I thought of her then. My master says he never saw such a smile for gladdening the heart. But may be it's not looks you're asking about. The best thing I can say of her looks is, that she's just one a stranger would stop in the street to ask help from if he needed it. All the little childer creeps as close as they can to her; she'll have as many as three or four hanging to her apron all at once.'

'Is she cocket* at all?'

'Cocket, bless you! you never saw a creature less set up in all your life. Her father's cocket enough. No! she's not cocket anyway. You've not heard much of Susan Palmer, I reckon, if you think she's cocket. She's just one to come quietly in, and do the very thing most wanted; little things, maybe, that any one could do, but that few would think on, for another. She'll bring her thimble wi' her, and mend up after the childer o'nights,—and she writes all Betty Harker's letters to her grandchild out at service,—and she's in nobody's way, and that's a great matter, I take it. Here's the childer running past! School is loosed. You'll find her now, missus, ready to hear and to help. But we none on us frab her* by going near her in school-time.'

Poor Mrs Leigh's heart began to beat, and she could almost have turned round and gone home again. Her country breeding had made her shy of strangers, and this Susan Palmer appeared to her like a real born lady by all accounts. So she knocked with a timid feeling at the indicated door, and when it was opened, dropped a simple curtsey without speaking. Susan had her little niece in her arms, curled up with fond endearment against her breast, but she put her gently down to the ground, and instantly placed a chair in the best corner of the room for Mrs Leigh, when she told her who she was. 'It's not Will as has asked me to come,' said the mother, apologetically, 'I'd a wish just to speak to you myself!'

Susan coloured up to her temples, and stooped to pick up the little toddling girl. In a minute or two Mrs Leigh began again.

'Will thinks you would na respect us if you knew all; but I think you could na help feeling for us in the sorrow God has put upon us; so I just put on my bonnet, and came off unknownst to the lads. Every one says you're very good, and that the Lord has keeped you from falling from his ways; but maybe you've never yet been tried and tempted as some is. I'm perhaps speaking too plain, but my heart's welly* broken, and I can't be choice in my words as them who are happy can. Well now! I'll tell you the truth. Will dreads you to hear it, but I'll just tell it you. You mun know,'—but here the poor woman's words failed her, and she could do nothing but sit rocking herself backwards and forwards, with sad eyes, straight-gazing into Susan's face, as if they tried to tell the tale of agony which the quivering lips refused to utter. Those wretched, stony eyes forced the tears down Susan's cheeks, and, as if this sympathy gave the mother strength, she went on in a low voice, 'I had a daughter once, my heart's darling. Her father thought I made too much on* her, and that she'd grow marred* staying at home; so he said she mun go among strangers, and learn to rough it. She were young, and liked the thought of seeing a bit of the world; and her father heard on a place in Manchester. Well! I'll not weary you. That poor girl were led astray; and first thing we heard on it, was when a letter of her father's was sent back by her missus, saying she'd left her place, or, to speak right, the master had turned her into the street soon as he had heard of her condition—and she not seventeen!'

She now cried aloud; and Susan wept too. The little child looked up into their faces, and, catching their sorrow, began to whimper and wail. Susan took it softly up, and hiding her face in its little neck, tried to restrain her tears, and think of comfort for the mother. At last she said,—

'Where is she now?'

'Lass! I dunnot know,' said Mrs Leigh, checking her sobs to communicate this addition to her distress. 'Mrs Lomax told me she went—'

'Mrs Lomax—what Mrs Lomax?'

'Her as lives in Brabazon-street. She told me my poor wench went to the workhouse fra there. I'll not speak again the dead; but if her father would but ha' letten me,—but he were one who had no notion—no, I'll not say that; best say nought. He forgave her on his death-bed. I dare say I did na go th' right way to work.'

'Will you hold the child for me one instant?' said Susan.

'Aye, if it will come to me. Childer used to be fond on me till I got the sad look on my face that scares them, I think.'

But the little girl clung to Susan; so she carried it upstairs with her. Mrs Leigh sate by herself—how long she did not know.

Susan came down with a bundle of far-worn baby-clothes.

'You must listen to me a bit, and not think too much about what I'm going to tell you. Nanny is not my niece, nor any kin to me, that I know of. I used to go out working by the day. One night, as I came home, I thought some woman was following me; I turned to look. The woman, before I could see her face (for she turned it to one side), offered me something. I held out my arms by instinct; she dropped a bundle into them, with a bursting sob that went straight to my heart. It was a baby. I looked round again; but the woman was gone. She had run away as quick as lightning. There was a little packet of clothes—very few—and as if they were made out of its mother's gowns, for they were large patterns to buy for a baby. I was always fond of babies; and I had not my wits about me, father says: for it was very cold, and when I'd seen as well as I could (for it was past ten) that there was no one in the street, I brought it in and warmed it. Father was very angry when he came, and said he'd take it to the workhouse the next morning, and flyted* me sadly about it. But when morning came I could not bear to part with it; it had slept in my arms all night; and I've heard what workhouse bringing-up is. So I told father I'd give up going out working, and stay at home and keep school, if I might only keep the baby; and after awhile, he said if I earned enough for him to have his comforts, he'd let me; but he's never taken to her. Now, don't tremble so,—I've but a little more to tell,—and maybe I'm wrong in telling it; but I used to work next door to Mrs Lomax's, in Brabazon-street, and the servants were all thick together; and I heard about Bessy (they called her) being sent away. I don't know that ever I saw her; but the time would be about fitting to this child's age, and I've sometimes fancied it was hers. And now, will you look at the little clothes that came with her—bless her!'

But Mrs Leigh had fainted. The strange joy and shame, and gushing love for the little child had overpowered her; it was some time before Susan could bring her round. Then she was all trembling, sick impatience to look at the little frocks. Among them was a slip of paper which Susan had forgotten to name, that had been pinned to the bundle. On it was scrawled in a round, stiff hand,—

'Call her Anne. She does not cry much, and takes a deal of notice. God bless you and forgive me.'

The writing was no clue at all; the name 'Anne,' common though it was, seemed something to build upon. But Mrs Leigh recognised one of the frocks instantly, as being made out of a gown that she and her daughter had bought together in Rochdale.

She stood up, and stretched out her hands in the attitude of blessing over Susan's bent head.

'God bless you, and show you His mercy in your need, as you have shown it to this little child.'

She took the little creature in her arms, and smoothed away her sad looks to a smile, and kissed it fondly, saying over and over again, 'Nanny, Nanny, my little Nanny.' At last the child was soothed, and looked in her face and smiled back again.

'It has her eyes,' said she to Susan.

'I never saw her to the best of my knowledge. I think it must be hers by the frock. But where can she be?'

'God knows,' said Mrs Leigh; 'I dare not think she's dead. I'm sure she isn't.'

'No! she's not dead. Every now and then a little packet is thrust in under our door, with may be two half-crowns in it; once it was half-a-sovereign. Altogether I've got seven-and-thirty shillings wrapped up for Nanny. I never touch it, but I've often thought the poor mother feels near to God when she brings this money. Father wanted to set the policeman to watch, but I said No, for I was afraid if she was watched she might not come, and it seemed such a holy thing to be checking her in, I could not find in my heart to do it.'

'Oh, if we could but find her! I'd take her in my arms, and we'd just lie down and die together.'

'Nay, don't speak so!' said Susan gently, 'for all that's come and gone, she may turn right at last. Mary Magdalen did, you know.'

'Eh! but I were nearer right about thee than Will. He thought you would never look on him again if you knew about Lizzie. But thou'rt not a Pharisee.'

'I'm sorry he thought I could be so hard,' said Susan in a low voice, and colouring up. Then Mrs Leigh was alarmed, and in her motherly anxiety, she began to fear lest she had injured Will in Susan's estimation.

'You see Will thinks so much of you—gold would not be good enough for you to walk on, in his eye. He said you'd never look at him as he was, let alone his being brother to my poor wench. He loves you so, it makes him think meanly on everything belonging to himself, as not fit to come near ye,—but he's a good lad, and a good son,—thou'lt be a happy woman if thou'lt have him,—so don't let my words go against him; don't!'

But Susan hung her head, and made no answer. She had not known until now, that Will thought so earnestly and seriously about her; and even now she felt afraid that Mrs Leigh's words promised her too much happiness, and that they could not be true. At any rate the instinct of modesty made her shrink from saying anything which might seem like a confession of her own feelings to a third person. Accordingly she turned the conversation on the child.

'I'm sure he could not help loving Nanny,' said she. 'There never was such a good little darling; don't you think she'd win his heart if he knew she was his niece, and perhaps bring him to think kindly on his sister?'

'I dunnot know,' said Mrs Leigh, shaking her head. 'He has a turn in his eye like his father, that makes me—. He's right down good though. But you see I've never been a good one at managing folk; one severe look turns me sick, and then I say just the wrong thing, I'm so fluttered. Now I should like nothing better than to take Nanny home with me, but Tom knows nothing but that his sister is dead, and I've not the knack of speaking rightly to Will. I dare not do it, and that's the truth. But you mun not think badly of Will. He's so good hissel, that he can't understand how any one can do wrong; and, above all, I'm sure he loves you dearly.'

'I don't think I could part with Nanny,' said Susan, anxious to stop this revelation of Will's attachment to herself. 'He'll come round to her soon; he can't fail; and I'll keep a sharp look-out after the poor mother, and try and catch her the next time she comes with her little parcels of money.'

'Aye, lass; we mun get hold of her; my Lizzie. I love thee dearly for thy kindness to her child: but, if thou canst catch her for me, I'll pray for thee when I'm too near my death to speak words; and, while I live, I'll serve thee next to her,—she mun come first, thou know'st. God bless thee, lass. My heart is lighter by a deal than it was when I comed in. Them lads will be looking for me home, and I mun go, and leave this little sweet one,' kissing it. 'If I can take courage, I'll tell Will all that has come and gone between us two. He may come and see thee, mayn't he?'

'Father will be very glad to see him, I'm sure,' replied Susan. The way in which this was spoken satisfied Mrs Leigh's anxious heart that she had done Will no harm by what she had said; and with many a kiss to the little one, and one more fervent, tearful blessing on Susan, she went homewards.

\* \* \*

## CHAPTER III

THAT night Mrs Leigh stopped at home; that only night for many months. Even Tom, the scholar, looked up from his books in amazement; but then he remembered that Will had not been well, and that his mother's attention having been called to the circumstance, it was only natural she should stay to watch him. And no watching could be more tender, or more complete. Her loving eyes seemed never averted from his face; his grave, sad, careworn face. When Tom went to bed the mother left her seat, and going up to Will, where he sat looking at the fire, but not seeing it, she kissed his forehead, and said,—

'Will! lad, I've been to see Susan Palmer!'

She felt the start under her hand which was placed on his shoulder, but he was silent for a minute or two. Then he said,—

'What took you there, mother?'

'Why, my lad, it was likely I should wish to see one you cared for; I did not put myself forward. I put on my Sunday clothes, and tried to behave as yo'd ha' liked me. At least I remember trying at first; but after, I forgot all.'

She rather wished that he would question her as to what made her forget all. But he only said,—

'How was she looking, mother?'

'Will, thou seest I never set eyes on her before; but she's a good, gentle-looking creature; and I love her dearly, as I've reason to.'

Will looked up with momentary surprise; for his mother was too shy to be usually taken with strangers. But after all it was natural in this case, for who could look at Susan without loving her? So still he did not ask any questions, and his poor mother had to take courage, and try again to introduce the subject near to her heart. But how?

'Will!' said she (jerking it out, in sudden despair of her own powers to lead to what she wanted to say), 'I told her all.'

'Mother! you've ruined me,' said he, standing up, and standing opposite to her with a stern white look of affright on his face.

'No! my own dear lad; dunnot look so scared, I have not ruined you!' she exclaimed, placing her two hands on his shoulders, and looking fondly into his face. 'She's not one to harden her heart against a mother's sorrow. My own lad, she's too good for that. She's not one to judge and scorn the sinner. She's too deep read in her New Testament for that. Take courage, Will; and thou mayst, for I watched her well, though it is not for one woman to let out another's secret. Sit thee down, lad, for thou look'st very white.'

He sat down. His mother drew a stool towards him, and sat at his feet.

'Did you tell her about Lizzie, then?' asked he, hoarse and low.

'I did, I told her all; and she fell a-crying over my deep sorrow, and the poor wench's sin. And then a light comed into her face, trembling and quivering with some new glad thought; and what dost thou think it was, Will, lad? Nay, I'll not misdoubt but that thy heart will give thanks as mine did, afore God and His angels, for her great goodness. That little Nanny is not her niece, she's our Lizzie's own child, my little grandchild.' She could no longer restrain her tears, and they fell hot and fast, but still she looked into his face.

'Did she know it was Lizzie's child? I do not comprehend,' said he, flushing red.

'She knows now: she did not at first, but took the little helpless creature in, out of her own pitiful, loving heart, guessing only that it was the child of shame, and she's worked for it, and kept it, and tended it ever sin' it were a mere baby, and loves it fondly. Will! won't you love it?' asked she beseechingly.

He was silent for an instant; then he said, 'Mother, I'll try. Give me time, for all these things startle me. To think of Susan having to do with such a child!'

'Aye, Will! and to think (as may be yet) of Susan having to do with the child's mother! For she is tender and pitiful, and speaks hopefully of my lost one, and will try and find her for me, when she comes, as she does sometimes, to thrust money under the door, for her baby. Think of that, Will. Here's Susan, good and pure as the angels in heaven, yet, like them, full of hope and mercy, and one who, like them, will rejoice over her as repents. Will, my lad, I'm not afeard of you now, and I must speak, and you must listen. I am your mother, and I dare to command you, because I know I am in the right and that God is on my side. If He should lead the poor wandering lassie to Susan's door, and she comes back crying and sorrowful, led by that good angel to us once more, thou shalt never say a casting-up word to her about her sin, but be tender and helpful towards one "who was lost and is found,"* so may God's blessing rest on thee, and so mayst thou lead Susan home as thy wife.'

She stood, no longer, as the meek, imploring, gentle mother, but firm and dignified, as if the interpreter of God's will. Her manner was so unusual and solemn, that it overcame all Will's pride and stubbornness. He rose softly while she was speaking, and bent his head as if in reverence at her words, and the solemn injunction which they conveyed. When she had spoken, he said in so subdued a voice that she was almost surprised at the sound, 'Mother, I will.'

'I may be dead and gone,—but all the same,—thou wilt take home the wandering sinner, and heal up her sorrows, and lead her to her Father's house. My lad! I can speak no more; I'm turned very faint.'

He placed her in a chair; he ran for water. She opened her eyes and smiled.

'God bless you, Will. Oh! I am so happy. It seems as if she were found; my heart is so filled with gladness.'

That night Mr Palmer stayed out late and long. Susan was afraid that he was at his old haunts and habits,—getting tipsy at some public-house: and this thought oppressed her, even though she had so much to make her happy in the consciousness that Will loved her. She sat up long, and then she went to bed, leaving all arranged as well as she could for her father's return. She looked at the little rosy sleeping girl who was her bed-fellow, with redoubled tenderness, and with many a prayerful thought. The little arms entwined her neck as she lay down, for Nanny was a light sleeper, and was conscious that she, who was loved with all the power of that sweet, childish heart, was near her, and by her, although she was too sleepy to utter any of her half-formed words.

And by-and-by she heard her father come home, stumbling uncertain, trying first the windows, and next the door-fastenings, with many a loud, incoherent murmur. The little innocent twined around her seemed all the sweeter and more lovely, when she thought sadly of her erring father. And presently he called aloud for a light; she had left matches and all arranged as usual on the dresser, but fearful of some accident from fire, in his unusually intoxicated state, she now got up softly, and putting on a cloak, went down to his assistance.

Alas! the little arms that were unclosed from her soft neck belonged to a light, easily awakened sleeper. Nanny missed her darling Susy, and terrified at being left alone in the vast, mysterious darkness, which had no bounds, and seemed infinite, she slipped out of bed, and tottered in her little nightgown towards the door. There was a light below, and there was Susy and safety! So she went onwards two steps towards the steep, abrupt stairs; and then dazzled with sleepiness, she stood, she wavered, she fell! Down on her head on the stone floor she fell! Susan flew to her, and spoke all soft, entreating, loving words; but her white lids covered up the blue violets of eyes, and there was no murmur came out of the pale lips. The warm tears that rained down did not awaken her; she lay stiff, and weary with her short life, on Susan's knee. Susan went sick with terror. She carried her upstairs, and laid her tenderly in bed; she dressed herself most hastily, with her trembling fingers. Her father was asleep on the settle down stairs; and useless, and worse than useless if awake. But Susan flew out of the door, and down the quiet, resounding street, towards the nearest doctor's house.

Quickly she went: but as quickly a shadow followed, as if impelled by some sudden terror. Susan rung wildly at the night-bell,—the shadow crouched near. The doctor looked out from an upstairs window.

'A little child has fallen down stairs at No. 9, Crown-street, and is very ill,—dying, I'm afraid. Please, for God's sake, sir, come directly. No. 9, Crown-street.'

'I'll be there directly,' said he, and shut the window.

'For that God you have just spoken about,—for His sake—tell me are you Susan Palmer? Is it my child that lies a-dying?' said the shadow springing forwards, and clutching poor Susan's arm.

'It is a little child of two years old,—I do not know whose it is; I love it as my own. Come with me, whoever you are; come with me.'

The two sped along the silent streets,—as silent as the night were they. They entered the house; Susan snatched up the light, and carried it upstairs. The other followed.

She stood with wild, glaring eyes by the bedside, never looking at Susan, but hungrily gazing at the little, white, still child. She stooped down, and put her hand tight on her own heart, as if to still its beating, and bent her ear to the pale lips. Whatever the result was, she did not speak; but threw off the bed-clothes wherewith Susan had tenderly covered up the little creature, and felt its left side.

Then she threw up her arms with a cry of wild despair.

'She is dead! she is dead!'

She looked so fierce, so mad, so haggard, that for an instant Susan was terrified—the next, the holy God had put courage into her heart, and her pure arms were round that guilty, wretched creature, and her tears were falling fast and warm upon her breast. But she was thrown off with violence.

'You killed her—you slighted her—you let her fall down those stairs! you killed her!'

Susan cleared off the thick mist before her, and gazing at the mother with her clear, sweet, angel-eyes, said mournfully,—

'I would have laid down my own life for her.'

'Oh, the murder is on my soul!' exclaimed the wild, bereaved mother, with the fierce impetuosity of one who has none to love her and to be beloved, regard to whom might teach self-restraint.

'Hush!' said Susan, her finger on her lips. 'Here is the doctor. God may suffer her to live.'

The poor mother turned sharp round. The doctor mounted the stair. Ah! that mother was right; the little child was really dead and gone.

And when he confirmed her judgment, the mother fell down in a fit. Susan, with her deep grief, had to forget herself, and forget her darling (her charge for years), and question the doctor what she must do with the poor wretch, who lay on the floor in such extreme of misery.

'She is the mother!' said she.

'Why did not she take better care of her child?' asked he, almost angrily.

But Susan only said, 'The little child slept with me; and it was I that left her.'

'I will go back and make up a composing draught; and while I am away you must get her to bed.'

Susan took out some of her own clothes, and softly undressed the stiff, powerless form. There was no other bed in the house but the one in which her father slept. So she tenderly lifted the body of her darling; and was going to take it down stairs, but the mother opened her eyes, and seeing what she was about, she said,—

'I am not worthy to touch her, I am so wicked; I have spoken to you as I never should have spoken; but I think you are very good; may I have my own child to be in my arms for a little while?'

Her voice was so strange a contrast to what it had been before she had gone into the fit, that Susan hardly recognised it; it was now so unspeakably soft, so irresistibly pleading, the features too had lost their fierce expression, and were almost as placid as death. Susan could not speak, but she carried the little child, and laid it in its mother's arms; then as she looked at them, something overpowered her, and she knelt down, crying aloud,—

'Oh, my God, my God, have mercy on her, and forgive, and comfort her.'

But the mother kept smiling, and stroking the little face, murmuring soft, tender words, as if it were alive; she was going mad, Susan thought; but she prayed on, and on, and ever still she prayed with streaming eyes.

The doctor came with the draught. The mother took it, with docile unconsciousness of its nature as medicine. The doctor sat by her; and soon she fell asleep. Then he rose softly, and beckoning Susan to the door, he spoke to her there.

'You must take the corpse out of her arms. She will not awake. That draught will make her sleep for many hours. I will call before noon again. It is now daylight. Good-bye.'

Susan shut him out; and then gently extricating the dead child from its mother's arms, she could not resist making her own quiet moan over her darling. She tried to learn off its little, placid face, dumb and pale before her.

> 'Not all the scalding tears of care
> Shall wash away that vision fair;
> Not all the thousand thoughts that rise,
> Not all the sights that dim her eyes,
> Shall e'er usurp the place
> Of that little angel-face.'*

And then she remembered what remained to be done. She saw that all was right in the house; her father was still dead asleep on the settle, in spite of all the noise of the night. She went out through the quiet streets, deserted still although it was broad daylight, and to where the Leighs lived. Mrs Leigh, who kept her country hours, was opening her window shutters. Susan took her by the arm, and, without speaking, went into the house-place. There she knelt down before the astonished Mrs Leigh, and cried as she had never done before; but the miserable night had overpowered her, and she who had gone through so much calmly, now that the pressure seemed removed could not find the power to speak.

'My poor dear! What has made thy heart so sore as to come and cry a-this-ons? Speak and tell me. Nay, cry on, poor wench, if thou canst not speak yet. It will ease the heart, and then thou canst tell me.'

'Nanny is dead!' said Susan. 'I left her to go to father, and she fell down stairs, and never breathed again. Oh, that's my sorrow! but I've more to tell. Her mother is come—is in our house! Come and see if it's your Lizzie.' Mrs Leigh could not speak, but, trembling, put on her things and went with Susan in dizzy haste back to Crown-street.

## CHAPTER IV

As they entered the house in Crown-street, they perceived that the door would not open freely on its hinges, and Susan instinctively looked behind to see the cause of the obstruction. She immediately recognised the appearance of a little parcel wrapped in a scrap of newspaper, and evidently containing money. She stooped and picked it up. 'Look!' said she, sorrowfully, 'the mother was bringing this for her child last night.'

But Mrs Leigh did not answer. So near to the ascertaining if it were her lost child or no, she could not be arrested, but pressed onwards with trembling steps and a beating, fluttering heart. She entered the bed-room, dark and still. She took no heed of the little corpse, over which Susan paused, but she went straight to the bed, and withdrawing the curtain, saw Lizzie,—but not the former Lizzie, bright, gay, buoyant, and undimmed. This Lizzie was old before her time; her beauty was gone; deep lines of care, and alas! of want (or thus the mother imagined) were printed on the cheek, so round, and fair, and smooth, when last she gladdened her mother's eyes. Even in her sleep she bore the look of woe and despair which was the prevalent expression of her face by day; even in her sleep she had forgotten how to smile. But all these marks of the sin and sorrow she had passed through only made her mother love her the more. She stood looking at her with greedy eyes, which seemed as though no gazing could satisfy their longing; and at last she stooped down and kissed the pale, worn hand that lay outside the bed-clothes. No touch disturbed the sleeper; the mother need not have laid the hand so gently down upon the counterpane. There was no sign of life, save only now and then a deep sob-like sigh. Mrs Leigh sate down beside the bed, and, still holding back the curtain, looked on and on, as if she could never be satisfied.

Susan would fain have stayed by her darling one; but she had many calls upon her time and thoughts, and her will had now, as ever, to be given up to that of others. All seemed to devolve the burden of their cares on her. Her father, ill-humoured from his last night's intemperance, did not scruple to reproach her with being the cause of little Nanny's death; and when, after bearing his upbraiding meekly for some time, she could no longer restrain herself, but began to cry, he wounded her even more by his injudicious attempts at comfort: for he said it was as well the child was dead; it was none of theirs, and why should they be troubled with it? Susan wrung her hands at this, and came and stood before her father, and implored him to forbear. Then she had to take all requisite steps for the coroner's inquest; she had to arrange for the dismissal of her school; she had to summon a little neighbour, and send his willing feet on a message to William Leigh, who, she felt, ought to be informed of his mother's whereabouts, and of the whole state of affairs. She asked her messenger to tell him to come and speak to her,—that his mother was at her house. She was thankful that her father sauntered out to have a gossip at the nearest coach-stand,* and to relate as many of the night's adventures as he knew; for as yet he was in ignorance of the watcher and the watched, who silently passed away the hours upstairs.

At dinner-time Will came. He looked red, glad, impatient, excited. Susan stood calm and white before him, her soft, loving eyes gazing straight into his.

'Will,' said she, in a low, quiet voice, 'your sister is upstairs.'

'My sister!' said he, as if affrighted at the idea, and losing his glad look in one of gloom. Susan saw it, and her heart sank a little, but she went on as calm to all appearance as ever.

'She was little Nanny's mother, as perhaps you know. Poor little Nanny was killed last night by a fall down stairs.' All the calmness was gone; all the suppressed feeling was displayed in spite of every effort. She sate down, and hid her face from him, and cried bitterly. He forgot everything but the wish, the longing to comfort her. He put his arm round her waist, and bent over her. But all he could say, was, 'Oh, Susan, how can I comfort you! Don't take on so,—pray don't!' He never changed the words, but the tone varied every time he spoke. At last she seemed to regain her power over herself; and she wiped her eyes, and once more looked upon him with her own quiet, earnest, unfearing gaze.

'Your sister was near the house. She came in on hearing my words to the doctor. She is asleep now, and your mother is watching her. I wanted to tell you all myself. Would you like to see your mother?'

'No!' said he. 'I would rather see none but thee. Mother told me thou know'st all.' His eyes were downcast in their shame.

But the holy and pure did not lower or veil her eyes.

She said, 'Yes, I know all—all but her sufferings. Think what they must have been!'

He made answer low and stern, 'She deserved them all; every jot.'

'In the eye of God, perhaps she does. He is the judge; we are not.'

'Oh!' she said with a sudden burst, 'Will Leigh! I have thought so well of you; don't go and make me think you cruel and hard. Goodness is not goodness unless there is mercy and tenderness with it. There is your mother who has been nearly heart-broken, now full of rejoicing over her child—think of your mother.'

'I do think of her,' said he. 'I remember the promise I gave her last night. Thou shouldst give me time. I would do right in time. I never think it o'er in quiet. But I will do what is right and fitting, never fear. Thou hast spoken out very plain to me; and misdoubted me, Susan; I love thee so, that thy words cut me. If I did hang back a bit from making sudden promises, it was because not even for love of thee, would I say what I was not feeling; and at first I could not feel all at once as thou wouldst have me. But I'm not cruel and hard; for if I had been, I should na' have grieved as I have done.'

He made as if he were going away; and indeed he did feel he would rather think it over in quiet. But Susan, grieved at her incautious words, which had all the appearance of harshness, went a step or two nearer—paused—and then, all over blushes, said in a low soft whisper,—

'Oh, Will! I beg your pardon. I am very sorry—won't you forgive me?'

She who had always drawn back, and been so reserved, said this in the very softest manner; with eyes now uplifted beseechingly, now dropped to the ground. Her sweet confusion told more than words could do; and Will turned back, all joyous in his certainty of being beloved, and took her in his arms and kissed her.

'My own Susan!' he said.

Meanwhile the mother watched her child in the room above.

It was late in the afternoon before she awoke; for the sleeping draught had been very powerful. The instant she awoke, her eyes were fixed on her mother's face with a gaze as unflinching as if she were fascinated.* Mrs Leigh did not turn away; nor move. For it seemed as if motion would unlock the stony command over herself which, while so perfectly still, she was enabled to preserve. But by-and-by Lizzie cried out in a piercing voice of agony,—

'Mother, don't look at me! I have been so wicked!' and instantly she hid her face, and grovelled among the bedclothes, and lay like one dead—so motionless was she.

Mrs Leigh knelt down by the bed, and spoke in the most soothing tones.

'Lizzie, dear, don't speak so. I'm thy mother, darling; don't be afeard of me. I never left off loving thee, Lizzie. I was always a-thinking of thee. Thy father forgave thee afore he died.' (There was a little start here, but no sound was heard.) 'Lizzie, lass, I'll do aught for thee; I'll live for thee; only don't be afeard of me. Whate'er thou art or hast been, we'll ne'er speak on't. We'll leave th' oud times behind us, and go back to the Upclose Farm. I but left it to find thee, my lass; and God has led me to thee. Blessed be His name. And God is good too, Lizzie. Thou hast not forgot thy Bible, I'll be bound, for thou wert always a scholar. I'm no reader, but I learnt off them texts to comfort me a bit, and I've said them many a time a day to myself. Lizzie, lass, don't hide thy head so, it's thy mother as is speaking to thee. Thy little child clung to me only yesterday; and if it's gone to be an angel, it will speak to God for thee. Nay, don't sob a-that-as; thou shalt have it again in Heaven; I know thou'lt strive to get there, for thy little Nanny's sake—and listen! I'll tell thee God's promises to them that are penitent—only doan't be afeard.'

Mrs Leigh folded her hands, and strove to speak very clearly, while she repeated every tender and merciful text she could remember. She could tell from the breathing that her daughter was listening; but she was so dizzy and sick herself when she had ended, that she could not go on speaking. It was all she could do to keep from crying aloud.

At last she heard her daughter's voice.

'Where have they taken her to?' she asked.

'She is down stairs. So quiet and peaceful, and happy she looks.'

'Could she speak? Oh, if God—if I might but have heard her little voice! Mother, I used to dream of it. May I see her once again—Oh mother, if I strive very hard, and God is very merciful, and I go to heaven, I shall not know her—I shall not know my own again—she will shun me as a stranger and cling to Susan Palmer and to you. Oh woe! Oh woe!' She shook with exceeding sorrow.

In her earnestness of speech she had uncovered her face, and tried to read Mrs Leigh's thoughts through her looks. And when she saw those aged eyes brimming full of tears, and marked the quivering lips, she threw her arms round the faithful mother's neck, and wept there as she had done in many a childish sorrow; but with a deeper, a more wretched grief.

Her mother hushed her on her breast; and lulled her as if she were a baby; and she grew still and quiet.

They sat thus for a long, long time. At last Susan Palmer came up with some tea and bread and butter for Mrs Leigh. She watched the mother feed her sick, unwilling child, with every fond inducement to eat which she could devise; they neither of them took notice of Susan's presence. That night they lay in each other's arms; but Susan slept on the ground beside them.

They took the little corpse (the little, unconscious sacrifice, whose early calling-home had reclaimed her poor, wandering mother) to the hills, which in her life-time she had never seen. They dared not lay her by the stern grandfather in Milne-Row churchyard, but they bore her to a lone moorland graveyard, where long ago the Quakers used to bury their dead. They laid her there on the sunny slope, where the earliest spring-flowers blow.

Will and Susan live at the Upclose Farm. Mrs Leigh and Lizzie dwell in a cottage so secluded that, until you drop into the very hollow where it is placed, you do not see it. Tom is a school-master in Rochdale, and he and Will help to support their mother. I only know that, if the cottage be hidden in a green hollow of the hills, every sound of sorrow in the whole upland is heard there—every call of suffering or of sickness for help is listened to by a sad, gentle-looking woman, who rarely smiles (and when she does, her smile is more sad than other people's tears), but who comes out of her seclusion whenever there's a shadow in any household. Many hearts bless Lizzie Leigh, but she—she prays always and ever for forgive-ness—such forgiveness as may enable her to see her child once more. Mrs Leigh is quiet and happy. Lizzie is to her eyes something precious,—as the lost piece of silver—found once more.* Susan is the bright one who brings sunshine to all. Children grow around her and call her blessed. One is called Nanny. Her, Lizzie often takes to the sunny graveyard in the uplands, and while the little creature gathers the daisies, and makes chains, Lizzie sits by a little grave and weeps bitterly.

# MORTON HALL

## CHAPTER I

OUR old Hall is to be pulled down, and they are going to build streets on the site. I said to my sister, 'Ethelinda!* if they really pull down Morton Hall, it will be a worse piece of work than the Repeal of the Corn Laws.'* And, after some consideration, she replied, that if she must speak what was on her mind, she would own that she thought the Papists had something to do with it; that they had never forgiven the Morton who had been with Lord Monteagle when he discovered the Gunpowder Plot;* for we knew that, somewhere in Rome, there was a book kept,* and which had been kept for generations, giving an account of the secret private history of every English family of note, and registering the names of those to whom the Papists owed either grudges or gratitude.

We were silent for some time; but I am sure the same thought was in both our minds; our ancestor, a Sidebotham, had been a follower of the Morton of that day; it had always been said in the family that he had been with his master when he went with the Lord Monteagle, and found Guy Fawkes and his dark lantern* under the Parliament House; and the question flashed across our minds, were the Sidebothams marked with a black mark in that terrible mysterious book which was kept under lock and key by the Pope and the Cardinals in Rome? It was terrible, yet, somehow, rather pleasant to think of. So many of the misfortunes which had happened to us through life, and which we had called 'mysterious dispensations,'* but which some of our neighbours had attributed to our want of prudence and foresight, were accounted for at once, if we were objects of the deadly hatred of such a powerful order as the Jesuits, of whom we had lived in dread ever since we had read the *Female Jesuit*.* Whether this last idea suggested what my sister said next I can't tell; we did know the female Jesuit's second cousin,* so might be said to have literary connections, and from that the startling thought might spring up in my sister's mind, for, said she, 'Biddy!' (my name is Bridget, and no one but my sister calls me Biddy) 'suppose you write some account of Morton Hall; we have known much in our time of the Mortons, and it will be a shame if they pass away completely from men's memories while we can speak or write.' I was pleased with the notion, I confess; but I felt ashamed to agree to it all at once, though even, as I objected for modesty's sake, it came into my mind how much I had heard of the old place in its former days, and how it was, perhaps, all I could now do for the Mortons, under whom our ancestors had lived as tenants for more than three hundred years. So at last I agreed; and, for fear of mistakes, I showed it to Mr Swinton, our young curate, who has put it quite in order for me.

Morton Hall is situated about five miles from the centre of Drumble.* It stands on the outskirts of a village, which, when the Hall was built, was probably as large as Drumble in those days; and even I can remember when there was a long piece of rather lonely road, with high hedges on either side, between Morton village and Drumble. Now, it is all street, and Morton seems but a suburb of the great town near.* Our farm stood where Liverpool Street runs now; and people used to come snipe-shooting just where the Baptist chapel is built. Our farm must have been older than the Hall, for we had a date of 1460 on one of the cross-beams. My father was rather proud of this advantage, for the Hall had no date older than 1554; and I remember his affronting Mrs Dawson, the house-keeper, by dwelling too much on this circumstance one evening when she came to drink tea with my mother, when Ethelinda and I were mere children. But my mother, seeing that Mrs Dawson would never allow that any house in the parish could be older than the Hall, and that she was getting very warm, and almost insinuating that the Sidebothams had forged the date to disparage the squire's family, and set themselves up as having the older blood, asked Mrs Dawson to tell us the story of old Sir John Morton before we went to bed. I slily reminded my father that Jack, our man, was not always so careful as might be in housing the Alderney* in good time in the autumn evenings. So he started up, and went off to see after Jack; and Mrs Dawson and we drew nearer the fire to hear the story about Sir John.

Sir John Morton had lived some time about the Restoration.* The Mortons had taken the right side; so when Oliver Cromwell came into power, he gave away their lands to one of his Puritan followers—a man who had been but a praying, canting, Scotch pedlar till the war broke out; and Sir John had to go and live with his royal master at Bruges. The upstart's name was Carr, who came to live at Morton Hall; and, I'm proud to say, we—I mean our ancestors—led him a pretty life. He had hard work to get any rent at all from the tenantry, who knew their duty better than to pay it to a Roundhead. If he took the law to them, the law officers fared so badly, that they were shy of coming out to Morton—all along that lonely road I told you of—again. Strange noises were heard about the Hall, which got the credit of being haunted; but, as those noises were never heard before or since that Richard Carr lived there, I leave you to guess if the evil spirits did not know well over whom they had power—over schismatic rebels, and no one else. They durst not trouble the Mortons, who were true and loyal, and were faithful followers of King Charles in word and deed. At last, Old Oliver died; and folks did say that, on that wild and stormy night, his voice was heard high up in the air, where you hear the flocks of wild geese skirl, crying out for his true follower Richard Carr to accompany him in the terrible chase the fiends were giving him before carrying him down to hell.* Anyway, Richard Carr died within a week—summoned by the dead or not, he went his way down to his master, and his master's master.

Then his daughter Alice came into possession. Her mother was somehow related to General Monk,* who was beginning to come into power about that time. So when Charles the Second came back to his throne, and many of the sneaking Puritans had to quit their ill-gotten land, and turn to the right about, Alice Carr was still left at Morton Hall to queen it there. She was taller than most women, and a great beauty, I have heard. But, for all her beauty, she was a stern, hard woman. The tenants had known her to be hard in her father's lifetime, but now that she was the owner, and had the power, she was worse than ever. She hated the Stuarts* worse than ever her father had done; had calves' head for dinner every thirtieth of January;* and when the first twenty-ninth of May came round, and every mother's son in the village gilded his oak-leaves,* and wore them in his hat, she closed the windows of the great hall with her own hands, and sat throughout the day in darkness and mourning. People did not like to go against her by force, because she was a young and beautiful woman. It was said the King got her cousin, the Duke of Albemarle,* to ask her to court, just as courteously as if she had been the Queen of Sheba, and King Charles, Solomon, praying her to visit him in Jerusalem.* But she would not go; not she! She lived a very lonely life, for now the King had got his own again, no servant but her nurse would stay with her in the Hall; and none of the tenants would pay her any money for all that her father had purchased the lands from the Parliament, and paid the price down in good red gold.

All this time, Sir John was somewhere in the Virginian plantations;* and the ships sailed from thence only twice a year: but his royal master had sent for him home; and home he came, that second summer after the restoration. No one knew if Mistress Alice had heard of his landing in England or not; all the villagers and tenantry knew, and were not surprised, and turned out in their best dresses, and with great branches of oak, to welcome him as he rode into the village one July morning, with many gay-looking gentlemen by his side, laughing, and talking, and making merry, and speaking gaily and pleasantly to the village people. They came in on the opposite side to the Drumble Road; indeed Drumble was nothing of a place then, as I have told you. Between the last cottage in the village and the gates to the old Hall, there was a shady part of the road, where the branches nearly met overhead, and made a green gloom. If you'll notice, when many people are talking merrily out of doors in sunlight, they will stop talking for an instant, when they come into the cool green shade, and either be silent for some little time, or else speak graver, and slower, and softer. And so old people say those gay gentlemen did; for several people followed to see Alice Carr's pride taken down. They used to tell how the cavaliers had to bow their plumed hats in passing under the unlopped and drooping boughs. I fancy Sir John expected that the lady would have rallied her friends, and got ready for a sort of battle to defend the entrance to the house; but she had no friends. She had no nearer relations than the Duke of Albemarle, and he was mad with her for having refused to come to court, and so save her estate, according to his advice.

Well, Sir John rode on in silence; the tramp of the many horses' feet, and the clumping sound of the clogs of the village people were all that was heard. Heavy as the great gate was, they swung it wide on its hinges, and up they rode to the Hall steps, where the lady stood, in her close, plain, Puritan dress, her cheeks one crimson flush, her great eyes flashing fire, and no one behind her, or with her, or near her, or to be seen, but the old trembling nurse, catching at

her gown in pleading terror. Sir John was taken aback; he could not
go out with swords and warlike weapons against a woman; his very
preparations for forcing an entrance made him ridiculous in his own
eyes, and, he well knew, in the eyes of his gay, scornful comrades too;
so he turned him round about, and bade them stay where they were,
while he rode close to the steps, and spoke to the young lady; and
there they saw him, hat in hand, speaking to her; and she, lofty and
unmoved, holding her own as if she had been a sovereign queen with
an army at her back. What they said, no one heard; but he rode back,
very grave and much changed in his look, though his grey eye
showed more hawk-like than ever, as if seeing the way to his end,
though as yet afar off. He was not one to be jested with before his
face; so when he professed to have changed his mind, and not to wish
to disturb so fair a lady in possession, he and his cavaliers rode back
to the village inn, and roystered there all day, and feasted the tenantry, cutting down the branches that had incommoded them in
their morning's ride, to make a bonfire of on the village green, in
which they burnt a figure, which some called Old Noll,* and others
Richard Carr: and it might do for either, folks said, for unless they
had given it the name of a man, most people would have taken it for
a forked log of wood.

But the lady's nurse told the villagers afterwards that Mistress
Alice went in from the sunny Hall steps into the chill house shadow,
and sat her down and wept as her poor faithful servant had never
seen her do before, and could not have imagined her proud young
lady ever doing. All through that summer's day she cried; and if for
very weariness she ceased for a time, and only sighed as if her heart
was breaking, they heard through the upper windows—which were
open because of the heat—the village bells ringing merrily through
the trees, and bursts of choruses to gay cavalier songs, all in favour
of the Stuarts. All the young lady said was once or twice, 'Oh God!
I am very friendless!'—and the old nurse knew it was true, and could
not contradict her; and always thought, as she said long after, that
such weary weeping showed there was some great sorrow at hand.

I suppose it was the dreariest sorrow that ever a proud woman had;
but it came in the shape of a gay wedding. How, the village never
knew. The gay gentlemen rode away from Morton the next day as
lightly and carelessly as if they had attained their end, and Sir John
had taken possession; and, by-and-by, the nurse came timorously

out to market in the village, and Mistress Alice was met in the wood walks just as grand and as proud as ever in her ways, only a little more pale, and a little more sad. The truth was, as I have been told, that she and Sir John had each taken a fancy to each other in that parley they held on the Hall steps; she, in the deep, wild way in which she took the impressions of her whole life, deep down, as if they were burnt in. Sir John was a gallant-looking man, and had a kind of foreign grace and courtliness about him. The way he fancied her was very different—a man's way, they tell me. She was a beautiful woman to be tamed, and made to come to his beck and call; and perhaps he read in her softening eyes that she might be won, and so all legal troubles about the possession of the estate come to an end in an easy, pleasant manner. He came to stay with friends in the neighbourhood; he was met in her favourite walks, with his plumed hat in his hand, pleading with her, and she looking softer and far more lovely than ever; and lastly, the tenants were told of the marriage then nigh at hand.

After they were wedded, he stayed for a time with her at the Hall, and then off back to court. They do say that her obstinate refusal to go with him to London was the cause of their first quarrel; but such fierce, strong wills would quarrel the first day of their wedded life. She said that the court was no place for an honest woman;* but surely Sir John knew best, and she might have trusted him to take care of her. However, he left her all alone; and at first she cried most bitterly, and then she took to her old pride, and was more haughty and gloomy than ever. By-and-by she found out hidden conventicles;* and, as Sir John never stinted her of money, she gathered the remnants of the old Puritan party about her, and tried to comfort herself with long prayers, snuffled through the nose, for the absence of her husband, but it was of no use. Treat her as he would, she loved him still with a terrible love. Once, they say, she put on her waiting-maid's dress, and stole up to London to find out what kept him there; and something she saw or heard that changed her altogether, for she came back as if her heart was broken. They say that the only person she loved with all the wild strength of her heart, had proved false to her; and if so, what wonder! At the best of times she was but a gloomy creature, and it was a great honour for her father's daughter to be wedded to a Morton. She should not have expected too much.

After her despondency came her religion. Every old Puritan preacher in the country was welcome at Morton Hall. Surely that was enough to disgust Sir John. The Mortons had never cared to have much religion, but what they had, had been good of its kind hitherto. So, when Sir John came down wanting a gay greeting and a tender show of love, his lady exhorted him, and prayed over him, and quoted the last Puritan text she had heard at him; and he swore at her, and at her preachers; and made a deadly oath that none of them should find harbour or welcome in any house of his. She looked scornfully back at him, and said she had yet to learn in what county of England the house he spoke of was to be found; but in the house her father purchased, and she inherited, all who preached the Gospel should be welcome, let kings make what laws, and kings' minions swear what oaths they would. He said nothing to this—the worst sign for her; but he set his teeth at her; and in an hour's time he rode away back to the French witch that had beguiled him.

Before he went away from Morton he set his spies. He longed to catch his wife in his fierce clutch, and punish her for defying him. She had made him hate her with her Puritanical ways. He counted the days till the messenger came, splashed up to the top of his deep leather boots, to say that my lady had invited the canting Puritan preachers of the neighbourhood to a prayer-meeting, and a dinner, and a night's rest at her house. Sir John smiled as he gave the messenger five gold pieces for his pains; and straight took post-horses,* and rode long days till he got to Morton; and only just in time; for it was the very day of the prayer-meeting. Dinners were then at one o'clock in the country.* The great people in London might keep late hours, and dine at three in the afternoon or so; but the Mortons they always clung to the good old ways, and as the church bells were ringing twelve when Sir John came riding into the village, he knew he might slacken bridle; and, casting one glance at the smoke which came hurrying up as if from a newly-mended fire, just behind the wood, where he knew the Hall kitchen chimney stood, Sir John stopped at the smithy, and pretended to question the smith about his horse's shoes; but he took little heed of the answers, being more occupied by an old serving-man from the Hall, who had been loitering about the smithy half the morning, as folk thought afterwards to keep some appointment with Sir John. When their talk was ended,

Sir John lifted himself straight in his saddle; cleared his throat, and spoke out aloud:—

'I grieve to hear your lady is so ill.' The smith wondered at this, for all the village knew of the coming feast at the Hall; the spring-chickens had been bought up, and the cade-lambs* killed; for the preachers in those days, if they fasted they fasted, if they fought they fought, if they prayed they prayed, sometimes for three hours at a standing; and if they feasted they feasted, and knew what good eating was, believe me.

'My lady ill?' said the smith, as if he doubted the old prim serving-man's word. And the latter would have chopped in with an angry asseveration (he had been at Worcester* and fought on the right side), but Sir John cut him short.

'My lady is very ill, good Master Fox. It touches her here,' continued he, pointing to his head. 'I am come down to take her to London, where the King's own physician shall prescribe for her.' And he rode slowly up to the hall.

The lady was as well as ever she had been in her life, and happier than she had often been; for in a few minutes some of those whom she esteemed so highly would be about her, some of those who had known and valued her father—her dead father, to whom her sorrowful heart turned in its woe, as the only true lover and friend she had ever had on earth. Many of the preachers would have ridden far,—was all in order in their rooms, and on the table in the great dining parlour? She had got into restless hurried ways of late. She went round below, and then she mounted the great oak staircase to see if the tower bed-chamber was all in order for old Master Hilton, the oldest among the preachers. Meanwhile, the maidens below were carrying in mighty cold rounds of spiced beef, quarters of lamb, chicken pies, and all such provisions, when, suddenly, they knew not how, they found themselves each seized by strong arms, their aprons thrown over their heads, after the manner of a gag, and themselves borne out of the house on to the poultry green behind, where, with threats of what worse might befall them, they were sent with many a shameful word (Sir John could not always command his men, many of whom had been soldiers in the French wars) back into the village. They scudded away like frightened hares. My lady was strewing the white-headed preacher's room with the last year's lavender, and stirring up the sweet-pot* on the dressing-table, when she heard a step on the echoing stairs. It was no measured tread of any Puritan; it was the clang of a man of war coming nearer and nearer, with loud rapid strides. She knew the step; her heart stopped beating, not for fear, but because she loved Sir John even yet; and she took a step forward to meet him, and then stood still and trembled, for the flattering false thought came before her that he might have come yet in some quick impulse of reviving love, and that his hasty step might be prompted by the passionate tenderness of a husband. But when he reached the door, she looked as calm and indifferent as ever.

'My lady,' said he, 'you are gathering your friends to some feast. May I know who are thus invited to revel in my house? Some graceless fellows, I see, from the store of meat and drink below—wine-bibbers and drunkards, I fear.'

But, by the working glance of his eye, she saw that he knew all; and she spoke with a cold distinctness.

'Master Ephraim Dixon, Master Zerubbabel Hopkins, Master Help-me-or-I-perish Perkins,* and some other godly ministers, come to spend the afternoon in my house.'

He went to her, and in his rage he struck her. She put up no arm to save herself, but reddened a little with the pain, and then drawing her neckerchief on one side, she looked at the crimson mark on her white neck.

'It serves me right,' she said. 'I wedded one of my father's enemies; one of those who would have hunted the old man to death. I gave my father's enemy house and lands, when he came as a beggar to my door; I followed my wicked, wayward heart in this, instead of minding my dying father's words. Strike again, and avenge him yet more!'

But he would not, because she bade him. He unloosed his sash, and bound her arms tight,—tight together, and she never struggled or spoke. Then pushing her so that she was obliged to sit down on the bed side,—

'Sit there,' he said, 'and hear how I will welcome the old hypocrites you have dared to ask to my house—my house and my ancestors' house, long before your father—a canting pedlar—hawked his goods about, and cheated honest men.'

And, opening the chamber window right above those Hall steps where she had awaited him in her maiden beauty scarce three short years ago, he greeted the company of preachers as they rode up to the

Hall with such terrible hideous language (my lady had provoked him past all bearing, you see), that the old men turned round aghast, and made the best of their way back to their own places.

Meanwhile, Sir John's serving-men below had obeyed their master's orders. They had gone through the house, closing every window, every shutter, and every door, but leaving all else just as it was—the cold meats on the table, the hot meats on the spit, the silver flagons on the side-board, all just as if it were ready for a feast; and then Sir John's head-servant, he that I spoke of before, came up and told his master all was ready.

'Is the horse and the pillion* all ready? Then you and I must be my lady's tire-women;'* and as it seemed to her in mockery, but in reality with a deep purpose, they dressed the helpless woman in her riding things all awry, and strange and disorderly, Sir John carried her down stairs; and he and his man bound her on the pillion; and Sir John mounted before. The man shut and locked the great house-door, and the echoes of the clang went through the empty Hall with an ominous sound. 'Throw the key,' said Sir John, 'deep into the mere* yonder. My lady may go seek it if she lists,* when next I set her arms at liberty. Till then I know whose house Morton Hall shall be called.'

'Sir John! it shall be called the Devil's House, and you shall be his steward.'

But the poor lady had better have held her tongue; for Sir John only laughed, and told her to rave on. As he passed through the village, with his serving-men riding behind, the tenantry came out and stood at their doors, and pitied him for having a mad wife, and praised him for his care of her, and of the chance he gave her of amendment by taking her up to be seen by the King's physician. But, somehow, the Hall got an ugly name; the roast and boiled meats, the ducks, the chickens had time to drop into dust, before any human being now dared to enter in; or, indeed, had any right to enter in, for Sir John never came back to Morton; and as for my lady, some said she was dead, and some said she was mad, and shut up in London, and some said Sir John had taken her to a convent abroad.

'And what did become of her?' asked we, creeping up to Mrs Dawson.

'Nay, how should I know?'

'But what do you think?' we asked pertinaciously.

'I cannot tell. I have heard that after Sir John was killed at the battle of the Boyne* she got loose, and came wandering back to Morton, to her old nurse's house; but, indeed, she was mad then, out and out, and I've no doubt Sir John had seen it coming on. She used to have visions and dream dreams: and some thought her a prophetess,* and some thought her fairly crazy. What she said about the Mortons was awful. She doomed* them to die out of the land, and their house to be razed to the ground, while pedlars and huxters,* such as her own people, her father, had been, should dwell where the knightly Mortons had once lived. One winter's night she strayed away, and the next morning they found the poor crazy woman frozen to death in Drumble meeting-house* yard; and the Mr Morton who had succeeded to Sir John had her decently buried where she was found, by the side of her father's grave.'

We were silent for a time. 'And when was the old Hall opened, Mrs Dawson, please?'

'Oh! when the Mr Morton, our Squire Morton's grandfather, came into possession.* He was a distant cousin of Sir John's, a much quieter kind of man. He had all the old rooms opened wide, and aired, and fumigated; and the strange fragments of musty food were collected and burnt in the yard; but somehow that old dining-parlour had always a charnel-house smell, and no one ever liked making merry in it—thinking of the grey old preachers, whose ghosts might be even then scenting the meats afar off, and trooping unbidden to a feast, that was not that of which they were baulked. I was glad for one when the squire's father built another dining-room; and no servant in the house will go an errand into the old dining-parlour after dark, I can assure ye.'

'I wonder if the way the last Mr Morton had to sell his land to the people at Drumble had anything to do with old Lady Morton's prophecy,' said my mother, musingly.

'Not at all,' said Mrs Dawson, sharply. 'My lady was crazy, and her words not to be minded. I should like to see the cotton-spinners of Drumble offer to purchase land from the squire. Besides, there's a strict entail* now. They can't purchase the land if they would. A set of trading pedlars, indeed!'

I remember Ethelinda and I looked at each other at this word 'pedlars;' which was the very word she had put into Sir John's mouth when taunting his wife with her father's low birth and calling. We thought, 'We shall see.'

Alas! we have seen.

Soon after that evening our good old friend Mrs Dawson died. I remember it well, because Ethelinda and I were put into mourning for the first time in our lives. A dear little brother of ours had died only the year before, and then my father and mother had decided that we were too young; that there was no necessity for their incurring the expense of black frocks. We mourned for the little delicate darling in our hearts, I know; and to this day I often wonder what it would have been to have had a brother. But when Mrs Dawson died it became a sort of duty we owed to the squire's family to go into black, and very proud and pleased Ethelinda and I were with our new frocks. I remember dreaming Mrs Dawson was alive again, and crying, because I thought my new frock would be taken away from me. But all this has nothing to do with Morton Hall.

When I first became aware of the greatness of the squire's station in life, his family consisted of himself, his wife (a frail, delicate lady), his only son, 'little master,' as Mrs Dawson was allowed to call him, 'the young squire,' as we in the village always termed him. His name was John Marmaduke. He was always called John; and after Mrs Dawson's story of the old Sir John, I used to wish he might not bear that ill-omened name. He used to ride through the village in his bright scarlet coat, his long fair curling hair falling over his lace collar, and his broad black hat and feather shading his merry blue eyes, Ethelinda and I thought then, and I always shall think, there never was such a boy. He had a fine high spirit, too, of his own, and once horsewhipped a groom twice as big as himself who had thwarted him. To see him and Miss Phillis go tearing through the village on their pretty Arabian horses, laughing as they met the west wind, and their long golden curls flying behind them, you would have thought them brother and sister, rather than nephew and aunt; for Miss Phillis was the squire's sister, much younger than himself; indeed, at the time I speak of, I don't think she could have been above seventeen, and the young squire, her nephew, was nearly ten. I remember Mrs Dawson sending for my mother and me up to the Hall that we might see Miss Phillis dressed ready to go with her brother to a ball given at some great lord's house to Prince William of Gloucester, nephew to good old George the Third.*

When Mrs Elizabeth, Mrs Morton's maid, saw us at tea in Mrs Dawson's room, she asked Ethelinda and me if we would not like to come into Miss Phillis's dressing-room, and watch her dress; and then she said, if we would promise to keep from touching anything, she would make interest* for us to go. We would have promised to stand on our heads, and would have tried to do so too, to earn such a privilege. So in we went, and stood together, hand-in-hand, up in a corner out of the way, feeling very red, and shy, and hot, till Miss Phillis put us at our ease by playing all manner of comical tricks, just to make us laugh, which at last we did outright, in spite of all our endeavours to be grave, lest Mrs Elizabeth should complain of us to my mother. I recollect the scent of the *maréchale* powder* with which Miss Phillis's hair was just sprinkled; and how she shook her head, like a young colt, to work the hair loose which Mrs Elizabeth was straining up over a cushion.* Then Mrs Elizabeth would try a little of Mrs Morton's rouge; and Miss Phillis would wash it off with a wet towel, saying that she liked her own paleness better than any performer's colour; and when Mrs Elizabeth wanted just to touch her cheeks once more, she hid herself behind the great arm-chair, peeping out, with her sweet, merry face, first at one side and then at another, till we all heard the squire's voice at the door, asking her, if she was dressed, to come and show herself to madam, her sister-in-law; for, as I said, Mrs Morton was a great invalid, and unable to go out to any grand parties like this. We were all silent in an instant; and even Mrs Elizabeth thought no more of the rouge, but how to get Miss Phillis's beautiful blue dress on quick enough. She had cherry-coloured knots* in her hair, and her breast-knots were of the same ribbon. Her gown was open in front, to a quilted white silk skirt. We felt very shy of her as she stood there fully dressed—she looked so much grander than anything we had ever seen; and it was like a relief when Mrs Elizabeth told us to go down to Mrs Dawson's parlour, where my mother was sitting all this time.

Just as we were telling how merry and comical Miss Phillis had been, in came a footman. 'Mrs Dawson,' said he, 'the squire bids me ask you to go with Mrs Sidebotham into the west parlour, to have a look at Miss Morton before she goes.' We went, too, clinging to my mother. Miss Phillis looked rather shy as we came in, and stood just by the door. I think we all must have shown her that we had never seen anything so beautiful as she was in our lives before; for she went very scarlet at our fixed gaze of admiration, and, to relieve herself, she began to play all manner of antics—whirling round, and making cheeses* with her rich silk petticoat; unfurling her fan (a present from madam, to complete her dress), and peeping first on one side and then on the other, just as she had done upstairs; and then catching hold of her nephew, and insisting that he should dance a minuet with her until the carriage came; which proposal made him very angry, as it was an insult to his manhood (at nine years old) to suppose he could dance. 'It was all very well for girls to make fools of themselves,' he said, 'but it did not do for men.' And Ethelinda and I thought we had never heard so fine a speech before. But the carriage came before we had half feasted our eyes enough; and the squire came from his wife's room to order the little master to bed, and hand his sister to the carriage.

I remember a good deal of talk about royal dukes and unequal marriages that night. I believe Miss Phillis did dance with Prince William; and I have often heard that she bore away the bell* at the ball, and that no one came near her for beauty and pretty, merry ways. In a day or two after I saw her scampering through the village, looking just as she did before she had danced with a royal duke. We all thought she would marry some one great, and used to look out for the lord who was to take her away. But poor madam died, and there was no one but Miss Phillis to comfort her brother, for the young squire was gone away to some great school down south; and Miss Phillis grew grave, and reined in her pony to keep by the squire's side, when he rode out on his steady old mare in his lazy, careless way.

We did not hear so much of the doings at the Hall now Mrs Dawson was dead; so I cannot tell how it was; but, by-and-by, there was a talk of bills that were once paid weekly, being now allowed to run to quarter-day;* and then, instead of being settled every quarter-day, they were put off to Christmas; and many said they had hard enough work to get their money then. A buzz went through the village that the young squire played high* at college, and that he made away with more money than his father could afford. But when he came down to Morton, he was as handsome as ever; and I, for one, never believed evil of him; though I'll allow others might cheat him, and he never suspect it. His aunt was as fond of him as ever; and he of her. Many is the time I have seen them out walking together, sometimes sad enough, sometimes merry as ever. By-and-by, my father heard of sales of small pieces of land, not included in the entail; and, at last, things got so bad, that the very crops were sold yet green upon the ground, for any price folks would give, so that there was but ready money paid. The squire at length gave way entirely, and never left the house; and the young master in London; and poor Miss Phillis used to go about trying to see after the workmen and labourers, and save what she could. By this time she would be above thirty; Ethelinda and I were nineteen and twenty-one when my mother died, and that was some years before this. Well, at last the squire died; they do say of a broken heart at his son's extravagance; and, though the lawyers kept it very close, it began to be rumoured that Miss Phillis's fortune had gone too. Any way, the creditors came down on the estate like wolves. It was entailed, and it could not be sold; but they put it into the hands of a lawyer, who was to get what he could out of it, and have no pity for the poor young squire, who had not a roof for his head. Miss Phillis went to live by herself in a little cottage in the village, at the end of the property, which the lawyer allowed her to have because he could not let it to any one, it was so tumble-down and old. We never knew what she lived on, poor lady; but she said she was well in health, which was all we durst ask about. She came to see my father just before he died, and he seemed made bold with the feeling that he was a dying man; so he asked, what I had longed to know for many a year, where was the young squire; he had never been seen in Morton since his father's funeral. Miss Phillis said he was gone abroad; but in what part he was then, she herself hardly knew; only she had a feeling that, sooner or later, he would come back to the old place; where she should strive to keep a home for him whenever he was tired of wandering about, and trying to make his fortune.

'Trying to make his fortune still?' asked my father, his questioning eyes saying more than his words. Miss Phillis shook her head, with a sad meaning in her face; and we understood it all. He was at some French gaming-table, if he was not at an English one.

Miss Phillis was right. It might be a year after my father's death when he came back, looking old and grey and worn. He came to our door just after we had barred it one winter's evening. Ethelinda and I still lived at the farm, trying to keep it up, and make it pay; but it was hard work. We heard a step coming up the straight pebble walk;

and then it stopped right at our door, under the very porch, and we heard a man's breathing, quick and short.

'Shall I open the door?' said I.

'No, wait!' said Ethelinda; for we lived alone, and there was no cottage near us. We held our breaths. There came a knock.

'Who's there?' I cried.

'Where does Miss Morton live—Miss Phillis?'

We were not sure if we would answer him; for she, like us, lived alone.

'Who's there?' again said I.

'Your master,' he answered, proud and angry. 'My name is John Morton. Where does Miss Phillis live?'

We had the door unbarred in a trice, and begged him to come in; to pardon our rudeness. We would have given him of our best, as was his due from us; but he only listened to the directions we gave him to his aunt's, and took no notice of our apologies.

\*   \*   \*

## CHAPTER II

UP to this time we had felt it rather impertinent to tell each other of our individual silent wonder as to what Miss Phillis lived on; but I know in our hearts we each thought about it, with a kind of respectful pity for her fallen low estate. Miss Phillis—that we remembered like an angel for beauty, and like a little princess for the imperious sway she exercised, and which was such sweet compulsion that we had all felt proud to be her slaves—Miss Phillis was now a worn, plain woman, in homely dress, tending towards old age; and looking— (at that time I dared not have spoken so insolent a thought, not even to myself)—but she did look as if she had hardly the proper nourishing food she required. One day, I remember Mrs Jones, the butcher's wife (she was a Drumble person) saying, in her saucy way, that she was not surprised to see Miss Morton so bloodless and pale, for she only treated herself to a Sunday's dinner of meat, and lived on slop and bread-and-butter all the rest of the week. Ethelinda put on her severe face—a look that I am afraid of to this day—and said, 'Mrs Jones, do you suppose Miss Morton can eat your half-starved meat? You do not know how choice and dainty she is, as becomes one born and bred like her. What was it we had to bring for her only last Saturday from the grand new butcher's, in Drumble, Biddy?'— (We took our eggs to market in Drumble every Saturday, for the cotton-spinners would give us a higher price than the Morton people: the more fools they!)

I thought it rather cowardly of Ethelinda to put the story-telling on me; but she always thought a great deal of saving her soul; more than I did, I am afraid, for I made answer, as bold as a lion, 'Two sweet breads, at a shilling a-piece; and a forequarter of house-lamb,* at eighteen-pence a pound.' So off went Mrs Jones, in a huff, saying, 'their meat was good enough for Mrs Donkin, the great mill-owner's widow, and might serve a beggarly Morton any day.' When we were alone, I said to Ethelinda, 'I'm afraid we shall have to pay for our lies at the great day of account;' and Ethelinda answered, very sharply—(she's a good sister in the main)—'Speak for yourself, Biddy. I never said a word. I only asked questions. How could I help it if you told lies? I'm sure I wondered at you, how glib you spoke out what was not true.' But I knew she was glad I told the lies, in her heart.

After the poor squire came to live with his aunt, Miss Phillis, we ventured to speak a bit to ourselves. We were sure they were pinched. They looked like it. He had a bad hacking cough at times; though he was so dignified and proud he would never cough when any one was near. I have seen him up before it was day, sweeping the dung off the roads, to try and get enough to manure the little plot of ground behind the cottage, which Miss Phillis had let alone, but which her nephew used to dig in and till; for, said he, one day, in his grand, slow way, 'he was always fond of experiments in agriculture.' Ethelinda and I do believe that the two or three score of cabbages he raised were all they had to live on that winter, besides the bit of meal and tea they got at the village shop.

One Friday night I said to Ethelinda, 'It is a shame to take these eggs to Drumble to sell, and never to offer one to the squire, on whose lands we were born.' She answered, 'I have thought so many a time; but how can we do it? I, for one, dare not offer them to the squire; and as for Miss Phillis, it would seem like impertinence.' 'I'll try at it,' said I.

So that night I took some eggs—fresh yellow eggs from our own pheasant hen, the like of which there were not for twenty miles round—and I laid them softly after dusk on one of the little stone seats in the porch of Miss Phillis's cottage. But, alas! when we went to market at Drumble, early the next morning, there were my eggs all shattered and splashed, making an ugly yellow pool in the road just in front of the cottage. I had meant to have followed it up by a chicken or so; but I saw now that it would never do. Miss Phillis came now and then to call on us; she was a little more high and distant than she had been when a girl, and we felt we must keep our place. I suppose we had affronted the young squire, for he never came near our house.

Well, there came a hard winter, and provisions rose; and Ethelinda and I had much ado to make ends meet.* If it had not been for my sister's good management, we should have been in debt, I know; but she proposed that we should go without dinner, and only have a breakfast and a tea, to which I agreed, you may be sure.

One baking day I had made some cakes for tea—potato-cakes we called them. They had a savoury, hot smell about them; and, to tempt Ethelinda, who was not quite well, I cooked a rasher of bacon. Just as we were sitting down, Miss Phillis knocked at our door. We let her in. God only knows how white and haggard she looked. The heat of our kitchen made her totter, and for a while she could not speak. But all the time she looked at the food on the table as if she feared to shut her eyes lest it should all vanish away. It was an eager stare like that of some animal, poor soul! 'If I durst,' said Ethelinda, wishing to ask her to share our meal, but being afraid to speak out. I did not speak, but handed her the good, hot, buttered cake; on which she seized, and putting it up to her lips as if to taste it, she fell back in her chair, crying.

We had never seen a Morton cry before; and it was something awful. We stood silent and aghast. She recovered herself, but did not taste the food; on the contrary, she covered it up with both her hands, as if afraid of losing it. 'If you'll allow me,' said she, in a stately kind of way, to make up for our having seen her crying, 'I'll take it to my nephew.' And she got up to go away; but she could hardly stand for very weakness, and had to sit down again; she smiled at us, and said she was a little dizzy, but it would soon go off; but as she smiled, the bloodless lips were drawn far back over her teeth, making her face seem somehow like a death's head. 'Miss Morton,' said I, 'do honour us by taking tea with us this once. The squire, your father, once took a luncheon with my father, and we are proud of it to this day.' I poured her out some tea, which she drank; the food she shrank away from as if the very sight of it turned her sick again. But when she rose to go, she looked at it with her sad, wolfish eyes, as if she could not leave it; and at last she broke into a low cry, and said, 'Oh, Bridget, we are starving! we are starving for want of food! I can bear it; I don't mind; but he suffers—oh, how he suffers! let me take him food for this one night.'

We could hardly speak; our hearts were in our throats, and the tears ran down our cheeks like rain. We packed up a basket, and carried it to her very door, never venturing to speak a word, for we knew what it must have cost her to say that. When we left her at the cottage, we made her our usual deep courtesy,* but she fell upon our necks, and kissed us. For several nights after she hovered round our house about dusk, but she would never come in again, and face us in candle or fire light, much less meet us by daylight. We took out food to her as regularly as might be, and gave it to her in silence, and with the deepest courtesies we could make, we felt so honoured. We had many plans now she had permitted us to know of her distress. We hoped she would allow us to go on serving her in some way as became us as Sidebothams. But one night she never came; we stayed out in the cold, bleak wind, looking into the dark for her thin, worn figure; all in vain. Late the next afternoon, the young squire lifted the latch, and stood right in the middle of our house-place.* The roof was low overhead, and made lower by the deep beams supporting the floor above; he stooped as he looked at us, and tried to form words, but no sound came out of his lips. I never saw such gaunt woe; no, never! At last he took me by the shoulder, and led me out of the house.

'Come with me!' he said, when we were in the open air, as if that gave him strength to speak audibly. I needed no second word. We entered Miss Phillis's cottage; a liberty I had never taken before. What little furniture was there, it was clear to be seen were cast-off fragments of the old splendour of Morton Hall. No fire. Grey wood ashes* lay on the hearth. An old settee, once white and gold, now doubly shabby in its fall from its former estate. On it lay Miss Phillis, very pale; very still; her eyes shut.

'Tell me!' he gasped. 'Is she dead? I think she is asleep; but she looks so strange—as if she might be—' He could not say the awful word again. I stooped, and felt no warmth; only a cold chill atmosphere seemed to surround her.

'She is dead!' I replied at length. 'Oh, Miss Phillis! Miss Phillis!' and, like a fool, I began to cry. But he sat down without a tear, and looked vacantly at the empty hearth. I dared not cry any more when I saw him so stony sad. I did not know what to do. I could not leave him; and yet I had no excuse for staying. I went up to Miss Phillis, and softly arranged the grey ragged locks about her face.

'Ay!' said he. 'She must be laid out. Who so fit to do it as you and your sister, children of good old Robert Sidebotham?'

'Oh, my master,' I said, 'this is no fit place for you. Let me fetch my sister to sit up with me all night; and honour us by sleeping at our poor little cottage.'

I did not expect he would have done it; but after a few minutes' silence he agreed to my proposal. I hastened home, and told Ethelinda, and both of us crying, we heaped up the fire, and spread the table with food, and made up a bed in one corner of the floor. While I stood ready to go, I saw Ethelinda open the great chest in which we kept our treasures; and out she took a fine Holland shift that had been one of my mother's wedding shifts; and, seeing what she was after, I went upstairs and brought down a piece of rare old lace, a good deal darned to be sure, but still old Brussels point, bequeathed to me long ago by my god-mother, Mrs Dawson. We huddled these things under our cloaks, locked the door behind us, and set out to do all we could now for poor Miss Phillis. We found the squire sitting just as we left him; I hardly knew if he understood me when I told him how to unlock our door, and gave him the key, though I spoke as distinctly as ever I could for the choking in my throat. At last he rose and went; and Ethelinda and I composed her poor thin limbs to decent rest, and wrapped her in the fine Holland shift; and then I plaited up my lace into a close cap to tie up the wasted features. When all was done we looked upon her from a little distance.

'A Morton to die of hunger!' said Ethelinda solemnly. 'We should not have dared to think that such a thing was within the chances of life. Do you remember that evening, when you and I were little children, and she a merry young lady peeping at us from behind her fan?'

We did not cry any more; we felt very still and awestruck. After a while I said, 'I wonder if, after all, the young squire did go to our house. He had a strange look about him. If I dared I would go and see.'

I opened the door; the night was black as pitch; the air very still. 'I'll go,' said I; and off I went, not meeting a creature, for it was long past eleven. I reached our house; the window was long and low, and the shutters were old and shrunk. I could peep between them well, and see all that was going on. He was there, sitting over the fire, never shedding a tear; but seeming as if he saw his past life in the embers. The food we had prepared was untouched. Once or twice, during my long watch (I was more than an hour away), he turned towards the food, and made as though he would have eaten it, and then shuddered back; but at last he seized it, and tore it with his teeth, and laughed and rejoiced over it like some starved animal. I could not keep from crying then. He gorged himself with great morsels; and when he could eat no more, it seemed as if his strength for suffering had come back. He threw himself on the bed, and such a passion of despair I never heard of, much less ever saw. I could not bear to witness it. The dead Miss Phillis lay calm and still. Her trials were over. I would go back and watch with Ethelinda.

When the pale grey morning dawn stole in, making us shiver and shake after our vigil, the squire returned. We were both mortal afraid of him, we knew not why. He looked quiet enough—the lines were worn deep before—no new traces were there. He stood and looked at his aunt for a minute or two. Then he went up into the loft above the room where we were; he brought a small paper parcel down; bade us keep on our watch yet a little time. First one and then the other of us went home to get some food. It was a bitter black frost; no one was out who could stop indoors; and those who were out cared not to stop to speak. Towards afternoon the air darkened, and a great snow-storm came on. We durst not be left only one alone; yet, at the cottage where Miss Phillis had lived, there was neither fire nor fuel. So we sat and shivered and shook till morning. The squire never came that night nor all next day.

'What must we do?' asked Ethelinda, broken down entirely. 'I shall die if I stop here another night. We must tell the neighbours and get help for the watch.'

'So we must,' said I, very low and grieved. I went out and told the news at the nearest house, taking care, you may be sure, never to speak of the hunger and cold Miss Phillis must have endured in silence. It was bad enough to have them come in, and make their remarks on the poor bits of furniture; for no one had known their bitter straits even as much as Ethelinda and me, and we had been shocked at the bareness of the place. I did hear that one or two of the more ill-conditioned had said, it was not for nothing we had kept the death to ourselves for two nights; that, to judge from the lace on her cap, there must have been some pretty pickings. Ethelinda would have contradicted this, but I bade her let it alone; it would save the memory of the proud Mortons from the shame that poverty is thought to be; and as for us, why we could live it down. But, on the whole, people came forward kindly; money was not wanting to bury her well, if not grandly, as became her birth; and many a one was bidden to the funeral who might have looked after her a little more in her life-time. Among others was Squire Hargreaves from Bothwick Hall over the moors. He was some kind of far-away cousin to the Morton's; so when he came he was asked to go chief mourner in Squire Morton's strange absence, which I should have wondered at the more if I had not thought him almost crazy when I watched his ways through the shutter that night. Squire Hargreaves started when they paid him the compliment of asking him to take the head of the coffin.

'Where is her nephew?' asked he.

'No one has seen him since eight o'clock last Thursday morning.'

'But I saw him at noon on Thursday,' said Squire Hargreaves, with a round oath. 'He came over the moors to tell me of his aunt's death, and to ask me to give him a little money to bury her, on the pledge of his gold shirt-buttons. He said I was a cousin, and could pity a gentleman in such sore need; that the buttons were his mother's first gift to him; and that I was to keep them safe, for some day he would make his fortune, and come back to redeem them. He had not known his aunt was so ill, or he would have parted with these buttons sooner, though he held them as more precious than he could tell me. I gave him money; but I could not find in my heart to take the buttons. He bade me not tell of all this; but when a man is missing it is my duty to give all the clue I can.'

And so their poverty was blazoned abroad! But folk forgot it all in the search for the squire on the moor-side. Two days they searched in vain; the third, upwards of a hundred men turned out, hand-in-hand, step to step, to leave no foot of ground unsearched. They found him stark and stiff, with Squire Hargreaves' money, and his mother's gold buttons, safe in his waistcoat pocket.

And we laid him down by the side of his poor aunt Phillis.

After the squire, John Marmaduke Morton, had been found dead in that sad way, on the dreary moors, the creditors seemed to lose all hold on the property; which indeed, during the seven years they had had it, they had drained as dry as a sucked orange. But for a long time no one seemed to know who rightly was the owner of Morton Hall and lands. The old house fell out of repair; the chimneys were full of starlings' nests; the flags in the terrace in front were hidden by the long grass; the panes in the windows were broken, no one knew how or why, for the children of the village got up a tale that the house was haunted. Ethelinda and I went sometimes in the summer mornings, and gathered some of the roses that were being strangled by the bindweed that spread over all; and we used to try and weed the old flower-garden a little; but we were no longer young, and the stooping made our backs ache. Still we always felt happier if we cleared but ever such a little space. Yet we did not go there willingly in the afternoons, and left the garden always long before the first slight shade of dusk.

We did not choose to ask the common people—many of them were weavers for the Drumble manufacturers, and no longer decent hedgers and ditchers—we did not choose to ask them, I say, who was squire now, or where he lived. But one day,* a great London lawyer came to the Morton Arms, and made a pretty stir. He came on behalf of a General Morton, who was squire now, though he was far away in India. He had been written to, and they had proved him heir, though he was a very distant cousin, farther back than Sir John, I think. And now he had sent word they were to take money of his that was in England, and put the house in thorough repair; for that three maiden sisters of his, who lived in some town in the north, would come and live at Morton Hall till his return. So the lawyer sent for a Drumble builder, and gave him directions. We thought it would have been prettier if he had hired John Cobb, the Morton builder and joiner, he that had made the squire's coffin, and the squire's father's before that. Instead, came a troop of Drumble men, knocking and tumbling about in the Hall, and making their jests up and down all those stately rooms. Ethelinda and I never went near the place till they were gone, bag and baggage. And then what a change! The old casement windows, with their heavy leaded panes half overgrown with vines and roses, were taken away, and great staring sash windows* were in their stead. New grates inside; all modern, newfangled, and smoking, instead of the brass dogs which held the mighty logs of wood in the old squire's time. The little square Turkey carpet under the dining-table, which had served Miss Phillis, was not good enough for these new Mortons; the dining-room was all carpeted over. We peeped into the old dining-parlour—that parlour where the dinner for the Puritan preachers had been laid out; the flag parlour, as it had been called of late years. But it had a damp, earthy smell, and was used as a lumber-room. We shut the door quicker than we had opened it. We came away disappointed. The Hall was no longer like our own honoured Morton Hall.

'After all, these three ladies are Mortons,' said Ethelinda to me. 'We must not forget that: we must go and pay our duty to them as soon as they have appeared in church.'

Accordingly we went. But we had heard and seen a little of them before we paid our respects at the Hall. Their maid had been down in the village; their maid, as she was called now; but a maid-of-all-work she had been until now, as she very soon let out when we questioned her. However, we were never proud; and she was a good honest farmer's daughter out of Northumberland. What work she did make with the Queen's English! The folk in Lancashire are said to speak broad, but I could always understand our own kindly tongue; whereas, when Mrs Turner told me her name, both Ethelinda and I could have sworn she said Donagh, and were afraid she was an Irishwoman. Her ladies were what you may call past the bloom of youth; Miss Sophronia—Miss Morton, properly—was just sixty; Miss Annabella, three years younger; and Miss Dorothy (or Baby, as they called her when they were by themselves), was two years younger still. Mrs Turner was very confidential to us, partly because, I doubt not, she had heard of our old connection with the family, and partly because she was an arrant talker, and was glad of anybody who would listen to her. So we heard the very first week how each of the ladies had wished for the east bed-room—that which faced the north-east—which no one slept in in the old squire's days; but there were two steps leading up into it, and, said Miss Sophronia, she would never let a younger sister have a room more elevated than she had herself. She was the eldest, and she had a right to the steps. So she bolted herself in for two days, while she unpacked her clothes, and then came out, looking like a hen that has laid an egg, and defies any one to take that honour from her.

But her sisters were very deferential to her in general; that must be said. They never had more than two black feathers in their bonnets; while she had always three. Mrs Turner said that once, when they thought Miss Annabella had been going to have an offer of marriage made her, Miss Sophronia had not objected to her wearing three that winter; but when it all ended in smoke,* Miss Annabella had to pluck it out as became a younger sister. Poor Miss Annabella! She had been a beauty (Mrs Turner said), and great things had been expected of her. Her brother, the general, and her mother had both spoilt her, rather than cross her unnecessarily, and so spoil her good looks; which old Mrs Morton had always expected would make the fortune of the family. Her sisters were angry with her for not having married some great rich gentleman; though, as she used to say to Mrs Turner, how could she help it? She was willing enough, but no rich gentleman came to ask her. We agreed that it really was not her fault; but her sisters thought it was; and now, that she had lost her beauty, they were always casting it up* what they would have done if they had had her gifts. There were some Miss Burrells they had heard of, each of whom had married a lord; and these Miss Burrells had not been such great beauties.* So Miss Sophronia used to work the question by the rule of three;* and put it in this way—If Miss Burrell, with a tolerable pair of eyes, a snub nose, and a wide mouth, married a baron, what rank of peer ought our pretty Annabella to have espoused? And the worst was, Miss Annabella—who had never had any ambition—wanted to have married a poor curate in her youth; but was pulled up by her mother and sisters, reminding her of the duty she owed to her family. Miss Dorothy had done her best—Miss Morton always praised her for it. With not half the good looks of Miss Annabella, she had danced with an honourable* at Harrogate three times running; and, even now, she persevered in trying; which was more than could be said of Miss Annabella, who was very broken-spirited.

I do believe Mrs Turner told us all this before we had ever seen the ladies. We had let them know, through Mrs Turner, of our wish to pay them our respects; so we ventured to go up to the front door, and rap modestly. We had reasoned about it before, and agreed that if we were going in our every-day clothes, to offer a little present of eggs, or to call on Mrs Turner (as she had asked us to do), the back door would have been the appropriate entrance for us. But going, however humbly, to pay our respects, and offer our reverential welcome to the Miss Mortons, we took rank as their visitors, and should go to the front door. We were shown up the wide stairs, along the gallery, up two steps, into Miss Sophronia's room. She put away some papers hastily as we came in. We heard afterwards that she was writing a book, to be called *The Female Chesterfield; or, Letters from a Lady of Quality to her Niece.** And the little niece sat there in a high chair, with a flat board tied to her back, and her feet in stocks* on the tail of the chair; so that she had nothing to do but listen to her aunt's letters; which were read aloud to her as they were written, in order to mark their effect on her manners. I was not sure whether Miss Sophronia liked our interruption; but I know little Miss Cordelia Mannisty did.

'Is the young lady crooked?' asked Ethelinda, during a pause in our conversation. I had noticed that my sister's eyes would rest on the child; although, by an effort, she sometimes succeeded in looking at something else occasionally.

'No! indeed, ma'am,' said Miss Morton. 'But she was born in India, and her backbone has never properly hardened. Besides, I and my two sisters each take charge of her for a week; and their systems of education—I might say non-education—differ so totally and entirely from my ideas, that when Miss Mannisty comes to me, I consider myself fortunate if I can undo the—hem!—that has been done during a fortnight's absence. Cordelia, my dear, repeat to these good ladies the geography lesson you learnt this morning.'

Poor little Miss Mannisty began to tell us a great deal about some river in Yorkshire of which we had never heard, though I dare say we ought to, and then a great deal more about the towns that it passed by, and what they were famous for; and all I can remember—indeed, could understand at the time—was that Pomfret was famous for Pomfret cakes;* which I knew before. But Ethelinda gasped for breath before it was done, she was so nearly choked up with astonishment; and when it was ended, she said, 'Pretty dear; it's wonderful!' Miss Morton looked a little displeased, and replied, 'Not at all. Good little girls can learn anything they choose, even French verbs. Yes, Cordelia, they can. And to be good is better than to be pretty. We don't think about looks here. You may get down, child, and go into the garden; and take care you put your bonnet on, or you'll be all over freckles.' We got up to take leave at the same time, and followed the little girl out of the room. Ethelinda fumbled in her pocket.

'Here's a sixpence, my dear, for you. Nay, I am sure you may take it from an old woman like me, to whom you've told over more geography than I ever thought there was out of the Bible.' For Ethelinda always maintained that the long chapters in the Bible which were all names, were geography; and though I knew well enough they were not, yet I had forgotten what the right word was,* so I let her alone; for one hard word did as well as another. Little miss looked as if she was not sure if she might take it; but I suppose we had two kindly old faces, for at last the smile came into her eyes—not to her mouth, she had lived too much with grave and quiet people for that—and, looking wistfully at us, she said,—

'Thank you. But won't you go and see aunt Annabella?' We said we should like to pay our respects to both her other aunts if we might take that liberty; and perhaps she would show us the way. But, at the door of a room, she stopped short, and said, sorrowfully, 'I mayn't go in; it is not my week for being with aunt Annabella;' and then she went slowly and heavily towards the garden-door.

'That child is cowed by somebody,' said I to Ethelinda.

'But she knows a deal of geography'—Ethelinda's speech was cut short by the opening of the door in answer to our knock. The once beautiful Miss Annabella Morton stood before us, and bade us enter. She was dressed in white, with a turned-up velvet hat, and two or three short drooping black feathers in it. I should not like to say she rouged, but she had a very pretty colour in her cheeks; that much can do neither good nor harm. At first she looked so unlike anybody I had ever seen, that I wondered what the child could have found to like in her; for like her she did, that was very clear. But, when Miss Annabella spoke, I came under the charm. Her voice was very sweet and plaintive, and suited well with the kind of things she said; all about charms of nature, and tears, and grief, and such sort of talk, which reminded me rather of poetry—very pretty to listen to, though I never could understand it as well as plain, comfortable prose. Still I hardly know why I liked Miss Annabella. I think I was sorry for her; though whether I should have been if she had not put it in my head, I don't know. The room looked very comfortable; a spinnet* in a corner to amuse herself with, and a good sofa to lie down upon. By-and-by, we got her to talk of her little niece, and she, too, had her system of education. She said she hoped to develop the sensibilities and to cultivate the tastes. While with her, her darling niece read works of imagination, and acquired all that Miss Annabella could impart of the fine arts. We neither of us quite knew what she was hinting at, at the time; but afterwards, by dint of questioning little miss, and using our own eyes and ears, we found that she read aloud to her aunt while she lay on the sofa. *Santo Sebastiano; or, the Young Protector,** was what they were deep in at this time; and, as it was in five volumes and the heroine spoke broken English—which required to be read twice over to make it intelligible—it lasted them a long time. She also learned to play on the spinnet; not much, for I never heard above two tunes, one of which was God save the King,* and the other was not. But I fancy the poor child was lectured by one aunt, and frightened by the other's sharp ways and numerous fancies. She might well be fond of her gentle, pensive (Miss Annabella told me she was pensive, so I know I am right in calling her so) aunt, with her soft voice, and her never-ending novels, and the sweet scents that hovered about the sleepy room.

No one tempted us towards Miss Dorothy's apartment when we left Miss Annabella; so we did not see the youngest Miss Morton this first day. We had each of us treasured up many little mysteries to be explained by our dictionary,* Mrs Turner.

'Who is little Miss Mannisty?' we asked in one breath, when we saw our friend from the Hall. And then we learnt that there had been a fourth—a younger Miss Morton, who was no beauty, and no wit, and no anything; so Miss Sophronia, her eldest sister, had allowed her to marry a Mr Mannisty, and ever after spoke of her as 'my poor sister Jane.' She and her husband had gone out to India, and both had died there; and the general had made it a sort of condition with his sisters that they should take charge of the child, or else none of them liked children except Miss Annabella.

'Miss Annabella likes children,' said I. 'Then that's the reason children like her.'

'I can't say she likes children; for we never have any in our house but Miss Cordelia; but her she does like dearly.'

'Poor little miss!' said Ethelinda, 'does she never get a game of play with other little girls?' And I am sure from that time Ethelinda considered her in a diseased state from this very circumstance, and that her knowledge of geography was one of the symptoms of the disorder; for she used often to say, 'I wish she did not know so much geography! I'm sure it is not quite right.'

Whether or not her geography was right, I don't know; but the child pined for companions. A very few days after we had called—and yet long enough to have passed her into Miss Annabella's week—I saw Miss Cordelia in a corner of the church green, playing, with awkward humility, along with some of the rough village girls, who were as expert at the game as she was unapt and slow. I hesitated a little, and at last I called to her.

'How do you, my dear?' I said. 'How come you here, so far from home?'

She reddened, and then looked up at me with her large, serious eyes.

'Aunt Annabel sent me into the wood to meditate—and—and—it was very dull—and I heard these little girls playing and laughing—and I had my sixpence with me, and—it was not wrong, was it, ma'am?—I came to them, and told one of them I would give it to her if she would ask the others to let me play with them.'

'But, my dear, they are—some of them—very rough little children, and not fit companions for a Morton.'

'But I am a Mannisty, ma'am!' she pleaded, with so much entreaty in her ways, that if I had not known what naughty, bad girls some of them were, I could not have resisted her longing for companions of her own age. As it was, I was angry with them for having taken her sixpence; but, when she had told me which it was, and saw that I was going to reclaim it, she clung to me, and said,—

'Oh! don't, ma'am—you must not. I gave it to her quite of my own self.'

So I turned away; for there was truth in what the child said. But to this day I have never told Ethelinda what became of her sixpence. I took Miss Cordelia home with me while I changed my dress to be fit to take her back to the Hall. And on the way, to make up for her disappointment, I began talking of my dear Miss Phillis, and her bright, pretty youth. I had never named her name since her death to any one but Ethelinda—and that only on Sundays and quiet times. And I could not have spoken of her to a grown-up person; but somehow to Miss Cordelia it came out quite natural. Not of her latter days, of course; but of her pony, and her little black King Charles's dogs, and all the living creatures that were glad in her presence when first I knew her. And nothing would satisfy the child but I must go into the Hall garden and show her where Miss Phillis's garden had been. We were deep in our talk, and she was stooping down to clear the plot from weeds, when I heard a sharp voice cry out, 'Cordelia! Cordelia! Dirtying your frock with kneeling on the wet grass! It is not my week; but I shall tell your aunt Annabella of you.'

And the window was shut down with a jerk. It was Miss Dorothy. And I felt almost as guilty as poor little Miss Cordelia; for I had heard from Mrs Turner that we had given great offence to Miss Dorothy by not going to call on her in her room that day on which we had paid our respects to her sisters; and I had a sort of an idea that seeing Miss Cordelia with me was almost as much of a fault as the kneeling down on the wet grass. So I thought I would take the bull by the horns.

'Will you take me to your aunt Dorothy, my dear?' said I.

The little girl had no longing to go into her aunt Dorothy's room, as she had so evidently had at Miss Annabella's door. On the contrary, she pointed it out to me at a safe distance, and then went away in the measured step she was taught to use in that house; where such things as running, going upstairs two steps at a time, or jumping down three, were considered undignified and vulgar. Miss Dorothy's room was the least prepossessing of any. Somehow it had a north-east look about it, though it did face direct south; and as for Miss Dorothy herself, she was more like a 'cousin Betty'* than anything else; if you know what a cousin Betty is, and perhaps it is too old-fashioned a word to be understood by any one who has learnt the foreign languages: but when I was a girl, there used to be poor crazy women rambling about the country, one or two in a district. They never did any harm that I know of; they might have been born idiots, poor creatures! or crossed in love, who knows? But they roamed the country, and were well known at the farm-houses, where they often got food and shelter for as long a time as their restless minds would allow them to stay in any one place; and the farmer's wife would, maybe, rummage up a ribbon, or a feather, or a smart old breadth of silk, to please the harmless vanity of these poor crazy women; and they would go about so bedizened sometimes that, as we called them always 'cousin Betty,' we made it into a kind of proverb for any one dressed in a fly-away, showy style, and said they were like a cousin Betty. So now you know what I mean that Miss Dorothy was like. Her dress was white, like Miss Annabella's; but, instead of the black velvet hat her sister wore, she had on, even in the house, a small black silk bonnet. This sounds as if it should be less like a cousin Betty than a hat; but wait till I tell you how it was lined—with strips of red silk, broad near the face, narrow near the brim; for all the world like the rays of the rising sun, as they are painted on the public-house sign. And her face was like the sun; as round as an apple; and with rouge on, without any doubt: indeed, she told me once, a lady was not dressed unless she had put her rouge on. Mrs Turner told us she studied reflections a great deal;* not that she was a thinking woman in general, I should say; and that this rayed lining was the fruit of her study. She had her hair pulled together, so that her forehead was quite covered with it; and I won't deny that I rather wished myself at home, as I stood facing her in the doorway. She pretended she did not know who I was, and made me tell all about myself; and then it turned out she knew all about me, and she hoped I had recovered from my fatigue the other day.

'What fatigue?' asked I, immovably. Oh! she had understood I was very much tired after visiting her sisters; otherwise, of course, I should not have felt it too much to come on to her room. She kept hinting at me in so many ways, that I could have asked her gladly to slap my face and have done with it, only I wanted to make Miss Cordelia's peace with her for kneeling down and dirtying her frock. I did say what I could to make things straight; but I don't know if I did any good. Mrs Turner told me how suspicious and jealous she was of everybody, and of Miss Annabella in particular, who had been set over her in her youth because of her beauty; but since it had faded, Miss Morton and Miss Dorothy had never ceased pecking at her; and Miss Dorothy worst of all. If it had not been for little Miss Cordelia's love, Miss Annabella might have wished to die; she did often wish she had had the small-pox as a baby. Miss Morton was stately and cold to her, as one who had not done her duty to her family, and was put in the corner for her bad behaviour. Miss Dorothy was continually talking at her, and particularly dwelling on the fact of her being the older sister. Now she was but two years older; and was still so pretty and gentle-looking, that I should have forgotten it continually but for Miss Dorothy.

The rules that were made for Miss Cordelia! She was to eat her meals standing, that was one thing! Another was, that she was to drink two cups of cold water before she had any pudding; and it just made the child loathe cold water. Then there were ever so many words she might not use; each aunt had her own set of words which were ungenteel or improper for some reason or another. Miss Dorothy would never let her say 'red;' it was always to be pink, or crimson, or scarlet. Miss Cordelia used at one time to come to us, and tell us she had a 'pain at her chest' so often, that Ethelinda and I began to be uneasy, and questioned Mrs Turner to know if her mother had died of consumption; and many a good pot of currant jelly have I given her, and only made her pain at the chest worse; for—would you believe it?—Miss Morton told her never to say she had got a stomach-ache, for that it was not proper to say so, I had heard it called by a worse name still in my youth, and so had Ethelinda; and we sat and wondered to ourselves how it was that some kinds of pain were genteel and others were not. I said that old families, like the Mortons, generally thought it showed good blood to have their complaints as high in the body as they could—brain-fevers and headaches had a better sound, and did perhaps belong more to the aristocracy. I thought I had got the right view in saying this, when Ethelinda would put in that she had often heard of Lord Toffey having the gout and being lame, and that nonplussed me. If there is one thing I do dislike more than another, it is a person saying something on the other side when I am trying to make up my mind—how can I reason if I am to be disturbed by another person's arguments?

But though I tell all these peculiarities of the Miss Mortons, they were good women in the main: even Miss Dorothy had her times of kindness, and really did love her little niece, though she was always laying traps to catch her doing wrong. Miss Morton I got to respect, if I never liked her. They would ask us up to tea; and we would put on our best gowns; and taking the house-key in my pocket, we used to walk slowly through the village, wishing that people who had been living in our youth could have seen us now, going by invitation to drink tea with the family at the Hall—not in the housekeeper's room, but with the family, mind you. But since they began to weave in Morton, everybody seemed too busy to notice us; so we were fain to be content with reminding each other how we should never have believed it in our youth that we could have lived to this day. After tea, Miss Morton would set us to talk of the real old family, whom they had never known; and you may be sure we told of all their pomp and grandeur and stately ways: but Ethelinda and I never spoke of what was to ourselves like the memory of a sad, terrible dream. So they thought of the squire in his coach-and-four as high sheriff, and madam lying in her morning-room in her Genoa velvet wrapping-robe, all over peacock's eyes (it was a piece of velvet the squire brought back from Italy, when he had been the grand tour), and Miss Phillis going to a ball at a great lord's house and dancing with a royal duke. The three ladies were never tired of listening to the tale of the splendour that had been going on here, while they and their mother had been starving in genteel poverty up in Northumberland; and as for Miss Cordelia, she sat on a stool at her aunt Annabella's knee, her hand in her aunt's, and listened, open-mouthed and unnoticed, to all we could say.

One day, the child came crying to our house. It was the old story; aunt Dorothy had been so unkind to aunt Annabella! The little girl said she would run away to India, and tell her uncle the general, and seemed in such a paroxysm of anger, and grief, and despair, that a sudden thought came over me. I thought I would try and teach her something of the deep sorrow that lies awaiting all at some part of their lives, and of the way in which it ought to be borne, by telling her of Miss Phillis's love and endurance for her wasteful, handsome nephew. So from little, I got to more, and I told her all; the child's great eyes filling slowly with tears, which brimmed over and came rolling down her cheeks unnoticed as I spoke. I scarcely needed to make her promise not to speak about all this to any one. She said, 'I could not—no! not even to aunt Annabella.' And to this day she never has named it again, not even to me; but she tried to make herself more patient, and more silently helpful in the strange household among whom she was cast.

By-and-by, Miss Morton grew pale, and grey, and worn, amid all her stiffness. Mrs Turner whispered to us that for all her stern, unmoved looks, she was ill unto death; that she had been secretly to see the great doctor at Drumble; and he had told her she must set her house in order. Not even her sisters knew this; but it preyed upon Mrs Turner's mind and she told us. Long after this, she kept up her week of discipline with Miss Cordelia; and walked in her straight, soldier-like way about the village, scolding people for having too large families, and burning too much coal, and eating too much butter. One morning she sent Mrs Turner for her sisters; and, while she was away, she rummaged out an old locket made of the four Miss Mortons' hair when they were all children; and, threading the eye of the locket with a piece of brown ribbon, she tied it round Cordelia's neck, and kissing her, told her she had been a good girl, and had cured herself of stooping; that she must fear God and honour the king;* and that now she might go and have a holiday. Even while the child looked at her in wonder at the unusual tenderness with which this was said, a grim spasm passed over her face, and Cordelia ran in affright to call Mrs Turner. But when she came, and the other two sisters came, she was quite herself again. She had her sisters in her room alone when she wished them good-by; so no one knows what she said, or how she told them (who were thinking of her as in health) that the signs of near-approaching death, which the doctor had foretold, were upon her. One thing they both agreed in saying—and it was much that Miss Dorothy agreed in anything—that she bequeathed her sitting-room, up the two steps, to Miss Annabella as being next in age. Then they left her room crying, and went both together into Miss Annabella's room, sitting hand in hand (for the first time since childhood I should think), listening for the sound of the little hand-bell which was to be placed close by her, in case, in her agony, she required Mrs Turner's presence. But it never rang. Noon became twilight. Miss Cordelia stole in from the garden with its long, black, green shadows, and strange eerie sounds of the night wind through the trees, and crept to the kitchen fire. At last Mrs Turner knocked at Miss Morton's door, and hearing no reply, went in and found her cold and dead in her chair.

I suppose that some time or other we had told them of the funeral the old squire had; Miss Phillis's father, I mean. He had had a procession of tenantry half-a-mile long to follow him to the grave. Miss Dorothy sent for me to tell her what tenantry of her brother's could follow Miss Morton's coffin; but what with people working in mills, and land having passed away from the family, we could but muster up twenty people, men and women and all; and one or two were dirty enough to be paid for their loss of time.

Poor Miss Annabella did not wish to go into the room up two steps; nor yet dared she stay behind; for Miss Dorothy, in a kind of spite for not having had it bequeathed to her, kept telling Miss Annabella it was her duty to occupy it; that it was Miss Sophronia's dying wish, and that she should not wonder if Miss Sophronia were to haunt Miss Annabella, if she did not leave her warm room, full of ease and sweet scent, for the grim north-east chamber. We told Mrs Turner we were afraid Miss Dorothy would lord it sadly over Miss Annabella, and she only shook her head; which, from so talkative a woman, meant a great deal. But, just as Miss Cordelia had begun to droop, the general came home, without any one knowing he was coming. Sharp and sudden was the word with him. He sent Miss Cordelia off to school; but not before she had had time to tell us that she loved her uncle dearly, in spite of his quick, hasty ways. He carried his sisters off to Cheltenham;* and it was astonishing how young they made themselves look before they came back again. He was always here, there, and everywhere: and very civil to us into the bargain; leaving the key of the Hall with us whenever they went from home. Miss Dorothy was afraid of him, which was a blessing, for it kept her in order, and really I was rather sorry when she died; and, as for Miss Annabella, she fretted after her till she injured her health, and Miss Cordelia had to leave school to come and keep her company. Miss Cordelia was not pretty; she had too sad and grave a look for that; but she had winning ways, and was to have her uncle's fortune some day, so I expected to hear of her being soon snapped up. But the general said her husband was to take the name of Morton; and what did my young lady do but begin to care for one of the great mill-owners at Drumble, as if there were not all the lords and commons to choose from besides? Mrs Turner was dead; and there was no one to tell us about it; but I could see Miss Cordelia growing thinner and paler every time they came back to Morton Hall; and I longed to tell her to pluck up a spirit, and be above a cotton-spinner. One day, not half a year before the general's death, she came to see us, and told us, blushing like a rose, that her uncle had given his consent; and so, although 'he' had refused to take the name of Morton, and had wanted to marry her without a penny, and without her uncle's leave, it had all come right at last, and they were to be married at once; and their house was to be a kind of home for her aunt Annabella, who was getting tired of being perpetually on the ramble with the general.

'Dear old friends!' said our young lady, 'you must like him. I am sure you will; he is so handsome, and brave, and good. Do you know, he says a relation of his ancestors lived at Morton Hall in the time of the Commonwealth.'

'His ancestors,' said Ethelinda. 'Has he got ancestors? That's one good point about him, at any rate. I didn't know cotton-spinners had ancestors.'

'What is his name?' asked I.

'Mr Marmaduke Carr,' said she, sounding each r with the old Northumberland burr, which was softened into a pretty pride and effort to give distinctness to each letter of the beloved name.

'Carr,' said I, 'Carr and Morton! Be it so! It was prophesied of old!' But she was too much absorbed in the thought of her own secret happiness to notice my poor sayings.

He was and is a good gentleman; and a real gentleman, too. They never lived at Morton Hall. Just as I was writing this, Ethelinda came in with two pieces of news. Never again say I am superstitious! There is no one living in Morton that knows the tradition of Sir John Morton and Alice Carr; yet the very first part of the Hall the Drumble builder has pulled down is the old stone dining-parlour where the great dinner for the preachers mouldered away—flesh from flesh, crumb from crumb! And the street they are going to build right through the rooms through which Alice Carr was dragged in her agony of despair at her husband's loathing hatred, is to be called Carr Street.

And Miss Cordelia has got a baby; a little girl; and writes in pencil two lines at the end of her husband's note, to say she means to call it Phillis.

Phillis Carr! I am glad he did not take the name of Morton. I like to keep the name of Phillis Morton in my memory very still and unspoken.

# MY FRENCH MASTER

## CHAPTER I

MY father's house was in the country, seven miles away from the nearest town. He had been an officer in the navy; but as he had met with some accident that would disable him from ever serving again, he gave up his commission, and his half-pay.* He had a small private fortune, and my mother had not been penniless; so he purchased a house, and ten or twelve acres of land, and set himself up as an amateur farmer on a very small scale. My mother rejoiced over the very small scale of his operations; and when my father regretted, as he did very often, that no more land was to be purchased in the neighbourhood, I could see her setting herself a sum in her head, 'If on twelve acres he manages to lose a hundred pounds a year, what would be our loss on a hundred and fifty?' But when my father was pushed hard on the subject of the money he spent in his sailor-like farming, he had one constant retreat:

'Think of the health, and the pleasure we all of us take in the cultivation of the fields around us! It is something for us to do, and to look forward to every day.' And this was so true that, as long as my father confined himself to these arguments, my mother left him unmolested: but to strangers he was still apt to enlarge on the returns his farm brought him in; and he had often to pull up in his statements when he caught the warning glance of my mother's eye, showing him that she was not so much absorbed in her own conversation as to be deaf to his voice. But as for the happiness that arose out of our mode of life, that was not to be calculated by tens or hundreds of pounds. There were only two of us, my sister and myself; and my mother undertook the greater part of our education. We helped her in her household cares during part of the morning; then came an old-fashioned routine of lessons, such as she herself had learnt when a girl—Goldsmith's 'History of England', Rollins's 'Ancient History', Lindley Murray's Grammar,* and plenty of sewing, and stitching.

My mother used sometimes to sigh, and wish that she could buy us a piano, and teach us what little music she knew; but many of my dear father's habits were expensive; at least, for a person possessed of no larger an income than he had. Besides the quiet and unsuspected drain of his agricultural pursuits, he was of a social turn; enjoying the dinners to which he was invited by his more affluent neighbours; and especially delighted in returning them the compliment, and giving them choice little entertainments, which would have been yet more frequent in their recurrence than they were, if it had not been for my mother's prudence. But we never were able to purchase the piano; it required a greater outlay of ready money than we ever possessed. I daresay we should have grown up ignorant of any language but our own if it had not been for my father's social habits, which led to our learning French in a very unexpected manner. He and my mother went to dine with General Ashburton, one of the forest rangers;* and there they met with an emigrant gentleman,* a Monsieur de Chalabre, who had escaped in a wonderful manner, and at terrible peril to his life; and was, consequently, in our small forest-circle, a great lion,* and a worthy cause of a series of dinner parties. His first entertainer, General Ashburton, had known him in France, under very different circumstances; and he was not prepared for the quiet and dignified request made by his guest, one afternoon after M. de Chalabre had been about a fortnight in the forest, that the General would recommend him as a French teacher, if he could conscientiously do so.

To the General's remonstrances, M. de Chalabre smilingly replied, by an assurance that his assumption of his new occupation could only be for a short time; that the good cause would—*must* triumph. It was before the fatal 21st of January, 1793;* and then, still smiling, he strengthened his position by quoting innumerable instances out of the classics, of heroes and patriots, generals and commanders, who had been reduced by Fortune's frolics to adopt some occupation far below their original one. He closed his speech with informing the General that, relying upon his kindness in acting as referee, he had taken lodgings for a few months at a small farm which was in the centre of our forest circle of acquaintances. The General was too thoroughly a gentleman to say anything more than that he should be most happy to do whatever he could to forward M. de Chalabre's plans, and as my father was the first person whom he met with after this conversation, it was announced to us, on the very evening of the day on which it had taken place, that we were forthwith to learn French; and I verily believe that, if my father could have persuaded my mother to join him, we should have formed a French class of father, mother, and two head of daughters, so touched had my father been by the General's account of M. de Chalabre's present desires, as compared with the high estate from which he had fallen. Accordingly, we were installed in the dignity of his first French pupils. My father was anxious that we should have a lesson every other day, ostensibly that we might get on all the more speedily, but really that he might have a larger quarterly bill to pay; at any rate, until M. de Chalabre had more of his time occupied with instruction. But my mother gently interfered, and calmed her husband down into two lessons a week, which was, she said, as much as we could manage. Those happy lessons! I remember them now, at the distance of more than fifty years. Our house was situated on the edge of the forest; our fields were, in fact, cleared out of it. It was not good land for clover; but my father would always sow one particular field with clover seed, because my mother was so fond of the fragrant scent in her evening walks, and through this a footpath ran which led into the forest.

A quarter of a mile beyond—a walk on the soft, fine, springy turf, and under the long, low branches of the beech-trees—and we arrived at the old red-brick farm where M. de Chalabre was lodging. Not that we went there to take our lessons; that would have been an offence to his spirit of politeness; but as my father and mother were his nearest neighbours, there was a constant interchange of small messages and notes, which we little girls were only too happy to take to our dear M. de Chalabre. Moreover, if our lessons with my mother were ended pretty early, she would say—'You have been good girls; now you may run to the high point in the clover-field, and see if M. de Chalabre is coming; and if he is, you may walk with him; but take care and give him the cleanest part of the path, for you know he does not like to dirty his boots.'

This was all very well in theory; but, like many theories, the difficulty was to put it in practice. If we slipped to the side of the path where the water lay longest, he bowed and retreated behind us to a still wetter place, leaving the clean part for us; yet when we got home, his polished boots would be without a speck, while our shoes were covered with mud.

Another little ceremony which we had to get accustomed to, was his habit of taking off his hat as we approached, and walking by us holding it in his hand. To be sure, he wore a wig, delicately pow-dered, frizzed, and tied in a queue behind;* but we had always a feeling that he would catch cold, and that he was doing us too great an honour, and that he did not know how old or rather how young we were, until one day we saw him (far away from our house) hand a countrywoman over a stile with the same kind of dainty, courteous politeness, lifting her basket of eggs over first; and then, taking up the silk-lined lapel of his coat, he spread it on the palm of his hand for her to rest her fingers upon; instead of which, she took his small white hand in her plump, vigorous gripe, and leant her full weight upon him. He carried her basket for her as far as their roads lay together; and from that time we were less shy in receiving his cour-tesies, perceiving that he considered them as deference due to our sex, however old or young, or rich or poor. So, as I said, we came down from the clover-field in rather a stately manner, and through the wicket-gate that opened into our garden, which was as rich in its scents of varied kinds as the clover-field had been in its one pure fragrance. My mother would meet us here; and somehow—our life was passed as much out of doors as in-doors, both winter and summer—we seemed to have our French lessons more frequently in the garden than in the house; for there was a sort of arbour on the lawn near the drawing-room window, to which we always found it easy to carry a table and chairs, and all the rest of the lesson paraphernalia, if my mother did not prohibit a lesson al fresco.

M. de Chalabre wore, as a sort of morning costume, a coat, waist-coat, and breeches, all made of a kind of coarse grey cloth, which he had bought in the neighbourhood. His three-cornered hat was brushed to a nicety, his wig sat as no one else's did. (My father's was always awry.) And the only thing wanting to his costume when he came was a flower. Sometimes I fancied he purposely omitted gath-ering one of the roses that clustered up the farm-house in which he lodged, in order to afford my mother the pleasure of culling her choicest carnations and roses to make him up his nosegay, or 'posy,' as he liked to call it. He had picked up that pretty country word, and adopted it as an especial favourite, dwelling on the first syllable with all the languid softness of an Italian accent. Many a time have Mary and I tried to say it like him, we did so admire his way of speaking.

Once seated round the table, whether in the house or out of it, we were bound to attend to our lessons; and somehow he made us perceive that it was a part of the same chivalrous code that made him so helpful to the helpless, to enforce the slightest claim of duty, to the full. No half-prepared lessons for him! The patience, and the resource with which he illustrated and enforced every precept; the untiring gentleness with which he made our stubborn English tongues pronounce, and mispronounce, and repronounce certain words; above all, the sweetness of temper which never varied, were such as I have never seen equalled. If we wondered at these qualities when we were children, how much greater has been our surprise at their existence since we have been grown up, and have learnt that, until his emigration, he was a man of rapid and impulsive action, with the imperfect education implied in the circumstance, that at fifteen he was a sous-lieutenant* in the Queen's regiment, and must, consequently, have had to apply himself hard and conscientiously to master the language which he had in after-life to teach.

Twice we had holidays to suit his sad convenience. Holidays with us were not at Christmas, and Midsummer, Easter, and Michaelmas.* If my mother was unusually busy, we had what we called a holiday, though, in reality, it involved harder work than our regular lessons; but we fetched, and carried, and ran errands, and became rosy, and dusty, and sang merry songs in the gaiety of our hearts. If the day was remarkably fine, my dear father—whose spirits were rather apt to vary with the weather—would come bursting in with his bright, kind, bronzed face, and carry the day by storm with my mother. 'It was a shame to coop such young things up in a house,' he would say, 'when every other young animal was frolicking in the air and sunshine. Grammar!—what was that but the art of arranging words?—and he never knew a woman but could do that fast enough. Geography!—he would undertake to teach us more geography in one winter evening, telling us of the countries where he had been, with just a map before him, than we could learn in ten years with that stupid book, all full of hard words. As for the French—why, that must be learnt; for he should not like M. de Chalabre to think we slighted the lessons he took so much pains to give us; but surely we could get up the earlier to learn our French.' We promised by acclamation; and my mother—sometimes smilingly, sometimes reluctantly—was always compelled to yield. And these were the usual occasions for our holidays. But twice we had a fortnight's entire cessation of French lessons: once in January, and once in October.*

Nor did we even see our dear French master during those periods. We went several times to the top of the clover-field, to search the dark green outskirts of the forest with our busy eyes; and if we could have seen his figure in that shade, I am sure we should have scampered to him, forgetful of the prohibition which made the forest forbidden ground. But we did not see him.

It was the fashion in those days to keep children much less informed than they are now on the subjects which interest their parents. A sort of hieroglyphic or cypher talk was used in order to conceal the meaning of much that was said if children were present. My mother was a proficient in this way of talking, and took, we fancied, a certain pleasure in perplexing my father by inventing a new cypher, as it were, every day. For instance, for some time, I was called Martia, because I was very tall of my age; and, just as my father began to understand the name—and, it must be owned, a good while after I had learnt to prick up my ears whenever Martia was named—my mother suddenly changed me into the 'buttress', from the habit I had acquired of leaning my languid length against a wall. I saw my father's perplexity about this 'buttress' for some days, and could have helped him out of it, but I durst not. And so, when the unfortunate Louis the Sixteenth was executed, the news was too terrible to be put into plain English, and too terrible also to be made known to us children, nor could we at once find the clue to the cypher in which it was spoken about. We heard about 'the Iris being blown down;'* and saw my father's honest loyal excitement about it, and the quiet reserve which always betokened some secret grief on my mother's part.

We had no French lessons; and somehow the poor, battered, storm-torn Iris was to blame for this. It was many weeks after this before we knew the full reason of M. de Chalabre's deep depression when he again came amongst us; why he shook his head when my mother timidly offered him some snowdrops on that first morning on which we began lessons again; why he wore the deep mourning of that day, when all of the dress that could be black was black, and the white muslin frills and ruffles were unstarched and limp, as if to bespeak the very abandonment of grief. We knew well enough the meaning of the next hieroglyphic announcement—'The wicked, cruel boys had broken off the White Lily's head!'* That beautiful queen, whose portrait once had been shown to us, with her blue eyes, and her fair resolute look, her profusion of lightly-powdered hair, her white neck adorned with strings of pearls. We could have cried, if we had dared, when we heard the transparent mysterious words. We did cry at night, sitting up in bed, with our arms round each other's necks, and vowing, in our weak, passionate, childish way, that if we lived long enough, that lady's death avenged should be. No one who cannot remember that time can tell the shudder of horror that thrilled through the country at hearing of this last execution. At the moment, there was no time for any consideration of the silent horrors endured for centuries by the people, who at length rose in their madness against their rulers. This last blow changed our dear M. de Chalabre. I never saw him again in quite the same gaiety of heart as before this time. There seemed to be tears very close behind his smiles for ever after. My father went to see him when he had been about a week absent from us—no reason given, for did not we, did not every one, know the horror the sun had looked upon! As soon as my father had gone, my mother gave it in charge to us to make the dressing-room belonging to our guest-chamber as much like a sitting-room as possible. My father hoped to bring back M. de Chalabre for a visit to us; but he would probably like to be a good deal alone; and we might move any article of furniture we liked, if we only thought it would make him comfortable.

I believe General Ashburton had been on a somewhat similar errand to my father's before; but he had failed. My father gained his point, as I afterwards learnt, in a very unconscious and characteristic manner. He had urged his invitation on M. de Chalabre, and received such a decided negative that he was hopeless, and quitted the subject. Then M. de Chalabre began to relieve his heart by telling him all the details; my father held his breath to listen—at last, his honest heart could contain itself no longer, and the tears ran down his face. His unaffected sympathy touched M. de Chalabre inexpressibly; and in an hour after we saw our dear French master coming down the clover-field slope, leaning on my father's arm, which he had involuntarily offered as a support to one in trouble—although he was slightly lame, and ten or fifteen years older than M. de Chalabre.

For a year after that time, M. de Chalabre never wore any flowers; and after that, to the day of his death, no gay or coloured rose or carnation could tempt him. We secretly observed his taste, and always took care to bring him white flowers for his posy. I noticed, too, that on his left arm, under his coat sleeve (sleeves were made very open then), he always wore a small band of black crape.* He lived to be eighty-one, but he had the black crape band on when he died.

M. de Chalabre was a favourite in all the forest circle. He was a great acquisition to the sociable dinner parties that were perpetually going on; and though some of the families piqued themselves on being aristocratic, and turned up their noses at any one who had been engaged in trade, however largely, M. de Chalabre, in right of his good blood, his loyalty, his daring *preux chevalier** actions, was ever an honoured guest. He took his poverty, and the simple habits it enforced, so naturally and gaily, as a mere trifling accident of his life, about which neither concealment nor shame could be necessary, that the very servants—often so much more pseudo-aristocratic than their masters—loved and respected the French gentleman, who, perhaps, came to teach in the mornings, and in the evenings made his appearance dressed with dainty neatness as a dinner guest. He came lightly prancing through the forest mire; and, in our little hall, at any rate, he would pull out a neat minute case containing a blacking-brush and blacking, and repolish his boots, speaking gaily, in his broken English, to the footman all the time. That blacking-case was his own making; he had a genius for using his fingers. After our lessons were over, he relaxed into the familiar house friend, the merry play-fellow. We lived far from any carpenter or joiner; if a lock was out of order, M. de Chalabre made it right for us.* If any box was wanted, his ingenious fingers had made it before our lesson day. He turned silk-winders* for my mother, made a set of chessmen for my father, carved an elegant watch-case out of a rough beef-bone, dressed up little cork dolls for us—in short, as he said, his heart would have been broken but for his joiner's tools. Nor were his ingenious gifts employed for us alone. The farmer's wife where he lodged had numerous contrivances in her house which he had made. One particularly which I remember was a paste-board,* made after a French pattern, which would not slip about on a dresser, as he had observed her English paste-board do. Susan, the farmer's ruddy daughter, had her work-box, too, to show us; and her cousin-lover had a wonderful stick, with an extraordinary demon head carved upon it;—all by M. de Chalabre. Farmer, farmer's wife, Susan, Robert, and all were full of his praises.

We grew from children into girls—from girls into women; and still M. de Chalabre taught on in the forest; still he was beloved and honoured; still no dinner-party within five miles was thought complete without him, and ten miles' distance strove to offer him a bed sooner than miss his company. The pretty, merry Susan of sixteen had been jilted by the faithless Robert, and was now a comely, demure damsel of thirty-one or two; still waiting upon M. de Chalabre, and still constant in respectfully singing his praises. My own poor mother was dead; my sister was engaged to be married to a young lieutenant, who was with his ship in the Mediterranean. My father was as youthful as ever in heart, and, indeed, in many of his ways; only his hair was quite white, and the old lameness was more frequently troublesome than it had been. An uncle of his had left him a considerable fortune, so he farmed away to his heart's content, and lost an annual sum of money with the best grace and the lightest heart in the world. There were not even the gentle reproaches of my mother's eyes to be dreaded now.

Things were in this state when the peace of 1814* was declared. We had heard so many and such contradictory rumours that we were inclined to doubt even the *Gazette*\* at last, and were discussing probabilities with some vehemence, when M. de Chalabre entered the room unannounced and breathless:

'My friends, give me joy!' he said. 'The Bourbons'—he could not go on; his features, nay, his very fingers, worked with agitation, but he could not speak. My father hastened to relieve him.

'We have heard the good news (you see, girls, it is quite true this time). I do congratulate you, my dear friend. I *am* glad.' And he seized M. de Chalabre's hand in his own hearty gripe, and brought the nervous agitation of the latter to a close by unconsciously administering a pretty severe dose of wholesome pain.

'I go to London. I go straight this afternoon to see my sovereign. My sovereign holds a court to-morrow at Grillon's Hotel;* I go to pay him my *devoirs*.\* I put on my uniform of Gardes du Corps,\* which have lain by these many years; a little old, a little worm-eaten, but never mind; they have been seen by Marie Antoinette, which gives them a grace for ever.' He walked about the room in a nervous, hurried way. There was something on his mind, and we signed to my father to be silent for a moment or two, and let it come out. 'No!' said M. de Chalabre, after a moment's pause. 'I cannot say adieu; for I shall return to say, dear friends, my adieux. I did come a poor emigrant; noble Englishmen took me for their friend, and welcomed me to their houses. Chalabre is one large mansion, and my English friends will not forsake me; they will come and see me in my own country; and, for their sakes, not an English beggar shall pass the doors of Chalabre without being warmed and clothed and fed. I will not say adieu. I go now but for two days.'

## CHAPTER II

MY father insisted upon driving M. de Chalabre in his gig to the nearest town through which the London mail passed; and, during the short time that elapsed before my father was ready, he told us something more about Chalabre. He had never spoken of his ancestral home to any of us before; we knew little of his station in his own country. General Ashburton had met with him in Paris, in a set where a man was judged of by his wit and talent for society, and general brilliance of character, rather than by his wealth and hereditary position. Now we learned for the first time that he was heir to considerable estates in Normandy; to an old Château Chalabre; all of which he had forfeited by his emigration, it was true, but that was under another regime.

'Ah! if my dear friend, your poor mother, were alive now, I could send her such slips of rare and splendid roses from Chalabre. Often when I did see her nursing up some poor little specimen, I longed in secret for my rose garden at Chalabre. And the orangerie!* Ah! Miss Fanny,* the bride must come to Chalabre who wishes for a beautiful wreath.' This was an allusion to my sister's engagement; a fact well known to him, as the faithful family friend.

My father came back in high spirits; and began to plan that very evening how to arrange his crops for the ensuing year, so as best to spare time for a visit to Château Chalabre; and as for us, I think we believed that there was no need to delay our French journey beyond the autumn of the present year.

M. de Chalabre came back in a couple of days; a little damped, we girls fancied, though we hardly liked to speak about it to my father. However, M. de Chalabre explained it to us by saying that he had found London more crowded and busy than he had expected; that it was smoky and dismal after leaving the country, where the trees were already coming into leaf; and, when we pressed him a little more respecting the reception at Grillon's, he laughed at himself for having forgotten the tendency of the Count de Provence* in former days to become stout, and so being dismayed at the mass of corpulence which Louis the Eighteenth presented, as he toiled up the long drawing-room of the hotel.

'But what did he say to you?' Fanny asked. 'How did he receive you when you were presented?'

A flash of pain passed over his face; but it was gone directly.

'Oh! his majesty did not recognize my name. It was hardly to be expected he would; though it is a name of note in Normandy; and I have—well! that is worth nothing. The Duc de Duras* reminded him of a circumstance or two, which I had almost hoped his majesty would not have forgotten; but I myself forgot the pressure of long years of exile; it was no wonder he did not remember me. He said he hoped to see me at the Tuileries.* His hopes are my laws. I go to prepare for my departure. If his majesty does not need my sword, I turn it into a ploughshare* at Chalabre. Ah! my friend, I will not forget there all the agricultural science I have learned from you.'

A gift of a hundred pounds would not have pleased my father so much as this last speech. He began forthwith to inquire about the nature of the soil, &c., in a way which made our poor M. de Chalabre shrug his shoulders in despairing ignorance.

'Never mind!' said my father. 'Rome was not built in a day. It was a long time before I learnt all that I know now. I was afraid I could not leave home this autumn, but I perceive you'll need some one to advise you about laying out the ground for next year's crops.'

So M. de Chalabre left our neighbourhood, with the full understanding that we were to pay him a visit in his Norman château in the following September; nor was he content until he had persuaded every one who had shown him kindness to promise him a visit at some appointed time. As for his old landlord at the farm, the comely dame and buxom Susan—they, we found, were to be franked* there and back, under the pretence that the French dairy-maids had no notion of cleanliness, any more than that the French farming men were judges of stock; so it was absolutely necessary to bring over some one from England to put the affairs of the Château Chalabre in order; and Farmer Dobson and his wife considered the favour quite reciprocal.

For some time we did not hear from our friend. The war had made the post between France and England very uncertain; so we were obliged to wait, and we tried to be patient; but, somehow, our autumn visit to France was silently given up; and my father gave us long expositions of the disordered state of affairs in a country which had suffered so much as France, and lectured us severely on the folly of having expected to hear so soon. We knew, all the while, that the exposition was repeated to soothe his own impatience, and that the admonition to patience was what he felt that he himself was needing.

At last the letter came. There was a brave attempt at cheerfulness in it, which nearly made me cry, more than any complaints would have done. M. de Chalabre had hoped to retain his commission as sous-lieutenant in the Gardes du Corps—a commission signed by Louis the Sixteenth himself, in 1791. But the regiment was to be remodelled, or re-formed, I forget which; and M. de Chalabre assured us that his was not the only case where applicants had been refused. He had then tried for a commission in the Cent Suisses, the Gardes du Porte, the Mousquetaires*—but all were full. 'Was it not a glorious thing for France to have so many brave sons ready to fight on the side of honour and loyalty?' To which question Fanny replied 'that it was a shame;' and my father, after a grunt or two, comforted himself by saying, 'that M. de Chalabre would have the more time to attend to his neglected estate.'

That winter was full of incidents in our home. As it often happens when a family has seemed stationary, and secure from change for years, and then at last one important event happens, another is sure to follow. Fanny's lover returned, and they were married, and left us alone—my father and I. Her husband's ship was stationed in the Mediterranean, and she was to go and live at Malta, with some of his relations there. I know not if it was the agitation of parting with her, but my father was stricken down from health into confirmed invalidism, by a paralytic stroke, soon after her departure, and my interests were confined to the fluctuating reports of a sick room. I did not care for the foreign intelligence which was shaking Europe with an universal tremor. My hopes, my fears were centred in one frail human body—my dearly beloved, my most loving father. I kept a letter in my pocket for days from M. de Chalabre, unable to find the time to decipher his French hieroglyphics; at last I read it aloud to my poor father, rather as a test of his power of enduring interest, than because I was impatient to know what it contained. The news in it was depressing enough, as everything else seemed to be that gloomy winter. A rich manufacturer of Rouen had bought the Château Chalabre; forfeited to the nation by its former possessor's emigration. His son, M. du Fay, was well-affected towards Louis the Eighteenth—at least as long as his government was secure and promised to be stable, so as not to affect the dyeing and selling of Turkey-red* wools; and so the natural legal consequence was, that M. du Fay, Fils,* was not to be disturbed in his purchased and paid-for property. My father cared to hear of this disappointment to our poor friend—cared just for one day, and forgot all about it the next. Then came the return from Elba—the hurrying events of that spring—the battle of Waterloo;* and to my poor father, in his second childhood, the choice of a daily pudding was far more important than all.

One Sunday, in that August of 1815, I went to church. It was many weeks since I had been able to leave my father for so long a time before. Since I had been last there to worship, it seemed as if my youth had passed away—gone without a warning—leaving no trace behind. After service, I went through the long grass to the unfrequented part of the churchyard where my dear mother lay buried. A garland of brilliant yellow immortelles* lay on her grave; and the unwonted offering took me by surprise. I knew of the foreign custom, although I had never seen the kind of wreath before. I took it up, and read one word in the black floral letters; it was simply 'Adieu.' I knew, from the first moment I saw it, that M. de Chalabre must have returned to England. Such a token of regard was like him, and could spring from no one else. But I wondered a little that we had never heard or seen anything of him; nothing, in fact, since Lady Ashburton had told me that her husband had met with him in Belgium, hurrying to offer himself as a volunteer to one of the eleven generals appointed by the Duc de Feltre* to receive such applications. General Ashburton himself had since this died at Brussels, in consequence of wounds received at Waterloo. As the recollection of all these circumstances gathered in my mind, I found I was drawing near the field-path which led out of the direct road home, to farmer Dobson's; and thither I suddenly determined to go, and hear if they had learnt anything respecting their former lodger. As I went up the garden-walk leading to the house, I caught M. de Chalabre's eye; he was gazing abstractedly out of the window of what used to be his sitting-room. In an instant he had joined me in the garden. If my youth had flown, his youth, and middle-age as well, had vanished altogether. He looked older by at least twenty years than when he had left us twelve months ago. How much of this was owing to the change in the arrangement of his dress, I cannot tell. He had formerly been remarkably dainty in all these things; now he was careless, even to the verge of slovenliness. He asked after my sister, after my father, in a manner which evinced the deepest, most respectful interest; but, somehow, it appeared to me as if he hurried question after question, rather to stop any inquiries which I, in my turn, might wish to make.

'I return here to my duties; to my only duties. The good God has not seen me fit to undertake any higher. Henceforth I am the faithful French teacher; the diligent, punctual French teacher: nothing more. But I do hope to teach the French language as becomes a gentleman and a Christian; to do my best. Henceforth the grammar and the syntax are my estate, my coat of arms.' He said this with a proud humility which prevented any reply. I could only change the subject, and urge him to come and see my poor sick father. He replied,—

'To visit the sick, that is my duty as well as my pleasure. For the mere society—I renounce all that. That is now beyond my position, to which I accommodate myself with all my strength.'

Accordingly, when he came to spend an hour with my father, he brought a small bundle of printed papers, announcing the terms on which M. Chalabre (the 'de' was dropped now and for evermore)* was desirous of teaching French, and a little paragraph at the bottom of the page solicited the patronage of schools. Now this was a great coming-down. In former days, non-teaching at schools had been the line which marked that M. de Chalabre had taken up teaching rather as an amateur profession, than with any intention of devoting his life to it. He respectfully asked me to distribute these papers where I thought fit. I say 'respectfully' advisedly; there was none of the old deferential gallantry, as offered by a gentleman to a lady, his equal in birth and fortune—instead, there was the matter-of-fact request and statement which a workman offers to his employer. Only in my father's room, he was the former M. de Chalabre; he seemed to understand how vain would be all attempts to recount or explain the circumstances which had led him so decidedly to take a lower level in society. To my father, to the day of his death, M. de Chalabre maintained the old easy footing; assumed a gaiety which he never even pretended to feel anywhere else; listened to my father's childish interests with a true and kindly sympathy for which I ever felt grateful, although he purposely put a deferential reserve between him and me, as a barrier to any expression of such feeling on my part.

His former lessons had been held in such high esteem by those who were privileged to receive them, that he was soon sought after on all sides. The schools of the two principal county towns* put forward their claims, and considered it a favour to receive his instructions. Morning, noon, and night he was engaged; even if he had not proudly withdrawn himself from all merely society engagements, he would have had no leisure for them. His only visits were paid to my father, who looked for them with a kind of childish longing. One day, to my surprise, he asked to be allowed to speak to me for an instant alone. He stood silent for a moment, turning his hat in his hand.

'You have a right to know—you, my first pupil; next Tuesday, I marry myself to Miss Susan Dobson—good, respectable woman, to whose happiness I mean to devote my life, or as much of it as is not occupied with the duties of instruction.' He looked up at me, expecting congratulations, perhaps; but I was too much stunned with my surprise: the buxom, red-armed, apple-cheeked Susan, who, when she blushed, blushed the colour of beet-root; who did not know a word of French; who regarded the nation (always excepting the gentleman before me) as frog-eating Mounseers, the national enemies of England! I afterwards thought that perhaps this very ignorance constituted one of her charms. No word, nor allusion, nor expressive silence, nor regretful sympathetic sighs, could remind M. de Chalabre of the bitter past, which he was evidently striving to forget. And, most assuredly, never man had a more devoted and admiring wife than poor Susan made M. de Chalabre. She was a little awed by him, to be sure; never quite at her ease before him; but I imagine husbands do not dislike such a tribute to their Jupiter-ship.* Madame Chalabre received my call, after their marriage, with a degree of sober, rustic, happy dignity, which I could not have foreseen in Susan Dobson. They had taken a small cottage on the borders of the forest; it had a garden round it; and the cow, pigs, and poultry, which were to be her charge, found their keep in the forest. She had a rough country servant to assist her in looking after them; and in what scanty leisure he had, her husband attended to the garden and the bees.

Madame Chalabre took me over the neatly furnished cottage with evident pride. 'Moussire,' as she called him, had done this; Moussire had fitted up that. Moussire was evidently a man of resource. In a little closet of a dressing-room belonging to Moussire, there hung a pencil drawing, elaborately finished to the condition of a bad pocket-book engraving. It caught my eye, and I lingered to look at it. It represented a high, narrow house, of considerable size, with four pepper-box turrets at each corner; and a stiff avenue formed the foreground.

'Château Chalabre?' said I, inquisitively.

'I never asked,' my companion replied. 'Moussire does not always like to be asked questions. It is the picture of some place he is very fond of, for he won't let me dust it for fear I should smear it.'

M. de Chalabre's marriage did not diminish the number of his visits to my father. Until that beloved parent's death, he was faithful in doing all he could to lighten the gloom of the sick-room. But a chasm, which he had opened, separated any present intercourse with him from the free, unreserved friendship that had existed formerly. And yet for his sake I used to go and see his wife. I could not forget early days, nor the walks to the top of the clover-field, nor the daily posies, nor my mother's dear regard for the emigrant gentleman; nor a thousand little kindnesses which he had shown to my absent sister and myself. He did not forget either in the closed and sealed chambers of his heart. So, for his sake, I tried to become a friend to his wife; and she learned to look upon me as such. It was my employment in the sick chamber to make clothes for the little expected Chalabre baby; and its mother would fain (as she told me) have asked me to carry the little infant to the font, but that her husband somewhat austerely reminded her that they ought to seek a *marraine*\* among those of their own station in society. But I regarded the pretty little Susan as my god-child nevertheless in my heart; and secretly pledged myself always to take an interest in her. Not two months after my father's death, a sister was born; and the human heart in M. de Chalabre subdued his pride; the child was to bear the pretty name of his French mother, although France could find no place for him, and had cast him out. That youngest little girl was called Aimée.

When my father died, Fanny and her husband urged me to leave Brookfield, and come and live with them at Valetta.\* The estate was left to us; but an eligible tenant offered himself; and my health, which had suffered materially during my long nursing, did render it desirable for me to seek some change to a warmer climate. So I went abroad, ostensibly for a year's residence only; but, somehow, that year has grown into a lifetime. Malta and Genoa have been my dwelling-places ever since. Occasionally, it is true, I have paid visits to England, but I have never looked upon it as my home since I left it thirty years ago. During these visits I have seen the Chalabres. He had become more absorbed in his occupation than ever; had published a French grammar on some new principle, of which he presented me with a copy, taking some pains to explain how it was to be used. Madame looked plump and prosperous; the farm, which was under her management, had thriven; and as for the two daughters, behind their English shyness, they had a good deal of French piquancy and *esprit*.* I induced them to take some walks with me, with a view of asking them some questions which should make our friendship an individual reality, not merely an hereditary feeling; but the little monkeys put me through my catechism, and asked me innumerable questions about France, which they evidently regarded as their country. 'How do you know all about French habits and customs?' asked I. 'Does Monsieur de—does your father talk to you much about France?'

'Sometimes, when we are alone with him—never when any one is by,' answered Susan, the elder, a grave, noble-looking girl, of twenty or thereabouts. 'I think he does not speak about France before my mother, for fear of hurting her.'

'And I think,' said little Aimée, 'that he does not speak at all, when he can help it; it is only when his heart gets too full with recollections, that he is obliged to talk to us, because many of the thoughts could not be said in English.'

'Then, I suppose, you are two famous French scholars?'

'Oh, yes! Papa always speaks to us in French; it is our own language.'

But with all their devotion to their father and to his country, they were most affectionate, dutiful daughters to their mother. They were her companions, her comforts in the pleasant household labours; most practical, useful young women. But in a privacy not the less sacred, because it was understood rather than prescribed, they kept all the enthusiasm, all the romance of their nature, for their father. They were the confidantes of that poor exile's yearnings for France; the eager listeners for what he chose to tell them of his early days.

His words wrought up Susan to make the resolution that, if ever she felt herself free from home duties and responsibilities, she would become a Sister of Charity,* like Anne-Marguérite de Chalabre, her father's great-aunt, and model of woman's sanctity. As for Aimée, come what might, she never would leave her father; and that was all she was clear about in picturing her future.

Three years ago I was in Paris. An English friend of mine who lives there—English by birth, but married to a German professor, and very French in manners and ways*—asked me to come to her house one evening. I was far from well and disinclined to stir out.

'Oh, but come!' said she. 'I have a good reason; really a tempting reason. Perhaps this very evening a piece of poetical justice will be done in my *salon*. A living romance! Now, can you resist?'

'What is it?' said I; for she was rather in the habit of exaggerating trifles into romances.

'A young lady is coming; not in the first youth, but still young, very pretty; daughter of a French *émigré*, whom my husband knew in Belgium, and who has lived in England ever since.'

'I beg your pardon, but what is her name?' interrupted I, roused to interest.

'De Chalabre. Do you know her?'

'Yes; I am much interested in her. I will gladly come to meet her. How long has she been in Paris? Is it Susan or Aimée?'

'Now I am not to be baulked of the pleasure of telling you my romance; my hoped-for bit of poetical justice. You must be patient, and you will have answers to all your questions.'

I sank back in my easy chair. Some of my friends are rather long-winded, and it is as well to be settled in a comfortable position before they begin to talk.

'I told you a minute ago, that my husband had become acquainted with M. de Chalabre in Belgium, in 1815. They have kept up a correspondence ever since; not a very brisk one, it is true, for M. de Chalabre was a French master in England, and my husband a professor in Paris; but still they managed to let each other know how they were going on, and what they were doing, once, if not twice every year. For myself; I never saw M. de Chalabre.'

'I know him well,' said I. 'I have known him all my life.'

'A year ago his wife died (she was an English-woman); she had had a long and suffering illness; and his eldest daughter had devoted herself to her with the patient sweetness of an angel, as he told us, and I can well believe. But after her mother's death, the world, it seems, became distasteful to her: she had been inured to the half-lights, the hushed voices, the constant thought for others required in a sick-room, and the noise and rough bustle of healthy people jarred upon her. So she pleaded with her father to allow her to become a Sister of Charity. She told him that he would have given a welcome to any suitor who came to offer to marry her, and bear her away from her home, and her father and sister; and now, when she was called by religion, would he grudge to part with her? He gave his consent, if not his full approbation; and he wrote to my husband to beg me to receive her here, while we sought out a convent into which she could be received. She has been with me two months, and endeared herself to me unspeakably; she goes home next week unless—'

'But, I beg your pardon; did you not say she wished to become a Sister of Charity?'

'It is true; but she was too old to be admitted into their order. She is eight-and-twenty. It has been a grievous disappointment to her; she has borne it very patiently and meekly, but I can see how deeply she has felt it. And now for my romance. My husband had a pupil some ten years ago, a M. du Fay, a clever, scientific young man, one of the first merchants of Rouen. His grandfather purchased M. de Chalabre's ancestral estate. The present M. du Fay came on business to Paris two or three days ago, and invited my husband to a little dinner; and somehow this story of Suzette Chalabre came out, in consequence of inquiries my husband was making for an escort to take her to England. M. du Fay seemed interested with the story; and asked my husband if he might pay his respects to me, some evening when Suzette should be in, and so is coming to-night, he, and a friend of his, who was at the dinner party the other day; will you come?'

I went, more in the hope of seeing Susan Chalabre, and hearing some news about my early home, than with any expectation of poetical justice. And in that I was right; and yet I was wrong. Susan Chalabre was a grave, gentle woman, of an enthusiastic and devoted appearance, not unlike that portrait of his daughter which arrests every eye in Ary Scheffer's sacred pictures.* She was silent and sad; her cherished plan of life was uprooted. She talked to me a little in a soft and friendly manner, answering any questions I asked; but, as for gentlemen, her indifference and reserve made it impossible for them to enter into any conversation with her; and the meeting was indisputably 'flat.'

'Oh! my romance! my poetical justice! Before the evening was half over, I would have given up all my castles in the air for one well-sustained conversation of ten minutes long. Now don't laugh at me, for I can't bear it to-night.' Such was my friend's parting speech. I did not see her again for two days. The third she came in glowing with excitement.

'You may congratulate me after all; if it was not poetical justice, it is prosaic justice; and, except for the empty romance, that is a better thing!'

'What do you mean?' said I. 'Surely M. du Fay has not proposed for Susan?'

'No! but that charming M. de Frez, his friend, has; that is to say, not proposed but spoken; no, not spoken, but it seems he asked M. du Fay—whose confidant he was—if he was intending to pro-ceed in his idea of marrying Suzette; and on hearing that he was not, M. de Frez said that he should come to us, and ask us to put him in the way of prosecuting the acquaintance, for that he had been charmed with her; looks, voice, silence, he admires them all; and we have arranged that he is to be the escort to England; he has business there, he says; and as for Suzette (she knows nothing of all this, of course, for who dared tell her?), all her anxiety is to return home, and the first person travelling to England will satisfy her, if it does us. And, after all, M. de Frez lives within five leagues of the Château Chalabre, so she can go and see the old place whenever she will.'

When I went to bid Susan good-by, she looked as unconscious and dignified as ever. No idea of a lover had ever crossed her mind. She considered M. de Frez as a kind of necessary incumbrance for the journey. I had not much hopes for him; and yet he was an agreeable man enough, and my friends told me that his character stood firm and high.

In three months, I was settled for the winter in Rome. In four, I heard that the marriage of Susan Chalabre had taken place. What were the intermediate steps between the cold, civil indifference with which I had last seen her regarding her travelling companion, and the full love with which such a woman as Suzette Chalabre must love a man before she could call him husband, I never learnt. I wrote to my old French master to congratulate him, as I believed I honestly might, on his daughter's marriage. It was some months before I received his answer. It was—

'Dear friend, dear old pupil, dear child of the beloved dead, I am an old man of eighty, and I tremble towards the grave. I cannot write many words; but my own hand shall bid you come to the home of Aimée and her husband. They tell me to ask you to come and see the old father's birth-place, while he is yet alive to show it to you. I have the very apartment in Château Chalabre that was mine when I was a boy, and my mother came in to bless me every night. Susan lives near us. The good God bless my sons-in-law, Bertrand de Frez and Alphonse du Fay, as He has blessed me all my life long. I think of your father and mother, my dear; and you must think no harm when I tell you I have had masses said for the repose of their souls. If I make a mistake, God will forgive.'

My heart could have interpreted this letter, even without the pretty letter of Aimée and her husband which accompanied it; and which told how, when M. du Fay came over to his friend's wedding, he had seen the younger sister, and in her seen his fate. The soft caressing, timid Aimée was more to his taste than the grave and stately Susan. Yet little Aimée managed to rule imperiously at Château Chalabre; or, rather, her husband was delighted to indulge her every wish; while Susan, in her grand way, made rather a pomp of her conjugal obedience. But they were both good wives, good daughters.

This last summer, you might have seen an old, old man, dressed in grey, with white flowers in his button-hole (gathered by a grandchild as fair as they), leading an elderly lady about the grounds of Château Chalabre, with tottering, unsteady eagerness of gait.

'Here!' said he to me, 'just here my mother bade me adieu when first I went to join my regiment. I was impatient to go. I mounted—I rode to yonder great chestnut, and then, looking back, I saw my mother's sorrowful countenance. I sprang off; threw the reins to the groom, and ran back for one more embrace. "My brave boy!" she said; "my own! Be faithful to God and your king!" I never saw her more; but I shall see her soon; and I think I may tell her I have been faithful both to my God and my king.'

Before now, he has told his mother all.

# HALF A LIFE-TIME AGO

## CHAPTER I

HALF a life-time ago, there lived in one of the Westmoreland dales a single woman, of the name of Susan Dixon. She was owner of the small farm-house where she resided, and of some thirty or forty acres of land by which it was surrounded. She had also an hereditary right to a sheep-walk, extending to the wild fells that overhang Blea Tarn. In the language of the country, she was a Stateswoman.* Her house is yet to be seen on the Oxenfell road, between Skelwith and Coniston. You go along a moorland track, made by the carts that occasionally came for turf from the Oxenfell. A brook babbles and brattles* by the wayside, giving you a sense of companionship, which relieves the deep solitude in which this way is usually traversed. Some miles on this side of Coniston there is a farmstead—a grey stone house, and a square of farm-buildings surrounding a green space of rough turf, in the midst of which stands a mighty, funereal umbrageous yew, making a solemn shadow, as of death, in the very heart and centre of the light and heat of the brightest summer day. On the side away from the house, this yard slopes down to a dark-brown pool, which is supplied with fresh water from the over-flowings of a stone cistern, into which some rivulet of the brook before mentioned continually and melodiously falls bubbling. The cattle drink out of this cistern. The household bring their pitchers and fill them with drinking-water by a dilatory, yet pretty, process. The water-carrier brings with her a leaf of the hound's-tongue fern, and, inserting it in the crevice of the grey rock, makes a cool, green spout for the sparkling stream.

The house is no specimen, at the present day, of what it was in the lifetime of Susan Dixon. Then, every small diamond pane in the windows glittered with cleanliness. You might have eaten off the floor; you could see yourself in the pewter plates and the polished oaken awmry, or dresser, of the state kitchen into which you entered. Few strangers penetrated further than this room. Once or twice, wandering tourists, attracted by the lonely picturesqueness of the situation, and the exquisite cleanliness of the house itself, made their way into this house-place, and offered money enough (as they thought) to tempt the hostess to receive them as lodgers. They would give no trouble, they said; they would be out rambling or sketching all day long; would be perfectly content with a share of the food which she provided for herself; or would procure what they required from the Waterhead Inn at Coniston. But no liberal sum—no fair words—moved her from her stony manner, or her monotonous tone of indifferent refusal. No persuasion could induce her to show any more of the house than that first room; no appearance of fatigue procured for the weary an invitation to sit down and rest; and if one more bold and less delicate did so without being asked, Susan stood by, cold and apparently deaf, or only replying by the briefest monosyllables, till the unwelcome visitor had departed. Yet those with whom she had dealings, in the way of selling her cattle or her farm produce, spoke of her as keen after a bargain—a hard one to have to do with; and she never spared herself exertion or fatigue, at market or in the field, to make the most of her produce. She led the haymakers with her swift, steady rake, and her noiseless evenness of motion. She was about among the earliest in the market, examining samples of oats, pricing them, and then turning with grim satisfaction to her own cleaner corn.

She was served faithfully and long by those who were rather her fellow-labourers than her servants. She was even and just in her dealings with them. If she was peculiar and silent, they knew her, and knew that she might be relied on. Some of them had known her from her childhood; and deep in their hearts was an unspoken—almost unconscious—pity for her, for they knew her story, though they never spoke of it.

Yes; the time had been when that tall, gaunt, hard-featured, angular woman—who never smiled, and hardly ever spoke an unnecessary word—had been a fine-looking girl, bright-spirited and rosy; and when the hearth at the Yew Nook had been as bright as she, with family love and youthful hope and mirth. Fifty or fifty-one years ago, William Dixon and his wife Margaret were alive; and Susan, their daughter, was about eighteen years old—ten years older than the only other child, a boy named after his father. William and Margaret Dixon were rather superior people, of a character belonging—as far as I have seen—exclusively to the class of Westmoreland and Cumberland statesmen—just, independent, upright; not given to much speaking; kind-hearted, but not demonstrative; disliking change, and new ways, and new people; sensible and shrewd; each household self-contained, and its members having little curiosity as to their neighbours, with whom they rarely met for any social inter-course, save at the stated times of sheep-shearing and Christmas; having a certain kind of sober pleasure in amassing money, which occasionally made them miserable (as they call miserly people up in the north)* in their old age; reading no light or ephemeral literature; but the grave, solid books brought round by the pedlars (such as the 'Paradise Lost' and 'Regained,' 'The Death of Abel,' 'The Spiritual Quixote,' and 'The Pilgrim's Progress')* were to be found in nearly every house: the men occasionally going off laking,* *i.e.* playing, *i.e.* drinking for days together, and having to be hunted up by anx-ious wives, who dared not leave their husbands to the chances of the wild precipitous roads, but walked miles and miles, lantern in hand, in the dead of night, to discover and guide the solemnly-drunken husband home; who had a dreadful headache the next day, and the day after that came forth as grave, and sober, and virtuous-looking as if there were no such things as malt and spirituous liquors in the world; and who were seldom reminded of their misdoings by their wives, to whom such occasional outbreaks were as things of course, when once the immediate anxiety produced by them was over. Such were—such are—the characteristics of a class now passing away* from the face of the land, as their compeers, the yeomen, have done before them. Of such was William Dixon. He was a shrewd clever farmer, in his day and generation, when shrewdness was rather shown in the breeding and rearing of sheep and cattle than in the cultivation of land. Owing to this character of his, statesmen from a distance, from beyond Kendal, or from Borrowdale, of greater wealth than he, would send their sons to be farm-servants for a year or two with him, in order to learn some of his methods before setting up on land of their own. When Susan, his daughter, was about seventeen, one Michael Hurst was farm-servant at Yew Nook. He worked with the master, and lived with the family, and was in all respects treated as an equal, except in the field. His father was a wealthy statesman at Wythburne, up beyond Grasmere; and through Michael's servitude the families had become acquainted, and the Dixons went over to the High Beck sheep-shearing, and the Hursts came down by Red Bank and Loughrig Tarn and across the

Oxenfell when there was the Christmas-tide feasting at Yew Nook. The fathers strolled round the fields together, examined cattle and sheep, and looked knowing over each other's horses. The mothers inspected the dairies and household arrangements, each openly admiring the plans of the other, but secretly preferring their own. Both fathers and mothers cast a glance from time to time at Michael and Susan, who were thinking of nothing less than farm or dairy, but whose unspoken attachment was, in all ways, so suitable and natural a thing that each parent rejoiced over it, although with characteristic reserve it was never spoken about—not even between husband and wife.

Susan had been a strong, independent, healthy girl; a clever help to her mother, and a spirited companion to her father; more of a man in her (as he often said) than her delicate little brother ever would have. He was his mother's darling, although she loved Susan well. There was no positive engagement between Michael and Susan—I doubt whether even plain words of love had been spoken; when one winter-time Margaret Dixon was seized with inflammation consequent upon a neglected cold. She had always been strong and notable,* and had been too busy to attend to the earliest symptoms of illness. It would go off, she said to the woman who helped in the kitchen; or if she did not feel better when they had got the hams and bacon out of hand, she would take some herb-tea and nurse up a bit. But Death could not wait till the hams and bacon were cured: he came on with rapid strides, and shooting arrows of portentous agony. Susan had never seen illness—never knew how much she loved her mother till now, when she felt a dreadful, instinctive certainty that she was losing her. Her mind was thronged with recollections of the many times she had slighted her mother's wishes; her heart was full of the echoes of careless and angry replies that she had spoken. What would she not now give to have opportunities of service and obedience, and trials of her patience and love, for that dear mother who lay gasping in torture! And yet Susan had been a good girl and an affectionate daughter.

The sharp pain went off, and delicious ease came on; yet still her mother sunk. In the midst of this languid peace she was dying. She motioned Susan to her bedside, for she could only whisper; and then, while the father was out of the room, she spoke as much to the eager, hungering eyes of her daughter by the motion of her lips, as by the slow, feeble sounds of her voice.

'Susan, lass, thou must not fret. It is God's will, and thou wilt have a deal to do. Keep father straight if thou canst; and if he goes out Ulverstone ways, see that thou meet him before he gets to the Old Quarry. It's a dree bit* for a man who has had a drop. As for lile Will'—here the poor woman's face began to work and her fingers to move nervously as they lay on the bed-quilt—'lile Will will miss me most of all. Father's often vexed with him because he's not a quick, strong lad; he is not, my poor lile chap. And father thinks he's saucy, because he cannot always stomach oat-cake and porridge. There's better than three pound in th' old black teapot on the top shelf of the cupboard. Just keep a piece of loaf-bread* by you, Susan dear, for Will to come to when he's not taken his breakfast. I have, may be, spoilt him; but there'll be no one to spoil him now.'

She began to cry a low, feeble cry, and covered up her face that Susan might not see her. That dear face! those precious moments while yet the eyes could look out with love and intelligence. Susan laid her head down close by her mother's ear.

'Mother, I'll take tent* of Will. Mother, do you hear? He shall not want ought I can give or get for him, least of all the kind words which you had ever ready for us both. Bless you! bless you! my own mother.'

'Thou'lt promise me that, Susan, wilt thou? I can die easy if thou'lt take charge of him. But he's hardly like other folk; he tries father at times, though I think father'll be tender of him when I'm gone, for my sake. And, Susan, there's one thing more. I never spoke on it for fear of the bairn being called a tell-tale, but I just comforted him up. He vexes Michael at times, and Michael has struck him before now. I did not want to make a stir; but he's not strong, and a word from thee, Susan, will go a long way with Michael.'

Susan was as red now as she had been pale before; it was the first time that her influence over Michael had been openly acknowledged by a third person, and a flash of joy came athwart the solemn sadness of the moment. Her mother had spoken too much, and now came on the miserable faintness. She never spoke again coherently; but when her children and her husband stood by her bedside, she took lile Will's hand and put it into Susan's, and looked at her with imploring eyes. Susan clasped her arms round Will, and leaned her head upon his curly little one, and vowed within herself to be as a mother to him.

Henceforward she was all in all to her brother. She was a more spirited and amusing companion to him than his mother had been, from her greater activity, and perhaps, also, from her originality of character, which often prompted her to perform her habitual actions in some new and racy manner. She was tender to lile Will when she was prompt and sharp with everybody else—with Michael most of all; for somehow the girl felt that, unprotected by her mother, she must keep up her own dignity, and not allow her lover to see how strong a hold he had upon her heart. He called her hard and cruel, and left her so; and she smiled softly to herself, when his back was turned, to think how little he guessed how deeply he was loved. For Susan was merely comely and fine-looking; Michael was strikingly handsome, admired by all the girls for miles round, and quite enough of a country coxcomb to know it and plume himself accordingly. He was the second son of his father; the eldest would have High Beck farm, of course, but there was a good penny in the Kendal bank in store for Michael. When harvest was over, he went to Chapel Langdale to learn to dance; and at night, in his merry moods, he would do his steps on the flag floor of the Yew Nook kitchen, to the secret admiration of Susan, who had never learned dancing, but who flouted him perpetually, even while she admired, in accordance with the rule she seemed to have made for herself about keeping him at a distance so long as he lived under the same roof with her. One evening he sulked at some saucy remark of hers; he sitting in the chimney-corner with his arms on his knees, and his head bent forwards, lazily gazing into the wood-fire on the hearth, and luxuriating in rest after a hard day's labour; she sitting among the geraniums on the long, low window-seat, trying to catch the last slanting rays of the autumnal light to enable her to finish stitching a shirt-collar for Will, who lounged full length on the flags at the other side of the hearth to Michael, poking the burning wood from time to time with a long hazel-stick to bring out the leap of glittering sparks.

'And if you can dance a threesome reel, what good does it do ye?' asked Susan, looking askance at Michael, who had just been vaunting his proficiency. 'Does it help you plough, or reap, or even climb the rocks to take a raven's nest? If I were a man, I'd be ashamed to give in to such softness.'

'If you were a man, you'd be glad to do anything which made the pretty girls stand round and admire.'

'As they do to you, eh! Ho, Michael, that would not be my way o' being a man!'

'What would then?' asked he, after a pause, during which he had expected in vain that she would go on with her sentence. No answer.

'I should not like you as a man, Susy; you'd be too hard and headstrong.'

'Am I hard and headstrong?' asked she, with as indifferent a tone as she could assume, but which yet had a touch of pique in it. His quick ear detected the inflexion.

'No, Susy! You're wilful at times, and that's right enough. I don't like a girl without spirit. There's a mighty pretty girl comes to the dancing class; but she is all milk and water. Her eyes never flash like yours when you're put out; why, I can see them flame across the kitchen like a cat's in the dark. Now, if you were a man, I should feel queer before those looks of yours; as it is, I rather like them, because—'

'Because what?' asked she, looking up and perceiving that he had stolen close up to her.

'Because I can make all right in this way,' said he, kissing her suddenly.

'Can you?' said she, wrenching herself out of his grasp and panting, half with rage. 'Take that, by way of proof that making right is none so easy.' And she boxed his ears pretty sharply. He went back to his seat discomfited and out of temper. She could no longer see to look, even if her face had not burnt and her eyes dazzled, but she did not choose to move her seat, so she still preserved her stooping attitude and pretended to go on sewing.

'Eleanor Hebthwaite may be milk-and-water,' muttered he, 'but—Confound thee, lad! what art thou doing?' exclaimed Michael, as a great piece of burning wood was cast into his face by an unlucky poke of Will's. 'Thou great lounging, clumsy chap, I'll teach thee better!' and with one or two good round kicks he sent the lad whimpering away into the back-kitchen. When he had a little recovered himself from his passion, he saw Susan standing before him, her face looking strange and almost ghastly by the reversed position of the shadows, arising from the fire light shining upwards right under it.

'I tell thee what, Michael,' said she, 'that lad's motherless, but not friendless.'

'His own father leathers him, and why should not I, when he's given me such a burn on my face?' said Michael, putting up his hand to his cheek as if in pain.

'His father's his father, and there is nought more to be said. But if he did burn thee, it was by accident, and not o' purpose, as thou kicked him; it's a mercy if his ribs are not broken.'

'He howls loud enough, I'm sure. I might ha' kicked many a lad twice as hard and they'd ne'er ha' said ought but "damn ye;" but yon lad must needs cry out like a stuck pig if one touches him,' replied Michael, sullenly.

Susan went back to the window-seat, and looked absently out of the window at the drifting clouds for a minute or two, while her eyes filled with tears. Then she got up and made for the outer door which led into the back-kitchen. Before she reached it, however, she heard a low voice, whose music made her thrill, say—

'Susan, Susan!'

Her heart melted within her, but it seemed like treachery to her poor boy, like faithlessness to her dead mother, to turn to her lover while the tears which he had caused to flow were yet unwiped on Will's cheeks. So she seemed to take no heed but passed into the darkness, and, guided by the sobs, she found her way to where Willie sat crouched among disused tubs and churns.

'Come out wi' me, lad;' and they went into the orchard, where the fruit-trees were bare of leaves, but ghastly in their tattered covering of grey moss: and the soughing November wind came with long sweeps over the fells till it rattled among the crackling boughs, underneath which the brother and sister sate in the dark; he in her lap, and she hushing his head against her shoulder.

'Thou should'st na' play wi' fire. It's a naughty trick. Thou'lt suffer for it in worse ways nor this before thou'st done, I'm afeared. I should ha' hit thee twice as lungeous* kicks as Mike, if I'd been in his place. He did na' hurt thee, I am sure,' she assumed, half as a question.

'Yes, but he did. He turned me quite sick.' And he let his head fall languidly down on his sister's breast.

'Come, lad! come lad!' said she anxiously. 'Be a man. It was not much that I saw. Why, when first the red cow came, she kicked me far harder for offering to milk her before her legs were tied. See thee! here's a peppermint-drop, and I'll make thee a pasty to-night; only don't give way so, for it hurts me sore to think that Michael has done thee any harm, my pretty.'

Willie roused himself up, and put back the wet and ruffled hair from his heated face; and he and Susan rose up, and hand-in-hand went towards the house, walking slowly and quietly except for a kind of sob which Willie could not repress. Susan took him to the pump and washed his tear-stained face, till she thought she had obliterated all traces of the recent disturbance, arranging his curls for him, and then she kissed him tenderly, and led him in, hoping to find Michael in the kitchen, and make all straight between them. But the blaze had dropped down into darkness; the wood was a heap of grey ashes in which the sparks ran hither and thither; but even in the groping darkness, Susan knew by the sinking at her heart that Michael was not there. She threw another brand on the hearth and lighted the candle, and sate down to her work in silence. Willie cowered on his stool by the side of the fire, eyeing his sister from time to time, and sorry and oppressed, he knew not why, by the sight of her grave, almost stern face. No one came. They two were in the house alone. The old woman who helped Susan with the household work had gone out for the night to some friend's dwelling. William Dixon, the father, was up on the fells seeing after his sheep. Susan had no heart to prepare the evening meal.

'Susy, darling, are you angry with me?' said Willie, in his little piping, gentle voice. He had stolen up to his sister's side. 'I won't never play with the fire again; and I'll not cry if Michael does kick me. Only don't look so like dead mother—don't—don't—please don't!' he exclaimed, hiding his face on her shoulder.

'I'm not angry, Willie,' said she. 'Don't be feared on me. You want your supper, and you shall have it; and don't you be feared on Michael. He shall give reason for every hair of your head that he touches—he shall.'

When William Dixon came home, he found Susan and Willie sitting together, hand-in-hand, and apparently pretty cheerful. He bade them go to bed, for that he would sit up for Michael; and the next morning, when Susan came down, she found that Michael had started an hour before with the cart for lime. It was a long day's work; Susan knew it would be late, perhaps later than on the preceding night, before he returned—at any rate, past her usual bed-time; and on no account would she stop up a minute beyond that hour in the kitchen, whatever she might do in her bed-room. Here she sate and watched till past midnight; and when she saw him coming up the brow with the carts, she knew full well, even in that faint moonlight, that his gait was the gait of a man in liquor. But though she was annoyed and mortified to find in what way he had chosen to forget her, the fact did not disgust or shock her as it would have done many a girl, even at that day, who had not been brought up as Susan had, among a class who considered it no crime, but rather a mark of spirit, in a man to get drunk occasionally. Nevertheless, she chose to hold herself very high all the next day when Michael was, perforce, obliged to give up any attempt to do heavy work, and hung about the out-buildings and farm in a very disconsolate and sickly state. Willie had far more pity on him than Susan. Before evening, Willie and he were fast, and, on his side, ostentatious friends. Willie rode the horses down to water; Willie helped him to chop wood. Susan sate gloomily at her work, hearing an indistinct but cheerful conversation going on in the shippon,* while the cows were being milked. She almost felt irritated with her little brother, as if he were a traitor, and had gone over to the enemy in the very battle that she was fighting in his cause. She was alone with no one to speak to, while they prattled on regardless if she were glad or sorry.

Soon Willie burst in. 'Susan! Susan! come with me; I've something so pretty to show you. Round the corner of the barn—run! run!' He was dragging her along, half reluctant, half desirous of some change in that weary day. Round the corner of the barn; and caught hold of by Michael, who stood there awaiting her.

'O Willie!' cried she, 'you naughty boy. There is nothing pretty— what have you brought me here for? Let me go; I won't be held.'

'Only one word. Nay, if you wish it so much, you may go,' said Michael, suddenly loosing his hold as she struggled. But now she was free, she only drew off a step or two, murmuring something about Willie.

'You are going, then?' said Michael, with seeming sadness. 'You won't hear me say a word of what is in my heart.'

'How can I tell whether it is what I should like to hear?' replied she, still drawing back.

'That is just what I want you to tell me; I want you to hear it and then to tell me whether you like it or not.'

'Well, you may speak,' replied she, turning her back, and beginning to plait the hem of her apron.

He came close to her ear.

'I'm sorry I hurt Willie the other night. He has forgiven me. Can you?'

'You hurt him very badly,' she replied. 'But you are right to be sorry. I forgive you.'

'Stop, stop!' said he, laying his hand upon her arm. 'There is something more I've got to say. I want you to be my—what is it they call it, Susan?'

'I don't know,' said she, half laughing, but trying to get away with all her might now; and she was a strong girl, but she could not manage it.

'You do. My—what is it I want you to be?'

'I tell you I don't know, and you had best be quiet, and just let me go in, or I shall think you're as bad now as you were last night.'

'And how did you know what I was last night? It was past twelve when I came home. Were you watching? Ah, Susan! be my wife, and you shall never have to watch for a drunken husband. If I were your husband, I would come straight home, and count every minute an hour till I saw your bonny face. Now you know what I want you to be. I ask you to be my wife. Will you, my own dear Susan?'

She did not speak for some time. Then she only said, 'Ask father.' And now she was really off like a lapwing round the corner of the barn, and up in her own little room, crying with all her might, before the triumphant smile had left Michael's face where he stood.

The 'Ask father' was a mere form to be gone through. Old Daniel Hurst and William Dixon had talked over what they could respectively give their children long before this; and that was the parental way of arranging such matters. When the probable amount of worldly gear that he could give his child had been named by each father, the young folk, as they said, might take their own time in coming to the point which the old men, with the prescience of experience, saw they were drifting to; no need to hurry them, for they were both young, and Michael, though active enough, was too thoughtless, old Daniel said, to be trusted with the entire management of a farm. Meanwhile, his father would look about him, and see after all the farms that were to be let.

Michael had a shrewd notion of this preliminary understanding between the fathers, and so felt less daunted than he might otherwise have done at making the application for Susan's hand. It was all right, there was not an obstacle; only a deal of good advice, which the lover thought might have as well been spared, and which it must be confessed he did not much attend to, although he assented to every part of it. Then Susan was called down stairs, and slowly came dropping into view down the steps which led from the two family apartments into the house-place. She tried to look composed and quiet, but it could not be done. She stood side by side with her lover, with her head drooping, her cheeks burning, not daring to look up or move, while her father made the newly-betrothed a somewhat formal address in which he gave his consent, and many a piece of worldly wisdom beside. Susan listened as well as she could for the beating of her heart; but when her father solemnly and sadly referred to his own lost wife, she could keep from sobbing no longer; but throwing her apron over her face, she sate down on the bench by the dresser, and fairly gave way to pent-up tears. Oh, how strangely sweet to be comforted as she was comforted, by tender caress, and many a low-whispered promise of love! Her father sate by the fire, thinking of the days that were gone; Willie was still out of doors; but Susan and Michael felt no one's presence or absence—they only knew they were together as betrothed husband and wife.

In a week or two, they were formally told of the arrangements to be made in their favour. A small farm in the neighbourhood happened to fall vacant; and Michael's father offered to take it for him, and be responsible for the rent for the first year, while William Dixon was to contribute a certain amount of stock, and both fathers were to help towards the furnishing of the house. Susan received all this information in a quiet, indifferent way; she did not care much for any of these preparations, which were to hurry her through the happy hours; she cared least of all for the money amount of dowry and of substance. It jarred on her to be made the confidante of occasional slight repinings of Michael's, as one by one his future father-in-law set aside a beast or a pig for Susan's portion, which were not always the best animals of their kind upon the farm. But he also complained of his own father's stinginess, which somewhat, though not much, alleviated Susan's dislike to being awakened out of her pure dream of love to the consideration of worldly wealth.

But in the midst of all this bustle, Willie moped and pined. He had the same chord of delicacy running through his mind that made his body feeble and weak. He kept out of the way, and was apparently occupied in whittling and carving uncouth heads on hazel-sticks in an out-house. But he positively avoided Michael, and shrunk away even from Susan. She was too much occupied to notice this at first. Michael pointed it out to her, saying, with a laugh—

'Look at Willie! he might be a cast-off lover and jealous of me, he looks so dark and downcast at me.' Michael spoke this jest out loud, and Willie burst into tears, and ran out of the house.

'Let me go. Let me go!' said Susan (for her lover's arm was round her waist). 'I must go to him if he's fretting. I promised mother I would!' She pulled herself away, and went in search of the boy. She sought in byre and barn, through the orchard, where indeed in this leafless winter-time there was no great concealment; up into the room where the wool was usually stored in the later summer, and at last she found him, sitting at bay, like some hunted creature, up behind the wood-stack.

'What are ye gone for, lad, and me seeking you everywhere?' asked she, breathless.

'I did not know you would seek me. I've been away many a time, and no one has cared to seek me,' said he, crying afresh.

'Nonsense,' replied Susan, 'don't be so foolish, ye little good-for-nought.' But she crept up to him in the hole he had made underneath the great, brown sheafs of wood, and squeezed herself down by him. 'What for should folk seek after you, when you get away from them whenever you can?' asked she.

'They don't want me to stay. Nobody wants me. If I go with father, he says I hinder more than I help. You used to like to have me with you. But now, you've taken up with Michael, and you'd rather I was away; and I can just bide away; but I cannot stand Michael jeering at me. He's got you to love him and that might serve him.'

'But I love you, too, dearly, lad!' said she, putting her arm round his neck.

'Which on us do you like best?' said he, wistfully, after a little pause, putting her arm away, so that he might look in her face, and see if she spoke truth.

She went very red.

'You should not ask such questions. They are not fit for you to ask, nor for me to answer.'

'But mother bade you love me!' said he, plaintively.

'And so I do. And so I ever will do. Lover nor husband shall come betwixt thee and me, lad—ne'er a one of them. That I promise thee (as I promised mother before), in the sight of God and with her hearkening now, if ever she can hearken to earthly word again. Only I cannot abide to have thee fretting, just because my heart is large enough for two.'

'And thou'lt love me always?'

'Always, and ever. And the more—the more thou'lt love Michael,' said she, dropping her voice.

'I'll try,' said the boy, sighing, for he remembered many a harsh word and blow of which his sister knew nothing. She would have risen up to go away, but he held her tight, for here and now she was all his own, and he did not know when such a time might come again. So the two sate crouched up and silent, till they heard the horn blowing at the field-gate, which was the summons home to any wanderers belonging to the farm, and at this hour of the evening, signified that supper was ready. Then the two went in.

## CHAPTER II

SUSAN and Michael were to be married in April. He had already gone to take possession of his new farm, three or four miles away from Yew Nook—but that is neighbouring, according to the acceptation of the word in that thinly-populated district—when William Dixon fell ill. He came home one evening, complaining of head-ache and pains in his limbs, but seemed to loathe the posset which Susan prepared for him; the treacle-posset* which was the homely country remedy against an incipient cold. He took to his bed with a sensation of exceeding weariness, and an odd, unusual looking-back to the days of his youth, when he was a lad living with his parents, in this very house.

The next morning he had forgotten all his life since then, and did not know his own children; crying, like a newly-weaned baby, for his mother to come and soothe away his terrible pain. The doctor from Coniston said it was the typhus-fever, and warned Susan of its infectious character, and shook his head over his patient. There were no friends near to come and share her anxiety; only good, kind old Peggy, who was faithfulness itself, and one or two labourers' wives, who would fain have helped her, had not their hands been tied by their responsibility to their own families. But, somehow, Susan neither feared nor flagged. As for fear, indeed, she had no time to give way to it, for every energy of both body and mind was required. Besides, the young have had too little experience of the danger of infection to dread it much. She did indeed wish, from time to time, that Michael had been at home to have taken Willie over to his father's at High Beck; but then, again, the lad was docile and useful to her, and his fecklessness in many things might make him harshly treated by strangers; so, perhaps, it was as well that Michael was away at Appleby fair, or even beyond that—gone into Yorkshire after horses.

Her father grew worse; and the doctor insisted on sending over a nurse from Coniston. Not a professed nurse—Coniston could not have supported such a one; but a widow who was ready to go where the doctor sent her for the sake of the payment. When she came, Susan suddenly gave way; she was felled by the fever herself, and lay unconscious for long weeks. Her consciousness returned to her one spring afternoon; early spring; April—her wedding-month. There was a little fire burning in the small corner-grate, and the flickering of the blaze was enough for her to notice in her weak state. She felt that there was some one sitting on the window-side of her bed, behind the curtain, but she did not care to know who it was; it was even too great a trouble for her languid mind to consider who it was likely to be. She would rather shut her eyes, and melt off again into the gentle luxury of sleep. The next time she wakened, the Coniston nurse perceived her movement, and made her a cup of tea, which she drank with eager relish; but still they did not speak, and once more Susan lay motionless—not asleep, but strangely, pleasantly conscious of all the small chamber and household sounds; the fall of a cinder on the hearth, the fitful singing of the half-empty kettle, the cattle tramping out to field again after they had been milked, the aged step on the creaking stair—old Peggy's, as she knew. It came to her door; it stopped; the person outside listened for a moment, and then lifted the wooden latch, and looked in. The watcher by the bedside arose, and went to her. Susan would have been glad to see Peggy's face once more, but was far too weak to turn, so she lay and listened.

'How is she?' whispered one trembling, aged voice.

'Better,' replied the other. 'She's been awake, and had a cup of tea. She'll do now.'

'Has she asked after him?'

'Hush! No; she has not spoken a word.'

'Poor lass! poor lass!'

The door was shut. A weak feeling of sorrow and self-pity came over Susan. What was wrong? Whom had she loved? And dawning, dawning, slowly rose the sun of her former life, and all particulars were made distinct to her. She felt that some sorrow was coming to her, and cried over it before she knew what it was, or had strength enough to ask. In the dead of night—and she had never slept again—she softly called to the watcher, and asked—

'Who?'

'Who what?' replied the woman, with a conscious affright, ill-veiled by a poor assumption of ease. 'Lie still, there's a darling, and go to sleep. Sleep's better for you than all the doctor's stuff.'

'Who?' repeated Susan. 'Something is wrong. Who?'

'Oh, dear!' said the woman. 'There's nothing wrong. Willie has taken the turn and is doing nicely.'

'Father?'

'Well! he's all right now,' she answered, looking another way, as if seeking for something.

'Then it's Michael! Oh, me! oh, me!' She set up a succession of weak, plaintive, hysterical cries before the nurse could pacify her, by declaring that Michael had been at the house not three hours before to ask after her, and looked as well and as hearty as ever man did.

'And you heard of no harm to him since?' inquired Susan.

'Bless the lass, no, for sure! I've ne'er heard his name named since I saw him go out of the yard as stout a man as ever trod shoe-leather.'

It was well, as the nurse said afterwards to Peggy, that Susan had been so easily pacified by the equivocating answer in respect to her father. If she had pressed the questions home in his case as she did in Michael's, she would have learnt that he was dead and buried more than a month before. It was well, too, that in her weak state of convalescence (which lasted long after this first day of consciousness) her perceptions were not sharp enough to observe the sad change that had taken place in Willie. His bodily strength returned, his appetite was something enormous, but his eyes wandered continually;

his regard could not be arrested; his speech became slow, impeded, and incoherent. People began to say, that the fever had taken away the little wit Willie Dixon had ever possessed, and that they feared that he would end in being a 'natural', as they call an idiot in the Dales.

The habitual affection and obedience to Susan lasted longer than any other feeling that the boy had had previous to his illness; and, perhaps, this made her be the last to perceive what every one else had long anticipated. She felt the awakening rude when it did come. It was in this wise:—

One June evening, she sate out of doors under the yew-tree, knitting. She was pale still from her recent illness; and her languor, joined to the fact of her black dress, made her look more than usually interesting. She was no longer the buoyant self-sufficient Susan, equal to every occasion. The men were bringing in the cows to be milked, and Michael was about in the yard giving orders and directions with somewhat the air of a master, for the farm belonged of right to Willie, and Susan had succeeded to the guardianship of her brother. Michael and she were to be married as soon as she was strong enough—so, perhaps, his authoritative manner was justified; but the labourers did not like it, although they said little. They remembered him a stripling on the farm, knowing far less than they did, and often glad to shelter his ignorance of all agricultural matters behind their superior knowledge. They would have taken orders from Susan with far more willingness; nay, Willie himself might have commanded them; and from the old hereditary feeling toward the owners of land, they would have obeyed him with far greater cordiality than they now showed to Michael. But Susan was tired with even three rounds of knitting, and seemed not to notice, or to care, how things went on around her; and Willie—poor Willie!—there he stood lounging against the door-sill, enormously grown and developed, to be sure, but with restless eyes and ever-open mouth, and every now and then setting up a strange kind of howling cry, and then smiling vacantly to himself at the sound he had made. As the two old labourers passed him, they looked at each other ominously, and shook their heads.

'Willie, darling,' said Susan, 'don't make that noise—it makes my head ache.'

She spoke feebly, and Willie did not seem to hear; at any rate, he continued his howl from time to time.

'Hold thy noise, wilt 'a?' said Michael, roughly, as he passed near him, and threatening him with his fist. Susan's back was turned to the pair. The expression of Willie's face changed from vacancy to fear, and he came shambling up to Susan, and put her arm round him, and, as if protected by that shelter, he began making faces at Michael. Susan saw what was going on, and, as if now first struck by the strangeness of her brother's manner, she looked anxiously at Michael for an explanation. Michael was irritated at Willie's defiance of him, and did not mince the matter.

'It's just that the fever has left him silly—he never was as wise as other folk, and now I doubt if he will ever get right.'

Susan did not speak, but she went very pale, and her lip quivered. She looked long and wistfully at Willie's face, as he watched the motion of the ducks in the great stable-pool. He laughed softly to himself every now and then.

'Willie likes to see the ducks go overhead,' said Susan, instinctively adopting the form of speech she would have used to a young child.

'Willie, boo! Willie, boo!' he replied, clapping his hands, and avoiding her eye.

'Speak properly, Willie,' said Susan, making a strong effort at self-control, and trying to arrest his attention.

'You know who I am—tell me my name!' She grasped his arm almost painfully tight to make him attend. Now he looked at her, and, for an instant, a gleam of recognition quivered over his face; but the exertion was evidently painful, and he began to cry at the vainness of the effort to recall her name. He hid his face upon her shoulder with the old affectionate trick of manner. She put him gently away, and went into the house into her own little bedroom. She locked the door, and did not reply at all to Michael's calls for her, hardly spoke to old Peggy, who tried to tempt her out to receive some homely sympathy, and through the open casement there still came the idiotic sound of 'Willie, boo! Willie, boo!'

\*    \*    \*

## CHAPTER III

AFTER the stun of the blow came the realisation of the consequences. Susan would sit for hours trying patiently to recall and piece together fragments of recollection and consciousness in her brother's mind. She would let him go and pursue some senseless bit of play, and wait until she could catch his eye or his attention again, when she would resume her self-imposed task. Michael complained that she never had a word for him, or a minute of time to spend with him now; but she only said she must try, while there was yet a chance, to bring back her brother's lost wits. As for marriage in this state of uncertainty, she had no heart to think of it. Then Michael stormed, and absented himself for two or three days; but it was of no use. When he came back, he saw that she had been crying till her eyes were all swollen up, and he gathered from Peggy's scoldings (which she did not spare him) that Susan had eaten nothing since he went away. But she was as inflexible as ever.

'Not just yet. Only not just yet. And don't say again that I do not love you,' said she, suddenly hiding herself in his arms.

And so matters went on through August. The crop of oats was gathered in; the wheat-field was not ready as yet, when one fine day Michael drove up in a borrowed shandry,* and offered to take Willie a ride. His manner, when Susan asked him where he was going to, was rather confused; but the answer was straight and clear enough.

He had business in Ambleside. He would never lose sight of the lad, and have him back safe and sound before dark. So Susan let him go.

Before night they were at home again: Willie in high delight at a little rattling paper windmill that Michael had bought for him in the street, and striving to imitate this new sound with perpetual buzzings. Michael, too, looked pleased. Susan knew the look, although afterwards she remembered that he had tried to veil it from her, and had assumed a grave appearance of sorrow whenever he caught her eye. He put up his horse; for, although he had three miles further to go, the moon was up—the bonny harvest-moon—and he did not care how late he had to drive on such a road by such a light. After the supper which Susan had prepared for the travellers was over, Peggy went up-stairs to see Willie safe in bed; for he had to have the same care taken of him that a little child of four years old requires.

Michael drew near to Susan.

'Susan,' said he, 'I took Will to see Dr Preston, at Kendal. He's the first doctor in the county. I thought it were better for us—for you—to know at once what chance there were for him.'

'Well!' said Susan, looking eagerly up. She saw the same strange glance of satisfaction, the same instant change to apparent regret and pain. 'What did he say?' said she. 'Speak! can't you?'

'He said he would never get better of his weakness.'

'Never!'

'No; never. It's a long word, and hard to bear. And there's worse to come, dearest. The doctor thinks he will get badder from year to year. And he said, if he was us—you—he would send him off in time to Lancaster Asylum. They've ways there both of keeping such people in order and making them happy. I only tell you what he said,' continued he, seeing the gathering storm in her face.

'There was no harm in his saying it,' she replied, with great self-constraint, forcing herself to speak coldly instead of angrily. 'Folk is welcome to their opinions.'

They sate silent for a minute or two, her breast heaving with suppressed feeling.

'He's counted a very clever man,' said Michael at length.

'He may be. He's none of my clever men, nor am I going to be guided by him, whatever he may think. And I don't thank them that went and took my poor lad to have such harsh notions formed about him. If I'd been there, I could have called out the sense that is in him.'

'Well! I'll not say more to-night, Susan. You're not taking it rightly, and I'd best be gone, and leave you to think it over. I'll not deny they are hard words to hear, but there's sense in them, as I take it; and I reckon you'll have to come to 'em. Anyhow, it's a bad way of thanking me for my pains, and I don't take it well in you, Susan,' said he, getting up, as if offended.

'Michael, I'm beside myself with sorrow. Don't blame me, if I speak sharp. He and me is the only ones, you see. And mother did so charge me to have a care of him! And this is what he's come to, poor lile chap!' She began to cry, and Michael to comfort her with caresses.

'Don't,' said she. 'It's no use trying to make me forget poor Willie is a natural. I could hate myself for being happy with you, even for just a little minute. Go away, and leave me to face it out.'

'And you'll think it over, Susan, and remember what the doctor says?'

'I can't forget,' said she. She meant she could not forget what the doctor had said about the hopelessness of her brother's case; Michael had referred to the plan of sending Willie to an asylum, or madhouse, as they were called in that day and place. The idea had been gathering force in Michael's mind for some time; he had talked it over with his father, and secretly rejoiced over the possession of the farm and land which would then be his in fact, if not in law, by right of his wife. He had always considered the good penny her father could give her in his catalogue of Susan's charms and attractions. But of late he had grown to esteem her as the heiress of Yew Nook. He, too, should have land like his brother—land to possess, to cultivate, to make profit from, to bequeath. For some time he had wondered that Susan had been so much absorbed in Willie's present, that she had never seemed to look forward to his future, state. Michael had long felt the boy to be a trouble; but of late he had absolutely loathed him. His gibbering, his uncouth gestures, his loose, shambling gait, all irritated Michael inexpressibly. He did not come near the Yew Nook for a couple of days. He thought that he would leave her time to become anxious to see him and reconciled to his plan. They were strange lonely days to Susan. They were the first she had spent face to face with the sorrows that had turned her from a girl into a woman; for hitherto Michael had never let twenty-four hours pass by without coming to see her since she had had the fever. Now that he was absent, it seemed as though some cause of irritation was removed from Will, who was much more gentle and tractable than he had been for many weeks. Susan thought that she observed him making efforts at her bidding, and there was something piteous in the way in which he crept up to her, and looked wistfully in her face, as if asking her to restore him the faculties that he felt to be wanting.

'I never will let thee go, lad. Never! There's no knowing where they would take thee to, or what they would do with thee. As it says in the Bible, "Nought but death shall part thee and me!"'*

The country-side was full, in those days, of stories of the brutal treatment offered to the insane; stories that were, in fact, but too well founded, and the truth of one of which only would have been a sufficient reason for the strong prejudice existing against all such places. Each succeeding hour that Susan passed, alone, or with the poor affectionate lad for her sole companion, served to deepen her solemn resolution never to part with him. So, when Michael came, he was annoyed and surprised by the calm way in which she spoke, as if following Dr Preston's advice was utterly and entirely out of the question.

He had expected nothing less than a consent, reluctant it might be, but still a consent; and he was extremely irritated. He could have repressed his anger, but he chose rather to give way to it; thinking that he could thus best work upon Susan's affection, so as to gain his point. But, somehow, he over-reached himself; and now he was astonished in his turn at the passion of indignation that she burst into.

'Thou wilt not bide in the same house with him, say'st thou? There's no need for thy biding, as far as I can tell. There's solemn reason why I should bide with my own flesh and blood, and keep to the word I pledged my mother on her death-bed; but, as for thee, there's no tie that I know on to keep thee fro' going to America or Botany Bay this very night, if that were thy inclination. I will have no more of your threats to make me send my bairn away. If thou marry me, thou'lt help me to take charge of Willie. If thou doesn't choose to marry me on those terms—why, I can snap my fingers at thee, never fear. I'm not so far gone in love as that. But I will not have thee, if thou say'st in such a hectoring way that Willie must go out of the house—and the house his own too—before thou'lt set foot in it. Willie bides here, and I bide with him.'

'Thou hast maybe spoken a word too much,' said Michael, pale with rage. 'If I am free, as thou say'st, to go to Canada or Botany Bay, I reckon I'm free to live where I like, and that will not be with a natural who may turn into a madman some day, for aught I know. Choose between him and me, Susy, for I swear to thee, thou shan't have both.'

'I have chosen,' said Susan, now perfectly composed and still. 'Whatever comes of it, I bide with Willie.'

'Very well,' replied Michael, trying to assume an equal composure of manner. 'Then I'll wish you a very good night.' He went out of the house door, half-expecting to be called back again; but, instead, he heard a hasty step inside, and a bolt drawn.

'Whew!' said he to himself, 'I think I must leave my lady alone for a week or two, and give her time to come to her senses. She'll not find it so easy as she thinks to let me go.'

So he went past the kitchen-window in nonchalant style, and was not seen again at Yew Nook for some weeks. How did he pass the time? For the first day or two, he was unusually cross with all things and people that came athwart him. Then wheat-harvest began, and he was busy, and exultant about his heavy crop. Then a man came from a distance to bid for the lease of his farm, which, by his father's advice, had been offered for sale, as he himself was so soon likely to remove to the Yew Nook. He had so little idea that Susan really would remain firm to her determination, that he at once began to haggle with the man who came after his farm, showed him the crop just got in, and managed skilfully enough to make a good bargain for himself. Of course, the bargain had to be sealed at the public-house; and the companions he met with there soon became friends enough to tempt him into Langdale, where again he met with Eleanor Hebthwaite.

How did Susan pass the time? For the first day or so, she was too angry and offended to cry. She went about her household duties in a quick, sharp, jerking, yet absent way; shrinking one moment from Will, overwhelming him with remorseful caresses the next. The third day of Michael's absence, she had the relief of a good fit of crying; and after that, she grew softer and more tender; she felt how harshly she had spoken to him, and remembered how angry she had been. She made excuses for him. 'It was no wonder,' she said to herself, 'that he had been vexed with her; and no wonder he would not give in, when she had never tried to speak gently or to reason with him. She was to blame, and she would tell him so, and tell him once again all that her mother had bade her to be to Willie, and all the horrible stories she had heard about madhouses, and he would be on her side at once.'

And so she watched for his coming, intending to apologise as soon as ever she saw him. She hurried over her household work, in order to sit quietly at her sewing, and hear the first distant sound of his well-known step or whistle. But even the sound of her flying needle seemed too loud—perhaps she was losing an exquisite instant of anticipation; so she stopped sewing, and looked longingly out through the geranium leaves, in order that her eye might catch the first stir of the branches in the wood-path by which he generally came. Now and then a bird might spring out of the covert; otherwise the leaves were heavily still in the sultry weather of early autumn. Then she would take up her sewing, and, with a spasm of resolution, she would determine that a certain task should be fulfilled before she would again allow herself the poignant luxury of expectation. Sick at heart was she when the evening closed in, and the chances of that day diminished. Yet she stayed up longer than usual, thinking that if he were coming—if he were only passing along the distant road—the sight of a light in the window might encourage him to make his appearance even at that late hour, while seeing the house all darkened and shut up might quench any such intention.

Very sick and weary at heart, she went to bed; too desolate and despairing to cry, or make any moan. But in the morning hope came afresh. Another day—another chance! And so it went on for weeks. Peggy understood her young mistress's sorrow full well, and respected it by her silence on the subject. Willie seemed happier now that the irritation of Michael's presence was removed; for the poor idiot had a sort of antipathy to Michael, which was a kind of heart's echo to the repugnance in which the latter held him. Altogether, just at this time, Willie was the happiest of the three.

As Susan went into Coniston, to sell her butter, one Saturday, some inconsiderate person told her that she had seen Michael Hurst the night before. I said inconsiderate, but I might rather have said unobservant; for any one who had spent half-an-hour in Susan Dixon's company might have seen that she disliked having any reference made to the subjects nearest her heart, were they joyous or grievous. Now she went a little paler than usual (and she had never recovered her colour since she had had the fever), and tried to keep silence. But an irrepressible pang forced out the question—

'Where?'

'At Thomas Applethwaite's, in Langdale. They had a kind of harvest-home, and he were there among the young folk, and very thick wi' Nelly Hebthwaite, old Thomas's niece. Thou'lt have to look after him a bit, Susan!'

She neither smiled nor sighed. The neighbour who had been speaking to her was struck with the grey stillness of her face. Susan herself felt how well her self-command was obeyed by every little muscle, and said to herself in her Spartan manner, 'I can bear it without either wincing or blenching.' She went home early, at a tearing, passionate pace, trampling and breaking through all obstacles of briar or bush. Willie was moping in her absence—hanging listlessly on the farm-yard gate to watch for her. When he saw her, he set up one of his strange, inarticulate cries, of which she was now learning the meaning, and came towards her with his loose, galloping run, head and limbs all shaking and wagging with pleasant excitement.

Suddenly she turned from him, and burst into tears. She sate down on a stone by the wayside, not a hundred yards from home, and buried her face in her hands, and gave way to a passion of pent-up sorrow; so terrible and full of agony were her low cries, that the idiot stood by her, aghast and silent. All his joy gone for the time, but not, like her joy, turned into ashes. Some thought struck him. Yes! the sight of her woe made him think, great as the exertion was. He ran, and stumbled, and shambled home, buzzing with his lips all the time. She never missed him. He came back in a trice, bringing with him his cherished paper windmill, bought on that fatal day when Michael had taken him into Kendal to have his doom of perpetual idiocy pronounced. He thrust it into Susan's face, her hands, her lap, regardless of the injury his frail plaything thereby received. He leapt before her to think how he had cured all heart-sorrow, buzzing louder than ever. Susan looked up at him, and that glance of her sad eyes sobered him. He began to whimper, he knew not why: and she now, comforter in her turn, tried to soothe him by twirling his windmill. But it was broken; it made no noise; it would not go round. This seemed to afflict Susan more than him. She tried to make it right, although she saw the task was hopeless; and while she did so, the tears rained down unheeded from her bent head on the paper toy.

'It won't do,' said she, at last. 'It will never do again.' And, somehow, she took the accident and her words as omens of the love that was broken, and that she feared could never be pieced together more. She rose up and took Willie's hand, and the two went slowly into the house.

To her surprise, Michael Hurst sate in the house-place. House-place is a sort of better kitchen, where no cookery is done, but which is reserved for state occasions. Michael had gone in there because he was accompanied by his only sister, a woman older than himself, who was well married beyond Keswick, and who now came for the first time to make acquaintance with Susan. Michael had primed his sister with his wishes regarding Will, and the position in which he stood with Susan; and arriving at Yew Nook in the absence of the latter, he had not scrupled to conduct his sister into the guest-room, as he held Mrs Gale's worldly position in respect and admiration, and therefore wished her to be favourably impressed with all the signs of property which he was beginning to consider as Susan's greatest charms.

He had secretly said to himself, that if Eleanor Hebthwaite and Susan Dixon were equal in point of riches, he would sooner have Eleanor by far. He had begun to consider Susan as a termagant; and when he thought of his intercourse with her, recollections of her somewhat warm and hasty temper came far more readily to his mind than any remembrance of her generous, loving nature.

And now she stood face to face with him; her eyes tear-swollen, her garments dusty, and here and there torn in consequence of her rapid progress through the bushy bypaths. She did not make a favourable impression on the well-clad Mrs Gale, dressed in her best silk gown, and therefore unusually susceptible to the appearance of another. Nor were Susan's manners gracious or cordial. How could they be, when she remembered what had passed between Michael and herself the last time they met? For her penitence had faded away under the daily disappointment of these last weary weeks.

But she was hospitable in substance. She bade Peggy hurry on the kettle, and busied herself among the tea-cups, thankful that the presence of Mrs Gale, as a stranger, would prevent the immediate recurrence to the one subject which she felt must be present in Michael's mind as well as in her own. But Mrs Gale was withheld by no such feelings of delicacy. She had come ready-primed with the case, and had undertaken to bring the girl to reason. There was no time to be lost. It had been prearranged between the brother and sister that he was to stroll out into the farm-yard before his sister introduced the subject; but she was so confident in the success of her arguments, that she must needs have the triumph of a victory as soon as possible; and, accordingly, she brought a hail-storm of good reasons to bear upon Susan. Susan did not reply for a long time; she was so indignant at this intermeddling of a stranger in the deep family sorrow and shame. Mrs Gale thought she was gaining the day, and urged her arguments more pitilessly. Even Michael winced for Susan, and wondered at her silence. He shrunk out of sight, and into the shadow, hoping that his sister might prevail, but annoyed at the hard way in which she kept putting the case.

Suddenly Susan turned round from the occupation she had pretended to be engaged in, and said to him in a low voice, which yet not only vibrated itself, but made its hearers thrill through all their obtuseness—

'Michael Hurst! does your sister speak truth, think you?'

Both women looked at him for his answer; Mrs Gale without anxiety, for had she not said the very words they had spoken together before? had she not used the very arguments that he himself had suggested? Susan, on the contrary, looked to his answer as settling her doom for life; and in the gloom of her eyes you might have read more despair than hope.

He shuffled his position. He shuffled in his words.

'What is it you ask? My sister has said many things.'

'I ask you,' said Susan, trying to give a crystal clearness both to her expressions and her pronunciations, 'if, knowing as you do how Will is afflicted, you will help me to take that charge of him which I promised my mother on her death-bed that I would do; and which means, that I shall keep him always with me, and do all in my power to make his life happy. If you will do this, I will be your wife; if not, I remain unwed.'

'But he may get dangerous; he can be but a trouble; his being here is a pain to you, Susan, not a pleasure.'

'I ask you for either yes or no,' said she, a little contempt at his evading her question mingling with her tone. He perceived it, and it nettled him.

'And I have told you. I answered your question the last time I was here. I said I would ne'er keep house with an idiot; no more I will. So now you've gotten your answer.'

'I have,' said Susan. And she sighed deeply.

'Come, now,' said Mrs Gale, encouraged by the sigh; 'one would think you don't love Michael, Susan, to be so stubborn in yielding to what I'm sure would be best for the lad.'

'Oh! she does not care for me,' said Michael. 'I don't believe she ever did.'

'Don't I? Haven't I?' asked Susan, her eyes blazing out fire. She left the room directly, and sent Peggy in to make the tea; and catching at Will, who was lounging about in the kitchen, she went upstairs with him and bolted herself in, straining the boy to her heart, and keeping almost breathless, lest any noise she made might cause him to break out into the howls and sounds which she could not bear that those below should hear.

A knock at the door. It was Peggy.

'He wants for to see you, to wish you good-bye.'

'I cannot come. Oh, Peggy, send them away.'

It was her only cry for sympathy; and the old servant understood it. She sent them away, somehow; not politely, as I have been given to understand.

'Good go with them,' said Peggy, as she grimly watched their retreating figures. 'We're rid of bad rubbish, anyhow.' And she turned into the house, with the intention of making ready some refreshment for Susan, after her hard day at the market, and her harder evening. But in the kitchen, to which she passed through the empty house-place, making a face of contemptuous dislike at the used teacups and fragments of a meal yet standing there, she found Susan, with her sleeves tucked up and her working apron on, busied in preparing to make clap-bread,* one of the hardest and hottest domestic tasks of a Daleswoman. She looked up, and first met and then avoided Peggy's eye; it was too full of sympathy. Her own cheeks were flushed, and her own eyes were dry and burning.

'Where's the board, Peggy? We need clap-bread; and, I reckon, I've time to get through with it to-night.' Her voice had a sharp, dry tone in it, and her motions a jerking angularity about them.

Peggy said nothing, but fetched her all that she needed. Susan beat her cakes thin with vehement force. As she stooped over them, regardless even of the task in which she seemed so much occupied, she was surprised by a touch on her mouth of something—what she did not see at first. It was a cup of tea, delicately sweetened and cooled, and held to her lips, when exactly ready, by the faithful old woman. Susan held it off a hand's-breadth, and looked into Peggy's eyes, while her own filled with the strange relief of tears.

'Lass!' said Peggy, solemnly, 'thou hast done well. It is not long to bide, and then the end will come.'

'But you are very old, Peggy,' said Susan, quivering.

'It is but a day sin' I were young,' replied Peggy; but she stopped the conversation by again pushing the cup with gentle force to Susan's dry and thirsty lips. When she had drunken she fell again to her labour, Peggy heating the hearth, and doing all that she knew would be required, but never speaking another word. Willie basked close to the fire, enjoying the animal luxury of warmth, for the autumn evenings were beginning to be chilly. It was one o'clock before they thought of going to bed on that memorable night.

*       *       *

## CHAPTER IV

THE vehemence with which Susan Dixon threw herself into occupation could not last for ever. Times of languor and remembrance would come—times when she recurred with a passionate yearning to bygone days, the recollection of which was so vivid and delicious, that it seemed as though it were the reality, and the present bleak bareness the dream. She smiled anew at the magical sweetness of some touch or tone which in memory she felt and heard, and drank the delicious cup of poison, although at the very time she knew what the consequences of racking pain would be.

'This time, last year,' thought she, 'we went nutting together—this very day last year; just such a day as to-day. Purple and gold were the lights on the hills; the leaves were just turning brown; here and there on the sunny slopes the stubble-fields looked tawny; down in a cleft of yon purple slate-rock the beck fell like a silver glancing thread; all just as it is to-day. And he climbed the slender, swaying nut-trees, and bent the branches for me to gather; or made a passage through the hazel copses, from time to time claiming a toll. Who could have thought he loved me so little?—who?—who?'

Or, as the evening closed in, she would allow herself to imagine that she heard his coming step, just that she might recall the feeling of exquisite delight which had passed by without the due and passionate relish at the time. Then she would wonder how she could have had strength, the cruel, self-piercing strength, to say what she had done; to stab herself with that stern resolution, of which the scar would remain till her dying day. It might have been right; but, as she sickened, she wished she had not instinctively chosen the right. How luxurious a life haunted by no stern sense of duty must be! And many led this kind of life; why could not she? O, for one hour again of his sweet company! If he came now, she would agree to whatever he proposed.

It was a fever of the mind. She passed through it, and came out healthy, if weak. She was capable once more of taking pleasure in following an unseen guide through briar and brake.* She returned with tenfold affection to her protecting care of Willie. She acknowledged to herself that he was to be her all-in-all in life. She made him her constant companion. For his sake, as the real owner of Yew Nook, and she as his steward and guardian, she began that course of careful saving, and that love of acquisition, which afterwards gained for her the reputation of being miserly. She still thought that he might regain a scanty portion of sense—enough to require some simple pleasures and excitement, which would cost money. And money should not be wanting. Peggy rather assisted her in the formation of her parsimonious habits than otherwise; economy was the order of the district, and a certain degree of respectable avarice the characteristic of her age. Only Willie was never stinted nor hindered of anything that the two women thought could give him pleasure, for want of money.

There was one gratification which Susan felt was needed for the restoration of her mind to its more healthy state, after she had passed through the whirling fever, when duty was as nothing, and anarchy reigned; a gratification that, somehow, was to be her last burst of unreasonableness; of which she knew and recognised pain as the sure consequence. She must see him once more—herself unseen.

The week before the Christmas of this memorable year, she went out in the dusk of the early winter evening, wrapped close in shawl and cloak. She wore her dark shawl under her cloak, putting it over her head in lieu of a bonnet; for she knew that she might have to wait long in concealment. Then she tramped over the wet fell-path, shut in by misty rain for miles and miles, till she came to the place where he was lodging; a farm-house in Langdale, with a steep, stony lane leading up to it: this lane was entered by a gate out of the main road, and by the gate were a few bushes—thorns; but of them the leaves had fallen, and they offered no concealment: an old wreck of a yew-tree grew among them, however, and underneath that Susan cowered down, shrouding her face, of which the colour might betray her, with a corner of her shawl. Long did she wait; cold and cramped she became, too damp and stiff to change her posture readily. And after all, he might never come! But, she would wait till daylight, if need were; and she pulled out a crust, with which she had providently supplied herself. The rain had ceased—a dull, still, brooding weather had succeeded; it was a night to hear distant sounds. She heard horses' hoofs striking and splashing in the stones, and in the pools of the road at her back. Two horses; not well ridden, or evenly guided, as she could tell.

Michael Hurst and a companion drew near; not tipsy, but not sober. They stopped at the gate to bid each other a maudlin farewell.

Michael stooped forward to catch the latch with the hook of the stick which he carried; he dropped the stick, and it fell with one end close to Susan—indeed, with the slightest change of posture she could have opened the gate for him. He swore a great oath, and struck his horse with his closed fist, as if that animal had been to blame; then he dismounted, opened the gate, and fumbled about for his stick. When he had found it (Susan had touched the other end) his first use of it was to flog his horse well, and she had much ado to avoid its kicks and plunges. Then, still swearing, he staggered up the lane, for it was evident he was not sober enough to remount.

By daylight Susan was back and at her daily labours at Yew Nook. When the spring came, Michael Hurst was married to Eleanor Hebthwaite. Others, too, were married, and christenings made their firesides merry and glad; or they travelled, and came back after long years with many wondrous tales. More rarely, perhaps, a Dalesman changed his dwelling. But to all households more change came than to Yew Nook. There the seasons came round with monotonous sameness; or, if they brought mutation, it was of a slow, and decaying, and depressing kind. Old Peggy died. Her silent sympathy, concealed under much roughness, was a loss to Susan Dixon. Susan was not yet thirty when this happened, but she looked a middle-aged, not to say an elderly woman. People affirmed that she had never recovered her complexion since that fever, a dozen years ago, which killed her father, and left Will Dixon an idiot. But besides her grey sallowness, the lines in her face were strong, and deep, and hard. The movements of her eyeballs were slow and heavy; the wrinkles at the corners of her mouth and eyes were planted firm and sure; not an ounce of unnecessary flesh was there on her bones—every muscle started strong and ready for use. She needed all this bodily strength, to a degree that no human creature now Peggy was dead, knew of: for Willie had grown up large and strong in body, and, in general, docile enough in mind; but, every now and then, he became first moody, and then violent. These paroxysms lasted but a day or two; and it was Susan's anxious care to keep their very existence hidden and unknown. It is true, that occasional passers-by on that lonely road heard sounds at night of knocking about of furniture, blows, and cries, as of some tearing demon within the solitary farm-house; but these fits of violence usually occurred in the night; and whatever had been their consequence, Susan had tidied and redded up* all signs of aught unusual before the morning. For, above all, she dreaded lest some one might find out in what danger and peril she occasionally was, and might assume a right to take away her brother from her care. The one idea of taking charge of him had deepened and deepened with years. It was graven into her mind as the object for which she lived. The sacrifice she had made for this object only made it more precious to her. Besides, she separated the idea of the docile, affectionate, loutish, indolent Will, and kept it distinct from the terror which the demon that occasionally possessed him inspired her with. The one was her flesh and her blood—the child of her dead mother; the other was some fiend who came to torture and convulse the creature she so loved. She believed that she fought her brother's battle in holding down those tearing hands, in binding whenever she could those uplifted restless arms prompt and prone to do mischief. All the time she subdued him with her cunning or her strength, she spoke to him in pitying murmurs, or abused the third person, the fiendish enemy, in no unmeasured tones. Towards morning the paroxysm was exhausted, and he would fall asleep, perhaps only to waken with evil and renewed vigour. But when he was laid down, she would sally out to taste the fresh air, and to work off her wild sorrow in cries and mutterings to herself. The early labourers saw her gestures at a distance, and thought her as crazed as the idiot-brother who made the neighbourhood a haunted place. But did any chance person call at Yew Nook later on in the day, he would find Susan Dixon cold, calm, collected; her manner curt, her wits keen.

Once this fit of violence lasted longer than usual. Susan's strength both of mind and body was nearly worn out; she wrestled in prayer that somehow it might end before she, too, was driven mad; or, worse, might be obliged to give up life's aim, and consign Willie to a madhouse. From that moment of prayer (as she afterwards superstitiously thought) Willie calmed—and then he drooped—and then he sank—and, last of all, he died in reality from physical exhaustion.

But he was so gentle and tender as he lay on his dying bed; such strange, child-like gleams of returning intelligence came over his face, long after the power to make his dull, inarticulate sounds had departed, that Susan was attracted to him by a stronger tie than she had ever felt before. It was something to have even an idiot loving her with dumb, wistful, animal affection; something to have any creature looking at her with such beseeching eyes, imploring protection from the insidious enemy stealing on. And yet she knew that to him death was no enemy, but a true friend, restoring light and health to his poor clouded mind. It was to her that death was an enemy; to her, the survivor, when Willie died; there was no one to love her. Worse doom still, there was no one left on earth for her to love.

You now know why no wandering tourist could persuade her to receive him as a lodger; why no tired traveller could melt her heart to afford him rest and refreshment; why long habits of seclusion had given her a moroseness of manner, and how care for the interests of another had rendered her keen* and miserly.

But there was a third act in the drama of her life.

## CHAPTER V

In spite of Peggy's prophecy that Susan's life should not seem long, it did seem wearisome and endless, as the years slowly uncoiled their monotonous circles. To be sure, she might have made change for herself, but she did not care to do it. It was, indeed, more than 'not caring', which merely implies a certain degree of *vis inertiae** to be subdued before an object can be attained, and that the object itself does not seem to be of sufficient importance to call out the requisite energy. On the contrary, Susan exerted herself to avoid change and variety. She had a morbid dread of new faces, which originated in her desire to keep poor dead Willie's state a profound secret. She had a contempt for new customs; and, indeed, her old ways prospered so well under her active hand and vigilant eye, that it was difficult to know how they could be improved upon. She was regularly present in Coniston market with the best butter and the earliest chickens of the season. Those were the common farm produce that every farmer's wife about had to sell; but Susan, after she had disposed of the more feminine articles, turned to on the man's side. A better judge of a horse or cow there was not in all the country round. Yorkshire itself might have attempted to jockey her,* and would have failed. Her corn was sound and clean; her potatoes well preserved to the latest spring. People began to talk of the hoards of money Susan Dixon must have laid up somewhere; and one young ne'er-do-weel of a farmer's son undertook to make love to the woman of forty,

who looked fifty-five, if a day. He made up to her by opening a gate
on the road-path home, as she was riding on a bare-backed horse, her
purchase not an hour ago. She was off before him, refusing his civil-
ity; but the remounting was not so easy, and rather than fail she did
not choose to attempt it. She walked, and he walked alongside,
improving his opportunity, which, as he vainly thought, had been
consciously granted to him. As they drew near Yew Nook, he ventured on some expression of a wish to keep company with her. His
words were vague and clumsily arranged. Susan turned round, and
coolly asked him to explain himself. He took courage, as he thought
of her reputed wealth, and expressed his wishes this second time
pretty plainly. To his surprise, the reply she made was in a series of
smart strokes across his shoulders, administered through the medium
of a supple hazel-switch.

'Take that!' said she, almost breathless, 'to teach thee how thou
darest make a fool of an honest woman old enough to be thy mother.
If thou com'st a step nearer the house, there's a good horse-pool, and
there's two stout fellows who'll like no better fun than ducking thee.
Be off wi' thee!'

And she strode into her own premises, never looking round to see
whether he obeyed her injunction or not.

Sometimes three or four years would pass over without her hearing Michael Hurst's name mentioned. She used to wonder at such
times whether he were dead or alive. She would sit for hours by the
dying embers of her fire on a winter's evening, trying to recall the
scenes of her youth; trying to bring up living pictures of the faces
she had then known—Michael's most especially. She thought it was
possible, so long had been the lapse of years, that she might now
pass by him in the street unknowing and unknown. His outward
form she might not recognise, but himself she should feel in the thrill
of her whole being. He could not pass her unawares.

What little she did hear about him, all testified a downward tendency. He drank—not at stated times when there was no other work
to be done, but continually, whether it was seed-time or harvest. His
children were all ill at the same time; then one died, while the others
recovered, but were poor sickly things. No one dared to give Susan
any direct intelligence of her former lover; many avoided all mention
of his name in her presence; but a few spoke out either in indifference
to, or ignorance of, those bygone days. Susan heard every word,

every whisper, every sound that related to him. But her eye never changed, nor did a muscle of her face move.

Late one November night she sate over her fire; not a human being besides herself in the house; none but she had ever slept there since Willie's death. The farm-labourers had foddered the cattle and gone home hours before. There were crickets chirping all round the warm hearth-stones; there was the clock ticking with the peculiar beat Susan had known from her childhood, and which then and ever since she had oddly associated with the idea of a mother and child talking together, one loud tick, and quick—a feeble, sharp one following.

The day had been keen, and piercingly cold. The whole lift* of heaven seemed a dome of iron. Black and frost-bound was the earth under the cruel east wind. Now the wind had dropped, and as the darkness had gathered in, the weather-wise old labourers prophesied snow. The sounds in the air arose again, as Susan sate still and silent. They were of a different character to what they had been during the prevalence of the east wind. Then they had been shrill and piping; now they were like low distant growling; not unmusical, but strangely threatening. Susan went to the window, and drew aside the little curtain. The whole world was white—the air was blinded with the swift and heavy fall of snow. At present it came down straight, but Susan knew those distant sounds in the hollows and gulleys of the hills portended a driving wind and a more cruel storm. She thought of her sheep; were they all folded? the new-born calf, was it bedded well? Before the drifts were formed too deep for her to pass in and out—and by the morning she judged that they would be six or seven feet deep—she would go out and see after the comfort of her beasts. She took a lantern, and tied a shawl over her head, and went out into the open air. She had tenderly provided for all her animals, and was returning, when, borne on the blast as if some spirit-cry—for it seemed to come rather down from the skies than from any creature standing on earth's level—she heard a voice of agony; she could not distinguish words; it seemed rather as if some bird of prey was being caught in the whirl of the icy wind, and torn and tortured by its vio-lence. Again! up high above! Susan put down her lantern, and shouted loud in return; it was an instinct, for if the creature were not human, which she had doubted but a moment before, what good could her responding cry do? And her cry was seized on by the tyran-nous wind, and borne farther away in the opposite direction to that from which the call of agony had proceeded. Again she listened; no sound: then again it rang through space; and this time she was sure it was human. She turned into the house, and heaped turf and wood on the fire, which, careless of her own sensations, she had allowed to fade and almost die out. She put a new candle in her lantern; she changed her shawl for a maud,* and leaving the door on latch, she sallied out. Just at the moment when her ear first encountered the weird noises of the storm, on issuing forth into the open air, she thought she heard the words, 'O God! O help!' They were a guide to her, if words they were, for they came straight from a rock not a quarter of a mile from Yew Nook, but only to be reached, on account of its precipitous character, by a round-about path. Thither she steered, defying wind and snow, guided by here a thorn-tree, there an old, doddered oak, which had not quite lost their identity under the whelming mask of snow. Now and then she stopped to listen; but never a word or sound heard she, till right from where the copse-wood grew thick and tangled at the base of the rock, round which she was winding, she heard a moan. Into the brake—all snow in appearance—almost a plain of snow looked on from the little eminence where she stood—she plunged, breaking down the bush, stumbling, bruising herself, fighting her way; her lantern held between her teeth, and she herself using head as well as hands to butt away a passage, at whatever cost of bodily injury. As she climbed or staggered, owing to the unevenness of the snow-covered ground, where the briars and weeds of years were tangled and matted together, her foot felt something strangely soft and yielding. She lowered her lantern; there lay a man, prone on his face, nearly covered by the fast-falling flakes; he must have fallen from the rock above, as, not knowing of the circuitous path, he had tried to descend its steep, slippery face. Who could tell? it was no time for thinking. Susan lifted him up with her wiry strength; he gave no help—no sign of life; but for all that he might be alive: he was still warm; she tied her maud round him; she fastened the lantern to her apron-string; she held him tight: half-carrying, half-dragging—what did a few bruises signify to him, compared to dear life, to precious life! She got him through the brake, and down the path. There, for an instant, she stopped to take breath; but, as if stung by the Furies,* she pushed on again with almost superhuman strength. Clasping him round the waist, and leaning his dead weight against the lintel of the door, she tried to undo the latch; but now, just at this moment, a trembling faintness came over her, and a fearful dread took possession of her—that here, on the very threshold of her home, she might be found dead, and buried under the snow, when the farm-servants came in the morning. This terror stirred her up to one more effort. Then she and her companion were in the warmth of the quiet haven of that kitchen; she laid him on the settle, and sank on the floor by his side. How long she remained in this swoon she could not tell; not very long she judged by the fire, which was still red and sullenly glowing when she came to herself. She lighted the candle, and bent over her late burden to ascertain if indeed he were dead. She stood long gazing. The man lay dead. There could be no doubt about it. His filmy eyes glared at her, unshut. But Susan was not one to be affrighted by the stony aspect of death. It was not that; it was the bitter, woeful recognition of Michael Hurst!

She was convinced he was dead; but after a while she refused to believe in her conviction. She stripped off his wet outer-garments with trembling, hurried hands. She brought a blanket down from her own bed; she made up the fire. She swathed him in fresh, warm wrappings, and laid him on the flags before the fire, sitting herself at his head, and holding it in her lap, while she tenderly wiped his loose, wet hair, curly still, although its colour had changed from nut-brown to iron-grey since she had seen it last. From time to time she bent over the face afresh, sick, and fain to believe that the flicker of the fire-light was some slight convulsive motion. But the dim staring eyes struck chill to her heart. At last she ceased her delicate, busy cares; but she still held the head softly, as if caressing it. She thought over all the possibilities and chances in the mingled yarn of their lives that might, by so slight a turn, have ended far otherwise. If her mother's cold had been early tended, so that the responsibility as to her brother's weal or woe had not fallen upon her; if the fever had not taken such rough, cruel hold on Will; nay, if Mrs Gale, that hard, worldly sister, had not accompanied him on his last visit to Yew Nook—his very last before this fatal, stormy night; if she had heard his cry—cry uttered by those pale, dead lips with such wild, despairing agony, not yet three hours ago!—O! if she had but heard it sooner, he might have been saved before that blind, false step had precipitated him down the rock! In going over this weary chain of unrealised possibilities, Susan learnt the force of Peggy's words.

Life was short, looking back upon it. It seemed but yesterday since all the love of her being had been poured out, and run to waste. The intervening years—the long monotonous years that had turned her into an old woman before her time—were but a dream.

The labourers coming in the dawn of the winter's day were surprised to see the fire-light through the low kitchen-window. They knocked, and hearing a moaning answer, they entered, fearing that something had befallen their mistress. For all explanation they got these words:

'It is Michael Hurst. He was belated, and fell down the Raven's Crag. Where does Eleanor, his wife, live?'

How Michael Hurst got to Yew Nook no one but Susan ever knew. They thought he had dragged himself there, with some sore, internal bruise sapping away his minuted life. They could not have believed the superhuman exertion which had first sought him out, and then dragged him hither. Only Susan knew of that.

She gave him into the charge of her servants, and went out and saddled her horse. Where the wind had drifted the snow on one side, and the road was clear and bare, she rode, and rode fast; where the soft, deceitful heaps were massed up, she dismounted and led her steed, plunging in deep, with fierce energy, the pain at her heart urging her onwards with a sharp, digging spur.

The grey, solemn, winter's noon was more night-like than the depth of summer's night; dim-purple brooded the low skies over the white earth, as Susan rode up to what had been Michael Hurst's abode while living. It was a small farm-house carelessly kept outside, slatternly tended within. The pretty Nelly Hebthwaite was pretty still; her delicate face had never suffered from any long-enduring feeling. If anything, its expression was that of plaintive sorrow; but the soft, light hair had scarcely a tinge of grey; the wood-rose tint of complexion yet remained, if not so brilliant as in youth; the straight nose, the small mouth were untouched by time. Susan felt the contrast even at that moment. She knew that her own skin was weather-beaten, furrowed, brown—that her teeth were gone, and her hair grey and ragged. And yet she was not two years older than Nelly—she had not been, in youth, when she took account of these things. Nelly stood wondering at the strange-enough horse-woman, who stopped and panted at the door, holding her horse's bridle, and refusing to enter.

'Where is Michael Hurst?' asked Susan, at last.

'Well, I can't rightly say. He should have been at home last night, but he was off, seeing after a public-house to be let at Ulverstone, for our farm does not answer, and we were thinking—'

'He did not come home last night?' said Susan, cutting short the story, and half-affirming, half-questioning, by way of letting in a ray of the awful light before she let it full in, in its consuming wrath.

'No! he'll be stopping somewhere out Ulverstone ways. I'm sure we've need of him at home, for I've no one but lile Tommy to help me tend the beasts. Things have not gone well with us, and we don't keep a servant now. But you're trembling all over, ma'am. You'd better come in, and take something warm, while your horse rests. That's the stable-door, to your left.'

Susan took her horse there; loosened his girths, and rubbed him down with a wisp of straw. Then she looked about her for hay; but the place was bare of food, and smelt damp and unused. She went to the house, thankful for the respite, and got some clap-bread, which she mashed up in a pailful of lukewarm water. Every moment was a respite, and yet every moment made her dread the more the task that lay before her. It would be longer than she thought at first. She took the saddle off, and hung about her horse, which seemed, somehow, more like a friend than anything else in the world. She laid her cheek against its neck, and rested there, before returning to the house for the last time.

Eleanor had brought down one of her own gowns, which hung on a chair against the fire, and had made her unknown visitor a cup of hot tea. Susan could hardly bear all these little attentions: they choked her, and yet she was so wet, so weak with fatigue and excitement, that she could neither resist by voice or by action. Two children stood awkwardly about, puzzled at the scene, and even Eleanor began to wish for some explanation of who her strange visitor was.

'You've, maybe, heard him speaking of me? I'm called Susan Dixon.'

Nelly coloured, and avoided meeting Susan's eye.

'I've heard other folk speak of you. He never named your name.'

This respect of silence came like balm to Susan: balm not felt or heeded at the time it was applied, but very grateful in its effects for all that.

'He is at my house,' continued Susan, determined not to stop or quaver in the operation—the pain which must be inflicted.

'At your house? Yew Nook?' questioned Eleanor, surprised. 'How came he there?'—half jealously. 'Did he take shelter from the coming storm? Tell me—there is something—tell me, woman!'

'He took no shelter. Would to God he had!'

'O! would to God! would to God!' shrieked out Eleanor, learning all from the woeful import of those dreary eyes. Her cries thrilled through the house; the children's piping wailings and passionate cries on 'Daddy! Daddy!' pierced into Susan's very marrow. But she remained as still and tearless as the great round face upon the clock.

At last, in a lull of crying, she said—not exactly questioning, but as if partly to herself—

'You loved him, then?'

'Loved him! he was my husband! He was the father of three bonny bairns that lie dead in Grasmere Churchyard. I wish you'd go, Susan Dixon, and let me weep without your watching me! I wish you'd never come near the place.'

'Alas! alas! it would not have brought him to life. I would have laid down my own to save his. My life has been so very sad! No one would have cared if I had died. Alas! alas!'

The tone in which she said this was so utterly mournful and despairing that it awed Nelly into quiet for a time. But by-and-by she said, 'I would not turn a dog out to do it harm; but the night is clear, and Tommy shall guide you to the Red Cow. But, oh, I want to be alone! If you'll come back tomorrow, I'll be better, and I'll hear all, and thank you for every kindness you have shown him—and I do believe you've showed him kindness—though I don't know why.'

Susan moved heavily and strangely.

She said something—her words came thick and unintelligible. She had had a paralytic stroke since she had last spoken. She could not go, even if she would. Nor did Eleanor, when she became aware of the state of the case, wish her to leave. She had her laid on her own bed, and weeping silently all the while for her lost husband, she nursed Susan like a sister. She did not know what her guest's worldly position might be; and she might never be repaid. But she sold many a little trifle to purchase such small comforts as Susan needed. Susan, lying still and motionless, learnt much. It was not a severe stroke; it might be the forerunner of others yet to come, but at some distance of time. But for the present she recovered, and regained much of her former health. On her sick-bed she matured her plans. When she returned to Yew Nook, she took Michael Hurst's widow and children with her to live there, and fill up the haunted hearth with living forms that should banish the ghosts.

And so it fell out that the latter days of Susan Dixon's life were better than the former.

# THE MANCHESTER MARRIAGE*

MR AND MRS OPENSHAW came from Manchester to settle in London. He had been, what is called in Lancashire, a Salesman for a large manufacturing firm, who were extending their business, and opening a warehouse in the city; where Mr Openshaw was now to superintend their affairs. He rather enjoyed the change; having a kind of curiosity about London, which he had never yet been able to gratify in his brief visits to the metropolis. At the same time, he had an odd, shrewd, contempt for the inhabitants; whom he always pictured to himself as fine, lazy people; caring nothing but for fashion and aristocracy, and lounging away their days in Bond Street, and such places; ruining good English, and ready in their turn to despise him as a provincial. The hours that the men of business kept in the city scandalized him too, accustomed as he was to the early dinners of Manchester folk and the consequently far longer evenings.* Still, he was pleased to go to London; though he would not for the world have confessed it, even to himself, and always spoke of the step to his friends as one demanded of him by the interests of his employers, and sweetened to him by a considerable increase of salary. This, indeed, was so liberal that he might have been justified in taking a much larger house than the one he did, had he not thought himself bound to set an example to Londoners of how little a Manchester man of business cared for show. Inside, however, he furnished it with an unusual degree of comfort, and, in the winter-time, he insisted on keeping up as large fires as the grates would allow, in every room where the temperature was in the least chilly. Moreover, his northern sense of hospitality was such, that, if he were at home, he could hardly suffer a visitor to leave the house without forcing meat and drink upon him. Every servant in the house was well warmed, well fed, and kindly treated; for their master scorned all petty saving in aught that conduced to comfort; while he amused himself by following out all his accustomed habits and individual ways, in defiance of what any of his new neighbours might think.

His wife was a pretty, gentle woman, of suitable age and character. He was forty-two, she thirty-five. He was loud and decided; she soft and yielding. They had two children; or rather, I should say, she had two; for the elder, a girl of eleven, was Mrs Openshaw's child by Frank Wilson, her first husband. The younger was a little boy, Edwin, who could just prattle, and to whom his father delighted to speak in the broadest and most unintelligible Lancashire dialect, in order to keep up what he called the true Saxon accent.*

Mrs Openshaw's Christian-name was Alice, and her first husband had been her own cousin. She was the orphan niece of a sea-captain in Liverpool; a quiet, grave little creature, of great personal attraction when she was fifteen or sixteen, with regular features and a blooming complexion. But she was very shy, and believed herself to be very stupid and awkward; and was frequently scolded by her aunt, her own uncle's second wife. So when her cousin, Frank Wilson, came home from a long absence at sea, and first was kind and protective to her; secondly, attentive, and thirdly, desperately in love with her, she hardly knew how to be grateful enough to him. It is true, she would have preferred his remaining in the first or second stages of behaviour; for his violent love puzzled and frightened her. Her uncle neither helped nor hindered the love affair; though it was going on under his own eyes. Frank's stepmother had such a variable temper, that there was no knowing whether what she liked one day she would like the next, or not. At length she went to such extremes of cross-ness, that Alice was only too glad to shut her eyes and rush blindly at the chance of escape from domestic tyranny offered her by a marriage with her cousin; and, liking him better than any one in the world, except her uncle (who was at this time at sea), she went off one morn-ing and was married to him; her only bridesmaid being the house-maid at her aunt's. The consequence was, that Frank and his wife went into lodgings, and Mrs Wilson refused to see them, and turned away Norah, the warm-hearted housemaid, whom they accordingly took into their service. When Captain Wilson returned from his voyage, he was very cordial with the young couple, and spent many an evening at their lodgings, smoking his pipe, and sipping his grog; but he told them that, for quietness' sake, he could not ask them to his own house; for his wife was bitter against them. They were not, however, very unhappy about this.

The seed of future unhappiness lay rather in Frank's vehement, passionate disposition; which led him to resent his wife's shyness and want of demonstrativeness as failures in conjugal duty. He was already tormenting himself, and her too, in a slighter degree, by apprehensions and imaginations of what might befall her during his approaching absence at sea. At last, he went to his father and urged him to insist upon Alice's being once more received under his roof; the more especially as there was now a prospect of her confinement while her husband was away on his voyage. Captain Wilson was, as he himself expressed it, 'breaking up,' and unwilling to undergo the excitement of a scene; yet he felt that what his son said was true. So he went to his wife. And before Frank set sail, he had the comfort of seeing his wife installed in her old little garret in his father's house. To have placed her in the one best spare room, was a step beyond Mrs Wilson's powers of submission or generosity. The worst part about it, however, was that the faithful Norah had to be dismissed. Her place as housemaid had been filled up; and, even if it had not, she had forfeited Mrs Wilson's good opinion for ever. She comforted her young master and mistress by pleasant prophecies of the time when they would have a household of their own; of which, whatever service she might be in meanwhile, she should be sure to form a part. Almost the last action Frank did, before setting sail, was going with Alice to see Norah once more at her mother's house; and then he went away.

Alice's father-in-law grew more and more feeble as winter advanced. She was of great use to her stepmother in nursing and amusing him; and, although there was anxiety enough in the household, there was, perhaps, more of peace than there had been for years; for Mrs Wilson had not a bad heart, and was softened by the visible approach of death to one whom she loved, and, touched by the lonely condition of the young creature, expecting her first confinement in her husband's absence. To this relenting mood Norah owed the permission to come and nurse Alice when her baby was born, and to remain to attend on Captain Wilson.

Before one letter had been received from Frank (who had sailed for the East Indies and China), his father died. Alice was always glad to remember that he had held her baby in his arms, and kissed and blessed it before his death. After that, and the consequent examination into the state of his affairs, it was found that he had left far less property than people had been led by his style of living to expect; and what money there was, was all settled upon his wife, and at her disposal after her death. This did not signify much to Alice, as Frank was now first mate of his ship, and, in another voyage or two, would be captain. Meanwhile he had left her rather more than two hundred pounds (all his savings) in the bank.

It became time for Alice to hear from her husband. One letter from the Cape* she had already received. The next was to announce his arrival in India. As week after week passed over, and no intelligence of the ship having got there reached the office of the owners, and the Captain's wife was in the same state of ignorant suspense as Alice herself, her fears grew most oppressive. At length the day came when, in reply to her inquiry at the Shipping Office, they told her that the owners had given up hope of ever hearing more of the 'Betsy-Jane,' and had sent in their claim upon the Underwriters.* Now that he was gone for ever, she first felt a yearning, longing love for the kind cousin, the dear friend, the sympathizing protector, whom she should never see again;—first felt a passionate desire to show him his child, whom she had hitherto rather craved to have all to herself—her own sole possession. Her grief was, however, noiseless, and quiet—rather to the scandal of Mrs Wilson; who bewailed her stepson as if he and she had always lived together in perfect harmony, and who evidently thought it her duty to burst into fresh tears at every strange face she saw; dwelling on his poor young widow's desolate state, and the helplessness of the fatherless child, with an unction,* as if she liked the excitement of the sorrowful story.

So passed away the first days of Alice's widowhood. By-and-by things subsided into their natural and tranquil course. But, as if this young creature was always to be in some heavy trouble, her ewe-lamb* began to be ailing, pining, and sickly. The child's mysterious illness turned out to be some affection of the spine, likely to affect health, but not to shorten life—at least, so the doctors said. But the long, dreary suffering of one whom a mother loves as Alice loved her only child, is hard to look forward to. Only Norah guessed what Alice suffered; no one but God knew.

And so it fell out, that when Mrs Wilson, the elder, came to her one day, in violent distress, occasioned by a very material diminution in the value of the property that her husband had left her,—a diminution which made her income barely enough to support herself, much less Alice—the latter could hardly understand how anything which did not touch health or life could cause such grief, and she received the intelligence with irritating composure. But when, that afternoon, the little sick child was brought in, and the grandmother—who after all loved it well—began a fresh moan over her losses to its unconscious ears—saying how she had planned to consult this or that doctor, and to give it this or that comfort or luxury in after years, but that now all chance of this had passed away—Alice's heart was touched, and she drew near to Mrs Wilson with unwonted caresses, and, in a spirit not unlike to that of Ruth,* entreated that, come what would, they might remain together. After much discussion in succeeding days, it was arranged that Mrs Wilson should take a house in Manchester, furnishing it partly with what furniture she had, and providing the rest with Alice's remaining two hundred pounds. Mrs Wilson was herself a Manchester woman, and naturally longed to return to her native town; some connections of her own, too, at that time required lodgings, for which they were willing to pay pretty handsomely. Alice undertook the active super-intendence and superior work of the household; Norah, willing, faithful Norah, offered to cook, scour, do anything in short, so that she might but remain with them.

The plan succeeded. For some years, their first lodgers remained with them, and all went smoothly,—with the one sad exception of the little girl's increasing deformity. How that mother loved that child, it is not for words to tell!

Then came a break of misfortune. Their lodgers left, and no one succeeded to them. After some months, it became necessary to remove to a smaller house; and Alice's tender conscience was torn by the idea that she ought not to be a burden to her mother-in-law, but to go out and seek her own maintenance. And leave her child! The thought came like the sweeping boom of a funeral bell over her heart.

By-and-by, Mr Openshaw came to lodge with them. He had started in life as the errand-boy and sweeper-out of a warehouse; had struggled up through all the grades of employment in it, fighting his way through the hard striving Manchester life with strong, pushing energy of character. Every spare moment of time had been sternly given up to self-teaching. He was a capital accountant, a good French and German scholar, a keen, far-seeing, tradesman,—understanding markets, and the bearing of events, both near and distant, on trade: and yet, with such vivid attention to present details, that I do not think he ever saw a group of flowers in the fields without thinking whether their colours would, or would not, form harmonious con-trasts in the coming spring muslins and prints. He went to debating societies, and threw himself with all his heart and soul into politics; esteeming, it must be owned, every man a fool or a knave who differed from him, and overthrowing his opponents rather by the loud strength of his language than the calm strength of his logic. There was something of the Yankee in all this. Indeed, his theory ran parallel to the famous Yankee motto*—'England flogs creation, and Manchester flogs England.' Such a man, as may be fancied, had had no time for falling in love, or any such nonsense. At the age when most young men go through their courting and matrimony, he had not the means of keeping a wife, and was far too practical to think of having one. And now that he was in easy circumstances, a rising man, he considered women almost as incumbrances to the world, with whom a man had better have as little to do as possible. His first impression of Alice was indistinct, and he did not care enough about her to make it distinct. 'A pretty yea-nay* kind of woman,' would have been his description of her, if he had been pushed into a corner. He was rather afraid, in the beginning, that her quiet ways arose from a listlessness and laziness of character, which would have been exceedingly discordant to his active, energetic nature. But, when he found out the punctuality with which his wishes were attended to, and her work was done; when he was called in the morning at the very stroke of the clock, his shaving-water scalding hot, his fire bright, his coffee made exactly as his peculiar fancy dictated (for he was a man who had his theory about everything based upon what he knew of science, and often perfectly original)—then he began to think: not that Alice had any peculiar merit, but that he had got into remarkably good lodgings; his restlessness wore away, and he began to consider himself as almost settled for life in them.

Mr Openshaw had been too busy, all his days, to be introspective. He did not know that he had any tenderness in his nature; and if he had become conscious of its abstract existence, he would have considered it as a manifestation of disease in some part of him. But he was decoyed into pity unawares; and pity led on to tenderness. That little helpless child—always carried about by one of the three busy women of the house, or else patiently threading coloured beads in the chair from which, by no effort of its own, could it ever move,—the great grave blue eyes, full of serious, not uncheerful, expression, giving to the small delicate face a look beyond its years,—the soft plaintive voice dropping out but few words, so unlike the continual prattle of a child,—caught Mr Openshaw's attention in spite of himself. One day—he half scorned himself for doing so—he cut short his dinner-hour to go in search of some toy, which should take the place of those eternal beads. I forget what he bought; but, when he gave the present (which he took care to do in a short, abrupt manner, and when no one was by to see him), he was almost thrilled by the flash of delight that came over that child's face, and he could not help, all through that afternoon, going over and over again the picture left on his memory, by the bright effect of unexpected joy on the little girl's face. When he returned home, he found his slippers placed by his sitting-room fire; and even more careful attention paid to his fancies than was habitual in those model lodgings. When Alice had taken the last of his tea-things away—she had been silent as usual till then—she stood for an instant with the door in her hand. Mr Openshaw looked as if he were deep in his book, though in fact he did not see a line; but was heartily wishing the woman would go, and not make any palaver of gratitude. But she only said:

'I am very much obliged to you, sir. Thank you very much,' and—was gone, even before he could send her away with a 'There, my good woman, that's enough!'

For some time longer he took no apparent notice of the child. He even hardened his heart into disregarding her sudden flush of colour and little timid smile of recognition, when he saw her by chance. But, after all, this could not last for ever; and, having a second time given way to tenderness, there was no relapse. The insidious enemy having thus entered his heart, in the guise of compassion to the child, soon assumed the more dangerous form of interest in the mother. He was aware of this change of feeling,—despised himself for it,—struggled with it; nay, internally yielded to it and cherished it, long before he suffered the slightest expression of it, by word, action, or look to escape him. He watched Alice's docile, obedient ways to her stepmother; the love which she had inspired in the rough Norah (roughened by the wear and tear of sorrow and years); but, above all, he saw the wild, deep, passionate affection existing between her and her child. They spoke little to any one else, or when any one else was by; but, when alone together, they talked, and murmured, and cooed, and chattered so continually, that Mr Openshaw first wondered what they could find to say to each other, and next became irritated because they were always so grave and silent with him. All this time, he was perpetually devising small new pleasures for the child. His thoughts ran, in a pertinacious way, upon the desolate life before her; and often he came back from his day's work loaded with the very thing Alice had been longing for, but had not been able to procure. One time, it was a little chair for drawing the little sufferer along the streets; and, many an evening that following summer, Mr Openshaw drew her along himself, regardless of the remarks of his acquaintances. One day in autumn, he put down his newspaper, as Alice came in with the breakfast, and said, in as indifferent a voice as he could assume:—

'Mrs Frank, is there any reason why we two should not put up our horses together?'

Alice stood still in perplexed wonder. What did he mean? He had resumed the reading of his newspaper, as if he did not expect any answer; so she found silence her safest course, and went on quietly arranging his breakfast, without another word passing between them. Just as he was leaving the house, to go to the warehouse as usual, he turned back and put his head into the bright, neat, tidy kitchen, where all the women breakfasted in the morning:—

'You'll think of what I said, Mrs Frank' (this was her name with the lodgers), 'and let me have your opinion upon it to-night.'

Alice was thankful that her mother and Norah were too busy talking together to attend much to this speech. She determined not to think about it at all through the day; and, of course, the effort not to think, made her think all the more. At night she sent up Norah with his tea. But Mr Openshaw almost knocked Norah down as she was going out at the door, by pushing past her and calling out, 'Mrs Frank!' in an impatient voice, at the top of the stairs.

Alice went up, rather than seem to have affixed too much meaning to his words.

'Well, Mrs Frank,' he said, 'what answer? Don't make it too long; for I have lots of office work to get through to-night.'

'I hardly know what you meant, sir,' said truthful Alice.

'Well! I should have thought you might have guessed. You're not new at this sort of work, and I am. However, I'll make it plain this time. Will you have me to be thy wedded husband, and serve me, and love me, and honour me, and all that sort of thing? Because, if you will, I will do as much by you, and be a father to your child—and that's more than is put in the Prayer-book. Now, I'm a man of my word; and what I say, I feel; and what I promise, I'll do. Now, for your answer!'

Alice was silent. He began to make the tea, as if her reply was a matter of perfect indifference to him; but, as soon as that was done, he became impatient.

'Well?' said he.

'How long, sir, may I have to think over it?'

'Three minutes!' (looking at his watch). 'You've had two already—that makes five. Be a sensible woman, say Yes, and sit down to tea with me, and we'll talk it over together; for, after tea, I shall be busy; say No' (he hesitated a moment to try and keep his voice in the same tone), 'and I shan't say another word about it, but pay up a year's rent for my rooms to-morrow, and be off. Time's up! Yes or no?'

'If you please, sir,—you have been so good to little Ailsie—'

'There, sit down comfortably by me on the sofa, and let us have our tea together. I am glad to find you are as good and sensible as I took you for.'

And this was Alice Wilson's second wooing.

Mr Openshaw's will was too strong, and his circumstances too good, for him not to carry all before him. He settled Mrs Wilson in a comfortable house of her own, and made her quite independent of lodgers. The little that Alice said with regard to future plans was in Norah's behalf.

'No,' said Mr Openshaw. 'Norah shall take care of the old lady as long as she lives; and, after that, she shall either come and live with us, or, if she likes it better, she shall have a provision for life—for your sake, missus. No one who has been good to you or the child shall go unrewarded. But even the little one will be better for some fresh stuff about her. Get her a bright, sensible girl as a nurse: one who won't go rubbing her with calf's-foot jelly as Norah does; wasting good stuff outside that ought to go in, but will follow doctors' directions; which, as you must see pretty clearly by this time, Norah won't; because they give the poor little wench pain. Now, I'm not above being nesh* for other folks myself. I can stand a good blow, and never change colour; but, set me in the operating-room in the Infirmary, and I turn as sick as a girl. Yet, if need were, I would hold the little wench on my knees while she screeched with pain, if it were to do her poor back good. Nay, nay, wench! keep your white looks for the time when it comes—I don't say it ever will But this I know, Norah will spare the child and cheat the doctor, if she can. Now, I say, give the bairn a year or two's chance, and then, when the pack of doctors have done their best—and, maybe, the old lady has gone—we'll have Norah back, or do better for her.'

The pack of doctors could do no good to little Ailsie. She was beyond their power. But her father (for so he insisted on being called, and also on Alice's no longer retaining the appellation of Mamma, but becoming henceforward Mother), by his healthy cheerfulness of manner, his clear decision of purpose, his odd turns and quirks of humour, added to his real strong love for the helpless little girl, infused a new element of brightness and confidence into her life; and, though her back remained the same, her general health was strengthened, and Alice—never going beyond a smile herself—had the pleasure of seeing her child taught to laugh.

As for Alice's own life, it was happier than it had ever been before. Mr Openshaw required no demonstration, no expressions of affection from her. Indeed, these would rather have disgusted him. Alice could love deeply, but could not talk about it. The perpetual requirement of loving words, looks, and caresses, and misconstruing their absence into absence of love, had been the great trial of her former married life. Now, all went on clear and straight, under the guidance of her husband's strong sense, warm heart, and powerful will. Year by year, their worldly prosperity increased. At Mrs Wilson's death, Norah came back to them, as nurse to the newly-born little Edwin; into which post she was not installed without a pretty strong oration on the part of the proud and happy father; who declared that if he found out that Norah ever tried to screen the boy by a falsehood, or to make him nesh either in body or mind, she should go that very day. Norah and Mr Openshaw were not on the most thoroughly cordial terms; neither of them fully recognizing or appreciating the other's best qualities.

This was the previous history of the Lancashire family who had now removed to London.

They had been there about a year, when Mr Openshaw suddenly informed his wife that he had determined to heal long-standing feuds, and had asked his uncle and aunt Chadwick to come and pay them a visit and see London. Mrs Openshaw had never seen this uncle and aunt of her husband's. Years before she had married him, there had been a quarrel. All she knew was, that Mr Chadwick was a small manufacturer in a country town in South Lancashire. She was extremely pleased that the breach was to be healed, and began making preparations to render their visit pleasant.

They arrived at last. Going to see London was such an event to them, that Mrs Chadwick had made all new linen fresh for the occasion—from nightcaps downwards; and as for gowns, ribbons, and collars, she might have been going into the wilds of Canada where never a shop is, so large was her stock. A fortnight before the day of her departure for London, she had formally called to take leave of all her acquaintance; saying she should need every bit of the intermediate time for packing up. It was like a second wedding in her imagination; and, to complete the resemblance which an entirely new wardrobe made between the two events, her husband brought her back from Manchester, on the last market-day before they set off, a gorgeous pearl and amethyst brooch, saying, 'Lunnon should see that Lancashire folks knew a handsome thing when they saw it.'

For some time after Mr and Mrs Chadwick arrived at the Openshaws' there was no opportunity for wearing this brooch; but at length they obtained an order to see Buckingham Palace,* and the spirit of loyalty demanded that Mrs Chadwick should wear her best clothes in visiting the abode of her sovereign. On her return, she hastily changed her dress; for Mr Openshaw had planned that they should go to Richmond, drink tea, and return by moonlight. Accordingly, about five o'clock, Mr and Mrs Openshaw and Mr and Mrs Chadwick set off.

The housemaid and cook sat below, Norah hardly knew where. She was always engrossed in the nursery, in tending her two children, and in sitting by the restless, excitable Ailsie till she fell asleep. By-and-by, the housemaid Bessy tapped gently at the door. Norah went to her, and they spoke in whispers.

'Nurse! there's some one down stairs wants you.'

'Wants me! Who is it?'

'A gentleman—'

'A gentleman? Nonsense!'

'Well! a man, then, and he asks for you, and he rang at the front-door bell, and has walked into the dining-room.'

'You should never have let him,' exclaimed Norah, 'master and missus out—'

'I did not want him to come in; but, when he heard you lived here, he walked past me, and sat down on the first chair, and said, "Tell her to come and speak to me." There is no gas lighted in the room, and supper is all set out.'

'He'll be off with the spoons!' exclaimed Norah, putting the housemaid's fear into words, and preparing to leave the room, first, however, giving a look to Ailsie, sleeping soundly and calmly.

Down stairs she went, uneasy fears stirring in her bosom. Before she entered the dining-room she provided herself with a candle, and, with it in her hand, she went in, looking around her in the darkness for her visitor.

He was standing up, holding by the table. Norah and he looked at each other; gradual recognition coming into their eyes.

'Norah?' at length he asked.

'Who are you?' asked Norah, with the sharp tones of alarm and incredulity. 'I don't know you:' trying, by futile words of disbelief, to do away with the terrible fact before her.

'Am I so changed?' he said, pathetically. 'I dare say I am. But, Norah, tell me!' he breathed hard, 'where is my wife? Is she—is she alive?'

He came nearer to Norah, and would have taken her hand; but she backed away from him; looking at him all the time with staring eyes, as if he were some horrible object. Yet he was a handsome, bronzed, good-looking fellow, with beard and moustache, giving him a foreign-looking aspect; but his eyes! there was no mistaking those eager, beautiful eyes—the very same that Norah had watched not half an hour ago, till sleep stole softly over them.

'Tell me, Norah—I can bear it—I have feared it so often. Is she dead?' Norah still kept silence. 'She is dead!' He hung on Norah's words and looks, as if for confirmation or contradiction.

'What shall I do?' groaned Norah. 'O, sir! why did you come? how did you find me out? where have you been? We thought you dead, we did indeed!' She poured out words and questions to gain time, as if time would help her.

'Norah! answer me this question straight, by yes or no—Is my wife dead?'

'No, she is not!' said Norah, slowly and heavily.

'O, what a relief! Did she receive my letters? But perhaps you don't know. Why did you leave her? Where is she? O, Norah, tell me all quickly!'

'Mr Frank!' said Norah at last, almost driven to bay by her terror lest her mistress should return at any moment, and find him there—unable to consider what was best to be done or said—rushing at something decisive, because she could not endure her present state: 'Mr Frank! we never heard a line from you, and the shipowners said you had gone down, you and every one else. We thought you were dead, if ever man was, and poor Miss Alice and her little sick, helpless child! O, sir, you must guess it,' cried the poor creature at last, bursting out into a passionate fit of crying, 'for indeed I cannot tell it. But it was no one's fault. God help us all this night!'

Norah had sat down. She trembled too much to stand. He took her hands in his. He squeezed them hard, as if, by physical pressure, the truth could be wrung out.

'Norah.' This time his tone was calm, stagnant as despair. 'She has married again!'

Norah shook her head sadly. The grasp slowly relaxed. The man had fainted.

There was brandy in the room. Norah forced some drops into Mr Frank's mouth, chafed his hands, and—when mere animal life returned, before the mind poured in its flood of memories and thoughts—she lifted him up, and rested his head against her knees. Then she put a few crumbs of bread taken from the supper-table, soaked in brandy, into his mouth. Suddenly he sprang to his feet.

'Where is she? Tell me this instant.' He looked so wild, so mad, so desperate, that Norah felt herself to be in bodily danger; but her time of dread had gone by. She had been afraid to tell him the truth, and then she had been a coward. Now, her wits were sharpened by the sense of his desperate state. He must leave the house. She would pity him afterwards; but now she must rather command and upbraid; for he must leave the house before her mistress came home. That one necessity stood clear before her.

'She is not here: that is enough for you to know. Nor can I say exactly where she is' (which was true to the letter if not to the spirit). 'Go away, and tell me where to find you to-morrow, and I will tell you all. My master and mistress may come back at any minute, and then what would become of me, with a strange man in the house?'

Such an argument was too petty to touch his excited mind.

'I don't care for your master and mistress. If your master is a man, he must feel for me—poor shipwrecked sailor that I am—kept for years a prisoner amongst savages, always, always, always thinking of my wife and my home—dreaming of her by night, talking to her, though she could not hear, by day. I loved her more than all heaven and earth put together. Tell me where she is, this instant, you wretched woman, who salved over* her wickedness to her, as you to do to me!'

The clock struck ten. Desperate positions require desperate measures.

'If you will leave the house now, I will come to you to-morrow and tell you all. What is more, you shall see your child now. She lies sleeping up-stairs. O, sir, you have a child, you do not know that as yet—a little weakly girl—with just a heart and soul beyond her years. We have reared her up with such care! We watched her, for we thought for many a year she might die any day, and we tended her, and no hard thing has come near her, and no rough word has ever been said to her. And now you come and will take her life into your hand, and will crush it. Strangers to her have been kind to her; but her own father—Mr Frank, I am her nurse, and I love her, and I tend her, and I would do anything for her that I could. Her mother's heart beats as hers beats; and, if she suffers a pain, her mother trembles all over. If she is happy, it is her mother that smiles and is glad. If she is growing stronger, her mother is healthy: if she dwindles, her mother languishes. If she dies—well, I don't know: it is not every one can lie down and die when they wish it. Come up stairs, Mr Frank, and see your child. Seeing her will do good to your poor heart. Then go away, in God's name, just this one night;—to-morrow, if need be, you can do anything—kill us all if you will, or show yourself a great, grand man, whom God will bless for ever and ever. Come, Mr Frank, the look of a sleeping child is sure to give peace.'

She led him up-stairs; at first almost helping his steps, till they came near the nursery door. She had well-nigh forgotten the existence of little Edwin. It struck upon her with affright as the shaded light fell over the other cot; but she skilfully threw that corner of the room into darkness, and let the light fall on the sleeping Ailsie. The child had thrown down the coverings, and her deformity, as she lay with her back to them, was plainly visible through her slight night-gown. Her little face, deprived of the lustre of her eyes, looked wan and pinched, and had a pathetic expression in it, even as she slept. The poor father looked and looked with hungry, wistful eyes, into which the big tears came swelling up slowly and dropped heavily down, as he stood trembling and shaking all over. Norah was angry with herself, for growing impatient of the length of time that long lingering gaze lasted. She thought that she waited for full half an hour before Frank stirred. And then—instead of going away—he sank down on his knees by the bedside, and buried his face in the clothes. Little Ailsie stirred uneasily. Norah pulled him up in terror. She could afford no more time, even for prayer, in her extremity of fear; for surely the next moment would bring her mistress home. She took him forcibly by the arm: but, as he was going, his eye lighted on the other bed: he stopped. Intelligence came back into his face. His hands clenched.

'His child?' he asked.

'Her child,' replied Norah. 'God watches over him,' said she instinctively; for Frank's looks excited her fears, and she needed to remind herself of the Protector of the helpless.

'God has not watched over me,' he said, in despair; his thoughts apparently recoiling on his own desolate, deserted state. But Norah had no time for pity. To-morrow she would be as compassionate as her heart prompted. At length she guided him down-stairs, and shut the outer door, and bolted it—as if by bolts to keep out facts.

Then she went back into the dining-room, and effaced all traces of his presence, as far as she could. She went up-stairs to the nursery and sat there, her head on her hand, thinking what was to come of all this misery. It seemed to her very long before her master and mistress returned; yet it was hardly eleven o'clock. She heard the loud, hearty Lancashire voices on the stairs; and, for the first time, she understood the contrast of the desolation of the poor man who had so lately gone forth in lonely despair.

It almost put her out of patience to see Mrs Openshaw come in, calmly smiling, handsomely dressed, happy, easy, to inquire after her children.

'Did Ailsie go to sleep comfortably?' she whispered to Norah.

'Yes.'

Her mother bent over her, looking at her slumbers with the soft eyes of love. How little she dreamed who had looked on her last! Then she went to Edwin, with perhaps less wistful anxiety in her countenance, but more of pride. She took off her things, to go down to supper. Norah saw her no more that night.

Beside having a door into the passage, the sleeping-nursery opened out of Mr and Mrs Openshaw's room, in order that they might have the children more immediately under their own eyes. Early the next summer morning, Mrs Openshaw was awakened by Ailsie's startled call of 'Mother! mother!' She sprang up, put on her dressing-gown, and went to her child. Ailsie was only half awake, and in a not unusual state of terror.

'Who was he mother? Tell me!'

'Who, my darling? No one is here. You have been dreaming, love. Waken up quite. See, it is broad daylight.'

'Yes,' said Ailsie, looking round her; then clinging to her mother, 'but a man was here in the night, mother.'

'Nonsense, little goose. No man has ever come near you!'

'Yes, he did. He stood there. Just by Norah. A man with hair and a beard. And he knelt down and said his prayers. Norah knows he was here, mother' (half angrily, as Mrs Openshaw shook her head in smiling incredulity).

'Well! we will ask Norah when she comes,' said Mrs Openshaw, soothingly. 'But we won't talk any more about him now. It is not five o'clock; it is too early for you to get up. Shall I fetch you a book and read to you?'

'Don't leave me, mother,' said the child, clinging to her. So Mrs Openshaw sat on the bedside talking to Ailsie, and telling her of what they had done at Richmond the evening before, until the little girl's eyes slowly closed and she once more fell asleep.

'What was the matter?' asked Mr Openshaw, as his wife returned robed.

'Ailsie wakened up in a fright, with some story of a man having been in the room to say his prayers,—a dream, I suppose.' And no more was said at the time.

Mrs Openshaw had almost forgotten the whole affair when she got up about seven o'clock. But, by-and-by, she heard a sharp altercation going on in the nursery—Norah speaking angrily to Ailsie, a most unusual thing. Both Mr and Mrs Openshaw listened in astonishment.

'Hold your tongue, Ailsie! let me hear none of your dreams; never let me hear you tell that story again!' Ailsie began to cry.

Mr Openshaw opened the door of communication, before his wife could say a word.

'Norah, come here!'

The nurse stood at the door, defiant. She perceived she had been heard, but she was desperate.

'Don't let me hear you speak in that manner to Ailsie again,' he said sternly, and shut the door.

Norah was infinitely relieved; for she had dreaded some questioning; and a little blame for sharp speaking was what she could well bear, if cross examination was let alone.

Down-stairs they went, Mr Openshaw carrying Ailsie; the sturdy Edwin coming step by step, right foot foremost, always holding his mother's hand. Each child was placed in a chair by the breakfast-table, and then Mr and Mrs Openshaw stood together at the window, awaiting their visitors' appearance and making plans for the day. There was a pause. Suddenly Mr Openshaw turned to Ailsie, and said:

'What a little goosey somebody is with her dreams, wakening up poor, tired mother in the middle of the night, with a story of a man being in the room.'

'Father! I'm sure I saw him,' said Ailsie, half crying. 'I don't want to make Norah angry; but I was not asleep, for all she says I was. I had been asleep,—and I wakened up quite wide awake, though I was so frightened. I kept my eyes nearly shut, and I saw the man quite plain. A great brown man with a beard. He said his prayers. And then he looked at Edwin. And then Norah took him by the arm and led him away, after they had whispered a bit together.'

'Now, my little woman must be reasonable,' said Mr Openshaw, who was always patient with Ailsie. 'There was no man in the house last night at all. No man comes into the house, as you know, if you think; much less goes up into the nursery. But sometimes we dream something has happened, and the dream is so like reality, that you are not the first person, little woman, who has stood out* that the thing has really happened.'

'But, indeed it was not a dream!' said Ailsie, beginning to cry.

Just then Mr and Mrs Chadwick came down, looking grave and discomposed. All during breakfast time, they were silent and uncomfortable. As soon as the breakfast things were taken away, and the children had been carried up-stairs, Mr Chadwick began, in an evidently preconcerted manner, to inquire if his nephew was certain that all his servants were honest; for, that Mrs Chadwick had that morning missed a very valuable brooch, which she had worn the day before. She remembered taking it off when she came home from Buckingham Palace. Mr Openshaw's face contracted into hard lines: grew like what it was before he had known his wife and her child. He rang the bell, even before his uncle had done speaking. It was answered by the housemaid.

'Mary, was any one here last night, while we were away?'

'A man, sir, came to speak to Norah.'

'To speak to Norah! Who was he? How long did he stay?'

'I'm sure I can't tell, sir. He came—perhaps about nine. I went up to tell Norah in the nursery, and she came down to speak to him. She let him out, sir. She will know who he was, and how long he stayed.'

She waited a moment to be asked any more questions, but she was not, so she went away.

A minute afterwards, Mr Openshaw made as though he were going out of the room; but his wife laid her hand on his arm:

'Do not speak to her before the children,' she said, in her low, quiet voice. 'I will go up and question her.'

'No! I must speak to her. You must know,' said he, turning to his uncle and aunt, 'my missus has an old servant, as faithful as ever woman was, I do believe, as far as love goes—but at the same time, who does not always speak truth, as even the missus must allow. Now, my notion is, that this Norah of ours has been come over by some good-for-nothing chap (for she's at the time o' life when they say women pray for husbands—"any, good Lord, any") and has let him into our house, and the chap has made off with your brooch, and m'appen many another thing beside. It's only saying that Norah is soft-hearted, and doesn't stick at a white lie—that's all, missus.'

It was curious to notice how his tone, his eyes, his whole face was changed, as he spoke to his wife; but he was the resolute man through all. She knew better than to oppose him; so she went up-stairs, and told Norah her master wanted to speak to her, and that she would take care of the children in the meanwhile.

Norah rose to go, without a word. Her thoughts were these:

'If they tear me to pieces, they shall never know through me. He may come,—and then, just Lord have mercy upon us all! for some of us are dead folk to a certainty. But *he* shall do it; not me.'

You may fancy, now, her look of determination, as she faced her master alone in the dining-room; Mr and Mrs Chadwick having left the affair in their nephew's hands, seeing that he took it up with such vehemence.

'Norah! Who was that man that came to my house last night?'

'Man, sir!' As if infinitely surprised; but it was only to gain time.

'Yes; the man that Mary let in; that she went up-stairs to the nursery to tell you about; that you came down to speak to; the same chap, I make no doubt, that you took into the nursery to have your talk out with; the one Ailsie saw, and afterwards dreamed about; thinking, poor wench! she saw him say his prayers, when nothing, I'll be bound, was further from his thoughts; the one that took Mrs Chadwick's brooch, value ten pounds. Now, Norah! Don't go off. I'm as sure, as my name's Thomas Openshaw, that you knew nothing of this robbery. But I do think you've been imposed on, and that's the truth. Some good-for-nothing chap has been making up to you, and you've been just like all other women, and have turned a soft place in your heart to him; and he came last night a-lovyering, and you had him up in the nursery, and he made use of his opportunities, and made off with a few things on his way down! Come, now, Norah: it's no blame to you, only you must not be such a fool again! Tell us,' he continued, 'what name he gave you, Norah. I'll be bound, it was not the right one; but it will be a clue for the police.'

Norah drew herself up. 'You may ask that question, and taunt me with my being single, and with my credulity, as you will, Master Openshaw. You'll get no answer from me. As for the brooch, and the story of theft and burglary; if any friend ever came to see me (which I defy you to prove, and deny), he'd be just as much above doing such a thing as you yourself, Mr Openshaw—and more so too; for I'm not at all sure as everything you have is rightly come by, or would be yours long, if every man had his own.' She meant, of course, his wife; but he understood her to refer to his property in goods and chattels.

'Now, my good woman,' said he, 'I'll just tell you truly, I never trusted you out and out; but my wife liked you, and I thought you had many a good point about you. If you once begin to sauce me, I'll have the police to you, and get out the truth in a court of justice, if you'll not tell it me quietly and civilly here. Now, the best thing you can do, is quietly to tell me who the fellow is. Look here! a man comes to my house; asks for you; you take him up-stairs; a valuable brooch is missing next day; we know that you, and Mary, and cook, are honest; but you refuse to tell us who the man is. Indeed, you've told one lie already about him, saying no one was here last night. Now, I just put it to you, what do you think a policeman would say to this, or a magistrate? A magistrate would soon make you tell the truth, my good woman.'

'There's never the creature born that should get it out of me,' said Norah. 'Not unless I choose to tell.'

'I've a great mind to see,' said Mr Openshaw, growing angry at the defiance. Then, checking himself, he thought before he spoke again:

'Norah, for your missus's sake I don't want to go to extremities. Be a sensible woman, if you can. It's no great disgrace, after all, to have been taken in. I ask you once more—as a friend—who was this man that you let into my house last night?'

No answer. He repeated the question in an impatient tone. Still no answer. Norah's lips were set in determination not to speak.

'Then there is but one thing to be done. I shall send for a policeman.'

'You will not,' said Norah, starting forward. 'You shall not, sir! No policeman shall touch me. I know nothing of the brooch, but I know this: ever since I was four-and-twenty, I have thought more of your wife than of myself: ever since I saw her, a poor motherless girl, put upon in her uncle's house, I have thought more of serving her than of serving myself! I have cared for her and her child, as nobody ever cared for me. I don't cast blame on you, sir, but I say it's ill giving up one's life to any one; for, at the end, they will turn round upon you, and forsake you. Why does not my missus come herself to suspect me? Maybe, she is gone for the police? But I don't stay here, either for police, or magistrate, or master. You're an unlucky lot. I believe there's a curse on you. I'll leave you this very day. Yes! I'll leave that poor Ailsie, too. I will! No good will ever come to you!'

Mr Openshaw was utterly astonished at this speech; most of which was completely unintelligible to him, as may easily be supposed. Before he could make up his mind what to say, or what to do, Norah had left the room. I do not think he had ever really intended to send for the police to this old servant of his wife's; for he had never for a moment doubted her perfect honesty. But he had intended to compel her to tell him who the man was, and in this he was baffled. He was, consequently, much irritated. He returned to his uncle and aunt in a state of great annoyance and perplexity, and told them he could get nothing out of the woman; that some man had been in the house the night before; but that she refused to tell who he was. At this moment his wife came in, greatly agitated, and asked what had happened to Norah; for that she had put on her things in passionate haste, and left the house.

'This looks suspicious,' said Mr Chadwick. 'It is not the way in which an honest person would have acted.'

Mr Openshaw kept silence. He was sorely perplexed. But Mrs Openshaw turned round on Mr Chadwick, with a sudden fierceness no one ever saw in her before.

'You don't know Norah, uncle! She is gone because she is deeply hurt at being suspected. Oh, I wish I had seen her—that I had spoken to her myself. She would have told me anything.' Alice wrung her hands.

'I must confess,' continued Mr Chadwick to his nephew, in a lower voice, 'I can't make you out. You used to be a word and a blow, and oftenest the blow first; and now, when there is every cause for suspicion, you just do nought. Your missus is a very good woman, I grant; but she may have been put upon as well as other folk, I suppose. If you don't send for the police, I shall.'

'Very well,' replied Mr Openshaw, surlily. 'I can't clear Norah. She won't clear herself, as I believe she might if she would. Only I wash my hands of it; for I am sure the woman herself is honest, and she's lived a long time with my wife, and I don't like her to come to shame.'

'But she will then be forced to clear herself. That, at any rate, will be a good thing.'

'Very well, very well! I am heart-sick of the whole business. Come, Alice, come up to the babies; they'll be in a sore way. I tell you, uncle,' he said, turning round once more to Mr Chadwick, suddenly and sharply, after his eye had fallen on Alice's wan, tearful, anxious face; 'I'll have no sending for the police, after all. I'll buy my aunt twice as handsome a brooch this very day; but I'll not have Norah suspected, and my missus plagued. There's for you!'

He and his wife left the room. Mr Chadwick quietly waited till he was out of hearing, and then said to his wife, 'For all Tom's heroics, I'm just quietly going for a detective, wench. Thou need'st know nought about it.'

He went to the police-station, and made a statement of the case. He was gratified by the impression which the evidence against Norah seemed to make. The men all agreed in his opinion, and steps were to be immediately taken to find out where she was. Most probably, as they suggested, she had gone at once to the man, who, to all appearance, was her lover. When Mr Chadwick asked how they would find her out, they smiled, shook their heads, and spoke of mysterious but infallible ways and means. He returned to his nephew's house with a very comfortable opinion of his own sagacity. He was met by his wife with a penitent face:

'O master, I've found my brooch! It was just sticking by its pin in the flounce of my brown silk, that I wore yesterday. I took it off in a hurry, and it must have caught in it: and I hung up my gown in the closet. Just now, when I was going to fold it up, there was the brooch! I'm very vexed, but I never dreamt but what it was lost!'

Her husband muttering something very like 'Confound thee and thy brooch too! I wish I'd never given it thee,' snatched up his hat, and rushed back to the station, hoping to be in time to stop the police from searching for Norah. But a detective was already gone off on the errand.

Where was Norah? Half mad with the strain of the fearful secret, she had hardly slept through the night for thinking what must be done. Upon this terrible state of mind had come Ailsie's questions, showing that she had seen the Man, as the unconscious child called her father. Lastly came the suspicion of her honesty. She was little less than crazy as she ran up stairs and dashed on her bonnet and shawl; leaving all else, even her purse, behind her. In that house she would not stay. That was all she knew or was clear about. She would not even see the children again, for fear it should weaken her. She dreaded above everything Mr Frank's return to claim his wife. She could not tell what remedy there was for a sorrow so tremendous, for her to stay to witness. The desire of escaping from the coming event was a stronger motive for her departure, than her soreness about the suspicions directed against her; although this last had been the final goad to the course she took. She walked away almost at headlong speed; sobbing as she went, as she had not dared to do during the past night for fear of exciting wonder in those who might hear her. Then she stopped. An idea came into her mind that she would leave London altogether, and betake herself to her native town of Liverpool. She felt in her pocket for her purse, as she drew near the Euston Square station with this intention. She had left it at home.

Her poor head aching, her eyes swollen with crying, she had to stand still, and think, as well as she could, where next she should bend her steps. Suddenly the thought flashed into her mind, that she would go and find our poor Mr Frank. She had been hardly kind to him the night before, though her heart had bled for him ever since. She remembered his telling her, when she inquired for his address, almost as she had pushed him out of the door, of some hotel in a street not far distant from Euston Square. Thither she went: with what intention she scarcely knew, but to assuage her conscience by telling him how much she pitied him. In her present state she felt herself unfit to counsel, or restrain, or assist, or do aught else but sympathize and weep. The people of the inn said such a person had been there; had arrived only the day before; had gone out soon after his arrival, leaving his luggage in their care; but had never come back. Norah asked for leave to sit down, and await the gentleman's return. The landlady—pretty secure in the deposit of luggage against any probable injury—showed her into a room, and quietly locked the door on the outside. Norah was utterly worn out, and fell asleep—a shivering, starting, uneasy slumber, which lasted for hours.

The detective, meanwhile, had come up with her some time before she entered the hotel, into which he followed her. Asking the land-lady to detain her for an hour or so, without giving any reason beyond showing his authority (which made the landlady applaud herself a good deal for having locked her in), he went back to the police-station to report his proceedings. He could have taken her directly; but his object was, if possible, to trace out the man who was supposed to have committed the robbery. Then he heard of the dis-covery of the brooch; and consequently did not care to return.

Norah slept till even the summer evening began to close in. Then started up. Some one was at the door. It would be Mr Frank; and she dizzily pushed back her ruffled grey hair, which had fallen over her eyes, and stood looking to see him. Instead, there came in Mr Openshaw and a policeman.

'This is Norah Kennedy,' said Mr Openshaw.

'O, sir,' said Norah, 'I did not touch the brooch; indeed I did not. O, sir, I cannot live to be thought so badly of;' and very sick and faint, she suddenly sank down on the ground. To her surprise, Mr Openshaw raised her up very tenderly. Even the policeman helped to lay her on the sofa; and, at Mr Openshaw's desire, he went for some wine and sandwiches; for the poor gaunt woman lay there almost as if dead with weariness and exhaustion.

'Norah,' said Mr Openshaw, in his kindest voice, 'the brooch is found. It was hanging to Mrs Chadwick's gown. I beg your pardon. Most truly I beg your pardon, for having troubled you about it. My wife is almost broken-hearted. Eat, Norah,—or, stay, first drink this glass of wine,' said he, lifting her head, and pouring a little down her throat.

As she drank, she remembered where she was, and who she was waiting for. She suddenly pushed Mr Openshaw away, saying, 'O, sir, you must go. You must not stop a minute. If he comes back, he will kill you.'

'Alas, Norah! I do not know who "he" is. But some one is gone away who will never come back: some one who knew you, and whom I am afraid you cared for.'

'I don't understand you, sir,' said Norah, her master's kind and sorrowful manner bewildering her yet more than his words. The policeman had left the room at Mr Openshaw's desire, and they two were alone.

'You know what I mean, when I say some one is gone who will never come back. I mean that he is dead!'

'Who?' said Norah, trembling all over.

'A poor man has been found in the Thames this morning—drowned.'

'Did he drown himself?' asked Norah, solemnly.

'God only knows,' replied Mr Openshaw, in the same tone. 'Your name and address at our house were found in his pocket: that, and his purse, were the only things that were found upon him. I am sorry to say it, my poor Norah; but you are required to go and identify him.'

'To what?' asked Norah.

'To say who it is. It is always done, in order that some reason may be discovered for the suicide—if suicide it was.—I make no doubt, he was the man who came to see you at our house last night.—it is very sad, I know.' He made pauses between each little clause, in order to try and bring back her senses, which he feared were wandering—so wild and sad was her look.

'Master Openshaw,' said she, at last, 'I've a dreadful secret to tell you—only you must never breathe it to any one, and you and I must hide it away for ever. I thought to have done it all by myself, but I see I cannot. You poor man—yes! the dead, drowned creature is, I fear, Mr Frank, my mistress's first husband!'

Mr Openshaw sat down, as if shot. He did not speak; but, after a while, he signed to Norah to go on.

'He came to me the other night—when—God be thanked! you were all away at Richmond. He asked me if his wife was dead or alive. I was a brute, and thought more of your all coming home than of his sore trial: I spoke out sharp, and said she was married again, and very content and happy: I all but turned him away: and now he lies dead and cold.'

'God forgive me!' said Mr Openshaw.

'God forgive us all!' said Norah. 'Yon poor man needs forgiveness, perhaps, less than any one among us. He had been among the savages—shipwrecked—I know not what—and he had written letters which had never reached my poor missus.'

'He saw his child!'

'He saw her—yes! I took him up, to give his thoughts another start; for I believed he was going mad on my hands. I came to seek him here, as I more than half promised. My mind misgave me when I heard he never came in. O, sir! it must be him!'

Mr Openshaw rang the bell. Norah was almost too much stunned to wonder at what he did. He asked for writing materials, wrote a letter, and then said to Norah:

'I am writing to Alice, to say I shall be unavoidably absent for a few days; that I have found you; that you are well, and send her your love, and will come home to-morrow. You must go with me to the Police Court; you must identify the body; I will pay high to keep names and details out of the papers.'

'But where are you going, sir?'

He did not answer her directly. Then he said:

'Norah! I must go with you, and look on the face of the man whom I have so injured,—unwittingly, it is true; but it seems to me as if I had killed him. I will lay his head in the grave, as if he were my only brother: and how he must have hated me! I cannot go home to my wife till all that I can do for him is done. Then I go with a dreadful secret on my mind. I shall never speak of it again, after these days are over. I know you will not, either.' He shook hands with her: and they never named the subject again, the one to the other.

Norah went home to Alice the next day. Not a word was said on the cause of her abrupt departure a day or two before. Alice had been charged by her husband, in his letter, not to allude to the supposed theft of the brooch; so she, implicitly obedient to those whom she loved both by nature and habit, was entirely silent on the subject, only treated Norah with the most tender respect, as if to make up for unjust suspicion.

Nor did Alice inquire into the reason why Mr Openshaw had been absent during his uncle and aunt's visit, after he had once said that it was unavoidable.

He came back grave and quiet; and from that time forth was curiously changed. More thoughtful, and perhaps less active; quite as decided in conduct, but with new and different rules for the guidance of that conduct. Towards Alice he could hardly be more kind than he had always been; but he now seemed to look upon her as some one sacred, and to be treated with reverence, as well as tenderness. He throve in business, and made a large fortune, one half of which was settled upon her.*

Long years after these events—a few months after her mother died—Ailsie and her 'father' (as she always called Mr Openshaw), drove to a cemetery a little way out of town, and she was carried to a certain mound by her maid, who was then sent back to the carriage. There was a head-stone, with F.W. and a date upon it. That was all. Sitting by the grave, Mr Openshaw told her the story; and for the sad fate of that poor father whom she had never seen, he shed the only tears she ever saw fall from his eyes.

# COUSIN PHILLIS

## PART I

IT is a great thing for a lad when he is first turned into the independence of lodgings. I do not think I ever was so satisfied and proud in
my life as when, at seventeen, I sate down in a little three-cornered
room above a pastry-cook's shop in the county town of Eltham. My
father had left me that afternoon, after delivering himself of a few
plain precepts, strongly expressed, for my guidance in the new
course of life on which I was entering. I was to be a clerk under the
engineer who had undertaken to make the little branch line from
Eltham to Hornby.* My father had got me this situation, which was
in a position rather above his own in life; or perhaps I should say,
above the station in which he was born and bred; for he was raising
himself every year in men's consideration and respect. He was a
mechanic by trade, but he had some inventive genius, and a great
deal of perseverance, and had devised several valuable improvements
in railway machinery. He did not do this for profit, though, as was
reasonable, what came in the natural course of things was acceptable;
he worked out his ideas, because, as he said, 'until he could put them
into shape, they plagued him by night and by day.' But this is enough
about my dear father; it is a good thing for a country where there are
many like him. He was a sturdy Independent* by descent and conviction; and this it was, I believe, which made him place me in the
lodgings at the pastry-cook's. The shop was kept by the two sisters
of our minister at home; and this was considered as a sort of safe-
guard to my morals, when I was turned loose upon the temptations
of the county town, with a salary of thirty pounds a year.

My father had given up two precious days, and put on his Sunday
clothes, in order to bring me to Eltham, and accompany me first to
the office, to introduce me to my new master (who was under some
obligations to my father for a suggestion), and next to take me to call
on the Independent minister of the little congregation at Eltham.
And then he left me; and though sorry to part with him, I now began
to taste with relish the pleasure of being my own master. I unpacked
the hamper that my mother had provided me with, and smelt the

pots of preserve with all the delight of a possessor who might break into their contents at any time he pleased. I handled and weighed in my fancy the home-cured ham, which seemed to promise me interminable feasts; and, above all, there was the fine savour of knowing that I might eat of these dainties when I liked, at my sole will, not dependent on the pleasure of any one else, however indulgent. I stowed my eatables away in the little corner cupboard—that room was all corners, and everything was placed in a corner, the fire-place, the window, the cupboard; I myself seemed to be the only thing in the middle, and there was hardly room for me. The table was made of a folding leaf under the window, and the window looked out upon the market-place; so the studies for the prosecution of which my father had brought himself to pay extra for a sitting-room for me, ran a considerable chance of being diverted from books to men and women. I was to have my meals with the two elderly Miss Dawsons in the little parlour behind the three-cornered shop downstairs; my breakfasts and dinners at least, for, as my hours in an evening were likely to be uncertain, my tea or supper was to be an independent meal.

Then, after this pride and satisfaction, came a sense of desolation. I had never been from home before, and I was an only child; and though my father's spoken maxim had been, 'Spare the rod, and spoil the child',* yet, unconsciously, his heart had yearned after me, and his ways towards me were more tender than he knew, or would have approved of in himself could he have known. My mother, who never professed sternness, was far more severe than my father: perhaps my boyish faults annoyed her more; for I remember, now that I have written the above words, how she pleaded for me once in my riper years, when I had really offended against my father's sense of right.

But I have nothing to do with that now. It is about cousin Phillis* that I am going to write, and as yet I am far enough from even saying who cousin Phillis was.

For some months after I was settled in Eltham, the new employment in which I was engaged—the new independence of my life—occupied all my thoughts. I was at my desk by eight o'clock, home to dinner at one, back at the office by two. The afternoon work was more uncertain than the morning's; it might be the same, or it might be that I had to accompany Mr Holdsworth, the managing engineer, to some point on the line between Eltham and Hornby. This I always enjoyed, because of the variety, and because of the country we traversed (which was very wild and pretty), and because I was thrown into companionship with Mr Holdsworth, who held the position of hero in my boyish mind. He was a young man of five-and-twenty or so, and was in a station above mine, both by birth and education; and he had travelled on the Continent, and wore mustachios and whiskers of a somewhat foreign fashion. I was proud of being seen with him. He was really a fine fellow in a good number of ways, and I might have fallen into much worse hands.

Every Saturday I wrote home, telling of my weekly doings—my father had insisted upon this; but there was so little variety in my life that I often found it hard work to fill a letter. On Sundays I went twice to chapel, up a dark narrow entry, to hear droning hymns, and long prayers, and a still longer sermon, preached to a small congregation, of which I was, by nearly a score of years, the youngest member. Occasionally, Mr Peters, the minister, would ask me home to tea after the second service. I dreaded the honour, for I usually sate on the edge of my chair all the evening, and answered solemn questions, put in a deep bass voice, until household prayer-time came, at eight o'clock, when Mrs Peters came in, smoothing down her apron, and the maid-of-all-work followed, and first a sermon, and then a chapter was read, and a long impromptu prayer followed, till some instinct told Mr Peters that supper-time had come, and we rose from our knees with hunger for our predominant feeling. Over supper the minister did unbend a little into one or two ponderous jokes, as if to show me that ministers were men, after all. And then at ten o'clock I went home, and enjoyed my long-repressed yawns in the three-cornered room before going to bed.

Dinah and Hannah Dawson, so their names were put on the board above the shop-door—I always called them Miss Dawson and Miss Hannah—considered these visits of mine to Mr Peters as the greatest honour a young man could have; and evidently thought that if after such privileges, I did not work out my salvation, I was a sort of modern Judas Iscariot. On the contrary, they shook their heads over my intercourse with Mr Holdsworth. He had been so kind to me in many ways, that when I cut into my ham, I hovered over the thought of asking him to tea in my room, more especially as the annual fair was being held in Eltham market-place, and the sight of the booths, the merry-go-rounds, the wild-beast shows, and such country pomps, was (as I thought at seventeen) very attractive. But when I ventured

to allude to my wish in even distant terms, Miss Hannah caught
me up, and spoke of the sinfulness of such sights, and something
about wallowing in the mire,* and then vaulted into France, and
spoke evil of the nation, and all who had ever set foot therein, till,
seeing that her anger was concentrating itself into a point, and that
that point was Mr Holdsworth, I thought it would be better to finish
my breakfast, and make what haste I could out of the sound of her
voice. I rather wondered afterwards to hear her and Miss Dawson
counting up their weekly profits with glee, and saying that a pastry-
cook's shop in the corner of the market-place, in Eltham fair
week, was no such bad thing. However, I never ventured to ask
Mr Holdsworth to my lodgings.

There is not much to tell about this first year of mine at Eltham.
But when I was nearly nineteen, and beginning to think of whiskers
on my own account, I came to know cousin Phillis, whose very existence had been unknown to me till then. Mr Holdsworth and I had
been out to Heathbridge for a day, working hard. Heathbridge was
near Hornby, for our line of railway was above half finished. Of
course, a day's outing was a great thing to tell about in my weekly
letters; and I fell to describing the country—a fault I was not often
guilty of. I told my father of the bogs, all over wild myrtle and soft
moss, and shaking ground over which we had to carry our line;
and how Mr Holdsworth and I had gone for our mid-day meals—for
we had to stay here for two days and a night—to a pretty village
hard by, Heathbridge proper; and how I hoped we should often
have to go there, for the shaking, uncertain ground was puzzling our
engineers—one end of the line going up as soon as the other was
weighted down. (I had no thought for the shareholders' interests, as
may be seen; we had to make a new line on firmer ground before the
junction railway was completed.) I told all this at great length, thankful to fill up my paper. By return letter, I heard that a second-cousin
of my mother's was married to the Independent minister of Hornby,
Ebenezer Holman by name, and lived at Heathbridge proper; the very
Heathbridge I had described, or so my mother believed, for she had
never seen her cousin Phillis Green, who was something of an heiress
(my father believed), being her father's only child, and old Thomas
Green had owned an estate of near upon fifty acres, which must have
come to his daughter. My mother's feeling of kinship seemed to have
been strongly stirred by the mention of Heathbridge; for my father

said she desired me, if ever I went thither again, to make inquiry for the Reverend Ebenezer Holman; and if indeed he lived there, I was further to ask if he had not married one Phillis Green; and if both these questions were answered in the affirmative, I was to go and introduce myself as the only child of Margaret Manning, born Moneypenny. I was enraged at myself for having named Heathbridge at all, when I found what it was drawing down upon me. One Independent minister, as I said to myself, was enough for any man; and here I knew (that is to say, I had been catechized on Sabbath mornings by) Mr Dawson, our minister at home; and I had had to be civil to old Peters at Eltham, and behave myself for five hours running whenever he asked me to tea at his house; and now, just as I felt the free air blowing about me up at Heathbridge, I was to ferret out another minister, and I should perhaps have to be catechized by him, or else asked to tea at his house. Besides, I did not like pushing myself upon strangers, who perhaps had never heard of my mother's name, and such an odd name as it was—Moneypenny; and if they had, had never cared more for her than she had for them, apparently, until this unlucky mention of Heathbridge.

Still, I would not disobey my parents in such a trifle, however irksome it might be. So the next time our business took me to Heathbridge, and we were dining in the little sanded inn-parlour,* I took the opportunity of Mr Holdsworth's being out of the room, and asked the questions which I was bidden to ask of the rosy-cheeked maid. I was either unintelligible or she was stupid; for she said she did not know, but would ask master; and of course the landlord came in to understand what it was I wanted to know; and I had to bring out all my stammering inquiries before Mr Holdsworth, who would never have attended to them, I dare say, if I had not blushed, and blundered, and made such a fool of myself.

'Yes,' the landlord said, 'the Hope Farm was in Heathbridge proper, and the owner's name was Holman, and he was an Independent minister, and, as far as the landlord could tell, his wife's Christian name was Phillis, anyhow her maiden name was Green.'

'Relations of yours?' asked Mr Holdsworth.

'No, sir—only my mother's second-cousins. Yes, I suppose they are relations. But I never saw them in my life.'

'The Hope Farm is not a stone's throw from here,' said the officious landlord, going to the window. 'If you carry your eye over yon bed of hollyhocks, over the damson-trees in the orchard yonder, you may see a stack of queer-like stone chimneys. Them is the Hope Farm chimneys; it's an old place, though Holman keeps it in good order.'

Mr Holdsworth had risen from the table with more promptitude than I had, and was standing by the window, looking. At the land-lord's last words, he turned round, smiling,—'It is not often that parsons know how to keep land in order, is it?'

'Beg pardon, sir, but I must speak as I find; and Minister Holman—we call the Church clergyman here "parson," sir; he would be a bit jealous if he heard a Dissenter called parson—Minister Holman knows what he's about as well as e'er a farmer in the neigh-bourhood. He gives up five days a week to his own work, and two to the Lord's; and it is difficult to say which he works hardest at. He spends Saturday and Sunday a-writing sermons and a-visiting his flock at Hornby; and at five o'clock on Monday morning he'll be guiding his plough in the Hope Farm yonder just as well as if he could neither read nor write. But your dinner will be getting cold, gentlemen.'

So we went back to table. After a while, Mr Holdsworth broke the silence:—'If I were you, Manning, I'd look up these relations of yours. You can go and see what they're like while we're waiting for Dobson's estimates, and I'll smoke a cigar in the garden meanwhile.'

'Thank you, sir. But I don't know them, and I don't think I want to know them.'

'What did you ask all those questions for, then?' said he, looking quickly up at me. He had no notion of doing or saying things without a purpose. I did not answer, so he continued,—'Make up your mind, and go off and see what this farmer-minister is like, and come back and tell me—I should like to hear.'

I was so in the habit of yielding to his authority, or influence, that I never thought of resisting, but went on my errand, though I remember feeling as if I would rather have had my head cut off. The landlord, who had evidently taken an interest in the event* of our discussion in a way that country landlords have, accompanied me to the house-door, and gave me repeated directions, as if I was likely to miss my way in two hundred yards. But I listened to him, for I was glad of the delay, to screw up my courage for the effort of facing unknown people and introducing myself. I went along the lane, I recollect, switching at all the taller roadside weeds, till, after a turn

or two, I found myself close in front of the Hope Farm. There was
a garden between the house and the shady, grassy lane; I afterwards
found that this garden was called the court; perhaps because
there was a low wall round it, with an iron railing on the top of the
wall, and two great gates between pillars crowned with stone balls
for a state entrance to the flagged path leading up to the front door.
It was not the habit of the place to go in either by these great gates
or by the front door; the gates, indeed, were locked, as I found,
though the door stood wide open. I had to go round by a side-path
lightly worn on a broad grassy way, which led past the court-wall,
past a horse-mount, half covered with stone-crop* and the little
wild yellow fumitory,* to another door—'the curate', as I found it
was termed by the master of the house, while the front door, 'handsome and all for show', was termed the 'rector'.* I knocked with
my hand upon the 'curate' door; a tall girl, about my own age, as I
thought, came and opened it, and stood there silent, waiting to know
my errand. I see her now—cousin Phillis. The westering sun shone
full upon her, and made a slanting stream of light into the room
within. She was dressed in dark blue cotton of some kind; up to her
throat, down to her wrists, with a little frill of the same wherever
it touched her white skin. And such a white skin as it was! I have
never seen the like. She had light hair, nearer yellow than any other
colour. She looked me steadily in the face with large, quiet eyes,
wondering, but untroubled by the sight of a stranger. I thought it
odd that so old, so full-grown as she was, she should wear a pinafore
over her gown.

Before I had quite made up my mind what to say in reply to her
mute inquiry of what I wanted there, a woman's voice called out,
'Who is it, Phillis? If it is any one for butter-milk send them round
to the back door.'

I thought I could rather speak to the owner of that voice than to
the girl before me; so I passed her, and stood at the entrance of a
room hat in hand, for this side-door opened straight into the hall or
house-place* where the family sate when work was done. There was
a brisk little woman of forty or so ironing some huge muslin cravats*
under the light of a long vine-shaded casement window. She looked
at me distrustfully till I began to speak. 'My name is Paul Manning,'
said I; but I saw she did not know the name. 'My mother's name was
Moneypenny,' said I,—'Margaret Moneypenny.'

'And she married one John Manning, of Birmingham,' said Mrs Holman, eagerly. 'And you'll be her son. Sit down! I am right glad to see you. To think of your being Margaret's son! Why, she was almost a child not so long ago. Well, to be sure, it is five-and-twenty years ago. And what brings you into these parts?'

She sate down herself, as if oppressed by her curiosity as to all the five-and-twenty years that had passed by since she had seen my mother. Her daughter Phillis took up her knitting—a long grey worsted man's stocking, I remember—and knitted away without looking at her work. I felt that the steady gaze of those deep grey eyes was upon me, though once, when I stealthily raised mine to hers, she was examining something on the wall above my head.

When I had answered all my cousin Holman's questions, she heaved a long breath, and said, 'To think of Margaret Moneypenny's boy being in our house! I wish the minister was here. Phillis, in what field is thy father to-day?'

'In the five-acre; they are beginning to cut the corn.'

'He'll not like being sent for, then, else I should have liked you to have seen the minister. But the five-acre is a good step off. You shall have a glass of wine and a bit of cake before you stir from this house, though. You're bound to go, you say, or else the minister comes in mostly when the men have their four o'clock.'

'I must go—I ought to have been off before now.'

'Here, then, Phillis, take the keys.' She gave her daughter some whispered directions, and Phillis left the room.

'She is my cousin, is she not?' I asked. I knew she was, but somehow I wanted to talk of her, and did not know how to begin.

'Yes—Phillis Holman. She is our only child—now.'

Either from that 'now', or from a strange momentary wistfulness in her eyes, I knew that there had been more children, who were now dead.

'How old is cousin Phillis?' said I, scarcely venturing on the new name, it seemed too prettily familiar for me to call her by it; but cousin Holman took no notice of it, answering straight to the purpose.

'Seventeen last May-day; but the minister does not like to hear me calling it May-day,'* said she, checking herself with a little awe. 'Phillis was seventeen on the first day of May last,' she repeated in an emended edition.

'And I am nineteen in another month,' thought I, to myself; I don't know why.

Then Phillis came in, carrying a tray with wine and cake upon it.

'We keep a house-servant,' said cousin Holman, 'but it is churning day, and she is busy.' It was meant as a little proud apology for her daughter's being the handmaiden.

'I like doing it, mother,' said Phillis, in her grave, full voice.

I felt as if I were somebody in the Old Testament—who, I could not recollect—being served and waited upon by the daughter of the host. Was I like Abraham's servant, when Rebekah gave him to drink at the well? I thought Isaac had not gone the pleasantest way to work in winning him a wife.* But Phillis never thought about such things. She was a stately, gracious young woman, in the dress and with the simplicity of a child.

As I had been taught, I drank to the health of my newfound cousin and her husband; and then I ventured to name my cousin Phillis with a little bow of my head towards her; but I was too awkward to look and see how she took my compliment. 'I must go now,' said I, rising.

Neither of the women had thought of sharing in the wine; cousin Holman had broken a bit of cake for form's sake.

'I wish the minister had been within,' said his wife, rising too. Secretly I was very glad he was not. I did not take kindly to ministers in those days, and I thought he must be a particular kind of man, by his objecting to the term May-day. But before I went, cousin Holman made me promise that I would come back on the Saturday following and spend Sunday with them; when I should see something of 'the minister'.

'Come on Friday, if you can,' were her last words as she stood at the curate-door, shading her eyes from the sinking sun with her hand.

Inside the house sate cousin Phillis, her golden hair, her dazzling complexion, lighting up the corner of the vine-shadowed room. She had not risen when I bade her good-by; she had looked at me straight as she said her tranquil words of farewell.

I found Mr Holdsworth down at the line, hard at work superintending. As soon as he had a pause, he said, 'Well, Manning, what are the new cousins like? How do preaching and farming seem to get on together? If the minister turns out to be practical as well as reverend, I shall begin to respect him.'

But he hardly attended to my answer, he was so much more occupied with directing his work-people. Indeed, my answer did not come very readily; and the most distinct part of it was the mention of the invitation that had been given me.

'Oh, of course you can go—and on Friday, too, if you like; there is no reason why not this week; and you've done a long spell of work this time, old fellow.'

I thought that I did not want to go on Friday; but when the day came, I found that I should prefer going to staying away, so I availed myself of Mr Holdsworth's permission, and went over to Hope Farm some time in the afternoon, a little later than my last visit. I found the 'curate' open to admit the soft September air, so tempered by the warmth of the sun, that it was warmer out of doors than in, although the wooden log lay smouldering in front of a heap of hot ashes on the hearth. The vine-leaves over the window had a tinge more yellow, their edges were here and there scorched and browned; there was no ironing about, and cousin Holman sate just outside the house, mending a shirt. Phillis was at her knitting indoors: it seemed as if she had been at it all the week. The many-speckled fowls were pecking about in the farmyard beyond, and the milk-cans glittered with brightness, hung out to sweeten. The court was so full of flowers that they crept out upon the low-covered wall and horse-mount, and were even to be found self-sown upon the turf that bordered the path to the back of the house. I fancied that my Sunday coat was scented for days afterwards by the bushes of sweet-briar and the fraxinella* that perfumed the air. From time to time cousin Holman put her hand into a covered basket at her feet, and threw handsful of corn down for the pigeons that cooed and fluttered in the air around, in expectation of this treat.

I had a thorough welcome as soon as she saw me. 'Now this is kind—this is right down friendly,' shaking my hand warmly. 'Phillis, your cousin Manning is come!'

'Call me Paul, will you?' said I; 'they call me so at home, and Manning in the office.'

'Well, Paul, then. Your room is all ready for you, Paul, for, as I said to the minister, "I'll have it ready whether he comes on Friday or not." And the minister said he must go up to the ash-field whether you were to come or not; but he would come home betimes to see if you were here. I'll show you to your room, and you can wash the dust off a bit.'

After I came down, I think she did not quite know what to do with me; or she might think that I was dull; or she might have work to do in which I hindered her; for she called Phillis, and bade her put on her bonnet, and go with me to the ash-field, and find father. So we set off, I in a little flutter of a desire to make myself agreeable, but wishing that my companion were not quite so tall; for she was above me in height. While I was wondering how to begin our conversation, she took up the words.

'I suppose, cousin Paul, you have to be very busy at your work all day long in general.'

'Yes, we have to be in the office at half-past eight; and we have an hour for dinner, and then we go at it again till eight or nine.'

'Then you have not much time for reading.'

'No,' said I, with a sudden consciousness that I did not make the most of what leisure I had.

'No more have I. Father always gets an hour before going a-field in the mornings, but mother does not like me to get up so early.'

'My mother is always wanting me to get up earlier when I am at home.'

'What time do you get up?'

'Oh!— ah!—sometimes half-past six: not often though;' for I remembered only twice that I had done so during the past summer.

She turned her head and looked at me.

'Father is up at three; and so was mother till she was ill. I should like to be up at four.'

'Your father up at three! Why, what has he to do at that hour?'

'What has he not to do? He has his private exercise* in his own room; he always rings the great bell which calls the men to milking; he rouses up Betty, our maid; as often as not he gives the horses their feed before the man is up—for Jem, who takes care of the horses, is an old man; and father is always loth to disturb him; he looks at the calves, and the shoulders, heels, traces,* chaff, and corn before the horses go a-field; he has often to whip-cord the plough-whips;* he sees the hogs fed; he looks into the swill-tubs, and writes his orders for what is wanted for food for man and beast; yes, and for fuel, too. And then, if he has a bit of time to spare, he comes in and reads with me—but only English; we keep Latin for the evenings, that we may have time to enjoy it; and then he calls in the men to breakfast, and cuts the boys' bread and cheese; and sees their wooden bottles filled, and sends them off to their work;—and by this time it is half-past six, and we have our breakfast. There is father,' she exclaimed, pointing out to me a man in his shirt-sleeves, taller by the head than the other two with whom he was working. We only saw him through the leaves of the ash-trees growing in the hedge, and I thought I must be confusing the figures, or mistaken: that man still looked like a very powerful labourer, and had none of the precise demureness of appearance which I had always imagined was the characteristic of a minister. It was the Reverend Ebenezer* Holman, however. He gave us a nod as we entered the stubble-field; and I think he would have come to meet us but that he was in the middle of giving some directions to his men. I could see that Phillis was built more after his type than her mother's. He, like his daughter, was largely made, and of a fair, ruddy complexion, whereas hers was brilliant and delicate. His hair had been yellow or sandy, but now was grizzled. Yet his grey hairs betokened no failure in strength. I never saw a more powerful man—deep chest, lean flanks, well-planted head. By this time we were nearly up to him; and he interrupted himself and stepped forwards; holding out his hand to me, but addressing Phillis.

'Well, my lass, this is cousin Manning, I suppose. Wait a minute, young man, and I'll put on my coat, and give you a decorous and formal welcome. But—Ned Hall, there ought to be a water-furrow* across this land: it's a nasty, stiff, clayey, dauby* bit of ground, and thou and I must fall to, come next Monday—I beg your pardon, cousin Manning—and there's old Jem's cottage wants a bit of thatch; you can do that job tomorrow while I am busy.' Then, suddenly changing the tone of his deep bass voice to an odd suggestion of chapels and preachers, he added, 'Now, I will give out the psalm, "Come all harmonious tongues", to be sung to "Mount Ephraim" tune.'*

He lifted his spade in his hand, and began to beat time with it; the two labourers seemed to know both words and music, though I did not; and so did Phillis: her rich voice followed her father's as he set the tune; and the men came in with more uncertainty, but still harmoniously. Phillis looked at me once or twice with a little surprise at my silence; but I did not know the words. There we five stood, bareheaded, excepting Phillis, in the tawny stubble-field, from which all the shocks of corn had not yet been carried—a dark wood on one side, where the woodpigeons were cooing; blue distance seen through the ash-trees on the other. Somehow, I think that if I had known the words, and could have sung, my throat would have been choked up by the feeling of the unaccustomed scene.

The hymn was ended, and the men had drawn off before I could stir. I saw the minister beginning to put on his coat, and looking at me with friendly inspection in his gaze, before I could rouse myself.

'I dare say you railway gentlemen don't wind up the day with singing a psalm together,' said he; 'but it is not a bad practice—not a bad practice. We have had it a bit earlier to-day for hospitality's sake—that's all.'

I had nothing particular to say to this, though I was thinking a great deal. From time to time I stole a look at my companion. His coat was black, and so was his waistcoat; neckcloth he had none, his strong full throat being bare above the snow-white shirt. He wore drab-coloured knee-breeches, grey worsted stockings (I thought I knew the maker), and strong-nailed shoes. He carried his hat in his hand, as if he liked to feel the coming breeze lifting his hair. After a while, I saw that the father took hold of the daughter's hand, and so, they holding each other, went along towards home. We had to cross a lane. In it were two little children, one lying prone on the grass in a passion of crying, the other standing stock still, with its finger in its mouth, the large tears slowly rolling down its cheeks for sympathy. The cause of their distress was evident; there was a broken brown pitcher, and a little pool of spilt milk on the road.

'Hollo! Hollo! What's all this?' said the minister. 'Why, what have you been about, Tommy,' lifting the little petticoated lad,* who was lying sobbing, with one vigorous arm. Tommy looked at him with surprise in his round eyes, but no affright—they were evidently old acquaintances.

'Mammy's jug!' said he, at last, beginning to cry afresh.

'Well! and will crying piece mammy's jug, or pick up spilt milk? How did you manage it, Tommy?'

'He' (jerking his head at the other) 'and me was running races.'

'Tommy said he could beat me,' put in the other.

'Now, I wonder what will make you two silly lads mind, and not run races again with a pitcher of milk between you,' said the minister, as if musing. 'I might flog you, and so save mammy the trouble; for I dare say she'll do it if I don't.' The fresh burst of whimpering from both showed the probability of this. 'Or I might take you to the Hope Farm, and give you some more milk; but then you'd be running races again, and my milk would follow that to the ground, and make another white pool. I think the flogging would be best—don't you?'

'We would never run races no more,' said the elder of the two.

'Then you'd not be boys; you'd be angels.'

'No, we shouldn't.'

'Why not?'

They looked into each other's eyes for an answer to this puzzling question. At length, one said, 'Angels is dead folk.'

'Come; we'll not get too deep into theology. What do you think of my lending you a tin can with a lid to carry the milk home in? That would not break, at any rate; though I would not answer for the milk not spilling if you ran races. That's it!'

He had dropped his daughter's hand, and now held out each of his to the little fellows. Phillis and I followed, and listened to the prattle which the minister's companions now poured out to him, and which he was evidently enjoying. At a certain point, there was a sudden burst of the tawny, ruddy-evening landscape. The minister turned round and quoted a line or two of Latin.*

'It's wonderful,' said he, 'how exactly Virgil has hit the enduring epithets, nearly two thousand years ago, and in Italy; and yet how it describes to a T what is now lying before us in the parish of Heathbridge, county—, England.'

'I dare say it does,' said I, all aglow with shame, for I had forgotten the little Latin I ever knew.

The minister shifted his eyes to Phillis's face; it mutely gave him back the sympathetic appreciation that I, in my ignorance, could not bestow.

'Oh! this is worse than the catechism,' thought I; 'that was only remembering words.'

'Phillis, lass, thou must go home with these lads, and tell their mother all about the race and the milk. Mammy must always know the truth,' now speaking to the children. 'And tell her, too, from me that I have got the best birch rod in the parish; and that if she ever thinks her children want a flogging she must bring them to me, and, if I think they deserve it, I'll give it them better than she can.' So Phillis led the children towards the dairy, somewhere in the back yard, and I followed the minister in through the 'curate' into the house-place.

'Their mother,' said he, 'is a bit of a vixen, and apt to punish her children without rhyme or reason. I try to keep the parish rod as well as the parish bull.'*

He sate down in the three-cornered chair* by the fire-side, and looked around the empty room.

'Where's the missus?' said he to himself. But she was there in a minute; it was her regular plan to give him his welcome home—by a look, by a touch, nothing more—as soon as she could after his return, and he had missed her now. Regardless of my presence, he went over the day's doings to her; and then, getting up, he said he must go and make himself 'reverend', and that then we would have a cup of tea in the parlour. The parlour was a large room with two casemented windows on the other side of the broad flagged passage leading from the rector-door to the wide staircase, with its shallow, polished oaken steps, on which no carpet was ever laid. The parlour-floor was covered in the middle by a home-made carpeting of needle-work and list.* One or two quaint family pictures of the Holman family hung round the walls; the fire-grate and irons were much ornamented with brass; and on a table against the wall between the windows, a great beau-pot* of flowers was placed upon the folio vol-umes of Matthew Henry's Bible.* It was a compliment to me to use this room, and I tried to be grateful for it; but we never had our meals there after that first day, and I was glad of it; for the large house-place, living room, dining-room, whichever you might like to call it, was twice as comfortable and cheerful. There was a rug in front of the great large fire-place, and an oven by the grate, and a crook, with the kettle hanging from it, over the bright wood-fire; everything that ought to be black and polished in that room was black and polished; and the flags, and window-curtains, and such things as were to be white and clean, were just spotless in their purity. Opposite to the fire-place, extending the whole length of the room, was an oaken shovel-board,* with the right incline for a skilful player to send the weights into the prescribed space. There were baskets of white work* about, and a small shelf of books hung against the wall, books used for reading, and not for propping up a beau-pot of flowers. I took down one or two of those books once when I was left alone in the house-place on the first evening—Virgil, Caesar, a Greek grammar—oh, dear! ah, me! and Phillis Holman's name in each of them! I shut them up, and put them back in their places, and walked as far away from the bookshelf as I could. Yes, and I gave my cousin Phillis a wide berth, although she was sitting at her work quietly enough, and her hair was looking more golden, her dark eyelashes longer, her round pillar of a throat whiter than ever. We had done tea, and we had returned into the house-place that the minister might smoke his pipe without fear of contaminating the drab damask window-curtains of the parlour. He had made himself 'reverend' by putting on one of the voluminous white muslin neckcloths that I had seen cousin Holman ironing that first visit I had paid to the Hope Farm, and by making one or two other unimportant changes in his dress. He sate looking steadily at me, but whether he saw me or not I cannot tell. At the time I fancied that he did, and was gauging me in some unknown fashion in his secret mind. Every now and then he took his pipe out of his mouth, knocked out the ashes, and asked me some fresh question. As long as these related to my acquirements or my reading, I shuffled uneasily and did not know what to answer. By-and-by he got round to the more practical subject of railroads, and on this I was more at home. I really had taken an interest in my work; nor would Mr Holdsworth, indeed, have kept me in his employment if I had not given my mind as well as my time to it; and I was, besides, full of the difficulties which beset us just then, owing to our not being able to find a steady bottom on the Heathbridge moss, over which we wished to carry our line. In the midst of all my eagerness in speaking about this, I could not help being struck with the extreme pertinence of his questions. I do not mean that he did not show ignorance of many of the details of engineering: that was to have been expected; but on the premises he had got hold of, he thought clearly and reasoned logically. Phillis—so like him as she was both in body and mind—kept stopping at her work and looking at me, trying to fully understand all that I said. I felt she did; and perhaps it made me take more pains in using clear expressions, and arranging my words, than I otherwise should.

'She shall see I know something worth knowing, though it mayn't be her dead-and-gone languages,' thought I.

'I see,' said the minister, at length. 'I understand it all. You've a clear, good head of your own, my lad,—choose how you came by it.'

'From my father,' said I, proudly. 'Have you not heard of his discovery of a new method of shunting?* It was in the *Gazette*. It was patented. I thought every one had heard of Manning's patent winch.'*

'We don't know who invented the alphabet,' said he, half smiling, and taking up his pipe.

'No, I dare say not, sir,' replied I, half offended; 'that's so long ago.' Puff—puff—puff.

'But your father must be a notable man. I heard of him once before; and it is not many a one fifty miles away whose fame reaches Heathbridge.'

'My father is a notable man, sir. It is not me that says so; it is Mr Holdsworth, and—and everybody.'

'He is right to stand up for his father,' said cousin Holman, as if she were pleading for me.

I chafed inwardly, thinking that my father needed no one to stand up for him. He was man sufficient for himself.

'Yes—he is right,' said the minister, placidly. 'Right, because it comes from his heart—right, too, as I believe, in point of fact. Else there is many a young cockerel that will stand upon a dunghill and crow about his father, by way of making his own plumage to shine. I should like to know thy father,' he went on, turning straight to me, with a kindly, frank look in his eyes.

But I was vexed, and would take no notice. Presently, having finished his pipe, he got up and left the room. Phillis put her work hastily down, and went after him. In a minute or two she returned, and sate down again. Not long after, and before I had quite recovered my good temper, he opened the door out of which he had passed, and called to me to come to him. I went across a narrow stone passage into a strange, many-cornered room, not ten feet in area, part study, part counting house, looking into the farm-yard; with a desk to sit at, a desk to stand at, a spittoon, a set of shelves with old divinity books upon them; another, smaller, filled with books on farriery,* farming, manures, and such subjects, with pieces of paper containing memoranda stuck against the whitewashed walls with wafers, nails, pins, anything that came readiest to hand; a box of carpenter's tools on the floor, and some manuscripts in short-hand on the desk.

He turned round, half laughing. 'That foolish girl of mine thinks I have vexed you'—putting his large, powerful hand on my shoulder. ' "Nay," says I, "kindly meant is kindly taken"*—is it not so?'

'It was not quite, sir,' replied I, vanquished by his manner; 'but it shall be in future.'

'Come, that's right. You and I shall be friends. Indeed, it's not many a one I would bring in here. But I was reading a book this morning, and I could not make it out; it is a book that was left here by mistake one day; I had subscribed to Brother Robinson's sermons; and I was glad to see this instead of them, for sermons though they be, they're . . . well, never mind! I took 'em both, and made my old coat do a bit longer; but all's fish that comes to my net.* I have fewer books than leisure to read them, and I have a prodigious big appetite. Here it is.'

It was a volume of stiff mechanics, involving many technical terms, and some rather deep mathematics. These last, which would have puzzled me, seemed easy enough to him; all that he wanted was the explanations of the technical words, which I could easily give.

While he was looking through the book to find the places where he had been puzzled, my wandering eye caught on some of the papers on the wall, and I could not help reading one, which has stuck by me ever since. At first, it seemed a kind of weekly diary; but then I saw that the seven days were portioned out for special prayers and intercessions: Monday for his family, Tuesday for enemies, Wednesday for the Independent churches, Thursday for all other churches, Friday for persons afflicted, Saturday for his own soul, Sunday for all wanderers and sinners, that they might be brought home to the fold.

We were called back into the house-place to have supper. A door opening into the kitchen was opened; and all stood up in both rooms, while the minister, tall, large, one hand resting on the spread table, the other lifted up, said, in the deep voice that would have been loud had it not been so full and rich, but without the peculiar accent or twang that I believe is considered devout by some people, 'Whether we eat or drink, or whatsoever we do, let us do all to the glory of God.'*

The supper was an immense meat-pie. We of the house-place were helped first; then the minister hit the handle of his buck-horn carving-knife on the table once, and said,—

'Now or never,' which meant, did any of us want any more; and when we had all declined, either by silence or by words, he knocked twice with his knife on the table, and Betty came in through the open door, and carried off the great dish to the kitchen, where an old man and a young one, and a help-girl, were awaiting their meal.

'Shut the door, if you will,' said the minister to Betty.

'That's in honour of you,' said cousin Holman, in a tone of satisfaction, as the door was shut. 'When we've no stranger with us, the minister is so fond of keeping the door open, and talking to the men and maids, just as much as to Phillis and me.'

'It brings us all together like a household just before we meet as a household in prayer,' said he, in explanation. 'But to go back to what we were talking about—can you tell me of any simple book on dynamics that I could put in my pocket, and study a little at leisure times in the day?'

'Leisure times, father?' said Phillis, with a nearer approach to a smile than I had yet seen on her face.

'Yes; leisure times, daughter. There is many an odd minute lost in waiting for other folk; and now that railroads are coming so near us, it behoves us to know something about them.'

I thought of his own description of his 'prodigious big appetite' for learning. And he had a good appetite of his own for the more material victual before him. But I saw, or fancied I saw, that he had some rule for himself in the matter both of food and drink.

As soon as supper was done the household assembled for prayer. It was a long impromptu evening prayer; and it would have seemed desultory enough had I not had a glimpse of the kind of day that preceded it, and so been able to find a clue to the thoughts that preceded the disjointed utterances; for he kept there kneeling down in the centre of a circle, his eyes shut, his outstretched hands pressed palm to palm—sometimes with a long pause of silence, as if waiting to see if there was anything else he wished to 'lay before the Lord' (to use his own expression)—before he concluded with the blessing. He prayed for the cattle and live creatures, rather to my surprise; for my attention had begun to wander, till it was recalled by the familiar words.

And here I must not forget to name an odd incident at the conclusion of the prayer, and before we had risen from our knees (indeed before Betty was well awake, for she made a nightly practice of having a sound nap, her weary head lying on her stalwart arms); the minister, still kneeling in our midst, but with his eyes wide open, and his arms dropped by his side, spoke to the elder man, who turned round on his knees to attend. 'John, didst see that Daisy had her warm mash to-night; for we must not neglect the means, John—two quarts of gruel, a spoonful of ginger, and a gill of beer—the poor beast needs it, and I fear it slipped out of my mind to tell thee; and here was I asking a blessing and neglecting the means, which is a mockery,' said he, dropping his voice.

Before we went to bed he told me he should see little or nothing more of me during my visit, which was to end on Sunday evening, as he always gave up both Saturday and Sabbath to his work in the ministry. I remembered that the landlord at the inn had told me this on the day when I first inquired about these new relations of mine; and I did not dislike the opportunity which I saw would be afforded me of becoming more acquainted with cousin Holman and Phillis, though I earnestly hoped that the latter would not attack me on the subject of the dead languages.

I went to bed, and dreamed that I was as tall as cousin Phillis, and had a sudden and miraculous growth of whisker, and a still more miraculous acquaintance with Latin and Greek. Alas! I wakened up still a short, beardless lad, with '*tempus fugit*'* for my sole remembrance of the little Latin I had once learnt. While I was dressing, a bright thought came over me: I could question cousin Phillis, instead of her questioning me, and so manage to keep the choice of the subjects of conversation in my own power.

Early as it was, every one had breakfasted, and my basin of bread and milk was put on the oven-top to await my coming down. Every one was gone about their work. The first to come into the house-place was Phillis with a basket of eggs. Faithful to my resolution, I asked,—

'What are those?'

She looked at me for a moment, and then said gravely,—

'Potatoes!'

'No! they are not,' said I. 'They are eggs. What do you mean by saying they are potatoes?'

'What do you mean by asking me what they were, when they were plain to be seen?' retorted she.

We were both getting a little angry with each other.

'I don't know. I wanted to begin to talk to you; and I was afraid you would talk to me about books as you did yesterday. I have not read much; and you and the minister have read so much.'

'I have not,' said she. 'But you are our guest; and mother says I must make it pleasant to you. We won't talk of books. What must we talk about?'

'I don't know. How old are you?'

'Seventeen last May. How old are you?'

'I am nineteen. Older than you by nearly two years,' said I, drawing myself up to my full height.

'I should not have thought you were above sixteen,' she replied, as quietly as if she were not saying the most provoking thing she possibly could. Then came a pause.

'What are you going to do now?' asked I.

'I should be dusting the bed-chambers; but mother said I had better stay and make it pleasant to you,' said she, a little plaintively, as if dusting rooms was far the easiest task.

'Will you take me to see the live-stock? I like animals, though I don't know much about them.'

'Oh, do you? I am so glad! I was afraid you would not like animals, as you did not like books.'

I wondered why she said this. I think it was because she had begun to fancy all our tastes must be dissimilar. We went together all through the farm-yard; we fed the poultry, she kneeling down with her pinafore full of corn and meal, and tempting the little timid, downy chickens upon it, much to the anxiety of the fussy ruffled hen, their mother. She called to the pigeons, who fluttered down at the sound of her voice. She and I examined the great sleek cart-horses; sympathized in our dislike of pigs; fed the calves; coaxed the sick cow, Daisy; and admired the others out at pasture; and came back tired and hungry and dirty at dinner-time, having quite forgotten that there were such things as dead languages, and consequently capital friends.

\* \* \*

# PART II

COUSIN HOLMAN gave me the weekly county newspaper to read aloud to her, while she mended stockings out of a high piled-up basket, Phillis helping her mother. I read and read, unregardful of the words I was uttering, thinking of all manner of other things; of the bright colour of Phillis's hair, as the afternoon sun fell on her bending head; of the silence of the house, which enabled me to hear the double tick of the old clock which stood half-way up the stairs; of the variety of inarticulate noises which cousin Holman made while I read, to show her sympathy, wonder, or horror at the newspaper intelligence. The tranquil monotony of that hour made me feel as if I had lived for ever, and should live for ever droning out paragraphs in that warm sunny room, with my two quiet hearers, and the curled-up pussy cat sleeping on the hearth-rug, and the clock on the house-stairs perpetually clicking out the passage of the moments. By-and-by Betty the servant came to the door into the kitchen, and made a sign to Phillis, who put her half-mended stocking down, and went away to the kitchen without a word. Looking at cousin Holman a minute or two afterwards, I saw that she had dropped her chin upon her breast, and had fallen fast asleep. I put the newspaper down, and was nearly following her example, when a waft of air from some unseen source, slightly opened the door of communication with the kitchen, that Phillis must have left unfastened; and I saw part of her figure as she sate by the dresser, peeling apples with quick dexterity of finger, but with repeated turnings of her head towards some book lying on the dresser by her. I softly rose, and as softly went into the kitchen, and looked over her shoulder; before she was aware of my neighbourhood, I had seen that the book was in a language unknown to me, and the running title was *L'Inferno.** Just as I was making out the relationship of this word to 'infernal', she started and turned round, and, as if continuing her thought as she spoke, she sighed out,—

'Oh! it is so difficult! Can you help me?' putting her finger below a line.

'Me! I! I don't even know what language it is in!'

'Don't you see it is Dante?' she replied, almost petulantly; she did so want help.

'Italian, then?' said I, dubiously; for I was not quite sure.

'Yes. And I do so want to make it out. Father can help me a little, for he knows Latin; but then he has so little time.'

'You have not much, I should think, if you have often to try and do two things at once, as you are doing now.'

'Oh! that's nothing! Father bought a heap of old books cheap. And I knew something about Dante before; and I have always liked Virgil so much. Paring apples is nothing, if I could only make out this old Italian. I wish you knew it.'

'I wish I did,' said I, moved by her impetuosity of tone. 'If, now, only Mr Holdsworth were here; he can speak Italian like anything, I believe.'

'Who is Mr Holdsworth?' said Phillis, looking up.

'Oh, he's our head engineer. He's a regular first-rate fellow! He can do anything;' my hero-worship and my pride in my chief all coming into play. Besides, if I was not clever and book-learned myself, it was something to belong to some one who was.

'How is it that he speaks Italian?' asked Phillis.

'He had to make a railway through Piedmont, which is in Italy, I believe; and he had to talk to all the workmen in Italian; and I have heard him say that for nearly two years he had only Italian books to read in the queer outlandish places he was in.'

'Oh, dear!' said Phillis; 'I wish—' and then she stopped. I was not quite sure whether to say the next thing that came into my mind; but I said it.

'Could I ask him anything about your book, or your difficulties?'

She was silent for a minute or so, and then she made reply,—

'No! I think not. Thank you very much, though. I can generally puzzle a thing out in time. And then, perhaps, I remember it better than if some one had helped me. I'll put it away now, and you must move off, for I've got to make the paste for the pies; we always have a cold dinner on Sabbaths.'

'But I may stay and help you, mayn't I?'

'Oh, yes; not that you can help at all, but I like to have you with me.'

I was both flattered and annoyed at this straightforward avowal. I was pleased that she liked me; but I was young coxcomb enough to have wished to play the lover, and I was quite wise enough to perceive that if she had any idea of the kind in her head she would never have spoken out so frankly. I comforted myself immediately, however, by finding out that the grapes were sour. A great tall girl in a pinafore, half a head taller than I was, reading books that I had never heard of, and talking about them too, as of far more interest than any mere personal subjects; that was the last day on which I ever thought of my dear cousin Phillis as the possible mistress of my heart and life. But we were all the greater friends for this idea being utterly put away and buried out of sight.

Late in the evening the minister came home from Hornby. He had been calling on the different members of his flock; and unsatisfactory work it had proved to him, it seemed from the fragments that dropped out of his thoughts into his talk.

'I don't see the men; they are all at their business, their shops, or their warehouses; they ought to be there. I have no fault to find with them; only if a pastor's teaching or words of admonition are good for anything, they are needed by the men as much as by the women.'

'Cannot you go and see them in their places of business, and remind them of their Christian privileges and duties, minister?' asked cousin Holman, who evidently thought that her husband's words could never be out of place.

'No!' said he, shaking his head. 'I judge them by myself. If there are clouds in the sky, and I am getting in the hay just ready for load-ing, and rain sure to come in the night, I should look ill upon brother Robinson if he came into the field to speak about serious things.'

'But, at any rate, father, you do good to the women, and perhaps they repeat what you have said to them to their husbands and children?'

'It is to be hoped they do, for I cannot reach the men directly; but the women are apt to tarry before coming to me, to put on ribbons and gauds;* as if they could hear the message I bear to them best in their smart clothes. Mrs Dobson to-day—Phillis, I am thankful thou dost not care for the vanities of dress!'

Phillis reddened a little as she said, in a low humble voice,—

'But I do, father, I'm afraid. I often wish I could wear pretty-coloured ribbons round my throat like the squire's daughters.'

'It's but natural, minister!' said his wife; 'I'm not above liking a silk gown better than a cotton one myself!'

'The love of dress is a temptation and a snare,'* said he, gravely. 'The true adornment is a meek and quiet spirit. And, wife,' said he, as a sudden thought crossed his mind, 'in that matter I, too, have sinned. I wanted to ask you, could we not sleep in the grey room, instead of our own?'

'Sleep in the grey room?—change our room at this time o' day?' cousin Holman asked, in dismay.

'Yes,' said he. 'It would save me from a daily temptation to anger. Look at my chin!' he continued; 'I cut it this morning—I cut it on Wednesday when I was shaving; I do not know how many times I have cut it of late, and all from impatience at seeing Timothy Cooper at his work in the yard.'

'He's a downright lazy tyke!'* said cousin Holman. 'He's not worth his wage. There's but little he can do, and what he can do, he does badly.'

'True,' said the minister. 'He is but, so to speak, a half-wit; and yet he has got a wife and children.'

'More shame for him!'

'But that is past change. And if I turn him off, no one else will take him on. Yet I cannot help watching him of a morning as he goes sauntering about his work in the yard; and I watch, and I watch, till the old Adam* rises strong within me at his lazy ways, and some day, I am afraid, I shall go down and send him about his business—let alone the way in which he makes me cut myself while I am shaving—and then his wife and children will starve. I wish we could move to the grey room.'

I do not remember much more of my first visit to the Hope Farm. We went to chapel in Heathbridge, slowly and decorously walking along the lanes, ruddy and tawny with the colouring of the coming autumn. The minister walked a little before us, his hands behind his back, his head bent down, thinking about the discourse to be delivered to his people, cousin Holman said; and we spoke low and quietly, in order not to interrupt his thoughts. But I could not help noticing the respectful greetings which he received from both rich and poor as we went along; greetings which he acknowledged with a kindly wave of his hand, but with no words of reply. As we drew near the town, I could see some of the young fellows we met cast admiring looks on Phillis; and that made me look too. She had on a white gown, and a short black silk cloak, according to the fashion of the day. A straw bonnet with brown ribbon strings; that was all. But what her dress wanted in colour, her sweet bonny face had. The walk made her cheeks bloom like the rose; the very whites of her eyes had a blue tinge in them, and her dark eyelashes brought out the depth of the blue eyes themselves. Her yellow hair was put away as straight as its natural curliness would allow. If she did not perceive the admiration she excited, I am sure cousin Holman did; for she looked as fierce and as proud as ever her quiet face could look, guarding her treasure, and yet glad to perceive that others could see that it was a treasure. That afternoon I had to return to Eltham to be ready for the next day's work. I found out afterwards that the minister and his family were all 'exercised in spirit,'* as to whether they did well in asking me to repeat my visits at the Hope Farm, seeing that of necessity I must return to Eltham on the Sabbath-day. However, they did go on asking me, and I went on visiting them, whenever my other engagements permitted me, Mr Holdsworth being in this case, as in all, a kind and indulgent friend. Nor did my new acquaintances oust him from my strong regard and admiration. I had room in my heart for all, I am happy to say, and as far as I can remember, I kept praising each to the other in a manner which, if I had been an older man, living more amongst people of the world, I should have thought unwise, as well as a little ridiculous. It was unwise, certainly, as it was almost sure to cause disappointment if ever they did become acquainted; and perhaps it was ridiculous, though I do not think we any of us thought it so at the time. The minister used to listen to my accounts of Mr Holdsworth's many accomplishments and various adventures in travel with the truest interest, and most kindly good faith; and Mr Holdsworth in return liked to hear about my visits to the farm, and description of my cousin's life there—liked it, I mean, as much as he liked anything that was merely narrative, without leading to action.

So I went to the farm certainly, on an average, once a month during that autumn; the course of life there was so peaceful and quiet, that I can only remember one small event, and that was one that I think I took more notice of than any one else: Phillis left off wearing the pinafores that had always been so obnoxious to me; I do not know why they were banished, but on one of my visits I found them replaced by pretty linen aprons in the morning, and a black silk one in the afternoon. And the blue cotton gown became a brown stuff* one as winter drew on; this sounds like some book I once read, in which a migration from the blue bed to the brown* was spoken of as a great family event.

Towards Christmas my dear father came to see me, and to consult Mr Holdsworth about the improvement which has since been known as 'Manning's driving wheel'. Mr Holdsworth, as I think I have before said, had a very great regard for my father, who had been employed in the same great machine-shop in which Mr Holdsworth had served his apprenticeship; and he and my father had many mutual jokes about one of these gentlemen-apprentices who used to set about his smith's work in white wash-leather gloves, for fear of spoiling his hands. Mr Holdsworth often spoke to me about my father as having the same kind of genius for mechanical invention as that of George Stephenson,* and my father had come over now to consult him about several improvements, as well as an offer of partnership. It was a great pleasure to me to see the mutual regard of these two men. Mr Holdsworth, young, handsome, keen, well-dressed, an object of admiration to all the youth of Eltham; my father, in his decent but unfashionable Sunday clothes, his plain, sensible face full of hard lines, the marks of toil and thought,—his hands, blackened beyond the power of soap and water by years of labour in the foundry; speaking a strong Northern dialect, while Mr Holdsworth had a long soft drawl in his voice, as many of the Southerners have, and was reckoned in Eltham to give himself airs.

Although most of my father's leisure time was occupied with conversations about the business I have mentioned, he felt that he ought not to leave Eltham without going to pay his respects to the relations who had been so kind to his son. So he and I ran up on an engine along the incomplete line as far as Heathbridge, and went, by invitation, to spend a day at the farm.

It was odd and yet pleasant to me to perceive how these two men, each having led up to this point such totally dissimilar lives, seemed to come together by instinct, after one quiet straight look into each other's faces. My father was a thin, wiry man of five foot seven; the minister was a broad-shouldered, fresh-coloured man of six foot one; they were neither of them great talkers in general—perhaps the minister the most so—but they spoke much to each other. My father went into the fields with the minister; I think I see him now, with his hands behind his back, listening intently to all explanations of tillage, and the different processes of farming; occasionally taking up an implement, as if unconsciously, and examining it with a critical eye, and now and then asking a question, which I could see was considered as pertinent by his companion. Then we returned to look at the cattle, housed and bedded in expectation of the snow-storm hanging black on the western horizon, and my father learned the points of a cow with as much attention as if he meant to turn farmer. He had his little book that he used for mechanical memoranda and measurements in his pocket, and he took it out to write down 'straight back', 'small muzzle', 'deep barrel',* and I know not what else, under the head 'cow'. He was very critical on a turnip-cutting machine, the clumsiness of which first incited him to talk; and when we went into the house he sate thinking and quiet for a bit, while Phillis and her mother made the last preparations for tea, with a little unheeded apology from cousin Holman, because we were not sitting in the best parlour, which she thought might be chilly on so cold a night. I wanted nothing better than the blazing, crackling fire that sent a glow over all the house-place, and warmed the snowy flags under our feet till they seemed to have more heat than the crimson rug right in front of the fire. After tea, as Phillis and I were talking together very happily, I heard an irrepressible exclamation from cousin Holman,—

'Whatever is the man about!'

And on looking round, I saw my father taking a straight burning stick out of the fire, and, after waiting for a minute, and examining the charred end to see if it was fitted for his purpose, he went to the hard-wood dresser, scoured to the last pitch of whiteness and cleanliness, and began drawing with the stick; the best substitute for chalk or charcoal within his reach, for his pocket-book pencil was not strong or bold enough for his purpose. When he had done, he began to explain his new model of a turnip-cutting machine to the minister, who had been watching him in silence all the time. Cousin Holman had, in the meantime, taken a duster out of a drawer, and, under pretence of being as much interested as her husband in the drawing, was secretly trying on an outside mark how easily it would come off, and whether it would leave her dresser as white as before. Then Phillis was sent for the book on dynamics* about which I had been consulted during my first visit, and my father had to explain many difficulties, which he did in language as clear as his mind, making drawings with his stick wherever they were needed as illustrations, the minister sitting with his massive head resting on his hands, his elbows on the table, almost unconscious of Phillis, leaning over and listening greedily, with her hand on his shoulder, sucking in information like her father's own daughter. I was rather sorry for cousin Holman; I had been so once or twice before; for do what she would, she was completely unable even to understand the pleasure her husband and daughter took in intellectual pursuits, much less to care in

the least herself for the pursuits themselves, and was thus unavoidably thrown out of some of their interests. I had once or twice
thought she was a little jealous of her own child, as a fitter companion
for her husband than she was herself; and I fancied the minister
himself was aware of this feeling, for I had noticed an occasional
sudden change of subject, and a tenderness of appeal in his voice as
he spoke to her, which always made her look contented and peaceful
again. I do not think that Phillis ever perceived these little shadows;
in the first place, she had such complete reverence for her parents
that she listened to them both as if they had been St Peter and
St Paul;* and besides, she was always too much engrossed with any
matter in hand to think about other people's manners and looks.

This night I could see, though she did not, how much she was
winning on my father. She asked a few questions which showed
that she had followed his explanations up to that point; possibly,
too, her unusual beauty might have something to do with his favourable impression of her; but he made no scruple of expressing his
admiration of her to her father and mother in her absence from the
room; and from that evening I date a project of his which came out
to me a day or two afterwards, as we sate in my little three-cornered
room in Eltham.

'Paul,' he began, 'I never thought to be a rich man; but I think it's
coming upon me. Some folk are making a deal of my new machine
(calling it by its technical name), and Ellison, of the Borough Green
Works, has gone so far as to ask me to be his partner.'

'Mr Ellison the Justice!—who lives in King Street? why, he drives
his carriage!' said I, doubting, yet exultant.

'Ay, lad, John Ellison. But that's no sign that I shall drive my
carriage.* Though I should like to save thy mother walking, for she's
not so young as she was. But that's a long way off; anyhow. I reckon
I should start with a third profit. It might be seven hundred, or it
might be more. I should like to have the power to work out some
fancies o' mine. I care for that much more than for th' brass. And
Ellison has no lads; and by nature the business would come to thee in
course o' time. Ellison's lasses are but bits o' things, and are not like
to come by husbands just yet; and when they do, maybe they'll not be
in the mechanical line. It will be an opening for thee, lad, if thou art
steady. Thou'rt not great shakes, I know, in th' inventing line; but
many a one gets on better without having fancies for something he

does not see and never has seen. I'm right down glad to see that mother's cousins are such uncommon folk for sense and goodness. I have taken the minister to my heart like a brother; and she is a womanly quiet sort of a body. And I'll tell you frank, Paul, it will be a happy day for me if ever you can come and tell me that Phillis Holman is like to be my daughter. I think if that lass had not a penny, she would be the making of a man; and she'll have yon house and lands, and you may be her match yet in fortune if all goes well.'

I was growing as red as fire; I did not know what to say, and yet I wanted to say something; but the idea of having a wife of my own at some future day, though it had often floated about in my own head, sounded so strange when it was thus first spoken about by my father. He saw my confusion, and half smiling said,—

'Well, lad, what dost say to the old father's plans? Thou art but young, to be sure; but when I was thy age, I would ha' given my right hand if I might ha' thought of the chance of wedding the lass I cared for—'

'My mother?' asked I, a little struck by the change of his tone of voice.

'No! not thy mother. Thy mother is a very good woman—none better. No! the lass I cared for at nineteen ne'er knew how I loved her, and a year or two after and she was dead, and ne'er knew. I think she would ha' been glad to ha' known it, poor Molly; but I had to leave the place where we lived for to try to earn my bread and I meant to come back but before ever I did, she was dead and gone: I ha' never gone there since. But if you fancy Phillis Holman, and can get her to fancy you, my lad, it shall go different with you, Paul, to what it did with your father.'

I took counsel with myself very rapidly, and I came to a clear conclusion.

'Father,' said I, 'if I fancied Phillis ever so much, she would never fancy me. I like her as much as I could like a sister; and she likes me as if I were her brother—her younger brother.'

I could see my father's countenance fall a little.

'You see she's so clever—she's more like a man than a woman—she knows Latin and Greek.'

'She'd forget 'em, if she'd a houseful of children,' was my father's comment on this.

'But she knows many a thing besides, and is wise as well as learned; she has been so much with her father. She would never think much of me, and I should like my wife to think a deal of her husband.'

'It is not just book-learning or the want of it as makes a wife think much or little of her husband,' replied my father, evidently unwilling to give up a project which had taken deep root in his mind. 'It's a something I don't rightly know how to call it—if he's manly, and sensible, and straightforward; and I reckon you're that, my boy.'

'I don't think I should like to have a wife taller than I am, father,' said I, smiling; he smiled too, but not heartily.

'Well,' said he, after a pause. 'It's but a few days I've been thinking of it, but I'd got as fond of my notion as if it had been a new engine as I'd been planning out. Here's our Paul, thinks I to myself, a good sensible breed o' lad, as has never vexed or troubled his mother or me; with a good business opening out before him, age nineteen, not so bad-looking, though perhaps not to call handsome, and here's his cousin, not too near cousin, but just nice, as one may say; aged seventeen, good and true, and well brought up to work with her hands as well as her head; a scholar—but that can't be helped, and is more her misfortune than her fault, seeing she is the only child of a scholar—and as I said afore, once she's a wife and a mother she'll forget it all, I'll be bound—with a good fortune in land and house when it shall please the Lord to take her parents to himself; with eyes like poor Molly's for beauty, a colour that comes and goes on a milk-white skin, and as pretty a mouth—'

'Why, Mr Manning, what fair lady are you describing?' asked Mr Holdsworth, who had come quickly and suddenly upon our *tête-à-tête*, and had caught my father's last words as he entered the room.

Both my father and I felt rather abashed; it was such an odd subject for us to be talking about; but my father, like a straightforward simple man as he was, spoke out the truth.

'I've been telling Paul of Ellison's offer, and saying how good an opening it made for him—'

'I wish I'd as good,' said Mr Holdsworth. 'But has the business a "pretty mouth"'?

'You're always so full of your joking, Mr Holdsworth,' said my father. 'I was going to say that if he and his cousin Phillis Holman liked to make it up between them, I would put no spoke in the wheel.'

'Phillis Holman!' said Mr Holdsworth. 'Is she the daughter of the minister-farmer out at Heathbridge? Have I been helping on the course of true love by letting you go there so often? I knew nothing of it.'

'There is nothing to know,' said I, more annoyed than I chose to show. 'There is no more true love in the case than may be between the first brother and sister you may choose to meet. I have been telling father she would never think of me; she's a great deal taller and cleverer; and I'd rather be taller and more learned than my wife when I have one.'

'And it is she, then, that has the pretty mouth your father spoke about? I should think that would be an antidote to the cleverness and learning. But I ought to apologize for breaking in upon your last night; I came upon business to your father.'

And then he and my father began to talk about many things that had no interest for me just then, and I began to go over again my conversation with my father. The more I thought about it, the more I felt that I had spoken truly about my feelings towards Phillis Holman. I loved her dearly as a sister, but I could never fancy her as my wife. Still less could I think of her ever—yes, *condescending*, that is the word—condescending to marry me. I was roused from a reverie on what I should like my possible wife to be, by hearing my father's warm praise of the minister, as a most unusual character; how they had got back from the diameter of driving-wheels to the subject of the Holmans I could never tell; but I saw that my father's weighty praises were exciting some curiosity in Mr Holdsworth's mind; indeed, he said, almost in a voice of reproach,—

'Why, Paul, you never told me what kind of a fellow this minister-cousin of yours was!'

'I don't know that I found out, sir,' said I. 'But if I had, I don't think you'd have listened to me, as you have done to my father.'

'No! most likely not, old fellow,' replied Mr Holdsworth, laughing. And again and afresh I saw what a handsome pleasant clear face his was; and though this evening I had been a bit put out with him—through his sudden coming, and his having heard my father's open-hearted confidence—my hero resumed all his empire over me by his bright merry laugh.

And if he had not resumed his old place that night, he would have done so the next day, when, after my father's departure, Mr Holdsworth spoke about him with such just respect for his character, such un-grudging admiration of his great mechanical genius, that I was compelled to say, almost unawares,—

'Thank you, sir. I am very much obliged to you.'

'Oh, you're not at all. I am only speaking the truth. Here's a Birmingham workman, self-educated, one may say—having never associated with stimulating minds, or had what advantages travel and contact with the world may be supposed to afford—working out his own thoughts into steel and iron, making a scientific name for himself—a fortune, if it pleases him to work for money—and keep-ing his singleness of heart, his perfect simplicity of manner; it puts me out of patience to think of my expensive schooling, my travels hither and thither, my heaps of scientific books, and I have done nothing to speak of. But it's evidently good blood; there's that Mr Holman, that cousin of yours, made of the same stuff.'

'But he's only cousin because he married my mother's second cousin,' said I.

'That knocks a pretty theory on the head, and twice over, too. I should like to make Holman's acquaintance.'

'I am sure they would be so glad to see you at Hope Farm,' said I, eagerly. 'In fact, they've asked me to bring you several times: only I thought you would find it dull.'

'Not at all. I can't go yet though, even if you do get me an invita-tion; for the —— Company want me to go to the —— Valley, and look over the ground a bit for them, to see if it would do for a branch line; it's a job which may take me away for some time; but I shall be backwards and forwards, and you're quite up to doing what is needed in my absence; the only work that may be beyond you is keeping old Jevons from drinking.'

He went on giving me directions about the management of the men employed on the line, and no more was said then, or for several months, about his going to Hope Farm. He went off into —— Valley, a dark overshadowed dale, where the sun seemed to set behind the hills before four o'clock on midsummer afternoon.

Perhaps it was this that brought on the attack of low fever which he had soon after the beginning of the new year; he was very ill for many weeks, almost many months; a married sister—his only rela-tion, I think—came down from London to nurse him, and I went over to him when I could, to see him, and give him 'masculine news', as he called it; reports of the progress of the line, which, I am glad to say, I was able to carry on in his absence, in the slow gradual way which suited the company best, while trade was in a languid state, and money dear in the market. Of course, with this occupation for my scanty leisure, I did not often go over to Hope Farm. Whenever I did go, I met with a thorough welcome; and many inquiries were made as to Holdsworth's illness, and the progress of his recovery.

At length, in June I think it was, he was sufficiently recovered to come back to his lodgings at Eltham, and resume part at least of his work. His sister, Mrs Robinson, had been obliged to leave him some weeks before, owing to some epidemic amongst her own children. As long as I had seen Mr Holdsworth in the rooms at the little inn at Hensleydale, where I had been accustomed to look upon him as an invalid, I had not been aware of the visible shake his fever had given to his health. But, once back in the old lodgings, where I had always seen him so buoyant, eloquent, decided, and vigorous in former days, my spirits sank at the change in one whom I had always regarded with a strong feeling of admiring affection. He sank into silence and despondency after the least exertion; he seemed as if he could not make up his mind to any action, or else that, when it was made up, he lacked strength to carry out his purpose. Of course, it was but the natural state of slow convalescence, after so sharp an illness; but, at the time, I did not know this, and perhaps I represented his state as more serious than it was to my kind relations at Hope Farm; who, in their grave, simple, eager way, immediately thought of the only help they could give.

'Bring him out here,' said the minister. 'Our air here is good to a proverb;* the June days are fine; he may loiter away his time in the hay-field, and the sweet smells will be a balm in themselves—better than physic.'

'And,' said cousin Holman, scarcely waiting for her husband to finish his sentence, 'tell him there is new milk and fresh eggs to be had for the asking; it's lucky Daisy has just calved, for her milk is always as good as other cows' cream; and there is the plaid room* with the morning sun all streaming in.'

Phillis said nothing, but looked as much interested in the project as any one. I took it upon myself. I wanted them to see him; him to know them. I proposed it to him when I got home. He was too languid after the day's fatigue, to be willing to make the little exertion of going amongst strangers; and disappointed me by almost declining to accept the invitation I brought. The next morning it was different; he apologized for his ungraciousness of the night before; and told me that he would get all things in train, so as to be ready to go out with me to Hope Farm on the following Saturday.

'For you must go with me, Manning,' said he; 'I used to be as impudent a fellow as need be, and rather liked going amongst strangers, and making my way; but since my illness I am almost like a girl, and turn hot and cold with shyness, as they do, I fancy.'

So it was fixed. We were to go out to Hope Farm on Saturday afternoon; and it was also understood that if the air and the life suited Mr Holdsworth, he was to remain there for a week or ten days, doing what work he could at that end of the line, while I took his place at Eltham to the best of my ability. I grew a little nervous, as the time drew near, and wondered how the brilliant Holdsworth would agree with the quiet quaint family of the minister; how they would like him, and many of his half-foreign ways. I tried to prepare him, by telling him from time to time little things about the goings-on at Hope Farm.

'Manning,' said he, 'I see you don't think I am half good enough for your friends. Out with it, man.'

'No,' I replied, boldly. 'I think you are good; but I don't know if you are quite of their kind of goodness.'

'And you've found out already that there is greater chance of disagreement between two "kinds of goodness", each having its own idea of right, than between a given goodness and a moderate degree of naughtiness—which last often arises from an indifference to right?'

'I don't know. I think you're talking metaphysics, and I am sure that is bad for you.'

' "When a man talks to you in a way that you don't understand about a thing which he does not understand, them's metaphysics."* You remember the clown's definition, don't you, Manning?'

'No, I don't,' said I. 'But what I do understand is, that you must go to bed; and tell me at what time we must start tomorrow, that I may go to Hepworth, and get those letters written we were talking about this morning.'

'Wait till to-morrow, and let us see what the day is like,' he answered, with such languid indecision as showed me he was over-fatigued. So I went my way.

The morrow was blue and sunny, and beautiful; the very perfection of an early summer's day. Mr Holdsworth was all impatience to be off into the country; morning had brought back his freshness and strength, and consequent eagerness to be doing. I was afraid we were going to my cousin's farm rather too early, before they would expect us; but what could I do with such a restless vehement man as Holdsworth was that morning? We came down upon the Hope Farm before the dew was off the grass on the shady side of the lane; the great house-dog was loose, basking in the sun, near the closed side door. I was surprised at this door being shut, for all summer long it was open from morning to night; but it was only on latch. I opened it, Rover watching me with half-suspicious, half-trustful eyes. The room was empty.

'I don't know where they can be,' said I. 'But come in and sit down while I go and look for them. You must be tired.'

'Not I. This sweet balmy air is like a thousand tonics. Besides, this room is hot, and smells of those pungent wood-ashes. What are we to do?'

'Go round to the kitchen. Betty will tell us where they are.'

So we went round into the farmyard, Rover accompanying us out of a grave sense of duty. Betty was washing out her milk-pans in the cold bubbling spring-water that constantly trickled in and out of a stone trough. In such weather as this most of her kitchen-work was done out of doors.

'Eh, dear!' said she, 'the minister and missus is away at Hornby! They ne'er thought of your coming so betimes! The missus had some errands to do, and she thought as she'd walk with the minister and be back by dinner-time.'

'Did not they expect us to dinner?' said I.

'Well, they did, and they did not, as I may say. Missus said to me the cold lamb would do well enough if you did not come; and if you did I was to put on a chicken and some bacon to boil; and I'll go do it now, for it is hard to boil bacon enough.'

'And is Phillis gone, too?' Mr Holdsworth was making friends with Rover.

'No! She's just somewhere about. I reckon you'll find her in the kitchen-garden, getting peas.'

'Let us go there,' said Holdsworth, suddenly leaving off his play with the dog.

So I led the way into the kitchen-garden. It was in the first promise of a summer profuse in vegetables and fruits. Perhaps it was not so much cared for as other parts of the property; but it was more attended to than most kitchen-gardens belonging to farm-houses. There were borders of flowers along each side of the gravel walks; and there was an old sheltering wall on the north side covered with tolerably choice fruit-trees; there was a slope down to the fish-pond at the end, where there were great strawberry-beds; and raspberry-bushes and rose-bushes grew wherever there was a space; it seemed a chance which had been planted. Long rows of peas stretched at right angles from the main walk, and I saw Phillis stooping down among them, before she saw us. As soon as she heard our cranching* steps on the gravel, she stood up, and shading her eyes from the sun, recognized us. She was quite still for a moment, and then came slowly towards us, blushing a little from evident shyness. I had never seen Phillis shy before.

'This is Mr Holdsworth, Phillis,' said I, as soon as I had shaken hands with her. She glanced up at him, and then looked down, more flushed than ever at his grand formality of taking his hat off and bowing; such manners had never been seen at Hope Farm before.

'Father and mother are out. They will be so sorry; you did not write, Paul, as you said you would.'

'It was my fault,' said Holdsworth, understanding what she meant as well as if she had put it more fully into words. 'I have not yet given up all the privileges of an invalid; one of which is indecision. Last night, when your cousin asked me at what time we were to start, I really could not make up my mind.'

Phillis seemed as if she could not make up her mind as to what to do with us. I tried to help her—

'Have you finished getting peas?' taking hold of the half-filled basket she was unconsciously holding in her hand; 'or may we stay and help you?'

'If you would. But perhaps it will tire you, sir?' added she, speaking now to Holdsworth.

'Not a bit,' said he. 'It will carry me back twenty years in my life, when I used to gather peas in my grandfather's garden. I suppose I may eat a few as I go along?'

'Certainly, sir. But if you went to the strawberry-beds you would find some strawberries ripe, and Paul can show you where they are.'

'I am afraid you distrust me. I can assure you I know the exact fulness at which peas should be gathered. I take great care not to pluck them when they are unripe. I will not be turned off, as unfit for my work.'

This was a style of half-joking talk that Phillis was not accustomed to. She looked for a moment as if she would have liked to defend herself from the playful charge of distrust made against her, but she ended by not saying a word. We all plucked our peas in busy silence for the next five minutes. Then Holdsworth lifted himself up from between the rows, and said, a little wearily,—

'I am afraid I must strike work. I am not as strong as I fancied myself.'

Phillis was full of penitence immediately. He did, indeed, look pale; and she blamed herself for having allowed him to help her.

'It was very thoughtless of me. I did not know—I thought, perhaps, you really liked it. I ought to have offered you something to eat, sir! Oh, Paul, we have gathered quite enough; how stupid I was to forget that Mr Holdsworth had been ill!' And in a blushing hurry she led the way towards the house. We went in, and she moved a heavy cushioned chair forwards, into which Holdsworth was only too glad to sink. Then with deft and quiet speed she brought in a little tray, wine, water, cake, home-made bread, and newly-churned butter. She stood by in some anxiety till, after bite and sup, the colour returned to Mr Holdsworth's face, and he would fain have made us some laughing apologies for the fright he had given us. But then Phillis drew back from her innocent show of care and interest, and relapsed into the cold shyness habitual to her when she was first thrown into the company of strangers. She brought out the last week's county paper (which Mr Holdsworth had read five days ago), and then quietly withdrew; and then he subsided into languor, leaning back and shutting his eyes as if he would go to sleep. I stole into the kitchen after Phillis; but she had made the round of the corner of the house outside, and I found her sitting on the horse-mount, with her basket of peas, and a basin into which she was shelling them. Rover lay at her feet, snapping now and then at the flies. I went to her, and tried to help her, but somehow the sweet crisp young peas found their way more frequently into my mouth than into the basket, while we talked together in a low tone, fearful of being overheard through the open casements of the house-place in which Holdsworth was resting.

'Don't you think him handsome?' asked I.

'Perhaps—yes—I have hardly looked at him,' she replied. 'But is not he very like a foreigner?'

'Yes, he cuts his hair foreign fashion,' said I.

'I like an Englishman to look like an Englishman.'

'I don't think he thinks about it. He says he began that way when he was in Italy, because everybody wore it so, and it is natural to keep it on in England.'

'Not if he began it in Italy because everybody there wore it so. Everybody here wears it differently.'

I was a little offended with Phillis's logical fault-finding with my friend; and I determined to change the subject.

'When is your mother coming home?'

'I should think she might come any time now; but she had to go and see Mrs Morton, who was ill, and she might be kept, and not be home till dinner. Don't you think you ought to go and see how Mr Holdsworth is going on, Paul? He may be faint again.'

I went at her bidding; but there was no need for it. Mr Holdsworth was up, standing by the window, his hands in his pockets; he had evidently been watching us. He turned away as I entered.

'So that is the girl I found your good father planning for your wife, Paul, that evening when I interrupted you! Are you of the same coy mind still? It did not look like it a minute ago.'

'Phillis and I understand each other,' I replied, sturdily. 'We are like brother and sister. She would not have me as a husband if there was not another man in the world; and it would take a deal to make me think of her—as my father wishes' (somehow I did not like to say 'as a wife'), 'but we love each other dearly.'

'Well, I am rather surprised at it—not at your loving each other in a brother-and-sister kind of way—but at your finding it so impossible to fall in love with such a beautiful woman.'

Woman! beautiful woman! I had thought of Phillis as a comely but awkward girl; and I could not banish the pinafore from my mind's eye when I tried to picture her to myself. Now I turned, as Mr Holdsworth had done, to look at her again out of the window: she had just finished her task, and was standing up, her back to us, holding the basket, and the basin in it, high in air, out of Rover's reach, who was giving vent to his delight at the probability of a change of place by glad leaps and barks, and snatches at what he imagined to be a withheld prize. At length she grew tired of their mutual play, and with a feint of striking him, and a 'Down, Rover! do hush!' she looked towards the window where we were standing, as if to reassure herself that no one had been disturbed by the noise, and seeing us, she coloured all over, and hurried away, with Rover still curving in sinuous lines about her as she walked.

'I should like to have sketched her,' said Mr Holdsworth, as he turned away. He went back to his chair, and rested in silence for a minute or two. Then he was up again.

'I would give a good deal for a book,' he said. 'It would keep me quiet.' He began to look round; there were a few volumes at one end of the shovel-board.

'Fifth volume of Matthew Henry's *Commentary*,' said he, reading their titles aloud. '*Housewife's complete Manual*; *Berridge on Prayer*; *L'Inferno*—Dante!' in great surprise. 'Why, who reads this?'

'I told you Phillis read it. Don't you remember? She knows Latin and Greek, too.'

'To be sure! I remember! But somehow I never put two and two together. That quiet girl, full of household work, is the wonderful scholar, then, that put you to rout with her questions when you first began to come here. To be sure, "Cousin Phillis!" What's here: a paper with the hard, obsolete words written out. I wonder what sort of a dictionary she has got. Baretti* won't tell her all these words. Stay! I have got a pencil here. I'll write down the most accepted meanings, and save her a little trouble.'

So he took her book and the paper back to the little round table, and employed himself in writing explanations and definitions of the words which had troubled her. I was not sure if he was not taking a liberty: it did not quite please me, and yet I did not know why. He had only just done, and replaced the paper in the book, and put the latter back in its place, when I heard the sound of wheels stopping in the lane, and looking out, I saw cousin Holman getting out of a neighbour's gig, making her little curtsey of acknowledgment, and then coming towards the house. I went to meet her.

'Oh, Paul!' said she, 'I am so sorry I was kept; and then Thomas Dobson said if I would wait a quarter of an hour he would—But where's your friend Mr Holdsworth? I hope he is come?'

Just then he came out, and with his pleasant cordial manner took her hand, and thanked her for asking him to come out here to get strong.

'I'm sure I am very glad to see you, sir. It was the minister's thought. I took it into my head you would be dull in our quiet house, for Paul says you've been such a great traveller; but the minister said that dulness would perhaps suit you while you were but ailing, and that I was to ask Paul to be here as much as he could. I hope you'll find yourself happy with us, I'm sure, sir. Has Phillis given you something to eat and drink, I wonder? there's a deal in eating a little often, if one has to get strong after an illness.' And then she began to question him as to the details of his indisposition in her simple, motherly way. He seemed at once to understand her, and to enter into friendly relations with her. It was not quite the same in the evening when the minister came home. Men have always a little natural antipathy to get over when they first meet as strangers. But in this case each was disposed to make an effort to like the other; only each was to each a specimen of an unknown class. I had to leave the Hope Farm on Sunday afternoon, as I had Mr Holdsworth's work as well as my own to look to in Eltham; and I was not at all sure how things would go on during the week that Holdsworth was to remain on his visit; I had been once or twice in hot water already at the near clash of opinions between the minister and my much-vaunted friend. On the Wednesday I received a short note from Holdsworth; he was going to stay on, and return with me on the following Sunday, and he wanted me to send him a certain list of books, his theodolite,* and other surveying instruments, all of which could easily be conveyed down the line to Heathbridge. I went to his lodgings and picked out the books. Italian, Latin, trigonometry; a pretty considerable parcel they made, besides the implements. I began to be curious as to the general progress of affairs at Hope Farm, but I could not go over till the Saturday. At Heathbridge I found Holdsworth, come to meet me. He was looking quite a different man to what I had left him; embrowned, sparkles in his eyes, so languid before. I told him how much stronger he looked.

'Yes!' said he. 'I am fidging fain* to be at work again. Last week I dreaded the thoughts of my employment: now I am full of desire to begin. This week in the country has done wonders for me.'

'You have enjoyed yourself, then?'

'Oh! it has been perfect in its way. Such a thorough country life! and yet removed from the dulness which I always used to fancy accompanied country life, by the extraordinary intelligence of the minister. I have fallen into calling him "the minister", like every one else.'

'You get on with him, then?' said I. 'I was a little afraid.'

'I was on the verge of displeasing him once or twice, I fear, with random assertions and exaggerated expressions, such as one always uses with other people, and thinks nothing of; but I tried to check myself when I saw how it shocked the good man; and really it is very wholesome exercise, this trying to make one's words represent one's thoughts, instead of merely looking to their effect on others.'

'Then you are quite friends now?' I asked.

'Yes, thoroughly; at any rate as far as I go. I never met with a man with such a desire for knowledge. In information, as far as it can be gained from books, he far exceeds me on most subjects; but then I have travelled and seen—Were not you surprised at the list of things I sent for?'

'Yes; I thought it did not promise much rest.'

'Oh! some of the books were for the minister, and some for his daughter. (I call her Phillis to myself, but I use euphuisms* in speaking about her to others. I don't like to seem familiar, and yet Miss Holman is a term I have never heard used.)'

'I thought the Italian books were for her.'

'Yes! Fancy her trying at Dante for her first book in Italian! I had a capital novel by Manzoni, *I Promessi Sposi*,* just the thing for a beginner; and if she must still puzzle out Dante, my dictionary is far better than hers.'

'Then she found out you had written those definitions on her list of words?'

'Oh! yes'—with a smile of amusement and pleasure. He was going to tell me what had taken place, but checked himself.

'But I don't think the minister will like your having given her a novel to read?'

'Pooh! What can be more harmless? Why make a bugbear of a word? It is as pretty and innocent a tale as can be met with. You don't suppose they take Virgil for gospel?'

By this time we were at the farm. I think Phillis gave me a warmer welcome than usual, and cousin Holman was kindness itself. Yet somehow I felt as if I had lost my place, and that Holdsworth had taken it. He knew all the ways of the house; he was full of little filial attentions to cousin Holman; he treated Phillis with the affectionate condescension of an elder brother; not a bit more; not in any way different. He questioned me about the progress of affairs in Eltham with eager interest.

'Ah!' said cousin Holman, 'you'll be spending a different kind of time next week to what you have done this! I can see how busy you'll make yourself! But if you don't take care you'll be ill again, and have to come back to our quiet ways of going on.'

'Do you suppose I shall need to be ill to wish to come back here?' he answered, warmly. 'I am only afraid you have treated me so kindly that I shall always be turning up on your hands.'

'That's right,' she replied. 'Only don't go and make yourself ill by over-work. I hope you'll go on with a cup of new milk every morning, for I am sure that is the best medicine; and put a teaspoonful of rum in it, if you like; many a one speaks highly of that, only we had no rum in the house.'

I brought with me an atmosphere of active life which I think he had begun to miss; and it was natural that he should seek my company, after his week of retirement. Once I saw Phillis looking at us as we talked together with a kind of wistful curiosity; but as soon as she caught my eye, she turned away, blushing deeply.

That evening I had a little talk with the minister. I strolled along the Hornby road to meet him; for Holdsworth was giving Phillis an Italian lesson, and cousin Holman had fallen asleep over her work.

Somehow, and not unwillingly on my part, our talk fell on the friend whom I had introduced to the Hope Farm.

'Yes! I like him!' said the minister, weighing his words a little as he spoke. 'I like him. I hope I am justified in doing it, but he takes hold of me, as it were; and I have almost been afraid lest he carries me away, in spite of my judgment.'

'He is a good fellow; indeed he is,' said I. 'My father thinks well of him; and I have seen a deal of him. I would not have had him come here if I did not know that you would approve of him.'

'Yes,' (once more hesitating,) 'I like him, and I think he is an upright man; there is a want of seriousness* in his talk at times, but, at the same time, it is wonderful to listen to him! He makes Horace and Virgil living, instead of dead, by the stories he tells me of his sojourn in the very countries where they lived, and where to this day, he says—But it is like dram-drinking.* I listen to him till I forget my duties, and am carried off my feet. Last Sabbath evening he led us away into talk on profane subjects ill befitting the day.'

By this time we were at the house, and our conversation stopped. But before the day was out, I saw the unconscious hold that my friend had got over all the family. And no wonder: he had seen so much and done so much as compared to them, and he told about it all so easily and naturally, and yet as I never heard any one else do; and his ready pencil was out in an instant to draw on scraps of paper all sorts of illustrations—modes of drawing up water in Northern Italy, wine-carts, buffaloes, stone-pines,* I know not what. After we had all looked at these drawings, Phillis gathered them together, and took them.

It is many years since I have seen thee, Edward Holdsworth, but thou wast a delightful fellow! Ay, and a good one too; though much sorrow was caused by thee!

*   *   *

## PART III

JUST after this I went home for a week's holiday. Everything was prospering there; my father's new partnership gave evident satisfaction to both parties. There was no display of increased wealth in our modest household; but my mother had a few extra comforts provided for her by her husband. I made acquaintance with Mr and Mrs Ellison, and first saw pretty Margaret Ellison, who is now my wife. When I returned to Eltham, I found that a step was decided upon, which had been in contemplation for some time; that Holdsworth and I should remove our quarters to Hornby; our daily presence, and as much of our time as possible, being required for the completion of the line at that end.

Of course this led to greater facility of intercourse with the Hope Farm people. We could easily walk out there after our day's work was done, and spend a balmy evening hour or two, and yet return before the summer's twilight had quite faded away. Many a time, indeed, we would fain have stayed longer—the open air, the fresh and pleasant country, made so agreeable a contrast to the close, hot town lodgings which I shared with Mr Holdsworth; but early hours, both at eve and morn, were an imperative necessity with the minister, and he made

no scruple at turning either or both of us out of the house directly
after evening prayer, or 'exercise', as he called it. The remembrance
of many a happy day, and of several little scenes, comes back upon me
as I think of that summer. They rise like pictures to my memory,
and in this way I can date their succession; for I know that corn harvest must have come after hay-making, apple-gathering after corn-
harvest.

The removal to Hornby took up some time, during which we had
neither of us any leisure to go out to the Hope Farm. Mr Holdsworth
had been out there once during my absence at home. One sultry
evening, when work was done, he proposed our walking out and
paying the Holmans a visit. It so happened that I had omitted to
write my usual weekly letter home in our press of business, and I
wished to finish that before going out. Then he said that he would
go, and that I could follow him if I liked. This I did in about an hour;
the weather was so oppressive, I remember, that I took off my coat as
I walked, and hung it over my arm. All the doors and windows at the
farm were open when I arrived there, and every tiny leaf on the trees
was still. The silence of the place was profound; at first I thought that
it was entirely deserted; but just as I drew near the door I heard a
weak sweet voice begin to sing; it was cousin Holman, all by herself
in the house-place, piping up a hymn, as she knitted away in the
clouded light. She gave me a kindly welcome, and poured out all the
small domestic news of the fortnight past upon me, and, in return,
I told her about my own people and my visit at home.

'Where were the rest?' at length I asked.

Betty and the men were in the field helping with the last load of
hay, for the minister said there would be rain before the morning.
Yes, and the minister himself, and Phillis, and Mr Holdsworth,
were all there helping. She thought that she herself could have done
something; but perhaps she was the least fit for hay-making of any
one; and somebody must stay at home and take care of the house,
there were so many tramps about; if I had not had something to do
with the railroad she would have called them navvies.* I asked her if
she minded being left alone, as I should like to go and help; and
having her full and glad permission to leave her alone, I went off,
following her directions: through the farmyard, past the cattle-pond,
into the ash-field, beyond into the higher field with two holly-bushes
in the middle. I arrived there: there was Betty with all the farming

men, and a cleared field, and a heavily laden cart; one man at the top
of the great pile ready to catch the fragrant hay which the others
threw up to him with their pitchforks; a little heap of cast-off clothes
in a corner of the field (for the heat, even at seven o'clock, was insuf-
ferable), a few cans and baskets, and Rover lying by them panting,
and keeping watch. Plenty of loud, hearty, cheerful talking; but no
minister, no Phillis, no Mr Holdsworth. Betty saw me first, and understanding who it was that I was in search of, she came towards me.

'They're out yonder—agait* wi' them things o' Measter
Holdsworth's.'

So 'out yonder' I went; out on to a broad upland common, full of
red sand-banks, and sweeps and hollows; bordered by dark firs,
purple in the coming shadows, but near at hand all ablaze with
flowering gorse, or, as we call it in the south, furze-bushes, which,
seen against the belt of distant trees, appeared brilliantly golden. On
this heath, a little way from the field-gate, I saw the three. I counted
their heads, joined together in an eager group over Holdsworth's
theodolite. He was teaching the minister the practical art of surveying
and taking a level. I was wanted to assist, and was quickly set to work
to hold the chain. Phillis was as intent as her father; she had hardly
time to greet me, so desirous was she to hear some answer to her
father's question.

So we went on, the dark clouds still gathering, for perhaps five
minutes after my arrival. Then came the blinding lightning and the
rumble and quick-following rattling peal of thunder right over our
heads. It came sooner than I expected, sooner than they had looked
for: the rain delayed not; it came pouring down; and what were we to
do for shelter? Phillis had nothing on but her indoor things—no
bonnet, no shawl. Quick as the darting lightning around us, Holdsworth
took off his coat and wrapped it round her neck and shoulders, and,
almost without a word, hurried us all into such poor shelter as one of
the overhanging sand-banks could give. There we were, cowered
down, close together, Phillis innermost, almost too tightly packed to
free her arms enough to divest herself of the coat, which she, in her
turn, tried to put lightly over Holdsworth's shoulders. In doing so
she touched his shirt.

'Oh, how wet you are!' she cried, in pitying dismay; 'and you've
hardly got over your fever! Oh, Mr Holdsworth, I am so sorry!' He
turned his head a little, smiling at her.

'If I do catch cold, it is all my fault for having deluded you into staying out here!' but she only murmured again, 'I am so sorry.'

The minister spoke now. 'It is a regular downpour. Please God that the hay is saved! But there is no likelihood of its ceasing, and I had better go home at once, and send you all some wraps; umbrellas will not be safe with yonder thunder and lightning.'

Both Holdsworth and I offered to go instead of him; but he was resolved, although perhaps it would have been wiser if Holdsworth, wet as he already was, had kept himself in exercise. As he moved off, Phillis crept out, and could see on to the storm-swept heath. Part of Holdsworth's apparatus still remained exposed to all the rain. Before we could have any warning, she had rushed out of the shelter and collected the various things, and brought them back in triumph to where we crouched. Holdsworth had stood up, uncertain whether to go to her assistance or not. She came running back, her long lovely hair floating and dripping, her eyes glad and bright, and her colour freshened to a glow of health by the exercise and the rain.

'Now, Miss Holman, that's what I call wilful,' said Holdsworth, as she gave them to him. 'No, I won't thank you' (his looks were thanking her all the time). 'My little bit of dampness annoyed you, because you thought I had got wet in your service; so you were determined to make me as uncomfortable as you were yourself. It was an unchristian piece of revenge!'

His tone of badinage (as the French call it) would have been palpable enough to any one accustomed to the world; but Phillis was not, and it distressed or rather bewildered her. 'Unchristian' had to her a very serious meaning; it was not a word to be used lightly; and though she did not exactly understand what wrong it was that she was accused of doing, she was evidently desirous to throw off the imputation. At first her earnestness to disclaim unkind motives amused Holdsworth; while his light continuance of the joke perplexed her still more; but at last he said something gravely, and in too low a tone for me to hear, which made her all at once become silent, and called out her blushes. After a while, the minister came back, a moving mass of shawls, cloaks, and umbrellas. Phillis kept very close to her father's side on our return to the farm. She appeared to me to be shrinking away from Holdsworth, while he had not the slightest variation in his manner from what it usually was in his graver moods; kind, protecting, and thoughtful towards her. Of course, there was a

great commotion about our wet clothes; but I name the little events
of that evening now because I wondered at the time what he had said
in that low voice to silence Phillis so effectually, and because, in thinking of their intercourse by the light of future events, that evening
stands out with some prominence.

I have said that after our removal to Hornby our communications
with the farm became almost of daily occurrence. Cousin Holman
and I were the two who had least to do with this intimacy. After
Mr Holdsworth regained his health, he too often talked above her
head in intellectual matters, and too often in his light bantering tone
for her to feel quite at her ease with him. I really believe that he
adopted this latter tone in speaking to her because he did not know
what to talk about to a purely motherly woman, whose intellect had
never been cultivated, and whose loving heart was entirely occupied
with her husband, her child, her household affairs and, perhaps, a
little with the concerns of the members of her husband's congregation, because they, in a way, belonged to her husband. I had noticed
before that she had fleeting shadows of jealousy even of Phillis, when
her daughter and her husband appeared to have strong interests and
sympathies in things which were quite beyond her comprehension.
I had noticed it in my first acquaintance with them, I say, and had
admired the delicate tact which made the minister, on such occasions, bring the conversation back to such subjects as those on which
his wife, with her practical experience of every-day life, was an
authority; while Phillis, devoted to her father, unconsciously followed his lead, totally unaware, in her filial reverence, of his motive
for doing so.

To return to Holdsworth. The minister had at more than one time
spoken of him to me with slight distrust, principally occasioned
by the suspicion that his careless words were not always those of
soberness and truth. But it was more as a protest against the fascination which the younger man evidently exercised over the elder
one—more as it were to strengthen himself against yielding to this
fascination—that the minister spoke out to me about this failing of
Holdsworth's, as it appeared to him. In return Holdsworth was subdued by the minister's uprightness and goodness, and delighted with
his clear intellect—his strong healthy craving after further knowledge. I never met two men who took more thorough pleasure and
relish in each other's society. To Phillis his relation continued that of

an elder brother: he directed her studies into new paths, he patiently drew out the expression of many of her thoughts, and perplexities, and unformed theories—scarcely ever now falling into the vein of banter which she was so slow to understand.

One day—harvest-time—he had been drawing on a loose piece of paper—sketching ears of corn, sketching carts drawn by bullocks and laden with grapes—all the time talking with Phillis and me, cousin Holman putting in her not pertinent remarks, when suddenly he said to Phillis,—

'Keep your head still; I see a sketch! I have often tried to draw your head from memory, and failed; but I think I can do it now. If I succeed I will give it to your mother. You would like a portrait of your daughter as Ceres,* would you not, ma'am?'

'I should like a picture of her; yes, very much, thank you, Mr Holdsworth; but if you put that straw in her hair,' (he was holding some wheat ears above her passive head, looking at the effect with an artistic eye,) 'you'll ruffle her hair. Phillis, my dear, if you're to have your picture taken, go upstairs, and brush your hair smooth.'

'Not on any account. I beg your pardon, but I want hair loosely flowing.'

He began to draw, looking intently at Phillis; I could see this stare of his discomposed her—her colour came and went, her breath quickened with the consciousness of his regard; at last, when he said, 'Please look at me for a minute or two, I want to get in the eyes,' she looked up at him, quivered, and suddenly got up and left the room. He did not say a word, but went on with some other part of the drawing; his silence was unnatural, and his dark cheek blanched a little. Cousin Holman looked up from her work, and put her spectacles down.

'What's the matter? Where is she gone?'

Holdsworth never uttered a word, but went on drawing. I felt obliged to say something; it was stupid enough, but stupidity was better than silence just then.

'I'll go and call her,' said I. So I went into the hall, and to the bottom of the stairs; but just as I was going to call Phillis, she came down swiftly with her bonnet on, and saying, 'I'm going to father in the five-acre,' passed out by the open 'rector,' right in front of the house-place windows, and out at the little white side-gate. She had been seen by her mother and Holdsworth, as she passed; so there was no need for explanation, only cousin Holman and I had a long discussion as to whether she could have found the room too hot, or what had occasioned her sudden departure. Holdsworth was very quiet during all the rest of that day; nor did he resume the portrait-taking by his own desire, only at my cousin Holman's request the next time that he came; and then he said he should not require any more formal sittings for only such a slight sketch as he felt himself capable of making. Phillis was just the same as ever the next time I saw her after her abrupt passing me in the hall. She never gave any explanation of her rush out of the room.

So all things went on, at least as far as my observation reached at the time, or memory can recall now, till the great apple-gathering of the year. The nights were frosty, the mornings and evenings were misty, but at mid-day all was sunny and bright, and it was one mid-day that both of us being on the line near Heathbridge, and knowing that they were gathering apples at the farm, we resolved to spend the men's dinner-hour in going over there. We found the great clothes-baskets full of apples, scenting the house, and stopping up the way; and an universal air of merry contentment with this the final produce of the year. The yellow leaves hung on the trees ready to flutter down at the slightest puff of air; the great bushes of Michaelmas daisies in the kitchen-garden were making their last show of flowers. We must needs taste the fruit off the different trees, and pass our judgment as to their flavour; and we went away with our pockets stuffed with those that we liked best. As we had passed to the orchard, Holdsworth had admired and spoken about some flower which he saw; it so happened he had never seen this old-fashioned kind since the days of his boyhood. I do not know whether he had thought anything more about this chance speech of his, but I know I had not—when Phillis, who had been missing just at the last moment of our hurried visit, re-appeared with a little nosegay of this same flower, which she was tying up with a blade of grass. She offered it to Holdsworth as he stood with her father on the point of departure. I saw their faces. I saw for the first time an unmistakable look of love in his black eyes; it was more than gratitude for the little attention; it was tender and beseeching—passionate. She shrank from it in confusion, her glance fell on me; and, partly to hide her emotion, partly out of real kindness at what might appear ungracious neglect of an older friend, she flew off to gather me a few late-blooming China roses. But it was the first time she had ever done anything of the kind for me.

We had to walk fast to be back on the line before the men's return, so we spoke but little to each other, and of course the afternoon was too much occupied for us to have any talk. In the evening we went back to our joint lodgings in Hornby. There, on the table, lay a letter for Holdsworth, which had been forwarded to him from Eltham. As our tea was ready, and I had had nothing to eat since morning, I fell to directly without paying much attention to my companion as he opened and read his letter. He was very silent for a few minutes; at length he said,

'Old fellow! I'm going to leave you!'

'Leave me!' said I. 'How? When?'

'This letter ought to have come to hand sooner. It is from Greathed the engineer' (Greathed was well known in those days; he is dead now, and his name half-forgotten); 'he wants to see me about some business; in fact, I may as well tell you, Paul, this letter contains a very advantageous proposal for me to go out to Canada, and superintend the making of a line there.'

I was in utter dismay.

'But what will our company say to that?'

'Oh, Greathed has the superintendence of this line, you know; and he is going to be engineer in chief to this Canadian line; many of the shareholders in this company are going in for the other, so I fancy they will make no difficulty in following Greathed's lead. He says he has a young man ready to put in my place.'

'I hate him,' said I.

'Thank you,' said Holdsworth, laughing.

'But you must not,' he resumed; 'for this is a very good thing for me, and, of course, if no one can be found to take my inferior work, I can't be spared to take the superior. I only wish I had received this letter a day sooner. Every hour is of consequence, for Greathed says they are threatening a rival line. Do you know, Paul, I almost fancy I must go up tonight? I can take an engine back to Eltham, and catch the night train. I should not like Greathed to think me luke-warm.'

'But you'll come back?' I asked, distressed at the thought of this sudden parting.

'Oh, yes! At least I hope so. They may want me to go out by the next steamer, that will be on Saturday.' He began to eat and drink standing, but I think he was quite unconscious of the nature of either his food or his drink.

'I will go to-night. Activity and readiness go a long way in our profession. Remember that, my boy! I hope I shall come back, but if I don't, be sure and recollect all the words of wisdom that have fallen from my lips. Now where's the portmanteau? If I can gain half an hour for a gathering up of my things in Eltham, so much the better. I'm clear of debt anyhow; and what I owe for my lodgings you can pay for me out of my quarter's salary, due November 4th.'

'Then you don't think you will come back?' I said, despondingly.

'I will come back some time, never fear,' said he, kindly. 'I may be back in a couple of days, having been found incompetent for the Canadian work; or I may not be wanted to go out so soon as I now anticipate. Anyhow you don't suppose I am going to forget you, Paul—this work out there ought not to take me above two years, and, perhaps, after that, we may be employed together again.'

Perhaps! I had very little hope. The same kind of happy days never returns. However, I did all I could in helping him: clothes, papers, books, instruments; how we pushed and struggled—how I stuffed. All was done in a much shorter time than we had calculated upon, when I had run down to the sheds to order the engine. I was going to drive him to Eltham. We sate ready for a summons. Holdsworth took up the little nosegay that he had brought away from the Hope Farm, and had laid on the mantel-piece on first coming into the room. He smelt at it, and caressed it with his lips.

'What grieves me is that I did not know—that I have not said good-by to—to them.'

He spoke in a grave tone, the shadow of the coming separation falling upon him at last.

'I will tell them,' said I. 'I am sure they will be very sorry.' Then we were silent.

'I never liked any family so much.'

'I knew you would like them.'

'How one's thoughts change,—this morning I was full of a hope, Paul.' He paused, and then he said,—

'You put that sketch in carefully?'

'That outline of a head?' asked I. But I knew he meant an abortive sketch of Phillis, which had not been successful enough for him to complete it with shading or colouring.

'Yes. What a sweet innocent face it is! and yet so—Oh, dear!'

He sighed and got up, his hands in his pockets, to walk up and down the room in evident disturbance of mind. He suddenly stopped opposite to me.

'You'll tell them how it all was. Be sure and tell the good minister that I was so sorry not to wish him good-by, and to thank him and his wife for all their kindness. As for Phillis,—please God in two years I'll be back and tell her myself all in my heart.'

'You love Phillis, then?' said I.

'Love her! Yes, that I do. Who could help it, seeing her as I have done? Her character as unusual and rare as her beauty! God bless her! God keep her in her high tranquillity, her pure innocence.—Two years! It is a long time.—But she lives in such seclusion, almost like the sleeping beauty,* Paul,'—(he was smiling now, though a minute before I had thought him on the verge of tears,)—'but I shall come back like a prince from Canada, and waken her to my love. I can't help hoping that it won't be difficult, eh, Paul?'

This touch of coxcombry displeased me a little, and I made no answer. He went on, half apologetically,—

'You see, the salary they offer me is large; and beside that, this experience will give me a name which will entitle me to expect a still larger in any future undertaking.'

'That won't influence Phillis.'

'No! but it will make me more eligible in the eyes of her father and mother.'

I made no answer.

'You give me your best wishes, Paul,' said he, almost pleading. 'You would like me for a cousin?'

I heard the scream and whistle of the engine ready down at the sheds.

'Ay, that I should,' I replied, suddenly softened towards my friend now that he was going away. 'I wish you were to be married to-morrow, and I were to be best man.'

'Thank you, lad. Now for this cursed portmanteau (how the minister would be shocked); but it is heavy!' and off we sped into the darkness.

He only just caught the night train at Eltham, and I slept, desolately enough, at my old lodgings at Miss Dawson's, for that night. Of course the next few days I was busier than ever, doing both his work and my own. Then came a letter from him, very short and affectionate. He was going out in the Saturday steamer, as he had more than half expected; and by the following Monday the man who was to succeed him would be down at Eltham. There was a P.S., with only these words:—

'My nosegay goes with me to Canada, but I do not need it to remind me of Hope Farm.'

Saturday came; but it was very late before I could go out to the farm. It was a frosty night, the stars shone clear above me, and the road was crisping beneath my feet. They must have heard my footsteps before I got up to the house. They were sitting at their usual employments in the house-place when I went in. Phillis's eyes went beyond me in their look of welcome, and then fell in quiet disappointment on her work.

'And where's Mr Holdsworth?' asked cousin Holman, in a minute or two. 'I hope his cold is not worse,—I did not like his short cough.'

I laughed awkwardly; for I felt that I was the bearer of unpleasant news.

'His cold had need be better—for he's gone—gone away to Canada!'

I purposely looked away from Phillis, as I thus abruptly told my news.

'To Canada!' said the minister.

'Gone away!' said his wife. But no word from Phillis.

'Yes!' said I. 'He found a letter at Hornby when we got home the other night—when we got home from here; he ought to have got it sooner; he was ordered to go up to London directly, and to see some people about a new line in Canada, and he's gone to lay it down; he has sailed to-day. He was sadly grieved not to have time to come out and wish you all good-by; but he started for London within two hours after he got that letter. He bade me thank you most gratefully for all your kindnesses; he was very sorry not to come here once again.'

Phillis got up and left the room with noiseless steps.

'I am very sorry,' said the minister.

'I am sure so am I!' said cousin Holman. 'I was real fond of that lad ever since I nursed him last June after that bad fever.'

The minister went on asking me questions respecting Holdsworth's future plans; and brought out a large old-fashioned atlas, that he might find out the exact places between which the new railroad

was to run. Then supper was ready; it was always on the table as soon
as the clock on the stairs struck eight, and down came Phillis—her
face white and set, her dry eyes looking defiance to me, for I am
afraid I hurt her maidenly pride by my glance of sympathetic interest
as she entered the room. Never a word did she say—never a question
did she ask about the absent friend, yet she forced herself to talk.

And so it was all the next day. She was as pale as could be, like one
who has received some shock; but she would not let me talk to her,
and she tried hard to behave as usual. Two or three times I repeated,
in public, the various affectionate messages to the family with which
I was charged by Holdsworth; but she took no more notice of them
than if my words had been empty air. And in this mood I left her on
the Sabbath evening.

My new master was not half so indulgent as my old one. He kept
up strict discipline as to hours, so that it was some time before
I could again go out, even to pay a call at the Hope Farm.

It was a cold misty evening in November. The air, even indoors,
seemed full of haze; yet there was a great log burning on the hearth,
which ought to have made the room cheerful. Cousin Holman and
Phillis were sitting at the little round table before the fire, working
away in silence. The minister had his books out on the dresser, seemingly deep in study, by the light of his solitary candle; perhaps
the fear of disturbing him made the unusual stillness of the room.
But a welcome was ready for me from all; not noisy, not demonstrative—that it never was; my damp wrappers were taken off; the next
meal was hastened, and a chair placed for me on one side of the fire,
so that I pretty much commanded a view of the room. My eye caught
on Phillis, looking so pale and weary, and with a sort of aching
tone (if I may call it so) in her voice. She was doing all the accustomed things—fulfilling small household duties, but somehow
differently—I can't tell you how, for she was just as deft and quick
in her movements, only the light spring was gone out of them.
Cousin Holman began to question me; even the minister put aside
his books, and came and stood on the opposite side of the fire-place,
to hear what waft of intelligence I brought. I had first to tell them
why I had not been to see them for so long—more than five weeks.
The answer was simple enough; business and the necessity of attending strictly to the orders of a new superintendent, who had not yet

learned trust, much less indulgence. The minister nodded his approval of my conduct, and said,—

'Right, Paul! "Servants, obey in all things your master according to the flesh."* I have had my fears lest you had too much licence under Edward Holdsworth.'

'Ah,' said cousin Holman, 'poor Mr Holdsworth, he'll be on the salt seas by this time!'

'No, indeed,' said I, 'he's landed. I have had a letter from him from Halifax.'

Immediately a shower of questions fell thick upon me. When? How? What was he doing? How did he like it? What sort of a voyage? &c.

'Many is the time we have thought of him when the wind was blowing so hard; the old quince-tree is blown down, Paul, that on the right-hand of the great pear-tree; it was blown down last Monday week, and it was that night that I asked the minister to pray in an especial manner for all them that went down in ships upon the great deep,* and he said then, that Mr Holdsworth might be already landed; but I said, even if the prayer did not fit him, it was sure to be fitting somebody out at sea, who would need the Lord's care. Both Phillis and I thought he would be a month on the seas.'

Phillis began to speak, but her voice did not come rightly at first. It was a little higher pitched than usual, when she said,—

'We thought he would be a month if he went in a sailing-vessel, or perhaps longer. I suppose he went in a steamer?'

'Old Obadiah Grimshaw was more than six weeks in getting to America,' observed cousin Holman.

'I presume he cannot as yet tell how he likes his new work?' asked the minister.

'No! he is but just landed; it is but one page long. I'll read it to you, shall I?—

'Dear Paul,—

'We are safe on shore, after a rough passage. Thought you would like to hear this, but homeward-bound steamer is making signals for letters. Will write again soon. It seems a year since I left Hornby. Longer since I was at the farm. I have got my nosegay safe. Remember me to the Holmans.

'Yours, E. H.'

'That's not much, certainly,' said the minister. 'But it's a comfort to know he's on land these blowy nights.'

Phillis said nothing. She kept her head bent down over her work; but I don't think she put a stitch in, while I was reading the letter. I wondered if she understood what nosegay was meant; but I could not tell. When next she lifted up her face, there were two spots of brilliant colour on the cheeks that had been so pale before. After I had spent an hour or two there, I was bound to return back to Hornby. I told them I did not know when I could come again, as we—by which I mean the company—had undertaken the Hensleydale line; that branch for which poor Holdsworth was surveying when he caught his fever.

'But you'll have a holiday at Christmas,' said my cousin. 'Surely they'll not be such heathens as to work you then?'

'Perhaps the lad will be going home,' said the minister, as if to mitigate his wife's urgency; but for all that, I believe he wanted me to come. Phillis fixed her eyes on me with a wistful expression, hard to resist. But, indeed, I had no thought of resisting. Under my new master I had no hope of a holiday long enough to enable me to go to Birmingham and see my parents with any comfort; and nothing could be pleasanter to me than to find myself at home at my cousin's for a day or two, then. So it was fixed that we were to meet in Hornby Chapel on Christmas Day, and that I was to accompany them home after service, and if possible to stay over the next day.

I was not able to get to chapel till late on the appointed day, and so I took a seat near the door in considerable shame, although it really was not my fault. When the service was ended, I went and stood in the porch to await the coming out of my cousins. Some worthy people belonging to the congregation clustered into a group just where I stood, and exchanged the good wishes of the season. It had just begun to snow, and this occasioned a little delay, and they fell into further conversation. I was not attending to what was not meant for me to hear, till I caught the name of Phillis Holman. And then I listened; where was the harm?

'I never saw any one so changed!'

'I asked Mrs Holman,' quoth another, ' "Is Phillis well?" and she just said she had been having a cold which had pulled her down; she did not seem to think anything of it.'

'They had best take care of her,' said one of the oldest of the good ladies; 'Phillis comes of a family as is not long-lived. Her mother's sister, Lydia Green, her own aunt as was, died of a decline just when she was about this lass's age.'

This ill-omened talk was broken in upon by the coming out of the minister, his wife and daughter, and the consequent interchange of Christmas compliments. I had had a shock, and felt heavy-hearted and anxious, and hardly up to making the appropriate replies to the kind greetings of my relations. I looked askance at Phillis. She had certainly grown taller and slighter, and was thinner; but there was a flush of colour on her face which deceived me for a time, and made me think she was looking as well as ever. I only saw her paleness after we had returned to the farm, and she had subsided into silence and quiet. Her grey eyes looked hollow and sad; her complexion was of a dead white. But she went about just as usual; at least, just as she had done the last time I was there, and seemed to have no ailment; and I was inclined to think that my cousin was right when she had answered the inquiries of the good-natured gossips, and told them that Phillis was suffering from the consequences of a bad cold, nothing more.

I have said that I was to stay over the next day; a great deal of snow had come down, but not all, they said, though the ground was covered deep with the white fall. The minister was anxiously housing his cattle, and preparing all things for a long continuance of the same kind of weather. The men were chopping wood, sending wheat to the mill to be ground before the road should become impassable for a cart and horse. My cousin and Phillis had gone upstairs to the apple-room to cover up the fruit from the frost. I had been out the greater part of the morning, and came in about an hour before dinner. To my surprise, knowing how she had planned to be engaged, I found Phillis sitting at the dresser, resting her head on her two hands and reading, or seeming to read. She did not look up when I came in, but murmured something about her mother having sent her down out of the cold. It flashed across me that she was crying, but I put it down to some little spirt of temper; I might have known better than to suspect the gentle, serene Phillis of crossness, poor girl; I stooped down, and began to stir and build up the fire, which appeared to have been neglected. While my head was down I heard a noise which made me pause and listen—a sob, an unmistakable, irrepressible sob. I started up.

'Phillis!' I cried, going towards her, with my hand out, to take hers for sympathy with her sorrow, whatever it was. But she was too quick for me, she held her hand out of my grasp, for fear of my detaining her; as she quickly passed out of the house, she said,

'Don't, Paul! I cannot bear it!' and passed me, still sobbing, and went out into the keen, open air.

I stood still and wondered. What could have come to Phillis? The most perfect harmony prevailed in the family, and Phillis especially, good and gentle as she was, was so beloved that if they had found out that her finger ached, it would have cast a shadow over their hearts. Had I done anything to vex her? No: she was crying before I came in. I went to look at her book—one of those unintelligible Italian books. I could make neither head nor tail of it. I saw some pencil-notes on the margin, in Holdsworth's handwriting.

Could that be it? Could that be the cause of her white looks, her weary eyes, her wasted figure, her struggling sobs? This idea came upon me like a flash of lightning on a dark night, making all things so clear we cannot forget them afterwards when the gloomy obscurity returns. I was still standing with the book in my hand when I heard cousin Holman's footsteps on the stairs, and as I did not wish to speak to her just then, I followed Phillis's example, and rushed out of the house. The snow was lying on the ground; I could track her feet by the marks they had made; I could see where Rover had joined her. I followed on till I came to a great stack of wood in the orchard—it was built up against the back wall of the outbuildings,—and I recollected then how Phillis had told me, that first day when we strolled about together, that underneath this stack had been her hermitage, her sanctuary, when she was a child; how she used to bring her book to study there, or her work, when she was not wanted in the house; and she had now evidently gone back to this quiet retreat of her childhood, forgetful of the clue given me by her footmarks on the new-fallen snow. The stack was built up very high; but through the interstices of the sticks I could see her figure, although I did not all at once perceive how I could get to her. She was sitting on a log of wood, Rover by her. She had laid her cheek on Rover's head, and had her arm round his neck, partly for a pillow, partly from an instinctive craving for warmth on that bitter cold day. She was making a low moan, like an animal in pain, or perhaps more like the sobbing of the wind. Rover, highly flattered by her caress, and also, perhaps, touched by sympathy, was flapping his heavy tail against the ground, but not otherwise moving a hair, until he heard my approach with his quick erected ears. Then, with a short, abrupt bark of distrust, he sprang up as if to leave his mistress. Both he and

I were immovably still for a moment. I was not sure if what I longed to do was wise: and yet I could not bear to see the sweet serenity of my dear cousin's life so disturbed by a suffering which I thought I could assuage. But Rover's ears were sharper than my breathing was noiseless: he heard me, and sprang out from under Phillis's restraining hand.

'Oh, Rover, don't you leave me, too,' she plained out.

'Phillis!' said I, seeing by Rover's exit that the entrance to where she sate was to be found on the other side of the stack. 'Phillis, come out! You have got a cold already; and it is not fit for you to sit there on such a day as this. You know how displeased and anxious it would make them all.'

She sighed, but obeyed; stooping a little, she came out, and stood upright, opposite to me in the lonely, leafless orchard. Her face looked so meek and so sad that I felt as if I ought to beg her pardon for my necessarily authoritative words.

'Sometimes I feel the house so close,' she said; 'and I used to sit under the wood-stack when I was a child. It was very kind of you, but there was no need to come after me. I don't catch cold easily.'

'Come with me into this cow-house, Phillis. I have got something to say to you; and I can't stand this cold, if you can.'

I think she would have fain run away again; but her fit of energy was all spent. She followed me unwillingly enough—that I could see. The place to which I took her was full of the fragrant breath of the cows, and was a little warmer than the outer air. I put her inside, and stood myself in the doorway, thinking how I could best begin. At last I plunged into it.

'I must see that you don't get cold for more reasons than one; if you are ill, Holdsworth will be so anxious and miserable out there' (by which I meant Canada)—

She shot one penetrating look at me, and then turned her face away with a slightly impatient movement. If she could have run away then she would, but I held the means of exit in my own power. 'In for a penny, in for a pound,' thought I, and I went on rapidly, anyhow.

'He talked so much about you, just before he left—that night after he had been here, you know—and you had given him those flowers.' She put her hands up to hide her face, but she was listening now—listening with all her ears.

'He had never spoken much about you before, but the sudden going away unlocked his heart, and he told me how he loved you, and how he hoped on his return that you might be his wife.'

'Don't,' said she, almost gasping out the word, which she had tried once or twice before to speak; but her voice had been choked. Now she put her hand backwards; she had quite turned away from me, and felt for mine. She gave it a soft lingering pressure; and then she put her arms down on the wooden division, and laid her head on it, and cried quiet tears. I did not understand her at once, and feared lest I had mistaken the whole case, and only annoyed her. I went up to her. 'Oh, Phillis! I am so sorry—I thought you would, perhaps, have cared to hear it; he did talk so feelingly, as if he did love you so much, and somehow I thought it would give you pleasure.'

She lifted up her head and looked at me. Such a look! Her eyes, glittering with tears as they were, expressed an almost heavenly happiness; her tender mouth was curved with rapture—her colour vivid and blushing; but as if she was afraid her face expressed too much, more than the thankfulness to me she was essaying to speak, she hid it again almost immediately. So it was all right then, and my conjecture was well-founded! I tried to remember something more to tell her of what he had said, but again she stopped me.

'Don't,' she said. She still kept her face covered and hidden. In half a minute she added, in a very low voice, 'Please, Paul, I think I would rather not hear any more—I don't mean but what I have—but what I am very much obliged—Only—only, I think I would rather hear the rest from himself when he comes back.'

And then she cried a little more, in quite a different way. I did not say any more, I waited for her. By-and-by she turned towards me—not meeting my eyes, however; and putting her hand in mine just as if we were two children, she said,—

'We had best go back now—I don't look as if I had been crying, do I?'

'You look as if you had a bad cold,' was all the answer I made.

'Oh! but I am quite well, only cold; and a good run will warm me. Come along, Paul.'

So we ran, hand in hand, till, just as we were on the threshold of the house, she stopped,—

'Paul, please, we won't speak about *that* again.'

\*　　\*　　\*

## PART IV

WHEN I went over on Easter Day I heard the chapel-gossips complimenting cousin Holman on her daughter's blooming looks, quite forgetful of their sinister prophecies three months before. And I looked at Phillis, and did not wonder at their words. I had not seen her since the day after Christmas Day. I had left the Hope Farm only a few hours after I had told her the news which had quickened her heart into renewed life and vigour. The remembrance of our conversation in the cow-house was vividly in my mind as I looked at her when her bright healthy appearance was remarked upon. As her eyes met mine our mutual recollections flashed intelligence from one to the other. She turned away, her colour heightening as she did so. She seemed to be shy of me for the first few hours after our meeting, and I felt rather vexed with her for her conscious avoidance of me after my long absence. I had stepped a little out of my usual line in telling her what I did; not that I had received any charge of secrecy, or given even the slightest promise to Holdsworth that I would not repeat his words. But I had an uneasy feeling sometimes when I thought of what I had done in the excitement of seeing Phillis so ill and in so much trouble. I meant to have told Holdsworth when I wrote next to him; but when I had my half-finished letter before me I sate with my pen in my hand hesitating. I had more scruple in revealing what I had found out or guessed at of Phillis's secret than in repeating to her his spoken words. I did not think I had any right to say out to him what I believed—namely, that she loved him dearly, and had felt his absence even to the injury of her health. Yet to explain what I had done in telling her how he had spoken about her that last night, it would be necessary to give my reasons, so I had settled within myself to leave it alone. As she had told me she should like to hear all the details and fuller particulars and more explicit declarations first from him, so he should have the pleasure of extracting the delicious tender secret from her maidenly lips. I would not betray my guesses, my surmises, my all but certain knowledge of the state of her heart. I had received two letters from him after he had settled to his business; they were full of life and energy; but in each there had been a message to the family at the Hope Farm of more than common regard; and a slight but distinct mention of Phillis herself, showing that she

stood single and alone in his memory. These letters I had sent on to
the minister, for he was sure to care for them, even supposing he had
been unacquainted with their writer, because they were so clever and
so picturesquely worded that they brought, as it were, a whiff of
foreign atmosphere into his circumscribed life. I used to wonder
what was the trade or business in which the minister would not have
thriven, mentally I mean, if it had so happened that he had been
called into that state. He would have made a capital engineer, that I
know; and he had a fancy for the sea, like many other land-locked
men to whom the great deep is a mystery and a fascination. He read
law-books with relish; and, once happening to borrow *De Lolme on
the British Constitution*\* (or some such title), he talked about jurispru-
dence till he was far beyond my depth. But to return to Holdsworth's
letters. When the minister sent them back he also wrote out a list of
questions suggested by their perusal, which I was to pass on in my
answers to Holdsworth, until I thought of suggesting direct correspondence between the two. That was the state of things as regarded
the absent one when I went to the farm for my Easter visit, and when
I found Phillis in that state of shy reserve towards me which I have
named before. I thought she was ungrateful; for I was not quite sure
if I had done wisely in having told her what I did. I had committed a
fault, or a folly, perhaps, and all for her sake; and here was she, less
friends with me than she had even been before. This little estrangement only lasted a few hours. I think that as soon as she felt pretty
sure of there being no recurrence, either by word, look, or allusion,
to the one subject that was predominant in her mind, she came back
to her old sisterly ways with me. She had much to tell me of her own
familiar interests; how Rover had been ill, and how anxious they had
all of them been, and how, after some little discussion between her
father and her, both equally grieved by the sufferings of the old dog,
he had been 'remembered in the household prayers', and how he had
begun to get better only the very next day, and then she would have
led me into a conversation on the right ends of prayer, and on special
providences,\* and I know not what; only I 'jibbed'\* like their old cart-
horse, and refused to stir a step in that direction. Then we talked
about the different broods of chickens, and she showed me the hens
that were good mothers, and told me the characters of all the poultry
with the utmost good faith; and in all good faith I listened, for I
believe there was a good deal of truth in all she said. And then we

strolled on into the wood beyond the ash-meadow, and both of us sought for early primroses, and the fresh green crinkled leaves. She was not afraid of being alone with me after the first day. I never saw her so lovely, or so happy. I think she hardly knew why she was so happy all the time. I can see her now, standing under the budding branches of the grey trees, over which a tinge of green seemed to be deepening day after day, her sun-bonnet fallen back on her neck, her hands full of delicate wood-flowers, quite unconscious of my gaze, but intent on sweet mockery of some bird in neighbouring bush or tree. She had the art of warbling, and replying to the notes of differ-ent birds, and knew their song, their habits and ways, more accur-ately than any one else I ever knew. She had often done it at my request the spring before; but this year she really gurgled, and whis-tled, and warbled just as they did, out of the very fulness and joy of her heart. She was more than ever the very apple of her father's eye; her mother gave her both her own share of love, and that of the dead child who had died in infancy. I have heard cousin Holman murmur, after a long dreamy look at Phillis, and tell herself how like she was growing to Johnnie, and soothe herself with plaintive inarticulate sounds, and many gentle shakes of the head, for the aching sense of loss she would never get over in this world. The old servants about the place had the dumb loyal attachment to the child of the land, common to most agricultural labourers; not often stirred into activity or expression. My cousin Phillis was like a rose that had come to full bloom on the sunny side of a lonely house, sheltered from storms. I have read in some book of poetry,—

> A maid whom there were none to praise,
> And very few to love.*

And somehow those lines always reminded me of Phillis; yet they were not true of her either. I never heard her praised; and out of her own household there were very few to love her; but though no one spoke out their approbation, she always did right in her parents' eyes out of her natural simple goodness and wisdom. Holdsworth's name was never mentioned between us when we were alone; but I had sent on his letters to the minister, as I have said; and more than once he began to talk about our absent friend, when he was smoking his pipe after the day's work was done. Then Phillis hung her head a little over her work, and listened in silence.

'I miss him more than I thought for; no offence to you, Paul. I said once his company was like dram-drinking; that was before I knew him; and perhaps I spoke in a spirit of judgment. To some men's minds everything presents itself strongly, and they speak accordingly; and so did he. And I thought in my vanity of censorship that his were not true and sober words; they would not have been if I had used them, but they were so to a man of his class of perceptions. I thought of the measure with which I had been meting to him* when Brother Robinson was here last Thursday, and told me that a poor little quotation I was making from the *Georgics* savoured of vain babbling and profane heathenism. He went so far as to say that by learning other languages than our own, we were flying in the face of the Lord's purpose when He had said, at the building of the Tower of Babel, that He would confound their languages so that they should not understand each other's speech.* As Brother Robinson was to me, so was I to the quick wits, bright senses, and ready words of Holdsworth.'

The first little cloud upon my peace came in the shape of a letter from Canada, in which there were two or three sentences that troubled me more than they ought to have done, to judge merely from the words employed. It was this:—'I should feel dreary enough in this out-of-the-way place if it were not for a friendship I have formed with a French Canadian of the name of Ventadour. He and his family are a great resource to me in the long evenings. I never heard such delicious vocal music as the voices of these Ventadour boys and girls in their part songs; and the foreign element retained in their characters and manner of living reminds me of some of the happiest days of my life. Lucille, the second daughter, is curiously like Phillis Holman.' In vain I said to myself that it was probably this likeness that made him take pleasure in the society of the Ventadour family. In vain I told my anxious fancy that nothing could be more natural than this intimacy, and that there was no sign of its leading to any consequence that ought to disturb me. I had a presentiment, and I was disturbed; and I could not reason it away. I dare say my presentiment was rendered more persistent and keen by the doubts which would force themselves into my mind, as to whether I had done well in repeating Holdsworth's words to Phillis. Her state of vivid happiness this summer was markedly different to the peaceful serenity of former days. If in my thoughtfulness at noticing this

I caught her eye, she blushed and sparkled all over, guessing that I was remembering our joint secret. Her eyes fell before mine, as if she could hardly bear me to see the revelation of their bright glances. And yet I considered again, and comforted myself by the reflection that, if this change had been anything more than my silly fancy, her father or her mother would have perceived it. But they went on in tranquil unconsciousness and undisturbed peace.

A change in my own life was quickly approaching. In the July of this year my occupation on the —— railway and its branches came to an end. The lines were completed, and I was to leave ——shire, to return to Birmingham, where there was a niche already provided for me in my father's prosperous business. But before I left the north it was an understood thing amongst us all that I was to go and pay a visit of some weeks at the Hope Farm. My father was as much pleased at this plan as I was; and the dear family of cousins often spoke of things to be done, and sights to be shown me, during this visit. My want of wisdom in having told 'that thing' (under such ambiguous words I concealed the injudicious confidence I had made to Phillis) was the only drawback to my anticipations of pleasure.

The ways of life were too simple at the Hope Farm for my coming to them to make the slightest disturbance. I knew my room, like a son of the house. I knew the regular course of their days, and that I was expected to fall into it, like one of the family. Deep summer peace brooded over the place; the warm golden air was filled with the murmur of insects near at hand, the more distant sound of voices out in the fields, the clear faraway rumble of carts over the stone-paved lanes miles away. The heat was too great for the birds to be singing; only now and then one might hear the wood-pigeons in the trees beyond the ash-field. The cattle stood knee-deep in the pond, flicking their tails about to keep off the flies. The minister stood in the hay-field, without hat or cravat, coat or waistcoat, panting and smiling. Phillis had been leading the row of farm-servants, turning the swathes of fragrant hay with measured movement. She went to the end—to the hedge, and then, throwing down her rake, she came to me with her free sisterly welcome. 'Go, Paul!' said the minister. 'We need all hands to make use of the sunshine to-day. "Whatsoever thine hand findeth to do, do it with all thy might."* It will be a healthy change of work for thee, lad; and I find best rest in change of work.' So off I went, a willing labourer, following Phillis's lead; it was

the primitive distinction of rank; the boy who frightened the spar-
rows off the fruit was the last in our rear. We did not leave off till the
red sun was gone down behind the fir-trees bordering the common.
Then we went home to supper—prayers—to bed; some bird singing
far into the night, as I heard it through my open window, and the
poultry beginning their clatter and cackle in the earliest morning.
I had carried what luggage I immediately needed with me from my
lodgings and the rest was to be sent by the carrier. He brought it to
the farm betimes that morning, and along with it he brought a letter
or two that had arrived since I had left. I was talking to cousin
Holman—about my mother's ways of making bread, I remember;
cousin Holman was questioning me, and had got me far beyond my
depth—in the house-place, when the letters were brought in by one
of the men, and I had to pay the carrier for his trouble before I could
look at them. A bill—a Canadian letter! What instinct made me so
thankful that I was alone with my dear unobservant cousin? What
made me hurry them away into my coat-pocket? I do not know. I felt
strange and sick, and made irrelevant answers, I am afraid. Then I
went to my room, ostensibly to carry up my boxes. I sate on the side
of my bed and opened my letter from Holdsworth. It seemed to me
as if I had read its contents before, and knew exactly what he had got
to say. I knew he was going to be married to Lucille Ventadour; nay,
that he *was* married; for this was the 5th of July, and he wrote word
that his marriage was fixed to take place on the 29th of June. I knew
all the reasons he gave, all the raptures he went into. I held the letter
loosely in my hands, and looked into vacancy, yet I saw the chaf-
finch's nest on the lichen-covered trunk of an old apple-tree opposite
my window, and saw the mother-bird come fluttering in to feed her
brood,—and yet I did not see it, although it seemed to me afterwards
as if I could have drawn every fibre, every feather. I was stirred up to
action by the merry sound of voices and the clamp* of rustic feet
coming home for the mid-day meal. I knew I must go down to
dinner; I knew, too, I must tell Phillis; for in his happy egotism, his
new-fangled foppery, Holdsworth had put in a P.S., saying that he
should send wedding-cards to me and some other Hornby and
Eltham acquaintances, and 'to his kind friends at Hope Farm'.
Phillis had faded away to one among several 'kind friends'. I don't
know how I got through dinner that day. I remember forcing myself
to eat, and talking hard; but I also recollect the wondering look in the

minister's eyes. He was not one to think evil without cause; but many a one would have taken me for drunk. As soon as I decently could I left the table, saying I would go out for a walk. At first I must have tried to stun reflection by rapid walking, for I had lost myself on the high moorlands far beyond the familiar gorse-covered common, before I was obliged for very weariness to slacken my pace. I kept wishing—oh! how fervently wishing I had never committed that blunder; that the one little half-hour's indiscretion could be blotted out. Alternating with this was anger against Holdsworth; unjust enough, I dare say. I suppose I stayed in that solitary place for a good hour or more, and then I turned homewards, resolving to get over the telling Phillis at the first opportunity, but shrinking from the fulfilment of my resolution so much that when I came into the house and saw Phillis (doors and windows open wide in the sultry weather) alone in the kitchen, I became quite sick with apprehension. She was standing by the dresser, cutting up a great household loaf into hunches of bread for the hungry labourers who might come in any minute, for the heavy thunder-clouds were overspreading the sky. She looked round as she heard my step.

'You should have been in the field, helping with the hay,' said she, in her calm, pleasant voice. I had heard her as I came near the house softly chanting some hymn-tune, and the peacefulness of that seemed to be brooding over her now.

'Perhaps I should. It looks as if it was going to rain.'

'Yes; there is thunder about. Mother has had to go to bed with one of her bad headaches. Now you are come in—'

'Phillis,' said I, rushing at my subject and interrupting her, 'I went a long walk to think over a letter I had this morning—a letter from Canada. You don't know how it has grieved me.' I held it out to her as I spoke. Her colour changed a little, but it was more the reflection of my face, I think, than because she formed any definite idea from my words. Still she did not take the letter. I had to bid her to read it, before she quite understood what I wished. She sate down rather suddenly as she received it into her hands; and, spreading it on the dresser before her, she rested her forehead on the palms of her hands, her arms supported on the table, her figure a little averted, and her countenance thus shaded. I looked out of the open window; my heart was very heavy. How peaceful it all seemed in the farmyard! Peace and plenty. How still and deep was the silence of the house!

Tick-tick went the unseen clock on the wide staircase. I had heard
the rustle once, when she turned over the page of thin paper. She
must have read to the end. Yet she did not move, or say a word, or
even sigh. I kept on looking out of the window, my hands in my
pockets. I wonder how long that time really was? It seemed to me
interminable—unbearable. At length I looked round at her. She
must have felt my look, for she changed her attitude with a quick
sharp movement, and caught my eyes.

'Don't look so sorry, Paul,' she said. 'Don't, please. I can't bear it.
There is nothing to be sorry for. I think not, at least. You have not
done wrong, at any rate.' I felt that I groaned, but I don't think she
heard me. 'And he,—there's no wrong in his marrying, is there? I'm
sure I hope he'll be happy. Oh! how I hope it!' These last words were
like a wail; but I believe she was afraid of breaking down, for she
changed the key in which she spoke, and hurried on. 'Lucille—that's
our English Lucy, I suppose? Lucille Holdsworth! It's a pretty name;
and I hope—I forget what I was going to say. Oh! it was this. Paul,
I think we need never speak about this again; only remember you are
not to be sorry. You have not done wrong; you have been very, *very*
kind; and if I see you looking grieved I don't know what I might
do;—I might break down, you know.'

I think she was on the point of doing so then, but the dark storm
came dashing down, and the thunder-cloud broke right above the
house, as it seemed. Her mother, roused from sleep, called out for
Phillis; the men and women from the hay-field came running into
shelter, drenched through. The minister followed, smiling, and not
unpleasantly excited by the war of elements; for, by dint of hard
work through the long summer's day, the greater part of the hay was
safely housed in the barn in the field. Once or twice in the succeeding
bustle I came across Phillis, always busy, and, as it seemed to me,
always doing the right thing. When I was alone in my own room at
night I allowed myself to feel relieved; and to believe that the worst
was over, and was not so very bad after all. But the succeeding days
were very miserable. Sometimes I thought it must be my fancy that
falsely represented Phillis to me as strangely changed, for surely, if
this idea of mine was well-founded, her parents—her father and
mother—her own flesh and blood—would have been the first to
perceive it. Yet they went on in their household peace and content;
if anything, a little more cheerfully than usual, for the 'harvest of the

first-fruits',* as the minister called it, had been more bounteous than usual, and there was plenty all around in which the humblest labourer was made to share. After the one thunderstorm, came one or two lovely serene summer days, during which the hay was all carried; and then succeeded long soft rains filling the ears of corn, and causing the mown grass to spring afresh. The minister allowed himself a few more hours of relaxation and home enjoyment than usual during this wet spell: hard earth-bound frost was his winter holiday; these wet days, after the hay harvest, his summer holiday. We sate with open windows, the fragrance and the freshness called out by the soft-falling rain filling the house-place; while the quiet ceaseless patter among the leaves outside ought to have had the same lulling effect as all other gentle perpetual sounds, such as mill-wheels and bubbling springs, have on the nerves of happy people. But two of us were not happy. I was sure enough of myself, for one. I was worse than sure,—I was wretchedly anxious about Phillis. Ever since that day of the thunderstorm there had been a new, sharp, discordant sound to me in her voice, a sort of jangle in her tone; and her restless eyes had no quietness in them; and her colour came and went without a cause that I could find out. The minister, happy in ignorance of what most concerned him, brought out his books; his learned volumes and classics. Whether he read and talked to Phillis, or to me, I do not know; but feeling by instinct that she was not, could not be, attending to the peaceful details, so strange and foreign to the turmoil in her heart, I forced myself to listen, and if possible to understand.

'Look here!' said the minister, tapping the old vellum-bound book he held; 'in the first *Georgic* he speaks of rolling and irrigation, a little further on he insists on choice of the best seed, and advises us to keep the drains clear. Again, no Scotch farmer could give shrewder advice than to cut light meadows while the dew is on, even though it involve night-work.* It is all living truth in these days.' He began beating time with a ruler upon his knee, to some Latin lines he read aloud just then. I suppose the monotonous chant irritated Phillis to some irregular energy, for I remember the quick knotting and breaking of the thread with which she was sewing. I never hear that snap repeated now, without suspecting some sting or stab troubling the heart of the worker. Cousin Holman, at her peaceful knitting, noticed the reason why Phillis had so constantly to interrupt the progress of her seam.

'It is bad thread, I'm afraid,' she said, in a gentle sympathetic voice. But it was too much for Phillis.

'The thread is bad—everything is bad—I am so tired of it all!' And she put down her work, and hastily left the room. I do not suppose that in all her life Phillis had ever shown so much temper before. In many a family the tone, the manner, would not have been noticed; but here it fell with a sharp surprise upon the sweet, calm atmosphere of home. The minister put down ruler and book, and pushed his spectacles up to his forehead. The mother looked distressed for a moment, and then smoothed her features and said in an explanatory tone,—'It's the weather, I think. Some people feel it different to others. It always brings on a headache with me.' She got up to follow her daughter, but half-way to the door she thought better of it, and came back to her seat. Good mother! she hoped the better to conceal the unusual spirt* of temper, by pretending not to take much notice of it. 'Go on, minister,' she said; 'it is very interesting what you are reading about, and when I don't quite understand it, I like the sound of your voice.' So he went on, but languidly and irregularly, and beat no more time with his ruler to any Latin lines. When the dusk came on, early that July night because of the cloudy sky, Phillis came softly back, making as though nothing had happened. She took up her work, but it was too dark to do many stitches; and she dropped it soon. Then I saw how her hand stole into her mother's, and how this latter fondled it with quiet little caresses, while the minister, as fully aware as I was of this tender pantomime, went on talking in a happier tone of voice about things as uninteresting to him, at the time, I verily believe, as they were to me; and that is saying a good deal, and shows how much more real what was passing before him was, even to a farmer, than the agricultural customs of the ancients.

I remember one thing more,—an attack which Betty the servant made upon me one day as I came in through the kitchen where she was churning, and stopped to ask her for a drink of buttermilk.

'I say, cousin Paul,' (she had adopted the family habit of addressing me generally as cousin Paul, and always speaking of me in that form,) 'something's amiss with our Phillis, and I reckon you've a good guess what it is. She's not one to take up wi' such as you,' (not complimentary, but that Betty never was, even to those for whom she felt the highest respect,) 'but I'd as lief* yon Holdsworth had never come near us. So there you've a bit o' my mind.'

And a very unsatisfactory bit it was. I did not know what to answer to the glimpse at the real state of the case implied in the shrewd woman's speech; so I tried to put her off by assuming surprise at her first assertion.

'Amiss with Phillis! I should like to know why you think anything is wrong with her. She looks as blooming as any one can do.'

'Poor lad! you're but a big child after all; and you've likely never heared of a fever-flush. But you know better nor that, my fine fellow! so don't think for to put me off wi' blooms and blossoms and such-like talk. What makes her walk about for hours and hours o' nights when she used to be abed and asleep? I sleep next room to her, and hear her plain as can be. What makes her come in panting and ready to drop into that chair,'—nodding to one close to the door,—'and it's "Oh! Betty, some water, please"? That's the way she comes in now, when she used to come back as fresh and bright as she went out. If yon friend o' yours has played her false, he's a deal for t' answer for; she's a lass who's as sweet and as sound as a nut, and the very apple of her father's eye, and of her mother's too, only wi' her she ranks second to th' minister. You'll have to look after yon chap, for I, for one, will stand no wrong to our Phillis.'

What was I to do, or to say? I wanted to justify Holdsworth, to keep Phillis's secret, and to pacify the woman all in the same breath. I did not take the best course, I'm afraid.

'I don't believe Holdsworth ever spoke a word of—of love to her in all his life. I'm sure he didn't.'

'Ay, ay! but there's eyes, and there's hands, as well as tongues; and a man has two o' th' one and but one o' t'other.'

'And she's so young; do you suppose her parents would not have seen it?'

'Well! if you axe me that, I'll say out boldly, "No." They've called her "the child" so long—"the child" is always their name for her when they talk on her between themselves, as if never anybody else had a ewe-lamb before them—that she's grown up to be a woman under their very eyes, and they look on her still as if she were in her long clothes. And you ne'er heard on a man falling in love wi' a babby in long clothes!'

'No!' said I, half laughing. But she went on as grave as a judge.

'Ay! you see you'll laugh at the bare thought on it—and I'll be bound th' minister, though he's not a laughing man, would ha' sniggled at* th' notion of falling in love wi' the child. Where's Holdsworth off to?'

'Canada,' said I, shortly.

'Canada here, Canada there,' she replied, testily. 'Tell me how far he's off, instead of giving me your gibberish. Is he a two days' journey away? or a three? or a week?'

'He's ever so far off—three weeks at the least,' cried I in despair. 'And he's either married, or just going to be. So there!' I expected a fresh burst of anger. But no; the matter was too serious. Betty sate down, and kept silence for a minute or two. She looked so miserable and downcast, that I could not help going on, and taking her a little into my confidence.

'It is quite true what I said. I know he never spoke a word to her. I think he liked her, but it's all over now. The best thing we can do—the best and kindest for her—and I know you love her, Betty—'

'I nursed her in my arms; I gave her little brother his last taste o' earthly food,' said Betty, putting her apron up to her eyes.

'Well! don't let us show her we guess that she is grieving; she'll get over it the sooner. Her father and mother don't even guess at it, and we must make as if we didn't. It's too late now to do anything else.'

'I'll never let on; I know nought. I've known true love mysel', in my day. But I wish he'd been farred* before he ever came near this house, with his "Please Betty" this, and "Please Betty" that, and drinking up our new milk as if he'd been a cat. I hate such beguiling ways.'

I thought it was as well to let her exhaust herself in abusing the absent Holdsworth; if it was shabby and treacherous in me, I came in for my punishment directly.

'It's a caution to a man how he goes about beguiling. Some men do it as easy and innocent as cooing doves. Don't you be none of 'em, my lad. Not that you've got the gifts to do it, either; you're no great shakes to look at, neither for figure, nor yet for face, and it would need be a deaf adder* to be taken in wi' your words, though there may be no great harm in 'em.' A lad of nineteen or twenty is not flattered by such an out-spoken opinion even from the oldest and ugliest of her sex; and I was only too glad to change the subject by my repeated injunctions to keep Phillis's secret. The end of our conversation was this speech of hers,—

'You great gaupus,* for all you're called cousin o' th' minister—
many a one is cursed wi' fools for cousins—d'ye think I can't see
sense except through your spectacles? I give you leave to cut out my
tongue, and nail it up on th' barn-door for a caution to magpies, if I
let out on that poor wench, either to herself, or any one that is hers,
as the Bible says.* Now you've heard me speak Scripture language,
perhaps you'll be content, and leave me my kitchen to myself.'

During all these days, from the 5th of July to the 17th, I must
have forgotten what Holdsworth had said about cards. And yet
I think I could not have quite forgotten; but, once having told
Phillis about his marriage, I must have looked upon the after consequence of cards as of no importance. At any rate they came upon
me as a surprise at last. The penny-post reform,* as people call it,
had come into operation a short time before; but the never-ending
stream of notes and letters which seem now to flow in upon most
households had not yet begun its course; at least in those remote
parts. There was a post-office at Hornby; and an old fellow, who
stowed away the few letters in any or all his pockets, as it best
suited him, was the letter-carrier to Heathbridge and the neighbourhood. I have often met him in the lanes thereabouts, and asked
him for letters. Sometimes I have come upon him, sitting on the
hedge-bank resting; and he has begged me to read him an address,
too illegible for his spectacled eyes to decipher. When I used to
inquire if he had anything for me, or for Holdsworth (he was not
particular to whom he gave up the letters, so that he got rid of
them somehow, and could set off homewards), he would say he
thought that he had, for such was his invariable safe form of answer;
and would fumble in breast-pockets, waistcoat-pockets, breeches-
pockets, and, as a last resource, in coat-tail pockets; and at length
try to comfort me, if I looked disappointed, by telling me, 'Hoo
had missed this toime, but was sure to write to-morrow;' 'Hoo'
representing an imaginary sweetheart.

Sometimes I had seen the minister bring home a letter which he
had found lying for him at the little shop that was the post-office at
Heathbridge, or from the grander establishment at Hornby. Once or
twice Josiah, the carter, remembered that the old letter-carrier had
trusted him with an epistle to 'Measter', as they had met in the lanes.
I think it must have been about ten days after my arrival at the farm,
and my talk to Phillis cutting bread-and-butter at the kitchen dresser,

before the day on which the minister suddenly spoke at the dinner-table, and said,—

'By-the-by, I've got a letter in my pocket. Reach me my coat here, Phillis.' The weather was still sultry, and for coolness and ease the minister was sitting in his shirt-sleeves. 'I went to Heathbridge about the paper they had sent me, which spoils all the pens—and I called at the post-office, and found a letter for me, unpaid,—and they did not like to trust it to old Zekiel. Ay! here it is! Now we shall hear news of Holdsworth,—I thought I'd keep it till we were all together.' My heart seemed to stop beating, and I hung my head over my plate, not daring to look up. What would come of it now? What was Phillis doing? How was she looking? A moment of suspense,—and then he spoke again. 'Why! what's this? Here are two visiting tickets* with his name on, no writing at all. No! it's not his name on both. MRS Holdsworth! The young man has gone and got married.' I lifted my head at these words; I could not help looking just for one instant at Phillis. It seemed to me as if she had been keeping watch over my face and ways. Her face was brilliantly flushed; her eyes were dry and glittering; but she did not speak; her lips were set together almost as if she was pinching them tight to prevent words or sounds coming out. Cousin Holman's face expressed surprise and interest.

'Well!' said she, 'who'd ha' thought it! He's made quick work of his wooing and wedding. I'm sure I wish him happy. Let me see'—counting on her fingers,—'October, November, December, January, February, March, April, May, June, July,—at least we're at the 28th,—it is nearly ten months after all, and reckon a month each way off—'

'Did you know of this news before?' said the minister, turning sharp round on me, surprised, I suppose, at my silence,—hardly suspicious, as yet.

'I knew—I had heard—something. It is to a French Canadian young lady,' I went on, forcing myself to talk. 'Her name is Ventadour.'

'Lucille Ventadour!' said Phillis, in a sharp voice, out of tune.

'Then you knew too!' exclaimed the minister.

We both spoke at once. I said, 'I heard of the probability of——, and told Phillis.' She said, 'He is married to Lucille Ventadour, of French descent; one of a large family near St. Meurice; am not I right?' I nodded. 'Paul told me,—that is all we know, is not it? Did you see the Howsons, father, in Heathbridge?' and she forced herself to talk more than she had done for several days, asking many questions, trying, as I could see, to keep the conversation off the one raw surface, on which to touch was agony. I had less self-command; but I followed her lead. I was not so much absorbed in the conversation but what I could see that the minister was puzzled and uneasy; though he seconded Phillis's efforts to prevent her mother from recurring to the great piece of news, and uttering continual exclamations of wonder and surprise. But with that one exception we were all disturbed out of our natural equanimity, more or less. Every day, every hour, I was reproaching myself more and more for my blundering officiousness. If only I had held my foolish tongue for that one half-hour; if only I had not been in such impatient haste to do something to relieve pain! I could have knocked my stupid head against the wall in my remorse. Yet all I could do now was to second the brave girl in her efforts to conceal her disappointment and keep her maidenly secret. But I thought that dinner would never, never come to an end. I suffered for her, even more than for myself. Until now everything which I had heard spoken in that happy household were simple words of true meaning. If we had aught to say, we said it; and if any one preferred silence, nay if all did so, there would have been no spasmodic, forced efforts to talk for the sake of talking, or to keep off intrusive thoughts or suspicions.

At length we got up from our places, and prepared to disperse; but two or three of us had lost our zest and interest in the daily labour. The minister stood looking out of the window in silence, and when he roused himself to go out to the fields where his labourers were working, it was with a sigh; and he tried to avert his troubled face as he passed us on his way to the door. When he had left us, I caught sight of Phillis's face, as, thinking herself unobserved, her countenance relaxed for a moment or two into sad, woful weariness. She started into briskness again when her mother spoke, and hurried away to do some little errand at her bidding. When we two were alone, cousin Holman recurred to Holdsworth's marriage. She was one of those people who like to view an event from every side of probability, or even possibility; and she had been cut short from indulging herself in this way during dinner.

'To think of Mr Holdsworth's being married! I can't get over it, Paul. Not but what he was a very nice young man! I don't like her name, though; it sounds foreign. Say it again, my dear. I hope she'll know how to take care of him, English fashion. He is not strong, and if she does not see that his things are well aired, I should be afraid of the old cough.'

'He always said he was stronger than he had ever been before, after that fever.'

'He might think so, but I have my doubts. He was a very pleasant young man, but he did not stand nursing very well. He got tired of being coddled, as he called it. I hope they'll soon come back to England, and then he'll have a chance for his health. I wonder now, if she speaks English; but, to be sure, he can speak foreign tongues like anything, as I've heard the minister say.'

And so we went on for some time, till she became drowsy over her knitting, on the sultry summer afternoon; and I stole away for a walk, for I wanted some solitude in which to think over things, and, alas! to blame myself with poignant stabs of remorse.

I lounged lazily as soon as I got to the wood. Here and there the bubbling, brawling brook circled round a great stone, or a root of an old tree, and made a pool; otherwise it coursed brightly over the gravel and stones. I stood by one of these for more than half an hour, or, indeed, longer, throwing bits of wood or pebbles into the water, and wondering what I could do to remedy the present state of things. Of course all my meditation was of no use; and at length the distant sound of the horn employed to tell the men far afield to leave off work, warned me that it was six o'clock, and time for me to go home. Then I caught wafts of the loud-voiced singing of the evening psalm. As I was crossing the ash-field, I saw the minister at some distance talking to a man. I could not hear what they were saying, but I saw an impatient or dissentient (I could not tell which) gesture on the part of the former, who walked quickly away, and was apparently absorbed in his thoughts, for though he passed within twenty yards of me, as both our paths converged towards home, he took no notice of me. We passed the evening in a way which was even worse than dinner-time. The minister was silent, depressed, even irritable. Poor cousin Holman was utterly perplexed by this unusual frame of mind and temper in her husband; she was not well herself, and was suffering from the extreme and sultry heat, which made her less talkative than usual. Phillis, usually so reverently tender to her parents, so soft, so gentle, seemed now to take no notice of the unusual state of things, but talked to me—to any one, on indifferent subjects, regardless of her father's gravity, of her mother's piteous looks of bewilderment. But once my eyes fell upon her hands, concealed under the table, and I could see the passionate, convulsive manner in which she laced and interlaced her fingers perpetually, wringing them together from time to time, wringing till the compressed flesh became perfectly white. What could I do? I talked with her, as I saw she wished; her grey eyes had dark circles round them, and a strange kind of dark light in them; her cheeks were flushed, but her lips were white and wan. I wondered that others did not read these signs as clearly as I did. But perhaps they did; I think, from what came afterwards, the minister did.

Poor cousin Holman! she worshipped her husband; and the outward signs of his uneasiness were more patent to her simple heart than were her daughter's. After a while she could bear it no longer. She got up, and, softly laying her hand on his broad stooping shoulder, she said,—

'What is the matter, minister? Has anything gone wrong?'

He started as if from a dream. Phillis hung her head, and caught her breath in terror at the answer she feared. But he, looking round with a sweeping glance, turned his broad, wise face up to his anxious wife, and forced a smile, and took her hand in a reassuring manner.

'I am blaming myself, dear. I have been overcome with anger this afternoon. I scarcely knew what I was doing, but I turned away Timothy Cooper. He has killed the Ribstone pippin at the corner of the orchard; gone and piled the quicklime for the mortar for the new stable wall against the trunk of the tree—stupid fellow! killed the tree outright—and it loaded with apples!'

'And Ribstone pippins are so scarce,' said sympathetic cousin Holman.

'Ay! But Timothy is but a half-wit; and he has a wife and children. He had often put me to it sore, with his slothful ways, but I had laid it before the Lord, and striven to bear with him. But I will not stand it any longer, it's past my patience. And he has notice to find another place. Wife, we won't talk more about it.' He took her hand gently off his shoulder, touched it with his lips; but relapsed into a silence as profound, if not quite so morose in appearance, as before. I could not tell why, but this bit of talk between her father and mother seemed to take all the factitious spirits out of Phillis. She did not speak now, but looked out of the open casement at the calm large moon, slowly moving through the twilight sky. Once I thought her eyes were filling with tears; but, if so, she shook them off, and arose with alacrity when her mother, tired and dispirited, proposed to go to bed immediately after prayers. We all said good-night in our separate ways to the minister, who still sate at the table with the great Bible open before him, not much looking up at any of our salutations, but returning them kindly. But when I, last of all, was on the point of leaving the room, he said, still scarcely looking up,—

'Paul, you will oblige me by staying here a few minutes. I would fain have some talk with you.'

I knew what was coming, all in a moment. I carefully shut-to the door, put out my candle, and sate down to my fate. He seemed to find some difficulty in beginning, for, if I had not heard that he wanted to speak to me, I should never have guessed it, he seemed so much absorbed in reading a chapter to the end. Suddenly he lifted his head up and said,—

'It is about that friend of yours, Holdsworth! Paul, have you any reason for thinking he has played tricks upon Phillis?'

I saw that his eyes were blazing with such a fire of anger at the bare idea, that I lost all my presence of mind, and only repeated,—

'Played tricks on Phillis!'

'Aye! you know what I mean: made love to her, courted her, made her think that he loved her, and then gone away and left her. Put it as you will, only give me an answer of some kind or another—a true answer, I mean—and don't repeat my words, Paul.'

He was shaking all over as he said this. I did not delay a moment in answering him,—

'I do not believe that Edward Holdsworth ever played tricks on Phillis, ever made love to her; he never, to my knowledge, made her believe that he loved her.'

I stopped; I wanted to nerve up my courage for a confession, yet I wished to save the secret of Phillis's love for Holdsworth as much as I could; that secret which she had so striven to keep sacred and safe; and I had need of some reflection before I went on with what I had to say.

He began again before I had quite arranged my manner of speech. It was almost as if to himself,—'She is my only child; my little daughter! She is hardly out of childhood; I have thought to gather

her under my wings* for years to come; her mother and I would lay
down our lives to keep her from harm and grief.' Then, raising his
voice, and looking at me, he said, 'Something has gone wrong with
the child; and it seemed to me to date from the time she heard of that
marriage. It is hard to think that you may know more of her secret
cares and sorrows than I do,—but perhaps you do, Paul, perhaps you
do,—only, if it be not a sin, tell me what I can do to make her happy
again; tell me.'

'It will not do much good, I am afraid,' said I, 'but I will own how
wrong I did; I don't mean wrong in the way of sin, but in the way of
judgment. Holdsworth told me just before he went that he loved
Phillis, and hoped to make her his wife, and I told her.'

There! it was out; all my part in it, at least; and I set my lips tight
together, and waited for the words to come. I did not see his face;
I looked straight at the wall opposite; but I heard him once begin to
speak, and then turn over the leaves in the book before him. How
awfully still that room was! The air outside, how still it was! The
open windows let in no rustle of leaves, no twitter or movement of
birds—no sound whatever. The clock on the stairs—the minister's
hard breathing—was it to go on for ever? Impatient beyond bearing
at the deep quiet, I spoke again,—

'I did it for the best, as I thought.'

The minister shut the book to hastily, and stood up. Then I saw
how angry he was.

'For the best, do you say? It was best, was it, to go and tell a young
girl what you never told a word of to her parents, who trusted you
like a son of their own?'

He began walking about, up and down the room close under the
open windows, churning up his bitter thoughts of me.

'To put such thoughts into the child's head,' continued he; 'to
spoil her peaceful maidenhood with talk about another man's love;
and such love, too,' he spoke scornfully now—'a love that is ready
for any young woman. Oh, the misery in my poor little daughter's
face to-day at dinner—the misery, Paul! I thought you were one to
be trusted—your father's son too, to go and put such thoughts into
the child's mind; you two talking together about that man wishing to
marry her.'

I could not help remembering the pinafore, the childish garment
which Phillis wore so long, as if her parents were unaware of her

progress towards womanhood. Just in the same way the minister spoke and thought of her now, as a child, whose innocent peace I had spoiled by vain and foolish talk. I knew that the truth was different, though I could hardly have told it now; but, indeed, I never thought of trying to tell; it was far from my mind to add one iota to the sorrow which I had caused. The minister went on walking, occasionally stopping to move things on the table, or articles of furniture, in a sharp, impatient, meaningless way, then he began again,—

'So young, so pure from the world! how could you go and talk to such a child, raising hopes, exciting feelings—all to end thus; and best so, even though I saw her poor piteous face look as it did. I can't forgive you, Paul; it was more than wrong—it was wicked—to go and repeat that man's words.'

His back was now to the door, and, in listening to his low angry tones, he did not hear it slowly open, nor did he see Phillis standing just within the room, until he turned round; then he stood still. She must have been half undressed; but she had covered herself with a dark winter cloak, which fell in long folds to her white, naked, noise-less feet. Her face was strangely pale: her eyes heavy in the black circles round them. She came up to the table very slowly, and leant her hand upon it, saying mournfully,—

'Father, you must not blame Paul. I could not help hearing a great deal of what you were saying. He did tell me, and perhaps it would have been wiser not, dear Paul! But—oh, dear! oh, dear! I am so sick with shame! He told me out of his kind heart, because he saw—that I was so very unhappy at his going away.'

She hung her head, and leant more heavily than before on her supporting hand.

'I don't understand,' said her father; but he was beginning to understand. Phillis did not answer till he asked her again. I could have struck him now for his cruelty; but then I knew all.

'I loved him, father!' she said at length, raising her eyes to the minister's face.

'Had he ever spoken of love to you? Paul says not!'

'Never.' She let fall her eyes, and drooped more than ever. I almost thought she would fall.

'I could not have believed it,' said he, in a hard voice, yet sighing the moment he had spoken. A dead silence for a moment. 'Paul! I was unjust to you. You deserved blame, but not all that I said.' Then again a silence. I thought I saw Phillis's white lips moving, but it might have been the flickering of the candlelight—a moth had flown in through the open casement, and was fluttering round the flame; I might have saved it, but I did not care to do so, my heart was too full of other things. At any rate, no sound was heard for long endless minutes. Then he said,—'Phillis! did we not make you happy here? Have we not loved you enough?'

She did not seem to understand the drift of this question; she looked up as if bewildered, and her beautiful eyes dilated with a painful, tortured expression. He went on, without noticing the look on her face; he did not see it, I am sure.

'And yet you would have left us, left your home, left your father and your mother, and gone away with this stranger, wandering over the world.'

He suffered, too; there were tones of pain in the voice in which he uttered this reproach. Probably the father and daughter were never so far apart in their lives, so unsympathetic. Yet some new terror came over her, and it was to him she turned for help. A shadow came over her face, and she tottered towards her father; falling down, her arms across his knees, and moaning out,—

'Father, my head! my head!' and then she slipped through his quick-enfolding arms, and lay on the ground at his feet.

I shall never forget his sudden look of agony while I live; never! We raised her up; her colour had strangely darkened; she was insensible. I ran through the back-kitchen to the yard pump, and brought back water. The minister had her on his knees, her head against his breast, almost as though she were a sleeping child. He was trying to rise up with his poor precious burden, but the momentary terror had robbed the strong man of his strength, and he sank back in his chair with sobbing breath.

'She is not dead, Paul! is she?' he whispered, hoarse, as I came near him.

I, too, could not speak, but I pointed to the quivering of the muscles round her mouth. Just then cousin Holman, attracted by some unwonted sound, came down. I remember I was surprised at the time at her presence of mind, she seemed to know so much better what to do than the minister, in the midst of the sick affright which blanched her countenance, and made her tremble all over. I think now that it was the recollection of what had gone before; the miserable thought that possibly his words had brought on this attack, whatever it might be, that so unmanned the minister. We carried her upstairs, and while the women were putting her to bed, still unconscious, still slightly convulsed, I slipped out, and saddled one of the horses, and rode as fast as the heavy-trotting beast could go, to Hornby, to find the doctor there, and bring him back. He was out, might be detained the whole night. I remember saying, 'God help us all!' as I sate on my horse, under the window, through which the apprentice's head had appeared to answer my furious tugs at the night-bell. He was a good-natured fellow. He said,—

'He may be home in half an hour, there's no knowing; but I daresay he will. I'll send him out to the Hope Farm directly he comes in. It's that good-looking young woman, Holman's daughter, that's ill, isn't it?'

'Yes.'

'It would be a pity if she was to go. She's an only child, isn't she? I'll get up, and smoke a pipe in the surgery, ready for the governor's coming home. I might go to sleep if I went to bed again.'

'Thank you, you're a good fellow!' and I rode back almost as quickly as I came.

It was a brain fever.* The doctor said so, when he came in the early summer morning. I believe we had come to know the nature of the illness in the night-watches that had gone before. As to hope of ultimate recovery, or even evil prophecy of the probable end, the cautious doctor would be entrapped into neither. He gave his directions, and promised to come again; so soon, that this one thing showed his opinion of the gravity of the case.

By God's mercy she recovered, but it was a long, weary time first. According to previously made plans, I was to have gone home at the beginning of August. But all such ideas were put aside now, without a word being spoken. I really think that I was necessary in the house, and especially necessary to the minister at this time; my father was the last man in the world, under such circumstances, to expect me home.

I say, I think I was necessary in the house. Every person (I had almost said every creature, for all the dumb beasts seemed to know and love Phillis) about the place went grieving and sad, as though a cloud was over the sun. They did their work, each striving to steer clear of the temptation to eye-service,* in fulfilment of the trust reposed in them by the minister. For the day after Phillis had been taken ill, he had called all the men employed on the farm into the empty barn; and there he had entreated their prayers for his only child; and then and there he had told them of his present incapacity for thought about any other thing in this world but his little daughter, lying nigh unto death, and he had asked them to go on with their daily labours as best they could, without his direction. So, as I say, these honest men did their work to the best of their ability, but they slouched along with sad and careful faces, coming one by one in the dim mornings to ask news of the sorrow that overshadowed the house; and receiving Betty's intelligence, always rather darkened by passing through her mind, with slow shakes of the head, and a dull wistfulness of sympathy. But, poor fellows, they were hardly fit to be trusted with hasty messages, and here my poor services came in. One time I was to ride hard to Sir William Bentinck's, and petition for ice out of his ice-house, to put on Phillis's head. Another it was to Eltham I must go, by train, horse, anyhow, and bid the doctor there come for a consultation, for fresh symptoms had appeared, which Mr Brown, of Hornby, considered unfavourable. Many an hour have I sate on the window-seat, half-way up the stairs, close by the old clock, listening in the hot stillness of the house for the sounds in the sick-room. The minister and I met often, but spoke together seldom. He looked so old—so old! He shared the nursing with his wife; the strength that was needed seemed to be given to them both in that day. They required no one else about their child. Every office about her was sacred to them; even Betty only went into the room for the most necessary purposes. Once I saw Phillis through the open door; her pretty golden hair had been cut off long before; her head was covered with wet cloths, and she was moving it backwards and forwards on the pillow, with weary, never-ending motion, her poor eyes shut, trying in the old accustomed way to croon out a hymn tune, but perpetually breaking it up into moans of pain. Her mother sate by her, tearless, changing the cloths upon her head with patient solicitude. I did not see the minister at first, but there he was in a dark corner, down upon his knees, his hands clasped together in passionate prayer. Then the door shut, and I saw no more.

One day he was wanted; and I had to summon him. Brother Robinson and another minister, hearing of his 'trial', had come to see him. I told him this upon the stair-landing in a whisper. He was strangely troubled.

'They will want me to lay bare my heart. I cannot do it. Paul, stay with me. They mean well; but as for spiritual help at such a time—it is God only, God only, who can give it.'

So I went in with him. They were two ministers from the neighbourhood; both older than Ebenezer Holman; but evidently inferior to him in education and worldly position. I thought they looked at me as if I were an intruder, but remembering the minister's words I held my ground, and took up one of poor Phillis's books (of which I could not read a word) to have an ostensible occupation. Presently I was asked to 'engage in prayer', and we all knelt down; Brother Robinson 'leading', and quoting largely as I remember from the Book of Job. He seemed to take for his text, if texts are ever taken for prayers, 'Behold thou hast instructed many; but now it is come upon thee, and thou faintest, it toucheth thee and thou art troubled.'* When we others rose up, the minister continued for some minutes on his knees. Then he too got up, and stood facing us, for a moment, before we all sate down in conclave. After a pause Robinson began,—

'We grieve for you, Brother Holman, for your trouble is great. But we would fain have you remember you are as a light set on a hill;* and the congregations are looking at you with watchful eyes. We have been talking as we came along on the two duties required of you in this strait; Brother Hodgson and me. And we have resolved to exhort you on these two points. First, God has given you the opportunity of showing forth an example of resignation.' Poor Mr Holman visibly winced at this word. I could fancy how he had tossed aside such brotherly preachings in his happier moments; but now his whole system was unstrung, and 'resignation' seemed a term which presupposed that the dreaded misery of losing Phillis was inevitable. But good stupid Mr Robinson went on. 'We hear on all sides that there are scarce any hopes of your child's recovery; and it may be well to bring you to mind of Abraham; and how he was willing to kill his only child when the Lord commanded. Take example by him, Brother Holman. Let us hear you say, "The Lord giveth and the Lord taketh away. Blessed be the name of the Lord!"'*

There was a pause of expectancy. I verily believe the minister tried to feel it; but he could not. Heart of flesh was too strong. Heart of stone he had not.*

'I will say it to my God, when He gives me strength,—when the day comes,' he spoke at last.

The other two looked at each other, and shook their heads. I think the reluctance to answer as they wished was not quite unexpected. The minister went on: 'There are hopes yet', he said, as if to himself. 'God has given me a great heart for hoping, and I will not look forward beyond the hour.' Then turning more to them,—and speaking louder, he added: 'Brethren, God will strengthen me when the time comes, when such resignation as you speak of is needed. Till then I cannot feel it; and what I do not feel I will not express; using words as if they were a charm.' He was getting chafed, I could see.

He had rather put them out by these speeches of his; but after a short time and some more shakes of the head, Robinson began again,—

'Secondly, we would have you listen to the voice of the rod,* and ask yourself for what sins this trial has been laid upon you; whether you may not have been too much given up to your farm and your cattle; whether this world's learning has not puffed you up to vain conceit and neglect of the things of God; whether you have not made an idol of your daughter?'

'I cannot answer—I will not answer!' exclaimed the minister. 'My sins I confess to God. But if they were scarlet (and they are so in His sight,' he added, humbly), 'I hold with Christ that afflictions are not sent by God in wrath as penalties for sin.'

'Is that orthodox, Brother Robinson?' asked the third minister, in a deferential tone of inquiry.

Despite the minister's injunction not to leave him, I thought matters were getting so serious that a little homely interruption would be more to the purpose than my continued presence, and I went round to the kitchen to ask for Betty's help.

' 'Od rot 'em!' said she; 'they're always a-coming at ill-convenient times; and they have such hearty appetites, they'll make nothing of what would have served master and you since our poor lass has been ill. I've but a bit of cold beef in th' house; but I'll do some ham and eggs, and that'll rout 'em from worrying the minister. They're a deal quieter after they've had their victual. Last time as old Robinson came, he was very reprehensible upon master's learning, which he couldn't compass to save his life, so he needn't have been afeard of that temptation, and used words long enough to have knocked a body down; but after me and missus had given him his fill of victual, and he'd had some good ale and a pipe, he spoke just like any other man, and could crack a joke with me.'

Their visit was the only break in the long weary days and nights. I do not mean that no other inquiries were made. I believe that all the neighbours hung about the place daily till they could learn from some out-comer how Phillis Holman was. But they knew better than to come up to the house, for the August weather was so hot that every door and window was kept constantly open, and the least sound outside penetrated all through. I am sure the cocks and hens had a sad time of it; for Betty drove them all into an empty barn, and kept them fastened up in the dark for several days, with very little effect as regarded their crowing and clacking. At length came a sleep which was the crisis, and from which she wakened up with a new faint life. Her slumber had lasted many, many hours. We scarcely dared to breathe or move during the time; we had striven to hope so long, that we were sick at heart, and durst not trust in the favourable signs: the even breathing, the moistened skin, the slight return of delicate colour into the pale, wan lips. I recollect stealing out that evening in the dusk, and wandering down the grassy lane, under the shadow of the over-arching elms to the little bridge at the foot of the hill, where the lane to the Hope Farm joined another road to Hornby. On the low parapet of that bridge I found Timothy Cooper, the stupid, half-witted labourer, sitting, idly throwing bits of mortar into the brook below. He just looked up at me as I came near, but gave me no greeting either by word or gesture. He had generally made some sign of recognition to me, but this time I thought he was sullen at being dismissed. Nevertheless I felt as if it would be a relief to talk a little to some one, and I sate down by him. While I was thinking how to begin, he yawned weariedly.

'You are tired, Tim?' said I.

'Aye,' said he. 'But I reckon I may go home now.'

'Have you been sitting here long?'

'Welly* all day long. Leastways sin' seven i' th' morning.'

'Why, what in the world have you been doing?'

'Nought.'

'Why have you been sitting here, then?'

'T' keep carts off.' He was up now, stretching himself, and shaking his lubberly limbs.

'Carts! what carts?'

'Carts as might ha' wakened yon wench! It's Hornby market day. I reckon yo're no better nor a half-wit yoursel'.' He cocked his eye at me as if he were gauging my intellect.

'And have you been sitting here all day to keep the lane quiet?'

'Ay. I've nought else to do. Th' minister has turned me adrift. Have yo' heard how th' lass is faring to-night?'

'They hope she'll waken better for this long sleep. Good night to you, and God bless you, Timothy,' said I.

He scarcely took any notice of my words, as he lumbered across a stile that led to his cottage. Presently I went home to the farm. Phillis had stirred, had spoken two or three faint words. Her mother was with her, dropping nourishment into her scarce conscious mouth. The rest of the household were summoned to evening prayer for the first time for many days. It was a return to the daily habits of happiness and health. But in these silent days our very lives had been an unspoken prayer. Now we met in the house-place, and looked at each other with strange recognition of the thankfulness on all our faces. We knelt down; we waited for the minister's voice. He did not begin as usual. He could not; he was choking. Presently we heard the strong man's sob. Then old John turned round on his knees, and said,—

'Minister, I reckon we have blessed the Lord wi' all our souls, though we've ne'er talked about it; and maybe He'll not need spoken words this night. God bless us all, and keep our Phillis safe from harm! Amen.'

Old John's impromptu prayer was all we had that night.

'Our Phillis,' as he called her, grew better day by day from that time. Not quickly; I sometimes grew desponding, and feared that she would never be what she had been before; no more she has, in some ways.

I seized an early opportunity to tell the minister about Timothy Cooper's unsolicited watch on the bridge during the long summer's day.

'God forgive me!' said the minister. 'I have been too proud in my own conceit. The first steps I take out of this house shall be to Cooper's cottage.'

I need hardly say Timothy was reinstated in his place on the farm; and I have often since admired the patience with which his master tried to teach him how to do the easy work which was henceforward carefully adjusted to his capacity.

Phillis was carried downstairs, and lay for hour after hour quite silent on the great sofa, drawn up under the windows of the house-place. She seemed always the same, gentle, quiet, and sad. Her energy did not return with her bodily strength. It was sometimes pitiful to see her parents' vain endeavours to rouse her to interest. One day the minister brought her a set of blue ribbons, reminding her with a tender smile of a former conversation in which she had owned to a love of such feminine vanities. She spoke gratefully to him, but when he was gone she laid them on one side, and languidly shut her eyes. Another time I saw her mother bring her the Latin and Italian books that she had been so fond of before her illness—or, rather, before Holdsworth had gone away. That was worst of all. She turned her face to the wall, and cried as soon as her mother's back was turned. Betty was laying the cloth for the early dinner. Her sharp eyes saw the state of the case.

'Now, Phillis!' said she, coming up to the sofa; 'we ha' done a' we can for you, and th' doctors has done a' they can for you, and I think the Lord has done a' He can for you, and more than you deserve, too, if you don't do something for yourself. If I were you, I'd rise up and snuff the moon, sooner than break your father's and your mother's hearts wi' watching and waiting till it pleases you to fight your own way back to cheerfulness. There, I never favoured long preachings, and I've said my say.'

A day or two after Phillis asked me, when we were alone, if I thought my father and mother would allow her to go and stay with them for a couple of months. She blushed a little as she faltered out her wish for change of thought and scene.

'Only for a short time, Paul. Then—we will go back to the peace of the old days. I know we shall; I can, and I will!'*

# EXPLANATORY NOTES

## LIZZIE LEIGH

3 *Milton's famous line . . . the interpreter, who stood between God and her*: Milton, *Paradise Lost*, iv. 299: 'He for God only, she for God in him'.

4 *house-place*: the common farmhouse living-room, described by Gaskell in 'Half a Life-time Ago' as 'a sort of better kitchen, in which no cookery is done' (p. 113).

*the Prodigal Son*: Luke 15: 11–32.

6 *fain to*: glad under the circumstances; glad or content to take a certain course in default of opportunity for anything better, or as the lesser of two evils (*OED*).

*pottered*: troubled, perplexed, or worried. A now rare regional usage, related to pothered.

*chaffering*: haggling.

7 *shippon . . . supper the cows*: *shippon*: a cattle-shed. *supper*: to give (horses, cattle, etc.) their evening feed and bed them down for the night. Northern dialect.

*sough*: a sighing or murmuring sound.

8 *noticed to him*: an obsolete usage, meaning to mention.

*a-this-ns*: like this (dialect; from the Old Norse). Cf. *Sylvia's Lovers*, ch. 14: 'Kester! oh, man! speak out, but dunnot leave me a this-ns.'

9 *'sided'*: put in order. Northern dialect.

*hope deferred*: Proverbs 13: 12: 'Hope deferred maketh the heart sick.'

13 *at after*: for after. In a footnote to *Mary Barton*, ch.4 Gaskell notes Shakespeare's use of the phrase in *Richard II*.

*cast it up*: rake up and utter as a reproach. Northern dialect.

*threep it up*: insist on discussing. Northern dialect.

*speered at*: questioned.

14 *telled me on*: told me of.

*Pharisee*: a self-righteous person; one who considers herself holier than others.

*mode*: glossy black silk.

15 *loosed*: let out, dismissed.

*call cousins*: claim relationship.

*gradely*: handsome.

*Whatten*: what kind of. Northern dialect.

15 *cocket*: stuck up.

    *frab her*: worry her.

16 *welly*: well nigh; almost; nearly (dialect).

    *on*: of.

    *marred*: spoilt, over-indulged.

17 *flyted*: scolded.

22 *"who was lost and is found"*: Luke 15: 24: 'For this my son was dead, and is alive again; he was lost, and is found.'

26 *'Not all the scalding . . . angel-face'*: from Bryan Waller Proctor ('Barry Cornwall'), 'On the Portrait of a Child' in *English Songs* (London, 1832).

28 *coach-stand*: a place where horse-drawn coaches wait for hire.

29 *fascinated*: laid under a spell, bewitched.

31 *the lost piece of silver—found once more*: Luke 15: 8–9: 'Either what woman having ten pieces of silver, if she lose one piece, doth not light a candle, and sweep the house, and seek diligently till she find it? And when she hath found it, she calleth her friends and her neighbours together, saying Rejoice with me; for I have found the piece which I had lost.'

## MORTON HALL

32 *Ethelinda*: medieval form of the Old English name *Æðelind*, perhaps reflecting the Sidebothams' pride in their 'older blood' (see below, p. 33). The name was rarely used after the Norman Conquest, but it was revived in the late eighteenth century, as a result of Charlotte Smith's *Ethelinda, or the Recluse of the Lake* (London, 1789).

    *the Repeal of the Corn Laws*: the Corn Laws, the first of which were introduced in 1815, were a series of statutes that kept corn prices at a high level, in order to protect English farmers from cheap foreign imports of grain. Though popular with the landed gentry and with the farming interest, they caused great distress amongst the poor, and were vigorously opposed by the Chartists and the Anti-Corn Law League. They were repealed in 1846. Bridget Sidebotham's sense that their repeal was a disaster establishes immediately her allegiance to the landed interest.

    *Lord Monteagle . . . the Gunpowder Plot*: *Lord Monteagle*: William Parker, Lord Monteagle (1575–1622), was brought up a Catholic, but professed his conversion to Protestantism. It was through his Catholic connections that he discovered the Gunpowder Plot and there was considerable contemporary suspicion that he had in fact been involved in it. He was, however, rewarded and protected by the government, and hailed as a national hero. He received an annuity of £500 for life and lands worth a further £200 per year. *the Gunpowder Plot*: a conspiracy by a group of English Catholics, including Guy Fawkes, to depose James I by blowing up the Houses of Parliament. The attempt, made on the night of 4/5 November 1605, failed;

the conspirators were seized, tortured, and executed, and James celebrated his survival by ordering the day to be marked by bonfires, and designated 5 November, by an Act of Parliament that remained in force until 1859, as a day of thanksgiving for 'the joyful day of deliverance'. After the 'Papal Aggression' of 1851, the celebrations held on the day became a focus for popular anti-Catholic feeling, and in many places led to rioting (see Denis G. Paz, *Popular Anti-Catholicism in Mid-Victorian England* (Stanford, Calif., 1992), ch. 8).

*somewhere in Rome, there was a book kept*: Bridget's sensational view of Roman Catholicism was shared by many in the early 1850s. The Pope's re-establishment of Roman Catholic bishoprics in England in 1850 was widely seen as an attack on Protestant England. The 'Papal Aggression', as it came to be called, led to a crescendo of anti-Catholic feeling in England, and there were numerous rumours of papist plots. The popular press portrayed Catholicism as a religion shrouded in secrecy, that sought to undermine the nation from within: *Punch*, for example, published a cartoon depicting the Pope as ' "The Guy Fawkes of 1850". Preparing to Blow Up All England'.

*Guy Fawkes and his dark lantern*: Guy Fawkes was captured outside Westminster Palace at about midnight on 4/5 November 1605, the night before the opening of Parliament. He was carrying a lighted dark lantern—a lantern with a slide or arrangement by which the light could be concealed. Hence the lines in the traditional song, 'Remember, remember the fifth of November', 'By God's providence he was catch'd | With a dark lantern and burning match.'

*'mysterious dispensations'*: 'mysterious dispensations of Providence' was a well-known phrase signifying God's inscrutable plan. In Evangelical discourse it indicated pious resignation, but by the early nineteenth century, it was being mocked as a cant term for 'nobody's fault'. Thus, Dickens invokes it comically in *Pickwick Papers* (1837), ch. 2: 'Like a general postman's coat—queer coats those—made by contract—no measuring—mysterious dispensations of Providence—all the short men get long coats—all the long men short ones.' Thus Florence Nightingale's *Notes on Nursing: What It Is, and What It Is Not* (London, 1860), 17. 'We should hear no longer of "Mysterious Dispensations," and of "Plague and Pestilence," being "in God's hands," when, so far as we know, He has put them into our own.'

*the Female Jesuit*: *The Female Jesuit, or Spy in the Family. A True Narrative of Recent Intrigues in a Protestant Household* by Jemima Luke (London, 1851) was presented as the true story of an imposture carried out by a young woman who claimed to have escaped from a convent, and was taken in by the author and her husband, a Congregational clergyman. The tale, which was followed in 1852 by *A Sequel to the Female Jesuit; Concerning Her Present History and Recent Discovery*, created a sensation. The announced mission of the Society of Jesus to propagate the Catholic faith throughout the world made the figure of the Jesuit a potent symbol of Catholic menace to Protestant England for nineteenth-century writers, and much lurid speculation on the subject was provoked by the 'female Jesuit' 's confession of her deceitful infiltration of English domesticity.

32 *we did know the female Jesuit's second cousin*: perhaps a joking reference to the fact that the impostor was reported to have an aunt and uncle in Manchester.

33 *Drumble*: this is the name given to Manchester in Gaskell's *Cranford*. Scholars have speculated about the precise location of Morton Hall and the Sidebothams' farm; but the origins of 'Morton Hall' appear to lie less in a particular place than in a story that Gaskell had heard from the Brontës' servant Tabby Aykroyd on her first visit to Charlotte Brontë in Haworth in September 1853. 'The whole story originated', she later wrote, 'in two little graphic sentences from the old Servant (aged 93) at Mr Brontë's at Haworth; I asked her why a certain field was called the Balcony Field (put a strong & long accent on cony) and she told me that when she was a girl "while the Farmers were still about the country & before they had begun to plague the land with their Mills &c" there had been a grand House with Balconies in that field, that she remembered seeing Miss —— (I forget the name) get into the Carriage, with her hair all taken up over a cushion, and in a blue sattin [sic] open gown, but Oh! she came to sore want, for her Nephew gambled away the property and then she lent him money, and at last he & she had nowhere to hide their heads but an old tumbledown Cottage (shewn to me) where folk do say she was clemmed to death, and many a one in Haworth remembered him going to Squire (Name forgotten again) to offer a bit of old plate for sale to bury his Aunt rather than that the Parrish should do it[.] The "Blue sattin gown" and the "clemming to death" were a striking contrast, were they not?' (Extract of a letter from Mrs Gaskell to Lady Hatherton, 27 December 1853, quoted in J. A. V. Chapple, 'Elizabeth Gaskell's *Morton Hall* and *The Poor Clare*', *Brontë Society Transactions*, 20, (1990), 47–9.)

*Morton seems but a suburb of the great town near*: Manchester was famed for its mushroom growth in the first half of the nineteenth century. 'Manchester already has 300,000 inhabitants and is growing at a prodigious rate,' wrote Alexis de Tocqueville in his 'Journey to England' on 2 July 1835 (*Journeys to England and Ireland*, trans. George Lawrence and K. P. Mayer, ed. Jacob Peter Mayer (London: Faber and Faber, 1957), 104).

*the Alderney*: a kind of cow bred in Alderney. In the early 1850s the Gaskells kept 'an Alderney, a very pretty young creature' in the field by their house on the edge of Manchester (*The Letters of Mrs Gaskell*, ed. J. V. A. Chapple and Arthur Pollard (Manchester: Manchester University Press, 1966), 199).

*the Restoration*: the first part of 'Morton Hall' tells of how Morton Hall passes into the hands of the Puritan Carrs during Cromwell's Protectorate, and of the return of the Mortons at the Restoration of Charles II (1660–85). The English Civil War (1642–8) ended with the execution of Charles I in 1649, and the establishment of the Commonwealth under Oliver Cromwell. Charles I's son, who was to become Charles II, was forced to flee to the Continent, and many Royalists (like John Morton) followed him. Royalist estates were confiscated and sold, often going to Cromwellians such as the Roundhead Richard Carr. After the death of Cromwell in September 1658 Charles II was recalled, and proclaimed king in May 1660.

34 *Old Oliver died . . . carrying him down to hell*: Cromwell died on 3 September 1658, the anniversary of his victories at Dunbar and Worcester, a day of tremendous wind and storm. 'Nature seemed to sympathise with the dying patriot and hero. The wind howled and roared around the palace; houses were unroofed; chimneys blown down; and trees, that had stood for half a century in the parks, were uptorn, and strewn over the earth' (J. T. Headley, *Life of Oliver Cromwell* (New York 1848), 426).

*General Monk*: George Monk of Monck (1608–70), famous general who fought successively in the Royalist, Parliamentarian, and Cromwellian causes, and finally supported the Restoration of Charles II. 'At last, General Monk got the army well into his own hands, and then in pursuance of a secret plan he seems to have entertained from the time of Oliver's death, declared for the King's cause,' writes Dickens, in *A Child's History of England*, going on to describe how, when the returning king landed at Dover, 'he kissed and embraced Monk' and 'made him ride in the coach with himself and his brothers' (ch. 34, pt. 2). It is because her kinsman Monk is a turncoat that Alice Carr is able to retain possession of Morton Hall.

*the Stuarts*: the Stuart monarchs were James I and Charles I (1603–49), Charles II and James II (1660–88), and William III and Mary II of Orange, and Anne (1689–1714).

*calves' head for dinner every thirtieth of January*: 30 January was the anniversary of the execution of Charles I. After the Restoration it was entered in the Book of Common Prayer as 'The Day of the Martyrdom of the Blessed King Charles I'; with 'A Form of Prayer, with Fasting, to be used yearly' upon that day. In parody of this, the republican Calves' Head Club met to eat roast calf's head on this day.

*the first twenty-ninth of May . . . oak-leaves*: on 30 May 1660 Parliament ordered 'the 29 of May, the King's birthday, to be for ever kept as a day of thanksgiving for our redemption from tyranny and the King's return to his Government, he entering London that day' (*House of Commons Journal* viii, 30 May 1660), and a special service (discontinued in 1859) was inserted into the Book of Common Prayer. 'It is usual with the vulgar people to wear oak-leaves in their hats on this day, and dress their horses' heads with them. This is in commemoration of the shelter afforded to

Charles by an oak while making his escape from England, after his defeat
at Worcester, by Cromwell' (William Hone, *Every-Day Book*).

34  *the Duke of Albemarle*: as Dickens notes sardonically in *A Child's History
of England*, Monk was made Duke of Albemarle for his support of the
Royalist cause.

35  *Queen of Sheba . . . Jerusalem*: in the biblical account, Solomon does not
ask the Queen of Sheba to visit him: she comes of her own accord. But he
is reported as giving her 'all her desire, whatsoever she asked' (I Kings 10:
13). The likening of the King to Solomon, who 'loved many strange
women', may be an allusion to Charles II's promiscuity.

*the Virginian plantations*: Virginia, one of the thirteen original American
colonies, was known as the Old Dominion because it remained loyal to
Charles II during the Commonwealth. For this reason, many Royalists,
like Sir John, fled there after the execution of Charles I.

36  *Old Noll*: popular nickname for Oliver Cromwell.

37  *the court was no place for an honest woman*: 'There never were such
profligate times in England as under Charles the Second,' writes Dickens,
in *A Child's History of England* (ch. 35). 'The sexual promiscuity of
Charles and his court, its applause of the sexually voracious male, its
attraction of sexually available women and its contempt for marital
fidelity in men or women, were both distinctive and new in English culture' (N. H. Keeble, *The Restoration: England in the 1660s* (Oxford:
Blackwell, 2002), 171–2).

*hidden conventicles*: Dissenting religious meetings, held in secret. The
Conventicles Act stipulated that 'any person above the age of sixteen who
was present at any religious service not according to the Prayer-Book,
was to be imprisoned for three months for the first offence, six for the
second, and to be transported for the third' (Dickens, *A Child's History of
England*, ch. 35). It was passed in 1664, expired in 1668, and was renewed
in a milder form in 1670 as 'An Act to prevent and suppress seditious
conventicles'.

38  *post-horses*: horses available for hire by travellers from towns or from inns
along the roads connecting them.

*Dinners were then at one o'clock in the country*: mealtimes in the country
were based around daylight and the need to accomplish the most important tasks before dark. Those who rose at dawn took their main meal in the
middle of the day. (See Andrea Broomfield, *Food and Cooking in Victorian
England* (Westport, Conn.: Praeger Publishers, 2007), ch. 3.)

39  *cade-lambs*: a cade-lamb is one brought up by hand, either as a pet or
because its mother has died. Its meat was believed to be especially
succulent.

*at Worcester*: the battle of Worcester (1651), at which Cromwell defeated
the Royalists. 'The escape of Charles after this battle of Worcester did
him good service long afterwards, for it induced many of the generous

English people to take a romantic interest in him,' notes Dickens, in
*A Child's History of England* (ch. 34).

*sweet-pot*: pot-pourri.

40 *Ephraim . . . Zerubbabel . . . Help-me-or-I-perish*: Puritan names. Ephraim
was the second son of Joseph, born in Egypt, and founder of the tribe of
Ephraim; Zerubbabel was the Jewish governor of Jehud at the time of the
building of the temple in the sixth century BC. On the Puritan fashion for
'scriptural phrases, pious ejaculations, or godly admonitions' as names,
see C. W. Bardsley, *Curiosities of Puritan Nomenclature* (London, 1880).
Such names, it seems, were actually comparatively rare in England, and
were indicative of religious extremism.

41 *pillion*: either a woman's saddle, or an attachment to an ordinary saddle to
allow a woman to be carried.

*tire-women*: (archaic) lady's maids.

*mere*: a lake or pond.

*lists*: (archaic) wishes, chooses.

42 *the battle of the Boyne*: fought on 1 July 1690, just outside the town of
Drogheda, between two rival claimants of the English, Scottish, and Irish
thrones, the Catholic King James II, who had lost the throne of England
in the bloodless 'Glorious Revolution' of 1688; and his son-in-law, the
Protestant King William III. James was defeated in the battle.

*some thought her a prophetess*: the New Testament enjoined women to
silence, but large numbers of women prophets emerged and became notorious during the Civil War and Commonwealth. Although such prophecy
was checked at the Restoration with the persecution of Dissenting sects,
women's prophesying continued into the last years of the century. See
Phyllis Mack, *Visionary Women: Ecstatic Prophecy in Seventeenth-Century
England* (Berkeley and Los Angeles: University of California Press, 1992).

*doomed*: (archaic) to doom, to pronounce sentence upon. A curse.

*huxters*: hucksters, pedlars; carrying the suggestion of ready to make a
profit in a mean and petty way.

*meeting-house*: a Dissenting chapel or place of worship.

*when . . . our Squire Morton's grandfather came into possession*: the second
story that Bridget Sidebotham tells begins in the time of George III. The
Sidebotham sisters are children too young to wear mourning when Phillis
Morton, aged 17, goes to a ball and dances with Prince William of
Gloucester, who would have been a young officer of 23 in 1799.

*a strict entail*: a legal arrangement to prevent the head of the family from
selling any part of the estate. Under a strict entail the male head of the
family was effectively a life tenant, enjoying its revenue but unable to
dispose of it.

43 *Prince William of Gloucester, nephew to good old George the Third*: William
Frederick, second duke of Gloucester and Edinburgh (1776–1834), was

the only son of William Henry, first duke of Gloucester and Edinburgh, a younger brother of George III. He entered the army at the age of 13, and he was frequently and rapidly promoted, being made a major-general at 20, and made lieutenant-general in 1799.

44 *make interest*: bring personal influence to bear.

*maréchale powder*: scented hair-powder.

*cushion*: a pad worn by women under the hair. The 'cushion' became the foundation of fashionable hairdressing in the 1770s and 1780s. Shaped like a heart or spear and puffed up like a pillow, the fabric or sometimes cork cushion was placed on the crown of the head. The hair, natural and acquired, could then be frizzed and piled over and around it. It remained pinned in place between hairdressings, sometimes for days or weeks at a time. 'It should be made clean, and delicately neat, or else, being placed on the warmest part of the head, it may breed and become troublesome,' writes James Stewart, in the course of an elaborate account of how to dress hair using the cushion (James Stewart, *Plocacosmos: Or the Whole Art of Hair Dressing* (London, 1782), 278). The style was still fashionable in the 1790s, though, as Lady Morgan reports, it was 'beginning to disappear, when Mr Pitt, by the hair-powder tax, gave a death-blow to the trade of hair-dressing' (*The Book of the Boudoir* (2 vols., London, 1829), 49).

*knots*: ribbon bows.

45 *making cheeses*: 'turning rapidly around and then suddenly sinking down, so that the petticoats are inflated all round somewhat in the shape of a cheese' (*OED*).

*bore away the bell*: took first place.

*quarter-day*: one of the four days fixed by custom as marking off the quarters of the year, on which tenancies begin and end and the payment of rent and other quarterly charges falls due. In England and Ireland the quarter days are traditionally Lady Day (25 Mar.), Midsummer Day (24 June), Michaelmas (29 Sept.), and Christmas (25 Dec.).

*played high*: gambled for high stakes.

48 *house-lamb*: a lamb kept in or near the house, and fattened for the table.

49 *provisions rose . . . much ado to make ends meet*: this part of the story seems to be set in the second decade of the nineteenth century. Bridget Sidebotham may be referring to the scarcity of 1816–17.

50 *courtesy*: an obeisance, a curtsey (obsolete).

*house-place*: see note to 'Lizzie Leigh', p. 4.

*Grey wood ashes*: evidence that the Mortons have been unable to afford coal.

54 *one day*: the last of the stories appears to begin in around 1840, years after the deaths of Phillis and her brother, when Cordelia Mannisty is a child

of about 10. She is a young married woman at the time of Bridget Sidebotham's narration in about 1852.

55 *great staring sash windows*: a sign of wealth. Sash windows in the early nineteenth century more usually consisted of six small panes. Large sheets of glass were expensive, until the removal of the duty on glass in 1845, when the price of the plate glass fell by three-quarters.

56 *ended in smoke*: came to nothing.

*casting it up*: raking it up reproachfully. Northern dialect.

*great beauties*: the sisters might be thinking of the Gunning sisters, who came of a relatively impoverished family, but became famous for their success in finding aristocratic husbands. The youngest, Catherine (died 1773), married a plain Irish esquire, Robert Travis. But the two elder sisters were famous beauties. Maria Gunning (1733–60) married the Earl of Coventry, and Elizabeth Gunning (1734–90) married successively the Dukes of Hamilton and Argyll. 'It was said that one of the Gunnings had graced the apartment with her beauty,' it is reported of the Cranford Assembly Rooms in *Cranford*, ch. 9.

*rule of three*: method of finding a fourth number from three given numbers, of which the first is in the same proportion to the second as the third is to the unknown fourth. In Miss Sophronia's calculation, Miss Burrell is to a baron as Arabella is to a nobleman of superior rank.

*an honourable*: courtesy title given to the younger sons of earls and to the children of peers below the rank of marquess.

57 *The Female Chesterfield; or, Letters from a Lady of Quality to her Niece*: Miss Sophronia's book is evidently modelled on the Earl of Chesterfield's famous *Letters to his Son* (1774), which became the model for many handbooks of etiquette.

*a flat board tied to her back, and her feet in stocks*: a back board was a board strapped across the back to straighten the figure; stocks were callisthenic devices used in girls' schools for straightening the feet.

*Pomfret cakes*: liquorice lozenges made at Pontefract since the sixteenth century.

58 *I had forgotten what the right word was*: the word that Bridget Sidebotham cannot remember is genealogy.

*spinnet*: a small keyboard instrument like a harpsichord.

59 *Santo Sebastiano; or, the Young Protector*: Gothic novel by Catherine Cuthbertson, published in 1806. Mrs Gaskell recommended it to a friend in a letter as 'so funny and so ridiculous that it carries one on through all that quantity of reading. I do not mean that it is *meant* to be funny, for it is rather highflown, and very sentimental; but the heroine speaks broken English all throughout, and faints so often &c.&c, and yet there is a degree of interest in the story to carry one along' (*Further Letters of Mrs Gaskell*, ed. John Chapple and Alan Shelston (Manchester: Manchester University

Press, 2003), 58). In *Cranford*, ch. 9 the novel enters into one of Miss Pole's extended streams of consciousness: 'He spoke such pretty broken English, I could not help thinking of Thaddeus of Warsaw and the Hungarian brothers, and Santo Sebastiani.'

59 *God save the King*: 'God save the King' was composed by Thomas Augustine Arne (1710–78). The first definitive published version appeared in 1744 in *Thesaurus Musicus* and the song was popularized in Scotland and England in the following year, with the landing of Charles Edward Stuart.

*dictionary*: a person or thing regarded as a repository of knowledge, convenient for consultation (*OED*).

61 *'cousin Betty'*: a common term for female lunatics (James Orchard Halliwell-Phillips, *A Dictionary of Archaic and Provincial Words* (London, 1860)). 'I dunnot think there's a man living—or dead, for that matter—as can say Fosters wronged him of a penny, or gave short measure to a child or a Cousin Betty' (*Sylvia's Lovers*, ch. 14).

62 *she studied reflections a great deal*: Miss Dorothy evidently shares the early nineteenth-century interest in optical experiments. In his popular *Letters on Natural Magic* (1832) David Brewster had described the striking optical illusions produced by reflections—although 'reflections' may be one of the Sidebothams' malapropisms. The rayed lining of the bonnet is apparently aimed at producing a flattering effect.

65 *fear God and honour the king*: 1 Peter 2: 17.

66 *Cheltenham*: a fashionable spa town, popular with retired army officers.

## MY FRENCH MASTER

68 *he gave up his commission, and his half-pay*: officers in the army and navy were not entitled to a pension as of right until 1871. Half-pay was a retaining fee paid to the officer, so long as he was still (in theory) available for future service.

*Goldsmith's 'History of England', Rollins's 'Ancient History', Lindley Murray's Grammar*: Oliver Goldsmith, *History of England in a series of letters from a nobleman to his son* (1764); Charles Rollin, *The ancient history of the Egyptians, Carthaginians, Assyrians, Babylonians, Medes and Persians, Macedonians, and Grecians*, translated from the French (1730–8), and into its eighth edition by 1788; Lindley Murray, *English Grammar* (1795). All were standard schoolroom texts of the late eighteenth century.

69 *one of the forest rangers*: the story is set in the New Forest in Hampshire, an ancient royal hunting forest, the 'government' of which was in 1791 'nearly what it originally was, excepting only that the abolition of forest-law hath restrained the power of its officers'. Under the Lord Warden (the Duke of Gloucester), there were 'two distinct appointments of officers; the one to preserve the *venison* of the forest; and the other to

preserve its *vert* . . . Of those officers who superintend the game, are first the two *rangers*. But the office of *ranger*, as well as that of *bow-bearer*, and a few others, have long been in disuse: at least they seem to be delegated to the keepers: of these there are fifteen' (William Gilpin, *Remarks on Forest Scenery; and other Woodland Views* (2 vols., London, 1791), ii. 17–18).

*an emigrant gentleman*: French nobles began to 'emigrate' to England after the fall of the Bastille on 14 July 1789, and their estates in France were confiscated. By 1797 it was estimated that there were 300,000 émigrés in England.

*a great lion*: a celebrity.

*the fatal 21st of January, 1793*: the date on which Louis XVI of France was guillotined.

71 *a wig, delicately powdered, frizzed, and tied in a queue behind*: after 1790, wigs and powder were worn mainly by older, more conservative men, and ladies being presented at court. In France the association of wigs with the aristocracy caused the fashion for both to evaporate during the Terror of 1793. In England, the tax on hair powder imposed in 1795 had a similar effect. *queue*: a pigtail.

72 *sous-lieutenant*: (French) a second lieutenant.

*Michaelmas*: 29 September, the feast of St Michael and All Angels.

*once in January, and once in October*: Louis XVI of France was guillotined on 21 January 1793, and his widow Marie Antoinette on 15 October 1793.

73 *'the Iris being blown down'*: a coded allusion to Louis XVI's death. The fleur-de-lis on the French royal coat of arms is a stylized version of the lily species *Iris pseudacorus*.

*'The wicked, cruel boys had broken off the White Lily's head!'*: another allusion to the fleur-de-lis, whose literal translation from the French is 'lily flower', this time referring to the execution of Marie Antoinette. The lily is a traditional symbol of beauty and purity.

75 *crape*: a gauzy, crimped silk fabric dyed black and used in mourning dress.

*preux chevalier*: (French) gallant knight; chivalrous.

*if a lock was out of order, M. de Chalabre made it right for us*: Louis XVI was an amateur locksmith, and had a little workshop for the purpose at Versailles.

*silk-winders*: reels.

*paste-board*: pastry-board.

76 *peace of 1814*: the Treaty of Paris in 1814 temporarily ended the war between France and the Allied armies. Napoleon was banished to the island of Elba, and the Bourbon monarchy was reinstated, in the person of Louis XVIII, younger brother of Louis XVI.

*the Gazette*: the *London Gazette*, official journal of the British government, first published in 1665.

76 *Grillon's Hotel*: Louis XVIII entered London on 20 April 1814, and proceeded in procession, accompanied by the Prince Regent, to Grillon's Hotel in Albemarle Street, where he held court for several days before departing for France on 24 April 1814.

*devoirs*: (French) respects, duty.

*Gardes du Corps*: the king's bodyguard, composed of noblemen.

77 *orangerie*: a place where orange trees were grown in tubs.

*Miss Fanny*: Gaskell has apparently forgotten that the narrator's sister is called 'Mary': she appears as 'Fanny' throughout Chapter 2.

78 *Count de Provence*: former title of Louis XVIII, brother of Louis XVI. The son of the latter, who died in prison in June 1795, was recognized by the Royalists as Louis XVII.

*Duc de Duras*: (1771–1838), a member of the Gardes du Corps, who, Fanny Burney tells, stood at the king's left hand 'and was the Grand Maître des Cérémonies' during the reception at Grillon's Hotel. M. de Chalabre's experience reflects Gaskell's reading of Burney's account. 'The presentations were short, and without much mark or likelihood. The men bowed low, and passed on; the ladies courtsied, and did the same. Those who were not known gave a card, I think, to the Duc de Duras, who named them; those of former acquaintance with his majesty simply made their obeisance. M. de Duras, who knew how much fatigue the King had to go through, hurried every one on, not only with speed but almost with ill-breeding, to my extreme astonishment' (Fanny Burney, *Diary and Letters of Madame d'Arblay* (London, 1854), vii. 27).

*the Tuileries*: royal palace in Paris.

*my sword . . . ploughshare*: Isaiah 2: 4.

*franked*: have their passages paid.

79 *Cent Suisses, the Gardes du Porte, the Mousquetaires*: elite, ceremonial regiments.

80 *Turkey-red*: famous, exceptionally colourfast dye produced by madder. The process was introduced into France in 1746, and perfected at and around Rouen, in Normandy.

*M. du Fay, Fils*: M. du Fay, the son.

*the return from Elba . . . the battle of Waterloo*: Napoleon escaped from Elba in early 1815 and entered Paris on 20 March. His short return to power, known as the Hundred Days, ended with his defeat at the battle of Waterloo on 18 June.

*immortelles*: everlasting flowers, that retain their colour when they are dried.

*Duc de Feltre*: Henri Clarke (1765–1818) had served under Napoleon but offered his services to Louis XVIII in 1814. From March to July 1815 he was the king's minister of war.

81 *the 'de' was dropped now and for evermore*: 'de' in French names was a marker of aristocracy.

82 *the two principal county towns*: Southampton and Winchester.

*Jupiter-ship*: lordship.

83 *marraine*: (French) godmother.

*Valetta*: capital of Malta.

84 *esprit*: (French) wit.

85 *a Sister of Charity*: the order of the Sisters of Charity, founded by St Vincent de Paul, sent women drawn from the higher classes of society out into the world to relieve destitution and suffering. Susan's desire to join the order is of a piece with her father's chivalric ideals. Gaskell, who was close to the Nightingale family and greatly admired Florence Nightingale, would have known of her attempt to train with the Sisters of Charity in June 1853. (In the event she caught measles and left after only two weeks, going to recuperate with Gaskell's friend Madame Mohl (see next note).) Gaskell may also have known, through her friendship with Anna Jameson, of the latter's attempts to revive the order in secular form. Jameson's *Sisters of Charity: Catholic and Protestant, Abroad and at Home* was published in March 1855, and went into several editions by 1859.

*An English friend of mine who lives there . . . French in manners and ways*: the description is evocative of Gaskell's friend Madame Mohl, born Mary Clarke, who married a German professor of Persian, Julius Mohl. Gaskell was a frequent visitor to their Paris home.

86 *Ary Scheffer's sacred pictures*: Ary Scheffer (1795–1858) was a popular painter of religious and romantic subjects, and a close friend of Madame Mohl's.

## HALF A LIFE-TIME AGO

89 *a Stateswoman*: Cumbrian term for a yeoman farmer occupying his own land. The 'statesmen' were famously celebrated by Wordsworth for their independence and self-sufficiency, and for their intense attachment to their small estates and families.

*brattles*: northern word, describing the rattling sound made by a rapid stream over stones.

91 *miserable (as they call miserly people up in the north)*: Gaskell, with her lively interest in etymology, is playing upon the fact that 'miser' derives from the Latin *miser* (miserable, wretched), and is an old northern term for a miserable or wretched person. Richard Chenevix Trench, in *On the Study of Words* (London, 1851), notes it as 'a remarkable fact, that men should have agreed to apply the word "miser", or miserable, to the man eminently addicted to the vice of covetousness' (p. 49).

*'Paradise Lost' . . . 'The Pilgrim's Progress': the 'Paradise Lost' and 'Regained'*: John Milton, *Paradise Lost* (1667) and *Paradise Regained* (1671). *The Death*

*of Abel*: Salomon Gessner, *Der Tod Abels* (1760), an epic on the Old Testament subject, was translated into English poetic prose by Mary Collyer as *The Death of Abel. In Five Books* (1761), and went into numerous editions. 'No book of foreign growth has ever become so popular in England as *The Death of Abel*,' declared the *Quarterly Review* in 1814. 'It has been repeatedly printed at country presses, with worn types and on coarse paper; and it is found at country fairs, and in the little shops of remote towns almost as certainly as the *Pilgrim's Progress* and *Robinson Crusoe*' (quoted in Bertha Reed [Mrs George R. Coffman], *The Influence of Solomon Gessner upon English Literature* (Philadelphia, 1905), 5). *The Spiritual Quixote*: Richard Graves, *The Spiritual Quixote, or the Summer's Ramble of Mr. Geoffry Wildgoose* (1772), a comic novel whose hero is an itinerant Methodist preacher. *The Pilgrim's Progress*: John Bunyan, *The Pilgrim's Progress from this World to That Which is to Come* (1678).

91  *laking*: dialect term for taking a holiday.

   *a class now passing away*: fifty years before, Wordsworth had lamented the dwindling of the numbers of 'statesmen', as the cottage industries that contributed to their subsistence were replaced by factories, and traditional farming practices gave way to agricultural 'improvement' that required injection of capital. As Stephen Gill has pointed out, much in 'Half a Life-Time Ago' is evocative of 'Michael', in *Lyrical Ballads 1800*, which at once celebrates and elegizes this class (Gill, *Wordsworth and the Victorians* (Oxford: Clarendon Press, 1998), 129).

92  *notable*: a now rare usage, meaning competent and efficient in household matters (*OED*).

93  *a dree bit*: a difficult stretch. Northern dialect. (Cf. William Gaskell, in the second of his *Two Lectures on the Lancashire Dialect* delivered in Manchester in 1854, and appended to *Mary Barton* in that year: 'A very expressive adjective . . . is "dree;" as, "This is a dree bit o' road.") In Anglo-Saxon "dreogan" meant to suffer or endure, having for its preterite "dreah".'

   *loaf-bread*: bread baked in the oven, as distinct from the porridge and oatcakes made on the griddle that were staple fare in Cumberland. 'Loaf-bread . . . is white, soft, full of cavities, has an agreeable taste, and is easily digested' (*Encyclopedia Britannica*, 1824).

   *take tent*: care for; 'tent' signifying attention. Northern dialect.

96  *lungeous*: rough, bad-tempered.

98  *shippon*: See note to p. 6.

102  *treacle-posset*: milk heated with treacle.

107  *shandry*: a light trap or cart on springs (*OED*).

109  *"Nought but death shall part thee and me!"*: Ruth 1: 17: 'Where thou diest, I will die, and there will I be buried: the LORD do so to me, and more also, if aught but death part thee and me.'

116  *clap-bread*: oatcakes cooked on a griddle.

117 *briar and brake*: cf. *A Midsummer Night's Dream*, 3. 1. 102. *brake*: a thicket; see below, p. 124.

119 *redded up*: tidied, set in order. Northern dialect.

121 *keen*: harsh (obsolete).

*vis inertiae*: that property of matter which makes it resist any change.

*Yorkshire itself might have attempted to jockey her*: *jockey*: to cheat. Possibly a reference to the proverbial phrase 'To come Yorkshire over anyone', meaning to cheat or swindle them (*Grose's Dictionary of the Vulgar Tongue* (London, 1811)).

123 *lift*: the sky, upper regions (obsolete).

124 *maud*: a plaid of the kind traditionally worn by shepherds.

*the Furies*: Roman name (*Furiae*) for the Greek Erinyes, three goddesses of vengeance, with snakes for hair and blood dripping from their eyes.

## THE MANCHESTER MARRIAGE

130 *Title*: 'The Manchester Marriage' was Gaskell's contribution to the extra Christmas number of *Household Words*, entitled '*A House to Let*, by Charles Dickens and Others', that appeared on 7 December 1858. The frame story tells how an elderly woman, Sophonisba, notices signs of life in a seemingly empty 'House to Let' opposite her own and employs a friend, Jabez Jarber, and her servant, Trottle, to find out its history. Dickens and Wilkie Collins wrote the first and last chapters, 'Over the Way' and 'Let at Last'. Gaskell contributed 'The Manchester Marriage', Dickens 'Going into Society', Adelaide Anne Procter 'Three Evenings in the House', and Collins 'Trottle's Report'. The *Household Words* version of 'The Manchester Marriage' varies slightly from the text given here, in that it contains a few references to Dickens's frame story; the opening sentence, for example, reads: 'Mr and Mrs Openshaw came from Manchester to London, and took the House to Let.' Gaskell removed these references when she republished the story in *Right at Last and Other Tales*.

*early dinners . . . far longer evenings*: in the mid-nineteenth century there was considerably more class and regional variation in mealtimes than there is today. Country folk usually dined earlier than Londoners.

131 *the true Saxon accent*: William Gaskell, in his *Two Lectures on the Lancashire Dialect*, notes that in Lancashire speech 'the pronunciation of many words, which would strike a southern ear as peculiar, is simply the retention of the old Saxon sounds of the vowels' (p. 14).

133 *the Cape*: the Cape of Good Hope. Cape Town, in South Africa, was a port of call en route to the Far East.

*the Underwriters*: the insurers of the ship.

*with an unction*: with relish.

*her ewe-lamb*: 2 Samuel 12: 3: 'The poor man had nothing, save one little ewe-lamb.'

134 *a spirit not unlike that of Ruth*: Ruth in the Old Testament cleaves to her husband's family after her husband's death, saying to Naomi, her mother-in-law: 'Intreat me not to leave thee, or to return from following after thee: for whither thou goest, I will go; and where thou lodgest, I will lodge: thy people shall be my people, and thy God, my God' (Ruth 1: 16).

135 *the famous Yankee motto*: to beat, lick, flog, or whip creation, was a United States colloquialism meaning to surpass everything (*OED*). The phrase was much quoted in England. Thus, for example, the *Morning Chronicle*, 21 December 1858: 'Here is a comparatively new country, inhabited by a race who boast themselves able to "flog all creation" in energy and activity.' Thus *Punch*, in a parody of 'Yankee Doodle', on 14 August 1858: 'United, brother JONATHAN, In firm amalgamation, I guess we Anglo-Saxons can | If need be, whip creation. Yankee doodle, &c.'

*yea-nay*: of indefinite or indeterminate character (*OED*).

138 *nesh*: soft, squeamish. 'This word, which has dropped out of use except as a provincialism, as in Lancashire, has been introduced by Dickens in his *House to Let*,' notes a correspondent in *Notes and Queries* in January 1859, listing its usage by Chaucer, Gower, and Lydgate, and observing that 'the modern form . . . "nice", meaning "dainty" is 'not half so forcible' (*Notes and Queries*, 2nd ser. 7 (Jan.–June 1859), 66).

140 *an order to see Buckingham Palace*: the 'Mode of Obtaining Admission' to Buckingham Palace 'during the absence of the Court' is listed in Black's *Picturesque Tourist and Road and Railway Guidebook through England and Wales* (Edinburgh, 1859) as 'by ticket signed by the Lord Chamberlain' (p. xxiii).

143 *salved over*: smoothed over. Cf. Charles Kingsley, *Alton Locke* (1850), ch. 14: 'I salved over that feeling, being desirous to see everything in the brightest light.' The accusation appears to be that Nora sanctioned the marriage by not admitting the possibility that the first husband might be alive, and that she is now similarly not admitting her mistress's 'wickedness' in marrying bigamously.

146 *stood out*: persisted in asserting.

155 *one half of which was settled on her*: Openshaw and Alice are not legally married, and he is unable to marry her without disclosing all. He has therefore made provision for her in a manner that does not depend on her being his wife.

## COUSIN PHILLIS

156 *Eltham to Hornby*: Eltham is usually assumed to be based on Knutsford, the Cheshire town in which Elizabeth Gaskell grew up. On 12 May 1862, a few months before the publication of the first instalment of *Cousin Phillis*, the Cheshire Midland Railway was opened between Knutsford and Altrincham, linking to Manchester South Junction and Altrincham Railway, which had opened in 1849.

*Independent*: the Independents developed out of the radical wing of the Puritan movement in Elizabethan England. Initially persecuted, the movement gained strength during the Civil War and the Commonwealth: its adherents included Oliver Cromwell. Independents subscribed to the Calvinist doctrines of the Trinity, the final authority of scripture, and salvation by faith alone; and observed two sacraments, baptism and the Lord's Supper. They had distinctive ideas on church government, believing that power should rest with each local congregation, rather than a church hierarchy; and a keen interest in education, as they were barred from the universities. In the early nineteenth century most Independents began to call themselves Congregationalists.

157 *'Spare the rod, and spoil the child'*: Proverbs 13: 24: 'He that spareth his rod hateth his son; but he that loveth him chasteneth him betimes.'

*Phillis*: the name comes from the Greek word for green leaf or bough. It recurs in classical pastoral, and was often given to shepherdesses in Renaissance and eighteenth-century pastoral. It is also associated with desertion in love, because of the Thracian princess, Phyllis, who hanged herself in despair when her betrothed, Demophoon, son of Theseus, did not appear at the appointed time.

159 *wallowing in the mire*: 2 Peter 2: 21–2: 'For it had been better for them not to have known the way of righteousness, than, after they have known it, to turn from the holy commandment delivered unto them. But it is happened unto them according to the true proverb, The dog is turned to his own vomit again; and the sow that was washed to her wallowing in the mire.'

160 *sanded inn-parlour*: nineteenth-century public houses customarily had a sanded parlour, in which the floor was sprinkled with sand to absorb spills.

161 *event*: outcome.

162 *stone-crop*: navelwort, a plant with fleshy circular leaves and spires of straw-coloured flowers, which grows in rocks, walls, and stony banks in the west of Britain.

*fumitory*: a common weed, whose delicate grey-green leaves have a smoky appearance. The name stems from the Latin *fumus terrae*: 'smoke of the earth'.

*'the curate'* . . . *'the rector'*: the Dissenting minister's jibe at what he sees as the Anglican practice of employing a rector for show, whilst the lowly curate does the bulk of the parish work.

*house-place*: in northern houses the front door opened directly into the house-place, a room whose centrality in the life of the house was indicated by its name.

*huge muslin cravats*: very long muslin cravats, or neckcloths, which swathed the neck and muffled the chin, were fashionable in the early years of the nineteenth century.

163 *May-day*: 1 May had for centuries been the day set aside for the celebra-
tion of the coming of spring, and was widely celebrated throughout
England. The Puritans attempted to suppress the May Day festival
because of its pagan origins, and it is clearly for this reason that the minister disapproves of it.

164 *Abraham's servant . . . winning him a wife*: Genesis 24 tells how Abraham
sends his oldest servant 'unto my country and my kingdom' to find a wife
for his son Isaac. Rebekah draws water at the well for him and his camels,
and is thus revealed as the wife destined for Isaac: she leaves her family,
and returns with the servant, to marry him.

165 *sweetbriar . . . fraxinella*: *sweetbriar*: eglantine, or *rosa rubiginosa*, climbing
rose with a strong scent. *fraxinella*: or white dittany, a perennial plant
with pinnate leaves like those of the ash, and a scent like lemon peel.
When bruised, it has a balsamic scent.

166 *exercise*: act of worship.

*traces*: the straps of the horses' harness.

*whip-cord the plough-whips*: put new hempen cord into the plough whips.

167 *Ebenezer*: a name popular amongst Dissenters, and often used for
Dissenting chapels. It is taken from 1 Samuel 7: 12 which tells how
Samuel, after the Israelite defeat of the Philistines, 'took a stone . . . and
called the name of it Ebenezer' to stand as a testimony to God's help.

*water-furrow*: a deep furrow made for conducting water from the ground
and keeping it dry (*OED*).

*dauby*: sticky.

*"Come all harmonious tongues", to be sung to "Mount Ephraim" tune*: 'Come
all harmonious tongues' was a hymn by Isaac Watts (1674–1748),
Independent minister and hymn writer; the tune of 'Mount Ephraim' was
composed by Benjamin Milgrove (1731–1810).

168 *the little petticoated lad*: it was customary throughout the nineteenth century for boys up to the age of 5 or 6 to be dressed in skirts.

169 *a line or two of Latin*: from Virgil's *Georgics*. These, written by Virgil
(Publius Vergilius Maro) between 37 and 30 BC, both idealized the countryside and provided practical instruction in agriculture. Sampson Low,
publishers of Gaskell's *Round the Sofa* and *Right at Last and Other Tales*,
had published *The Farm and Fruit of Old. A Translation in Verse of the
First and Second Georgics of Virgil. By a Market-Gardener*, in 1862.

170 *the parish bull*: it had been customary for centuries in many parishes to
keep a common parish bull, which was at first the responsibility of the
manor, then of the constable or the churchwarden. During the eighteenth
century there was considerable dispute as to who was responsible for the
parish's common bull. (See Nicholas Russell, *Like Engend'ring Like*
(Cambridge: Cambridge University Press, 1986), 151 ff.

*three-cornered chair*: or roundabout chair, designed to fit in a corner, dating from the mid-eighteenth century.

*list*: the material of which the selvage of cloth consists (*OED*).

*beau-pot*: a large ornamental vase for cut flowers.

*Matthew Henry's Bible*: the work referred to is not a bible, but the famous multi-volume practical and devotional *Exposition of the Old and New Testaments* by Matthew Henry (1662–1714), Nonconformist divine and commentator.

*shovel-board*: an old game in which a coin or other disk was driven by a blow with the hand along a highly polished board, floor, or table (sometimes 10 yards or more long). 'In former times, the residences of the noblility, or the mansions of the opulent, were not thought to be complete without a shovel-board table; and this fashionable piece of furniture was usually stationed in the great hall' (Joseph Strutt, *The Sports and Pastimes of the People of England* (London, 1801)).

*white work*: embroidery in which the thread was the same colour as the base fabric, usually white. In the nineteenth century it was used on baby-clothes, blouses, and pinafores, and became popular as a demonstration of skill.

171 *shunting*: shifting a train from one line to another.

172 *Manning's patent winch*: a winch is a hoisting or hauling apparatus, consisting of a drum around which a rope is passed and a crank by which it is turned. The Patent Law Amendment Act of 1852 had established a dedicated Patent Office and introduced a single patent system for the entire United Kingdom.

*farriery*: the art of shoeing horses.

*"kindly meant is kindly taken"*: well-known phrase. Cf. Flora Finching in *Little Dorrit* (1856): 'which being kindly meant it may hoped will be kindly taken' (ch. 23).

173 *all's fish that comes to my net*: I turn everything to some use.

'*Whether we eat or drink . . . the glory of God*': 1 Corinthians 10: 31.

175 '*tempus fugit*': time flies. A hackneyed phrase in common use, signalling the limits of Paul's classical learning.

177 *l'Inferno*: the first part of *The Divine Comedy*, by Dante Aligheieri (1265–1321), one of the great works of world literature.

179 *gauds*: trinkets.

*a temptation and a snare*: biblical phrase, from 1 Timothy 6: 9.

180 *tyke*: a mongrel, a low-bred fellow.

*the old Adam*: unregenerate human nature.

181 '*exercised in spirit*': Dissenting expression, meaning soul-searching.

*stuff*: a woollen fabric.

181 *some book I once read . . . from the blue bed to the brown*: Oliver Goldsmith, *The Vicar of Wakefield*, ch. 1: 'We had no revolutions to fear, nor fatigues to undergo; all our adventures were by the fireside, and all our migrations from the blue bed to the brown.'

182 *George Stephenson*: civil engineer and pioneer of steam locomotion (1781–1848).

183 *'deep barrel'*: the barrel is the belly and loins of a horse or cow.

*dynamics*: the study of the causes of motion. A major branch of engineering.

184 *St Peter and St Paul*: the leading Apostles.

*drive my carriage*: to keep a carriage required a considerable income. 'How the man who drives his close carriage looks down upon him who only drives his barouche or phaeton; how both contemn the poor occupier of a gig,' writes William Howitt in *The Rural Life of England* (London, 1838).

189 *to a proverb*: so much that it has become proverbial (obsolete).

*plaid room*: a room with plaid or check soft furnishings.

190 *"When a man talks to you . . . them's metaphysics"*: 'When he to whom one speaks does not understand, and he who speaks himself does not understand, that is metaphysics': attributed to Voltaire.

192 *cranching*: crunching.

195 *Baretti*: Joseph Baretti, *A Dictionary of the English and Italian Languages*, published in 1760, with a dedication to Dr Johnson, and reprinted several times in the eighteenth century.

196 *theodolite*: a surveying instrument, for measuring horizontal angles.

*fidging fain*: eager, restless.

197 *euphuisms*: the word intended here appears to be 'euphemisms'. Gaskell makes the same slip in *Wives and Daughters*, ch. 37: '"If anything did—go wrong, you know," said Cynthia, using an euphuism for death, as most people do.'

*I Promessi Sposi*: historical novel by Alessandro Manzoni (1785–1873), which first appeared in Italy in 1827 and was translated into English as *The Betrothed* in 1845.

198 *seriousness*: the term here possibly has something of its obsolete meaning of earnestness regarding the things of religion.

*dram-drinking*: tippling.

199 *stone-pines*: medium-sized pine, widely cultivated in southern Europe for its sweet almond-like seeds.

200 *navvies*: construction workers, especially those employed on the railways. 'The word "navvie" or "navigator", is supposed to have originated in the fact of many of these labourers having been originally employed in making the navigations, or canals, the construction of which immediately preceded the railway era,' writes Samuel Smiles, in *Lives of the Engineers*

(1862), ch. 15. 'Unburdened, as they usually were, by domestic ties, unsoftened by family affection, and without much moral or religious training, the navvies came to be distinguished by a sort of savage manners, which contrasted with those of the surrounding population.'

201 *agait*: engaged with (Lancashire dialect).

204 *Ceres*: the Roman goddess of agriculture and of all the fruits of the earth.

208 *the sleeping beauty*: the princess in Perrault's fairy tale, who is shut up by enchantment in a castle, where she sleeps for a hundred years, whilst an impenetrable wood grows around. She is at last woken by the kiss of a young prince, who marries her.

211 *"Servants, obey in all things your master according to the flesh"*: Colossians 3: 22: 'Servants, obey in all things your master according to the flesh; not with eye-service, as menpleasers; but in singleness of heart, fearing God.'

*them that went down in ships upon the great deep*: Psalm 107: 24–5: 'They that go down to the sea in ships, that do business in great waters, These see the works of the Lord, and his wonders in the deep.'

218 *De Lolme on the British Constitution*: Jean Louis de Lolme, *The Constitution of England*, published in Amsterdam in 1771 and translated into English in 1775, one of the most distinguished and influential eighteenth-century treatises on English political liberty.

*the right ends of prayer . . . special providences*: *right ends of prayer*: serious religious subjects. *special providences*, much debated in the nineteenth century, were acts of divine intervention that fell short of miracles.

*'jibbed'*: stopped short, refused to go on. Used of a horse in harness.

219 *I have read . . . . few to love*: the lines quoted are from 'She dwelt among th'untrodden ways', one of the 'Lucy poems' in Wordsworth's *Lyrical Ballads 1800*.

220 *the measure with which I had been meting to him*: Mark 4: 24: 'Take heed what ye hear: with what measure ye mete, it shall be measured to you.'

*at the building of the Tower of Babel . . . each other's speech*: Genesis 9: 1–9.

221 *"Whatsoever thine hand findeth to do, do it with all thy might"*: Ecclesiastes 9: 10.

222 *clamp*: a heavy, stamping tread.

225 *the 'harvest of the first-fruits'*: Exodus 23: 19: 'the feast of harvest, the first-fruits of thy labours, which thou hast sown in the field'.

*'in the first Georgic . . . even though it involve night-work*: Virgil, *Georgics*, i. 268–9. Gaskell is here closely echoing an article by the American essayist Donald Grant Mitchell (one of a series about his farm in Connecticut) that had appeared in the *Atlantic Monthly* in June 1863: 'There is sound farm-talk in Virgil. . . . We are hardly launched upon the first Georgic before we find a pretty suggestion of the theory of rotation . . . Rolling and irrigation both glide into the verse a few lines later. He insists upon the choice of the

best seed, advises to keep the drains clear, even upon holy-days (268), and urges, in common with a great many shrewd New-England farmers, to cut light meadows when the dew is on (288–9), even though it involve night-work' (Donald G. Mitchell, 'Wet-Weather Work', *Atlantic Monthly*, 40 (1863), 721).

226 *spirt*: a sudden outbreak.

*I'd as lief*: I'd rather.

228 *sniggled at*: covertly laughed at.

*farred*: far away.

*need be a deaf adder*: Psalm 58: 4–5.

229 *gaupus*: simpleton.

*I give you leave to cut out my tongue . . . as the Bible says*: Proverbs 10: 31: 'the froward tongue shall be cut out'. Magpies were notorious as chatterers.

*penny-post reform*: Rowland Hill's pamphlet, *Post Office Reform: its Importance and Practicability* was published in 1837, and paved the way for the Act which introduced the Uniform Penny Post on 10 January 1840. The new Post Office Regulations stipulated that 'a Letter not exceeding HALF AN OUNCE IN WEIGHT, may be sent from any part of the United Kingdom, to any other part, for ONE PENNY, if paid when posted, or for TWO PENCE if paid when delivered'. As a result of this substantial reduction in postal charges, there was a considerable increase in the volume of mail delivered. In 1839 76 million letters were posted in Britain; in 1840, after the introduction of the Penny Post, there were 168 million.

230 *two visiting tickets*: visiting cards bearing the names of bride and groom, sometimes linked with a ribbon, were customarily sent out as announcements of marriage. Gaskell may here have been thinking of Millais's painting of 1854, *Wedding Cards*, which portrays a desolate-faced, apparently jilted girl holding a just-opened envelope and wedding cards.

235 *gather her under my wings*: Luke 13: 34: 'How often would I have gathered thy children together, as a hen doth gather her brood under her wings.'

238 *a brain fever*: inflammation of the brain, or encephalitis, believed in the Victorian period to be brought on by a sudden shock.

*eye-service*: see note to p. 211 above.

240 *'Behold, thou hast instructed many . . . thou art troubled'*: Job 4: 3–5.

*as a light set on a hill*: Matthew 5: 14.

*"The Lord giveth and the Lord taketh away. Blessed be the name of the Lord!"*: Job 1: 21.

*Heart of flesh was too strong. Heart of stone he had not*: Gaskell is making oblique reference to a text much cited in the mid-nineteenth century, Ezekiel 36: 26: 'A new heart also will I give you, and a new spirit will I put within you: and I will take away the stony heart out of your flesh, and I will give you a heart of flesh.'

241 *voice of the rod*: 'the voice of the rod', meaning the lesson taught by affliction, probably derives from Micah 6: 9: 'The Lord's voice crieth unto the city, and the man of wisdom shall see thy name: hear ye the rod, and who hath appointed it.' The phrase recurs in Dissenting sermons and homilies in the middle years of the nineteenth century.

242 *Welly*: well nigh.

244 *I will!*: in a letter to George Smith, her publisher, written whilst *Cousin Phillis* was as yet unfinished, in December 1863, Gaskell, speaking in the persona of her narrator Paul Manning, sketched in a possible longer ending thus:

> She . . . goes to my fathers—& in a town, among utterly different people & scenery, cures herself,—but it is a sort of moral' Tis better to have loved & lost, than never to have loved at all—last scene long years after. The Minister dead, I married—we hear of the typhus fever in the village where Phillis lives, & I go to persuade her & her bedridden mother to come to us. I find her making practical use of the knowledge she had learnt from Holdsworth and, with the help of common labourers, levelling & draining the undrained village—a child (orphaned by the fever) in her arms another plucking at her gown—we hear afterwards that she has adopted these to be her own. (*Further Letters*, 259–60)

*The Oxford World's Classics Website*

## www.worldsclassics.co.uk

- Browse the full range of Oxford World's Classics online

- Sign up for our monthly e-alert to receive information on new titles

- Read extracts from the Introductions

- Listen to our editors and translators talk about the world's greatest literature with our Oxford World's Classics audio guides

- Join the conversation, follow us on Twitter at OWC_Oxford

- Teachers and lecturers can order inspection copies quickly and simply via our website

## www.worldsclassics.co.uk

American Literature

British and Irish Literature

Children's Literature

Classics and Ancient Literature

Colonial Literature

Eastern Literature

European Literature

Gothic Literature

History

Medieval Literature

Oxford English Drama

Poetry

Philosophy

Politics

Religion

The Oxford Shakespeare

A complete list of Oxford World's Classics, including Authors in Context, Oxford English Drama, and the Oxford Shakespeare, is available in the UK from the Marketing Services Department, Oxford University Press, Great Clarendon Street, Oxford OX2 6DP, or visit the website at www.oup.com/uk/worldsclassics.

In the USA, visit www.oup.com/us/owc for a complete title list.

Oxford World's Classics are available from all good bookshops. In case of difficulty, customers in the UK should contact Oxford University Press Bookshop, 116 High Street, Oxford OX1 4BR.

|  | Late Victorian Gothic Tales |
| JANE AUSTEN | Emma |
|  | Mansfield Park |
|  | Persuasion |
|  | Pride and Prejudice |
|  | Selected Letters |
|  | Sense and Sensibility |
| MRS BEETON | Book of Household Management |
| MARY ELIZABETH BRADDON | Lady Audley's Secret |
| ANNE BRONTË | The Tenant of Wildfell Hall |
| CHARLOTTE BRONTË | Jane Eyre |
|  | Shirley |
|  | Villette |
| EMILY BRONTË | Wuthering Heights |
| ROBERT BROWNING | The Major Works |
| JOHN CLARE | The Major Works |
| SAMUEL TAYLOR COLERIDGE | The Major Works |
| WILKIE COLLINS | The Moonstone |
|  | No Name |
|  | The Woman in White |
| CHARLES DARWIN | The Origin of Species |
| THOMAS DE QUINCEY | The Confessions of an English Opium-Eater |
|  | On Murder |
| CHARLES DICKENS | The Adventures of Oliver Twist |
|  | Barnaby Rudge |
|  | Bleak House |
|  | David Copperfield |
|  | Great Expectations |
|  | Nicholas Nickleby |
|  | The Old Curiosity Shop |
|  | Our Mutual Friend |
|  | The Pickwick Papers |

|  | Six French Poets of the Nineteenth Century |
| --- | --- |
| HONORÉ DE BALZAC | Cousin Bette<br>Eugénie Grandet<br>Père Goriot |
| CHARLES BAUDELAIRE | The Flowers of Evil<br>The Prose Poems and Fanfarlo |
| BENJAMIN CONSTANT | Adolphe |
| DENIS DIDEROT | Jacques the Fatalist<br>The Nun |
| ALEXANDRE DUMAS (PÈRE) | The Black Tulip<br>The Count of Monte Cristo<br>Louise de la Vallière<br>The Man in the Iron Mask<br>La Reine Margot<br>The Three Musketeers<br>Twenty Years After<br>The Vicomte de Bragelonne |
| ALEXANDRE DUMAS (FILS) | La Dame aux Camélias |
| GUSTAVE FLAUBERT | Madame Bovary<br>A Sentimental Education<br>Three Tales |
| VICTOR HUGO | The Essential Victor Hugo<br>Notre-Dame de Paris |
| J.-K. HUYSMANS | Against Nature |
| PIERRE CHODERLOS DE LACLOS | Les Liaisons dangereuses |
| MME DE LAFAYETTE | The Princesse de Clèves |
| GUILLAUME DU LORRIS and JEAN DE MEUN | The Romance of the Rose |

Anthony Trollope    The American Senator

An Autobiography

Barchester Towers

Can You Forgive Her?

The Claverings

Cousin Henry

The Duke's Children

The Eustace Diamonds

Framley Parsonage

He Knew He Was Right

Lady Anna

Orley Farm

Phineas Finn

Phineas Redux

The Prime Minister

Rachel Ray

The Small House at Allington

The Warden

The Way We Live Now